THE LAST BIRD OF PARADISE

A Novel by
Clifford Garstang

Black Rose Writing | Texas

©2024 by Clifford Garstang
All rights reserved. No part of this book may be reproduced, stored in a retrieval system or transmitted in any form or by any means without the prior written permission of the publishers, except by a reviewer who may quote brief passages in a review to be printed in a newspaper, magazine or journal.

The author grants the final approval for this literary material.

First printing

This is a work of fiction. Names, characters, businesses, places, events, and incidents are either the products of the author's imagination or used in a fictitious manner. Any resemblance to actual persons, living or dead, or actual events is purely coincidental.

ISBN: 978-1-68513-376-4
LIBRARY OF CONGRESS CONTROL NUMBER: 2023945418
PUBLISHED BY BLACK ROSE WRITING
www.blackrosewriting.com

Printed in the United States of America
Suggested Retail Price (SRP) $23.95

The Last Bird of Paradise is printed in Minion Pro

*As a planet-friendly publisher, Black Rose Writing does its best to eliminate unnecessary waste to reduce paper usage and energy costs, while never compromising the reading experience. As a result, the final word count vs. page count may not meet common expectations.

ALSO BY CLIFFORD GARSTANG

IN AN UNCHARTED COUNTRY

WHAT THE ZHANG BOYS KNOW

THE SHAMAN OF TURTLE VALLEY

HOUSE OF THE ANCIENTS AND OTHER STORIES

OLIVER'S TRAVELS

THE LAST BIRD OF PARADISE

A pair of wings, a different respiratory system, which enabled us to travel through space, would in no way help us, for if we visited Mars or Venus while keeping the same senses, they would clothe everything we could see in the same aspect as the things of the Earth. The only true voyage, the only bath in the Fountain of Youth, would be not to visit strange lands but to possess other eyes, to see the universe through the eyes of another, of a hundred others, to see the hundred universes that each of them sees, that each of them is; and this we do, with great artists; with artists like these we do really fly from star to star.

–**Marcel Proust,** ***La Prisonnière***

1

Aislinn Givens exited the Bryant Park station to a damp, earthy scent—a sign, she hoped, that spring had finally arrived. A little warmth and renewal, perhaps some sun, the promise of brighter days ahead, would all be most welcome after New York's hellish fall and winter. There was even less litter on the street than usual as she strode up 6th Avenue, fewer discarded handbills, not a single wadded napkin or food wrapper. Promising, indeed.

She grabbed a latte from the Starbucks in her building's lobby, nodded to Henry, the longtime security guard—"Morning glory, Miss A," he said, his Georgia drawl whistling between the gap in his front teeth—and rode the wood-paneled elevator to the 47th floor. She passed the vacant reception counter—Paulette didn't start until eight—headed down the east corridor, her working home since she came to the city after graduating from law school five, almost six, years ago, noted which of her colleagues had arrived before her and which were not yet at their desks, and entered her office.

A copy machine thrummed nearby, but otherwise the floor, the lowest of six occupied by Morrow, Dunn & O'Brien, one of the oldest and most prestigious law firms in New York City, was still quiet. This was her favorite time of day: a dim glow from her narrow window, phones silent, the firm not yet fully awake. She fitted her trench coat onto the hanger she kept behind the door and glanced at the tiny mirror she'd installed there, resettling a stray wisp of hair. She sat at her desk—an oak monstrosity she'd inherited from the office's previous occupant, a senior associate who had failed to make partner and had moved on to God-knew-where—booted up the computer, sipped her coffee, and began the workday. Which, in the slower economy of the post-9/11 world, was going to be a relatively light one. She had a department meeting at ten, lunch with Rebecca at noon, a loan closing at three, but that was it. She'd be home in time for an early dinner with Liam.

To prepare for the closing, a loan by the New York office of a California lender, she planned to take a last look through the stack of documents her assistant had left on her desk the previous night. Tawnisha, whom she shared with two other lawyers, was the best assistant she'd had at the firm—efficient and thorough and sassy as hell—and would be missed when she started law school at Cardozo in the fall. They'd discussed the possibility of her coming back as an associate after graduation, instantly doubling the number of black women lawyers at the firm, the other being a litigator in the securities department who had graduated at the top of her Georgetown class and clerked for a high-profile judge, but as an associate herself that was entirely out of Aislinn's control. Unless, as she hoped, she'd been made a partner by then. What she didn't say to Tawnisha was that the firm almost never hired from outside the top tier of law schools, as unfair and inherently discriminatory as that sort of parochialism was, and so her return to the firm was unlikely.

The lender in this project, a client of Frank McKee's who now looked to Aislinn, Frank's protégé and senior associate, for all their legal work in New York, had been delighted with her handling of the negotiations and had told her as much. Now the time had come to finalize the deal and sign the agreements, a ceremonial conclusion she always enjoyed, even with its inevitable air of suspense, the gnat of worry that something might go wrong at the last minute.

In a crisp, new accordion file were two pristine copies of the credit agreement she'd drafted, ready for signing, plus two copies marked to show the changes the borrower's lawyer had asked for and to which she and her client had agreed. Frank had told her about the days before sophisticated word-processing programs that marked the changes automatically, when the lawyers—the junior associate on the project, usually—would have to do it all by hand, red-lining with a ruler and a felt pen, a mind-numbing task that was nonetheless a critical responsibility. Then there was the mortgage on the warehouse the borrower was buying with the loan proceeds, plus another security agreement granting liens on various key assets—equipment, vehicles, inventory. There was a promissory note and a personal guaranty. And there was also a legal opinion that the borrower's lawyer would sign assuring the lender that all the agreements were fully enforceable under New York law. Legal opinions had always struck Aislinn as odd elements of these deals. They were a bit like wearing a down jacket over a bullet-proof vest, but any tool that reduced the risk of repayment default was welcomed by the lender, and in the lender/borrower relationship, there was no question who had the power.

• • • • •

The department's lawyers assembled in the largest conference room on their floor, and Aislinn noted that no one was absent. During busier times, there were always a couple of lawyers who had deadlines or closings and so skipped the weekly meeting, risking Frank's displeasure. Today, though, a sign of the times, the room was crowded and full of chatter. Partners and senior associates took their seats at the table, and the more junior lawyers occupied chairs along the wall. She remembered those days, clustered with the other new associates, notepad at the ready to record any nuggets of legal wisdom or questions to research later, but now she'd earned her place in the hierarchy, right beside Frank.

Frank, who had been chairman of the department for as long as Aislinn had been at the firm, was wearing one of his trademark blue pinstripe suits and a solid maroon tie, his silver hair short and neat, as always, steel-rimmed glasses in his hand, waiting for his team to settle down. Right at ten, he slipped on his glasses, the signal that the meeting would begin, thanked everyone for attending, and dived into a report on a recent New York Appeals Court case that might cause clients to rethink the bankruptcy provisions in their loan agreements. It was the sort of development that grabbed Aislinn's attention, wheels already turning toward the research that would be needed, documents to be reviewed, discussions with Frank about how best to address the problem. One of the younger partners brought to their attention an article in *The American Lawyer* about the global expansion of law practices and asked if Morrow, Dunn shouldn't be taking steps in that direction. With business so slow, Aislinn wondered if that would be a prudent investment, but then she had no say in the matter and kept that thought to herself. It was nearly imperceptible, but she noticed Frank shaking his head and knew the suggestion would go nowhere. He was a New York lawyer through and through and saw no need to look elsewhere for clients; if they were the best at what they did, and they were, the clients would come to them. The last item on Frank's agenda was a reminder that the department would have two summer clerks this year, both from Harvard Law School, and everyone would be expected to make them feel welcome, keep them busy and happy, even if it was unlikely that offers of permanent employment would be forthcoming given the downturn in business.

Now, the meeting over, Aislinn was planning to leave the building for lunch for the first time in months, for the first time since the Towers fell. It wasn't as though she'd been too busy to go out, as had often been the case during her first several years at the firm. In fact, Morrow, Dunn's deal flow had slowed to the point that rumors of layoffs were impossible to dismiss. Her billable hours were half what they'd been before the attacks, and that worried her, although most associates were in the same boat; even the partners were scrambling to keep themselves productive. She just hadn't been in the mood to face the sea of grief and fear that the city had become, content instead to grab a salad from the firm's commissary or make do with another latte from Starbucks.

She might never have gone out again, but her stepdaughter—would she ever get used to the idea that she had nearly grown stepchildren?—had phoned and wanted to meet. Rebecca was home for spring break and felt suffocated in Westchester with her mother. She needed to get out of the house, she said. Desperately. She needed to come into the city. To breathe. To see Ground Zero for herself. Her father was mired in meetings, predictably, so Aislinn agreed to fill in—grateful, in fact, for the distraction, the excuse to emerge from the cave.

Aislinn's relationship with her stepchildren was fragile, a condition she supposed was not uncommon, perhaps even normal, given that it was her affair with their father that had ended his marriage to their mother. Liam was a banker, and she'd met him at her very first loan closing, fresh out of law school and a newly minted member of the bar, learning the ropes from Frank. That project was a leveraged buyout financed by a consortium of lenders led by SJ Freeman Financial, one of the city's most illustrious investment banking houses and Liam's employer. She'd been overdressed for the closing, deliberately, in a crimson suit her roommate, Jessica, had urged her to wear, an attention grabber, just the thing to wrong-foot the opposition, most likely a bunch of flat-footed old white men. "Doing business with men is like playing lacrosse," Jessica had advised. A second-team All-American midfielder at the University of Virginia, where she and Aislinn had been teammates and friends, with an MBA from Wharton, Jessica knew what she was talking about. "Winning is all about controlling the sticks." They'd had a good laugh over that, but, joke or not, they both knew there was truth in it, and Aislinn had taken extra care when dressing that morning. The bold suit. A silk blouse that was revealing, but not *too* revealing.

Still a newcomer in New York then, she'd been intoxicated by what was happening, the real threshold of her career, and that surely contributed to her infatuation with the handsome banker. White, yes, but not old, or at least not as old as the other men in the room. His bespoke suit was perfectly fitted to his athletic frame, nearly as provocative as her own outfit, and suggested overflowing charm and confidence. Or maybe she was enchanted by the way he looked at her, the way he'd focused his attention on her during the celebratory dinner after the closing, thanking her profusely for her contribution to the transaction, which, as they both knew, was minimal.

The next day, he sent her a live orchid, her favorite flower, with a note he'd signed "Margaret Atwood," her favorite author—intelligence he'd extracted during the closing dinner. After that there had been insistent phone calls, clandestine meetings at out-of-the-way bars in Chelsea and SoHo, furtive but thrilling trips to Chicago, San Francisco, and Miami, traveling separately, booked into different hotels. His marriage was already over, he'd said. It was only a matter of time before they made it official, he'd said. He needed her, he'd said. When Liam's wife, Janice, discovered their affair and confronted him, Rebecca, then in high school, and her younger brother Jason, had been furious with their father. Who could blame them? He'd moved out of their suburban home into a distant apartment in Manhattan, and the kids refused to see him, to even speak to him. And of course, they wanted nothing to do with Aislinn, the other woman, a woman much younger than their mother, which only added to her feelings of guilt.

She didn't mind so much for herself, not craving the stepmother role, but the wedge she'd driven between Liam and his children tortured her. It was as if their world had ended. Aislinn and her brother, Rory, had felt the same in high school after their mother's decision to leave their father, an existential choice Aislinn had only recently come to appreciate and begin to forgive. It was devastating at the time, difficult to understand or accept, and it was especially hard because it exacerbated her father's deepening depression. But Rebecca and Jason's world hadn't ended with their parents' divorce, any more than hers had. Nor had the world come to an end on 9/11 when the Towers fell, although it had felt like it at the time. They could all mourn what they'd lost, the grieving might never be over, but they would go on.

And they did. Rebecca, now a junior psychology major at Dartmouth, had gradually warmed to Aislinn and occasionally phoned just to chat. Only a decade apart in age, they'd become friends. Jason had eventually reconciled with his father, too, although for a long time he kept his distance from Aislinn. Some things were too much to ask of a boy. Still, now that he was a little older, preparing to apply to colleges, and had revealed—to no one's surprise or dismay, not even his father's—that he was gay, he'd shown signs of coming around. A hug at Christmas. An email on her birthday.

When it was time to leave the office to meet Rebecca, she took another look in her mirror and brushed her hair. She'd kept it short in law school, partly as a matter of expediency, partly rebellion against faculty sexism, but recently she'd grown it long because Liam said he preferred it that way, and now it fell below her shoulders again, just as it had through high school and college. She liked it long, too, but it seemed to attract unwelcome attention from the older men in the office, which was alternately flattering and disheartening, as if her credentials and hard work meant nothing to them.

She returned to her desk and checked her email again, realizing as she did so that she was stalling. She'd withdrawn from the city after 9/11 for a reason. Was she ready to go back?

No more postponing the inevitable. She slipped on her trench coat, hesitated, thought about grabbing her umbrella, decided against it, and headed to the elevator, noting Paulette's surprised expression as she passed the reception counter. On the descent, she considered riding the elevator back up, returning to her office, calling Rebecca, and canceling. Something had come up, she'd say. A problem with her closing, more work to be done.

But no. It was time. In her work she was decisive. Why was lunch so hard?

In the building's lobby she nodded at Henry, registered the surprise on his face, too—she really had been cooped up too long—and pushed through the revolving doors to join the lunchtime throng on the sidewalk.

She inhaled the damp, chilly air. How she'd missed this energy in her workday seclusion, the flood of faces, the dodge and jostle, a chaotic modern dance only found in New York City. On her early morning trek to the office, and after work, she barely noticed anyone. She could have been anywhere. Especially since the attacks, she'd avoided eye contact. She didn't want to see anyone else's pain or reveal her own. She kept her gaze on the pavement, anywhere but on the fractured skyline. As if in a trance, she willed herself from Brooklyn to Midtown and back. But now, in the midday light, she saw the people were still there, driven, the same as always, maybe more than ever. The world really had gone on.

She passed the bookstore on the corner and thought about stopping on her way back to the office to pick up a new release her mother had recommended in one of their brief, awkward calls, short stories about independent southern women. At least the slowdown in business allowed her a little time to read, and she loved that her mother knew what might appeal to her, still thinking of her as a southern woman after all this time up north. Plus, the book might give them something to talk about, a way of healing the rift between them that had only grown wider since she'd been working in the city. Next to the bookstore was a dentist. Then a tiny noodle shop, a vitamin store, a tobacconist. Had all these stores been here before the attacks? Why did nothing seem familiar? It was as if an entirely different city had replaced the New York she knew and loved.

A horn blared in front of her as a yellow cab swerved to avoid a cyclist, a long-haired messenger who raised his middle finger to the hack. Aislinn dodged a leaking trash bag on the sidewalk, nearly collided with a dog-walker and his rambunctious charges, then turned another corner.

She approached the restaurant, a venerable bistro on 46th, and saw Rebecca waiting outside in her stylishly ragged jeans and lavender down vest, carrying an Urban Outfitters shopping bag. Such a pretty girl—no surprise given her handsome father and beauty-queen mother—even bundled up against the March chill. She had pulled her auburn hair into a ponytail; her cheeks were rosy with the cold. She waved when she spotted Aislinn.

"There you are," Aislinn said, as if she'd been searching all over. "I'm sorry I'm late." She looked at her watch. She wasn't late.

"No problem! It's so good to see you!"

They embraced and kissed each other's cheeks, like two old friends, and Aislinn took Rebecca's icy hand to pull her inside. The restaurant was dim and hushed, a farrago of smells: fresh bread, garlic, grilled meat, chocolate. A perky hostess ushered them through the dining room, dark wood, swirling red and gray shapes in the carpet. Three large paintings—bold patterns in orange and black—dominated the room from the rear wall. Rothkos? Or at any rate, Rothko knockoffs. They suggested a distant horizon, a vast empty landscape, a too perfect reminder of what had been erased from New York's skyline.

Settled at a booth, rubbing her hands for warmth, Aislinn asked Rebecca about school, about boys, about vacation plans. School was school—she was thinking about taking a semester off, or maybe a semester abroad, if her father would allow it—and there was this one guy she'd been seeing, a political science major and a drummer for a rock band. Too early to tell where that was going. As for vacation, her Cabo trip had fallen through because her over-protective father had vetoed it, and being stuck in Westchester with her needy mother was the pits, although it had been fun to hang out with Jason.

Not so far removed from college herself, Aislinn thought it all sounded familiar and wonderful. She couldn't do anything about Cabo, but she had wonderful memories of her one semester in London and promised to put in a good word with Liam. She was curious about this drummer. Remembering her own sexual awakening in college—she'd fallen for a skinny journalism major with long, wavy hair and insatiable appetites—she wanted details, something a friend might ask, but maybe not a stepmother.

"Did you go downtown this morning?" she asked instead. "You said you wanted to see it."

"I chickened out. I wanted to, but…I didn't. Have you been?"

The waiter appeared, a tall young man dressed in black from neck to toe, square-jawed with blond, spiky hair and smooth, tanned skin—an out-of-work actor, Aislinn guessed, because weren't they all, especially the pretty ones?—and dropped off menus and water glasses.

Seeing to other tables filling around them, the waiter gazed frequently back at Rebecca, who ignored—or pretended to ignore—his attention. Aislinn envied her stepdaughter, her life just beginning, so many options, so much ahead of her. Not that Aislinn was unhappy with her own choices. On the contrary. She adored her husband. She loved being a lawyer. She loved living in New York with its museums and theaters and concert halls, a kaleidoscope of restaurants, the entire world wrapped up in one enormous package. Aislinn was sorry she wasn't on better terms with her mother, but she loved being able to afford nice things and do things her parents never could. It was just that sometimes, occasionally, especially since the attacks, she felt something was missing, an opportunity that was slipping away. She couldn't say what, exactly. Something.

"No," Aislinn said. "Or yes. Your father and I went to a memorial service at St. Paul's for someone he worked with. But that's as close as I've been. I still don't know what to think about what happened." Which wasn't even close to being true, but the disaster was still too painful, too recent, and she didn't want to talk about it.

She picked up the menu and studied it, contemplated ordering a glass of wine, which she never did at lunch, ever, but spring was coming, she was closing another deal that afternoon, the world was looking a little less bleak, just a little, and here was beautiful Rebecca, young and innocent and happy, so maybe just this once.

"I know," Rebecca said. "It still seems so grim in the city. At school, we're sort of oblivious. I mean, everyone was affected in some way, even if remotely, and a sorority sister of mine lost…." She sipped her water while she gathered herself, and then the light came back to her eyes. "But at least you guys are getting away from it, right? Moving to Singapore! That's so exciting."

Aislinn lowered the menu. "Singapore?"

"Oh, God. Don't tell me."

Aislinn stared at her stepdaughter, whose expression had turned from light-hearted to horrified.

"What's this about Singapore, Becca?"

"Me and my big mouth. I shouldn't have said anything. I must have misunderstood him. Forget it." Rebecca pored over the menu, avoiding Aislinn's glare. "Is the Cobb salad good here?"

"Becca?"

Rebecca put her menu down. "Okay. Look, I guess I wasn't supposed to mention it, but he didn't tell me not to. When I called to see if we could have lunch today, he said he'd be tied up in a meeting about the move. He said he couldn't wait to get out of the city. That you both hated it here."

The fawning waiter reappeared and refilled their water glasses, complimented Rebecca on her cheerful yellow sweater, recited the lunch specials, took their orders, and asked Rebecca if there was anything else she wanted.

Just ask her for her phone number already, Aislinn silently commanded, and leave us alone. She ordered a glass of chardonnay after all.

"But I guess it's not a done deal if he hasn't even talked to you about it yet," Rebecca said when the waiter was gone. "Just a lame excuse not to have lunch with his daughter, I'm sure. Or I totally misunderstood. It's probably someone else moving to Singapore, someone who works for him. Okay? Can we just have lunch now? I'm starving."

• • • • •

An icy rain began as she hurried back to her office, and she cursed herself for not taking the umbrella. What had she been thinking? And what the hell was Liam thinking, planning a move to Singapore, somewhere on the other side of the planet, without talking to her first?

She had scarcely settled behind her desk when she called Liam's office, and she called every five minutes after that. She'd never known anyone more adept at dodging calls. He was in a meeting, his assistant said. He'd stepped away. He was tied up. She dialed his cell phone, but it went straight to voicemail, and she hung up without leaving a message. No doubt Rebecca had gotten to him first to tell him she'd spilled the beans about Singapore. Or Liam had planned it that way, telling his daughter about the move, knowing she couldn't keep a secret. Coward.

· · · ·

Paulette called to let her know her guests had arrived, and Aislinn asked Tawnisha to show them into a conference room. She paged through the documents again, unable to concentrate on the words. There was the closing to get through, and then she'd call Liam again, and in the meantime her head was spinning. Singapore? It made no sense. Why Singapore? She wasn't even sure where Singapore was except that it was far away. Why hadn't he talked to her?

Aislinn returned the documents to the folder, took another look in her little mirror, and headed down the corridor toward the conference room. She stopped in Frank's office to remind him she had the loan closing for his client, but he was expecting a call about a bankruptcy filing that was giving everyone heartburn and wouldn't be joining her. She was proud that Frank McKee, one of the top lawyers in the city, had confidence in her, a senior associate, to handle a project entirely on her own. It was a reminder that she belonged in this world, that she'd found a welcoming home in this firm, and whatever Liam's plans were, she had no intention of leaving. Not now. Not ever.

She moved on to the bullpen, a windowless office where her own career had begun that was now shared by four first-year associates, including Brian, the young lawyer Frank had assigned to help her on this deal. An eager Yale graduate—law school and undergrad, both—Brian popped up from his desk when she arrived. Well over six feet tall, he had a thin, angular face and broad shoulders, a swimmer's build, like her husband's. She'd noticed his thick red hair before, and it looked even more fiery today as he pulled on a navy-blue suit coat. On their way to the conference room, Aislinn reminded him of the terms of the deal, terms they'd discussed weeks ago and that he would know from studying the loan documents as she'd suggested, and recalled similar briefings she had received from Frank when she was starting out. Had Brian been at the department meeting that morning? Yes, she remembered seeing that red hair along the back wall with the other first-years.

As she entered the room, the men—her client was a man, the borrower was a man, his lawyer was a man—stood and greeted her. She shook their hands and introduced Brian, amused by their confusion. They were wondering if Brian, another man, might not be in charge here, even though all their previous dealings had been with Aislinn. She took a seat at the head of the long table, directed the men to sit, and their attention refocused on her, resolving the momentary uncertainty. She might be the only woman in the room, and much younger than her visitors, but this was her show, and now they knew it.

Negotiations having been completed, there was nothing further to discuss. Aislinn handed the documents to Brian, who distributed them to the borrower and his lawyer for a final review of the changes she'd made. While they read, she studied their faces, wondering what kind of men they were, whether they had wives with careers, whether they'd dragged them to New York against their wills, and her fury rose again. Surely Rebecca had been mistaken. Liam wouldn't do this to her. In this day and age, who would? When the borrower's lawyer looked up and nodded his approval, she reined herself in and smiled at him, presenting a pen to the borrower who signed all the agreements with a flourish, laughing when he dotted the last i. Her client signed. The lawyer read through his legal opinion one last time and signed that. The deal was done.

By this point in her career, she'd done enough deals that she no longer experienced the anxiety she once felt at closings—worries about typos or missing documents or last-minute lien searches that turned up unpleasant surprises—but a thrill still raced through her when the agreements were finalized and signed, even for a small loan like this one. She worked damn hard on every project to make sure the firm would keep her around for the long haul and eventually make her a partner. That meant keeping clients happy, doing first-rate work on every deal, big or small. And not running off to Singapore when her husband snapped his fingers.

They all shook hands, the client thanked her and asked to be remembered to Frank, Brian gathered up the documents, and the closing was over.

Back in her office to debrief, she watched Brian study the diplomas on the wall behind her desk—Harvard Law, *magna cum laude*, a BA from the University of Virginia—and the framed Georgia O'Keeffe poster from MOMA, a reminder to herself that once, when she was younger, she thought she might want to be an artist and had admired O'Keeffe's provocative work. There was also a signed Miro lithograph she treasured, with his trademark vibrant blue and red and yellow, a gift from Liam that really was too valuable to keep in the office, but too eloquent to leave at home where she'd rarely see it. When she took the time to really look at the Miro, she saw three sailing ships leaving the harbor, knifing through the waves bound for distant ports. Her anger about Singapore resurfaced, and she grew eager for Brian to leave so she could try Liam's office again.

"Could I ask you something?" Brian said.

"Of course," she said. She assumed he was curious about some aspect of the deal they'd just closed. After all, his involvement in the project was all about training. It was how all young lawyers learned. It was how she had learned. He was only a few years her junior but seemed even younger with his red hair and freckles, a dimpled chin. A shallow frat-boy coasting along on his good looks and, she suspected, family connections. And then she chided herself for making an assumption based on his appearance, something she herself had encountered all her life. Men had always made assumptions about her because of her gender, her blond hair, her figure. What did she really know about this man? Talk about shallow.

"Did you always want to be a lawyer?" Brian asked. "I mean, you work such long hours and these deals, one after another, they're kind of meaningless and all the same. I'm just wondering if there isn't something more fulfilling. Especially now."

Although Brian did all that was asked of him and carried himself with confidence, a bit of swagger that bore the unmistakable mark of privilege, his question was evidence to Aislinn that he wasn't cut out for this kind of work. Few lawyers were, she'd learned. Nearing the end of her fifth year as an associate at Morrow, Dunn & O'Brien, Aislinn's cohort had dwindled to a handful of survivors. There had been twenty of them to start, all recent graduates of the finest law schools in the country, including seven women. Not parity, but a respectable showing for a conservative New York law firm. One of the women left within a few months owing to an undisclosed health problem—stress-related, Aislinn was sure—and by the end of their first year, two more women and three men were gone. The next year, one of the remaining women, who had married shortly after being hired, took maternity leave from which she never returned, and another trio of male colleagues also disappeared. One of those, a brilliant lawyer who had been a clerk for an appeals court judge right out of the University of Chicago, accepted an offer to teach law in a prominent state university somewhere in the South. The other two, she'd heard, had been told by the partners they'd be better off looking for work elsewhere, that their prospects at Morrow, Dunn were dim. Neither departure had surprised her. They were both lazy, billing barely half the hours she did, expecting their Ivy League pedigrees to pave their way in an old-line firm like Morrow, Dunn. It didn't work that way anymore.

So, if Brian here hadn't already accepted the drudgery ahead of him, if he wasn't already committed to this life, he never would be. Maybe her first impression had been right after all. She wondered if she shouldn't advise him to keep that opinion about meaningless work to himself if he had any hope of succeeding in the firm, but from the sound of it, he'd made up his mind and was plotting a different course.

"Not always, no," she said. "My dad was a veterinarian, having grown up on a farm in Virginia, and my mom is a teacher, so I didn't know much about the law until my junior year of college. I took a class in law and economics from the most inspiring professor I'd ever had, and I began to understand the relationship between the legal system and power dynamics, how that's been true throughout history. She connected it to everything from migratory flows across continents, colonial exploitation, and post-colonial independence movements. It blew me away. Since then, working at a place like Morrow, Dunn has been my dream. It's not just about the deals we do, although they're sort of like snowflakes and no two transactions are exactly the same. What I find thrilling is using the law in creative ways to meet genuine needs, putting theory into practice, making the engine of the world hum."

Even talking about it sent a charge through her, one that she felt when negotiating with borrowers, tightening the terms of a deal as a hedge against failure. It was almost sexual, the feeling she had when she immersed herself in a project, but of course she couldn't say that to Brian. She couldn't really say that to anyone, although she'd once tried to explain it to Liam. "I love the law and can't imagine doing anything else with my life."

When the young lawyer left, she called Liam's office again. He was in a meeting.

· · · · ·

By the time she got to their Park Slope townhouse, her rage growing with every aggravating stop of the subway, she was shaking with fury. Hearing the clank of glasses from the kitchen, she marched toward the back of the house without taking off her coat.

"When the hell were you going to tell me about Singapore?"

Liam, necktie loose and flung over his shoulder, dress shirt sleeves rolled up, was stirring a Bolognese sauce, an open bottle of Chianti on the kitchen island. She'd forgotten they'd planned an early dinner.

"When it was a sure thing," he said, as if that were a perfectly reasonable response.

"And you don't think you should have consulted me before agreeing to something like this? When they made the offer, you didn't think to run it by your wife immediately? 'Oh, by the way, honey, would you mind terribly if we moved halfway around the world?' This isn't the dark ages, Liam. I'm not your slave. What the hell were you thinking?"

"I'm consulting you now, sweet. I haven't committed us to the move yet, but I honestly thought you'd be thrilled. I thought we both wanted to get out of New York. This is our chance. You said yourself how it had changed so much."

He was right about that. The energy of the place had evaporated for her, most of the joy along with it. But leave? That was the last thing she wanted. For days and weeks after the attacks, she'd barely spoken to anyone. She'd found it hard to breathe. She buried herself in work, taking on litigation assignments when the new deals dried up, just to keep busy. She sought refuge in her piano, the one Liam had bought for her when they moved to Brooklyn, but not even that helped, and looking at the ivory keys only reminded her of the Towers. She suspected every dark stranger, every cabdriver, every bodega clerk, of being a terrorist, and then felt guilty for her baseless suspicions. Aislinn had come to hate New York, and so had Liam, but she couldn't leave.

Now they were at the dining table, facing each other over their gory swirls of spaghetti. She was calmer, but still angry. How could he make this decision without her? Because clearly, he'd made up his mind. All his life he'd gotten what he wanted. His parents weren't wealthy by any means, working-class people from Boston, but they doted on him, and their only son had used his good looks and Irish charm to waltz through Boston College and then Tuck for his MBA. He was just like that kid at work, Brian. Had he ever been denied anything in his life? His sense of entitlement was infuriating. How could he do this to her?

"My job is here, Liam. My career. You know that."

"But you don't *need* to work. Things are going great for me at the bank. And this transfer is a huge promotion, besides being a ticket out of this purgatory. Way more money. With the promise of bigger things to come. We could even start a family." It wasn't the first time he'd mentioned children, and her answer was always the same: she wasn't ready, and he already had children. He popped a piece of buttery garlic bread into his mouth and wiped his fingers on a napkin.

"It's the twenty-first century, Liam. Women work, too. We have careers. I can't believe we're even having this conversation. Remember Janice, your ex-wife? Whom you tired of because she'd become a drudge, had no interests other than the kids?"

"Babe, that's different. You're not Janice."

"Exactly! I'm not Janice, I'm Aislinn Givens, and I'm on track to be a partner in one of the best law firms in the world in the most important *city* in the world. My career is at stake, Liam. I can't go running off to Singapore!"

Even as she said this, though, the doubts crept in. Was she really on track? In this economy, with business as slow as it was, how long would she be able to keep her job? Was she only kidding herself about her chances of making partner? She knew Frank adored her and appreciated her work, but there were other considerations, other partners in the firm who would be part of the decision. Did they feel the same way about her contributions to the firm? Maybe this was the perfect time to make a change, move on before they pushed her out the door.

Liam leaned on his elbows and folded his hands together. He was looking at his empty plate, as if in prayer, weighing what to say.

"You weren't there, Aislinn. You didn't see the people jumping from windows. You didn't see the buildings implode or hear that unholy sound, like the earth screaming. You didn't see the bodies, the bits of bodies raining down. You didn't breathe that putrid smoke, the fire and ash. And you didn't walk through the rubble."

He was right about that, too. He'd been downtown that morning and had gone through something she hadn't. She'd lost friends, of course. She'd lost Clark, a man she'd once loved dearly, whose office had been in the South Tower. Everyone had lost someone. Her brother had enlisted in the army after the attacks to join the fight against whomever it was they were going to fight, and God only knew what was going to happen to him. She worried about Rory every day. The whole thing was still so unimaginable, but she hadn't been there. She'd been in her office in Midtown, miles away. She didn't see it, and Liam was there.

"It was pure fucking hell, and I can't stay here. I have to leave. We have to leave."

"But why didn't you talk to me? Why didn't you ask?"

"I'm asking now." His voice broke. Was he near tears? He was afraid of what was happening, what could happen again.

"I don't want to leave, Liam. I can't leave." She pushed away from the table and left the mess for him to deal with.

2

Aislinn stopped at the threshold of Hannah Boseman's office and tapped on the open door. Hannah, on the phone, waved her in and pointed to the white leather chair facing her desk. Aislinn sat and half-listened to the conversation—a client considering a trademark infringement claim, apparently—while she let her eyes wander around the room. She loved this office, all white, the desk, the credenza, the chairs, with stunning abstracts on the walls by women artists Hannah knew personally. One of the few senior women partners in the firm, Hannah had been a sounding board for Aislinn since the day she arrived as a first-year associate. She had taken several of the new women lawyers to lunch that day, and Aislinn had recognized in Hannah the drive she herself possessed. The older woman had survived and prospered in the male-dominated firm by being smart and tough, one of the best lawyers in the business, and Aislinn had planned to do the same. But now?

Hannah swiveled in her chair and held up a finger, to which Aislinn nodded. There was something different about Hannah's hair today, freshly cut and maybe less gray than there had been. She touched her own hair, wondering, looking ahead to a time when she'd be sitting where Hannah was now. The older woman's elegant high-collared suit, the thick beaded necklace, the gold brooch—it all exuded success, authority, power.

When Hannah finished the call, Aislinn filled her in on her dilemma.

"Have you talked to Frank?" Hannah asked. Frank McKee was not only Aislinn's boss and chairman of her department, he was also a member of the firm's management committee. A brilliant commercial finance lawyer, he was her role model, her mentor in the firm, her guide through the firm's internal politics, and something of a father figure. But she was afraid to confide in him about this.

Aislinn shook her head. "You're the only one I've told. I don't want Frank to know I'm even thinking of leaving."

"Frank has great foresight. He might have some helpful advice about your prospects here."

Prospects? What was Hannah saying? Did she mean Frank might tell her not to expect to be at the firm long term? That she might as well move with her husband because there was no future for her at Morrow, Dunn & O'Brien? She'd had those doubts herself, given the slowdown, but even if that were true, even if she wasn't destined to make partner here, which would be a major disappointment, she was still a New York lawyer. That was her identity. She loved Morrow, Dunn, but there were other firms, other jobs in the city.

"I don't know what to do, Hannah. I can't go to Singapore."

"Can't? What happens to your marriage if you don't, love?"

"It's over, I guess. Liam says he's going, no matter what." He hadn't said so in exactly that way, but she knew him. He had decided, and there would be no changing his mind.

"And you told him you weren't? Was it clear?"

"No uncertain terms. He didn't budge. He thinks I'll come around eventually. But how can I? This is where I belong. This is my life. Liam says he hates it here now, that he hates what New York has become."

"He's not wrong, though, is he? Haven't things changed since the attacks? Haven't we all changed? I used to think we lived in a safe little bubble here, that what happened in the rest of the world didn't matter to me. What did I care what was going on in the Middle East or Africa, or anywhere else? I was being naïve. We all were." She paused, as if to underscore this new reality. No matter what Aislinn decided to do, the world was a different place now. "I know it's been your dream to make partner in a big firm, and you're an excellent lawyer, one of the best we have, but is it really worth the sacrifice of your marriage?"

Aislinn looked at Hannah, who had never married. She had come to the firm in the Vietnam War years after excelling at a second-tier New England law school, an anomaly at Morrow, Dunn even then, and had devoted her life to the place. Not only to her work in intellectual property, which was legendary, but to changing the firm's culture. To proving that a woman could succeed in this world. To nurturing younger women lawyers and artists. But there'd been a price. As far as Aislinn knew, she'd had no personal life, no lasting relationships. Work was everything. Aislinn, though, wanted a personal life *and* a career, maybe children one day, too, and she was determined to have it all.

On the other hand, Hannah was right. The world around her *had* changed. Had she changed with it?

"I don't know, Hannah. How can I know?"

· · · · ·

Why the hell did Liam wait so long to talk to her about moving to Singapore? A man her own age would not have done this. Clark, whom she'd nearly married when they were in their last year of law school, would not have done this. As true equals, they would have discussed it when the subject was first broached to make sure it made sense for both of them, and if it did not, they wouldn't pursue it. It was generational, she supposed. Liam was just enough older, raised by a domineering father in a traditional family that saw women's roles differently, and he didn't get it, merely paid lip service to equality. He'd referred to their marriage as a partnership, but apparently, not unlike her law firm, the views of some partners carried more weight than others. Even Hannah didn't seem to understand.

Aislinn's mother might be sympathetic, having declared her independence years ago after two decades of marriage, but they were barely on speaking terms, and Aislinn didn't want to give her yet another chance to fault her for marrying Liam. Rory would be no help. She got along well with her brother, but he had never dated anyone for more than a six-month stretch and wasn't likely to have useful advice in the relationship department. Besides, his post-9/11 decision to join the army meant that his own life was in upheaval just now. She needed to talk to someone her own age.

She called Jessica, her best friend since their days on the lacrosse team at the University of Virginia and her former roommate in the tiny Morningside Heights apartment they'd shared when they were both new to New York. They agreed to meet at The Cape, a South African wine bar near the Metropolitan Museum of Art, one that Jessica's current girlfriend, Nomandia, a woman originally from Johannesburg, had introduced her to.

"It's been too long, girl," Jessica said when she jumped from her seat at the bar to embrace Aislinn. It was a small place, narrow and cramped, with the sounds and smells of sizzling meat wafting from the open kitchen and lilting South African accents buzzing all around them. They ordered a bottle of a Stellenbosch sauvignon blanc and toasted their overdue reunion. Jessica's hair had gone the opposite direction from Aislinn's. During their lacrosse days, she had tamed her afro with a headband, but now her hair was in tight natural curls cut close to her dark scalp. More Nigerian princess than MBA marketing executive, Aislinn thought, but it was a potent, noble look that had served her well in the ranks of her Fortune 250 behemoth.

"Now, what's this crazy talk about Singapore?"

Aislinn filled her in on the offer Liam had received from his bank, or that he had finagled, she wasn't sure which. "I need help," she said. "We're barely speaking to each other at this point. I don't know what to do."

"I'll tell you what to do," Jessica said. "Tell that fine-looking husband of yours to go fuck himself. He thinks the world revolves around him, typical white-male bullshit, and it just doesn't work that way. Not anymore. No sir and fuck you. Welcome to the twenty-first century."

Aislinn laughed. "Oh, Jess, I knew I could count on you."

"Girl, I've got your back."

By the time the bottle was empty, Jessica had convinced her she had to say no to Liam, not just for herself, but on behalf of women and oppressed people everywhere. She couldn't go to Singapore. She had her own career, her own life, and it was right here in New York.

On the way home, though, staring into the dark subway tunnel, the hypnotic reflected lights flashing in her eyes, she wavered. Jessica was right, but wasn't Hannah right, too? Was Aislinn ready to sacrifice her marriage? She loved her husband. She did. He was clever and generous and, most of the time, thoughtful, and was great with his kids, once the trauma of the divorce had healed. Those were lessons he'd learned from his father, too, a gruff old soul who nonetheless took care of his family as best he could. The bottom line was that she loved being married to him. She wanted to stay married. Short of finding some way to manage a long-distance relationship—a *very* long-distance relationship—she had to convince him not to go.

Or was she letting her own ambition blind her to the inevitable? Her career or her marriage? Work or love? Women have had to make that choice forever, or at least since they'd begun entering the workforce to compete with men. Rarely did men have to choose, even now. How was that fair? It's *not* fair, Hannah had agreed. And it *has* to change. But did Aislinn want to lead the way? Could she pay the price?

Plus, despite Frank McKee's encouragement over the years, promotion was no sure thing, apparently. The calculus was unfathomable. If deal flow didn't pick up soon, associates would be lucky to keep their jobs, never mind being elevated to partnership. She could work twenty-four hours a day for the next three years, and it might not do any good. Wasn't that the real dilemma here? Given the dynamics of law firms, where associates were worked to death while the carrot of partnership was dangled in front of them, always out of reach, there was a chance she'd be asked to leave before too long. It might have nothing at all to do with her skills as a lawyer or being a woman. It boiled down to economics. As a highly paid senior associate, she'd become too expensive to keep around if she wasn't going to be producing new business for the firm, and right now, no one was producing new business.

• • • • •

At work the next day, Aislinn's mind strayed from the draft loan agreement on her desk, a first attempt by the young associate Brian based on the term sheet she'd given him. She had already scrawled extensive notes in the margins, recalling how she had learned the same lessons about legal drafting from Frank so many years earlier. She would meet with Brian, explain what she meant, and hope he took her criticism well. Not all young lawyers did, but they had to learn. It was part of the process.

Her gaze landed on the Miro lithograph, the ships sailing from the harbor. Where were those ships headed? Singapore? At home last night, Liam had tried to explain himself, marshaling again all the same arguments, but she'd stopped him. She didn't want to hear it. She just needed to think.

There was a knock on her office door. "Got a minute?" Hannah asked.

"For you, of course." Aislinn said. "To what do I owe the honor?"

Hannah dropped a business card on Aislinn's desk. "There's a gallery opening tonight I thought you'd find interesting. A friend tells me the work is stunning and, as it happens, the artist is from Singapore. It wouldn't hurt to get a little taste of what the place is like, would it?"

Whose side was Hannah on? Had Liam put her up to this? Aislinn picked up the card. SoHo. She was in no hurry to get home to yet another argument, so why not take in a little art?

• • • • •

Before Aislinn left the office, she did what she was good at: analyzing, dissecting, bringing her training to bear on the problem at hand. What was Hannah telling her, exactly? Was the gallery suggestion another hint about her future? That she needed to rethink her opposition to the Singapore move? And what did Liam want from her? How could he expect her simply to do his bidding, to abandon her career now, when she'd come this far? He'd always claimed to be proud of her success and independence, her ambition and drive. What had changed? Yes, New York wasn't the same since the attacks, but she had her own life, her own future, every bit as important and legitimate as his. And despite Hannah's doubts, or the seeds of doubt Hannah had planted, Aislinn was still confident she had done everything she needed to do to prevail at the firm. She was on track to join the partnership in another year or two, three at most, and add another crack to the legal profession's glass ceiling. Unless, that is, she packed up and moved ten thousand miles away.

What the hell was she supposed to do?

And then there it was, the twinge in her knee, real or imagined, she didn't know anymore, that sometimes surfaced in times of stress. The twinge became sharper, gnawing at her, the pain bleeding to her foot, then up into her thigh, until it was unbearable.

Aislinn could usually ignore the knee injury that had ended her college lacrosse career, but when the pain came, it came with a vengeance. At times, she felt the world spinning out of control, a certainty that there would be no way back from the darkness. In those times, she had no choice. The university doctors had weaned her from the Percocet after her surgery, but resourceful teammates, most of whom had dealt with their own injuries, had a source for buttons, as the girls called them, and they'd been a godsend. The stress of school, the mess that her parents' marriage had become, her mother's erratic behavior and then her father's death. It was too much to handle. When she'd gone on to Harvard Law and then moved to New York, Jessica, her reliable old teammate, her world-wise and well-connected friend, had kept her supplied. God only knew who Jess got them from.

Why was Liam doing this to her? Why was he putting her through this agony when he knew her world was already unsettled?

She clutched at her leg, massaging her knee, knowing that would bring no real relief, and, when none came, she unlocked her file cabinet and retrieved an accordion folder labeled Harvard. Inside, among correspondence, printouts, and old copies of the alumni magazine, was a slim envelope from which she now extracted a button. She took it with a swallow of cold coffee and willed it to work its magic. She closed her eyes and waited. When the pain did at last ebb, the screaming in her head softening to a tolerable buzz, she gathered her things and left the office.

• • • • •

She emerged from a cab in SoHo across the street from the gallery. Inside the storefront space, lights blazed over a milling crowd attired in conservative suits and cocktail dresses and a few in jeans and paint-spattered sweaters, part of the neighborhood's studio scene, she guessed. Curious about this artist from Singapore, she entered the gallery, shed her coat on a rack by the door, and accepted a glass of white wine from a slim young waiter. He was dark, Middle Eastern, she thought, and briefly wondered what nationality he might be, what religion. Did he pose a threat? Was he one of them?

Stop, Aislinn commanded herself. What the hell is wrong with you? He's just a boy, a waiter, for God's sake, not a terrorist. Maybe Liam was right. New York right now was driving everyone crazy, and clearly, she was no different. She drank her wine, half the glass in one gulp. She knew the risks of drinking with the button in her system, her mind already swimming dangerously, but at that moment, alcohol was exactly what she craved. She finished the wine, found the waiter, smiled at him, attempting amends for her unspoken insult, and took another glass.

She became aware of music and spotted a pale, gaunt woman in a black gown playing a Bach cello suite, a piece Aislinn had always loved, its sonorous strains rippling beneath the gurgle of commingled conversations. She strolled through the throng, not listening to voices, not seeing faces or bodies, all a dizzying blur, only aware of the Bach, the pleasant warmth still building inside her, the bright paintings on the walls, vibrant colors, vaguely tropical images on over-sized canvasses. Inspired by Gauguin, perhaps. Or Rousseau?

She stopped moving and looked more closely at the nearest painting. Not nearly so complex as Gauguin, always one of her favorites when she visited the Met. But the colors were vivid, practically throbbing, oranges and yellows and especially vibrant greens. No naked island women, but the scene was mysterious, inviting, a spectral avalanche of flowers, a deep green jungle with soaring palm trees, animal faces—she thought they were tigers or monkeys, but it was hard to be sure with the artist's impressionistic style—and a seductive blue lagoon, its surface as smooth as glass. Come drown yourself in my depths, it seemed to say.

As she studied the painting, first one monkey and then another leaped from tree to tree, and a brilliantly colored parrot, red and yellow and blue, flapped noisily from one side of the scene to the other, squawking a shrill warning. A shimmering serpent, something prehistoric and sinewy, rose in the lagoon and sank again, sending ardent ripples across the surface. At the water's edge, a naked savage raised his spear and then, when an explosion echoed across the lagoon and blood blossomed on his chest, collapsed. Smoke rose from the rifle of a uniformed soldier who had appeared on the opposite shore.

She'd thought the work cheerful at first glance, but it had turned sinister. Was it some kind of animation? Video art? It had looked like a normal oil painting, but who knew what technology was available now, especially from a place like Singapore, supposedly the Silicon Valley of Asia, according to Liam? She turned to see if anyone else had seen what she had, this miraculous moving picture. But no, there was no surprise on their faces, no recognition that anything out of the ordinary had occurred. Oblivious, they all sipped their drinks, continued their conversations, wandered through the gallery.

Now the painting was still again, back to its original motionless state, the colors vibrant but static. And yet, she'd seen it move. Hadn't she?

She turned around. On the opposite wall hung a painting of a city skyline, a stark contrast with the jungle. The colors were the same, though, bright and engaging, the glass of the city reflecting nature, and she realized the two scenes were in dialogue with each other: the jungle and the metropolis.

As she watched this painting, the parrot from the jungle painting entered the view and crashed into a skyscraper, erupting into flame. She gasped and stepped back, bumping against a man standing behind her. She wanted to ask if he'd seen it, but again, no one else seemed to notice, as if the painting's message had been meant only for her. And what was the message exactly? She'd imagined it, surely. So much stress from the Singapore decision, the pressure from Liam, 9/11 still a raw memory, maybe the pill she'd taken, the wine, it was making her hallucinate. She looked again, and now there was no bird, no fire.

Aislinn stumbled away from the painting, bumping against the man again, or a different man, hearing his grumbled complaint, apologizing, and drifted deeper into the gallery. Near the back wall, she found a group clustered around an Asian woman with short black hair, a bob cut that framed her face in a near-perfect circle.

"That's the artist," whispered a woman standing next to her, who then moved closer to the front. From a display on the buffet table, Aislinn picked up a gallery brochure on the cover of which was a photograph of this artist, Shan Lee, posed in front of one of her jungle paintings, a common motif for her, apparently. Chinese, Aislinn supposed, from her name and appearance, and wasn't there some connection between Singapore and China? It made her feel stupid not to know. Now Aislinn joined the huddle. The artist wore a black sheath cut very short. Gleaming red lipstick, a red scarf at her neck, red heels. Aislinn recognized the muscular calves of a fellow runner.

"Wasn't Singapore the place where they banned chewing gum?" asked the woman who had whispered to Aislinn. "Kind of heavy-handed, isn't it?"

The artist rolled her eyes but laughed along with the crowd. "Yes," she said, "and that's not the only rule Americans would have a hard time understanding." Her accent was British, almost, but not quite what Aislinn remembered from her semester in London. "You won't find a cleaner city anywhere, or one more orderly. And these days, there's a brilliant art scene. Galleries, schools, you name it. Most of these works I did there."

Was this woman, this Shan Lee, typical of Singapore? Did they all speak English like this? Were they this sophisticated and glamorous? Was the city really full of galleries and these stunning colors? It was absurd that she knew so little about the place. Probably Liam had been trying to tell her, but she hadn't listened.

A portly man in a charcoal suit asked, "What are the paintings about?"

The artist grimaced. Because of the question? Or the man who asked it? Aislinn recognized in this woman a kindred spirit, a woman who could not, or would not, hide her feelings or tolerate fools. "Isn't it obvious?" Lee asked. "Next question."

Obvious? No, Aislinn thought, not obvious, but she did sense in them, especially when they came alive for her, a feeling of resentment, the modern city encroaching on the natural world, crowding out the animals and the native people. Plus, there was a universal theme of post-colonialism, and that reminded her of some of the Mexican muralists who depicted the atrocities of the Spanish invaders. Did it have special meaning for Lee? Or for Singapore? Of course, the painter wasn't going to do the viewer's work for him, just as writers had no business telling readers what their books were about. The pieces either conveyed their meaning or they didn't, and these paintings were clearly telling a story.

Aislinn caught the artist's attention. "I apologize that I know so little about Singapore, but is it at all like New York?" Meaning, should

I even consider moving there with my husband, even though it will have to be kicking and screaming?

The crowd laughed and Aislinn felt her face flush, but the artist smiled warmly, tolerantly.

"Not New York, really. Given our British colonial history, I'd say it's more like London. A hot, humid, extremely tidy London."

More laughter. London didn't sound so bad. Aislinn recalled the city fondly: museums, music, theater, pubs, and historic sites. She liked this woman and imagined them becoming friends, getting to know other artists and fun, interesting women in Singapore. Maybe musicians and writers, too. A whole side of her life she'd been missing while proving herself at the firm.

If, that is, she decided to go.

• • • • •

After another night and morning of tension-filled silence at home, Liam called Aislinn at the office. He wanted to talk and suggested they meet in Chelsea at an out-of-the-way lounge they used to go to when he was still married to Janice. He knew she was angry, but she couldn't help feeling that he didn't get it. He couldn't understand; maybe no man could. Men of his generation were raised to believe their careers and jobs came first. Sure, maybe the women worked in an office somewhere, or taught school, or were nurses, and some managed to break into the professional ranks, but men like Liam thought it was a game for those women, something that wouldn't last and was just an amusement, while their real job was to raise children and support the husband in his career.

Why had she thought Liam might be different? It was her own fault. Deluding herself, blinded by—what, exactly? Breathtaking sex? His physical beauty? His gallantry? They'd agreed in their support of Bill Clinton back in '96, when their affair had begun, although Aislinn had her doubts about the President's character and Liam seemed to love everything about him. All of which, she realized now, should have been warning signals that this man did not consider her his equal and did not understand women. But no more. She was going to make him see that he'd underestimated her. He couldn't take her for granted. She had a career, too, and somehow—she wasn't sure how, at this point—he had to accommodate her needs.

• • • • •

Aislinn joined Liam at a candle-lit table. He had a drink in front of him and a glass of white wine was waiting for her. He stood and greeted her with a kiss.

"Mmm, I taste Scotch," she said as he helped her with her coat.

He held her chair for her as she sat. Gallant, she noted. Is that a gesture of equals?

"I got the chardonnay you like."

"Perfect," she said, and took a sip. It was just like him to remember the wine, a label only this bar stocked, to have it waiting for her. He could be so thoughtful when he put his mind to it. She couldn't imagine being apart from him, certainly not a world away.

"You look amazing tonight," he said.

Although the weather was still cool, she was wearing a spring dress, yellow, one he'd complimented before. They'd been married now for three years, but why did it feel like a first date? So much uncertainty and upheaval, and here they were dancing around the question that would determine their future.

He reached into his suit coat pocket and took out a box, which he placed next to her wineglass.

"What's this?"

"A peace offering," he said. "And an apology. I was a jerk for not talking to you about the Singapore move when I first knew it was a possibility. It would be great for my career, but you and I are a team, and of course I want you to be happy. And fulfilled. I wasn't thinking, and I'm sorry. It's just that the attack affected me more than I realized. This city has changed. I have, too."

Although the speech sounded rehearsed, which Aislinn thought endearing, she saw something new in his eyes. He was afraid of losing her, whether he went to Singapore or not. And he was afraid of staying here. His air of confidence first attracted her to him, his swagger, but it was this sensitive side, his softer interior, that had won her over when he'd asked her to marry him.

She looked at the box, but didn't move, so Liam opened it for her, lifting from it a diamond tennis bracelet that he slipped onto her wrist. It caught the flickering light of the candle and exploded like fireworks. The weight of it was cool against her skin.

"Liam! It's gorgeous. And too much. You shouldn't have done this."

"Gorgeous, yes. Just like you."

She leaned forward to reward him with a kiss, tasting the Scotch again. She thought about her conversation with Hannah. She *did* love Liam. Wasn't her marriage worth saving? Or was Jessica right? Should she tell him to go without her? That she wouldn't tolerate being undervalued?

The sparkling bracelet brought to mind a weekend they'd spent in Vermont, just before the attacks. An anniversary celebration, they'd planned to hike in the Green Mountains, and Liam had booked them into a rustic B&B near Killington. After the long drive north from the city, she felt terrible, drained, her head pounding and her throat scratchy, and she knew what was coming. In the morning, after a restless night, her throat now blazing, she couldn't bear the thought of getting out of bed, much less hiking. Liam, though, was perfect, attentive, solicitous. He brought her tea with honey and lemon, drove into town to get cough syrup and cold tablets, and late in the afternoon, when he'd convinced her to join him by the fire in the inn's living room, served her brandy and cake. He was sweet and thoughtful, and she'd fallen in love with him all over again.

"So," Liam asked now, "have you given Singapore any more thought?"

She sat back and admired the bracelet. On the one hand, it might just be a lovely gesture, like the care he'd shown her in Vermont that weekend, or the piano he'd bought for their townhouse. An apology and peace offering, as Liam had said. On the other hand, it was a bribe, wasn't it? Buying her submission with a bauble, like some Indian chief trading his birthright for a handful of wampum? He was still not taking her needs into account. He was still pushing Singapore on her. There was no way for them both to get what they wanted. He'd put her in an impossible position.

Her head was spinning, still uncertain. "My career is very important to me—"

"Aislinn—"

"Let me finish, Liam. I was furious with you when Rebecca told me about Singapore. How could you be so thoughtless? It was so unlike you. My career's important to me, and I thought you understood that." The bracelet's reflected light caught her eye again. She hadn't decided until just now what she was going to say to him. Moving with him meant sacrificing everything she'd worked so hard for. Not going meant, almost certainly, the end of her marriage. She took a deep breath.

"But so are you," she said. "I will go with you to Singapore."

She'd surprised them both, it seemed, and Liam reached for her hand.

"I will go," she resumed, her hand now in his, "on one condition—that I can find something productive to do with my time. I need to find a job. I've worked too hard to get where I am. I won't let this derail my career."

Liam lifted her hand and kissed her fingers.

"Yes, of course, my love. Yes."

· · · · ·

Telling Frank she was leaving the firm was the hardest thing she'd ever done. With her own father gone, she'd looked to him for guidance for these last few years at Morrow, Dunn. She couldn't believe her luck when she'd landed in Frank's department and discovered what a patient teacher he was. His specialty was cutting-edge structured-finance deals, and his services were in high demand. At first, her job was to watch and learn. Gradually, she took on more and more responsibility, handling smaller projects on her own, her own clients, assigned new lawyers like Brian to train. Every year during her performance review, Frank had assured her she was on track for partnership, one of the stars of her class. She billed more hours than anyone else, even in the slowdown since the attacks. She was both professional and collegial. Clients loved her. All she had to do was keep doing what she was doing.

Now, though, all that was about to change.

"Frank," she said, "I've got something to tell you." They'd been reviewing the loan agreement for a new leveraged buyout, one of the few deals that had come in recently, plotting strategy for their negotiations with the borrower's counsel. It was a sign that, maybe, business was picking up. Frank leaned back in his desk chair and waited.

"You know how much I love working here. My dream has been to spend my whole career at this firm." She looked into Frank's eyes, which revealed nothing. Did he suspect what was coming? Had Hannah tipped him off, or Liam? "However," she said, "Liam has accepted a promotion as assistant manager of SJ Freeman's Singapore joint venture." Still nothing in Frank's expression. "We're moving in late May. It kills me to say it, but I have to resign."

Now Frank leaned forward, elbows on his desk. "We'll miss you, Aislinn. I had high hopes for you here."

Was that it? Nothing more? He didn't sound surprised, and Aislinn again wondered if someone at the bank had told him about Liam's promotion. How long had he known? And how could he be so dismissive?

"I appreciate all you've done for me, Frank. Truly. Working here has been an amazing experience. I hope when we come back to New York, that I might return to the firm."

Frank was sliding the documents for the new project into a file folder, no longer looking at her.

"We'll see. But you know that's not how things usually work. By then, we'll have moved on. And so will you."

So. That was it, then. The end of her career at Morrow, Dunn & O'Brien.

3

5 August 1914
— On board The Duchess of Lancaster, bound for Singapore

I had intended long before now to begin writing in my journal, a promise I made to myself when first I boarded this ghastly ship, which we passengers have taken to calling "The Duchess," but events and my own incommodious frailties have prevented me from doing so. Or, to be as candid as I ought, knowing that only my eyes will see these scribblings, I have been most distraught since the day we departed Liverpool. I did not want to leave England, not with the world in such turmoil, and I most certainly did not want to voyage to the Far East, where I do not know a soul, save for my Uncle Cyril, who has settled in distant Singapore and has agreed to take me in like the poor refugee I am. Uncle Cyril, my mother's brother, who remembers me as little Lizzie Pennington, a sickly girl in plaits, not the grown-up Elizabeth I have become.

Alas, however, the choice was not mine to make. As a young woman, without a shilling of my own, I was at the mercy of what remained of my pitiable family, chiefly my maiden Aunt Margaret, who was scandalized by my supposed libertine ways and terrorized by the drumbeat of approaching war, and so, given no options whatsoever and no say in the matter in any event, I embarked.

The Duchess is not so grand a ship as those now plying the waves to North America, much larger and luxurious vessels that are meant to appeal to the very wealthy who travel for mere pleasure but must also accommodate the laboring class off to seek new opportunities in the West where there are none at home. Our ship is comfortable enough, I suppose, though cramped and poorly decorated, with little thought given to pleasing the eye, a failing to which these past several years under the tutelage of a brilliant painter have rendered me acutely attuned. I am fortunate to have my own stateroom, at least, as drab as it is, and the dining saloon, with its wood paneling, resembles the restaurant in a Manchester hotel I once visited with R. All in all, I remind myself, it could be far worse.

Immediately as we hit the open water, I took ill, a combination, no doubt, of the roiling seas and my equally roiling emotions. I am confident that I was not alone in my misery, however, as I could hear perfectly well the moaning and retching of my nearest on-board neighbors, and when I eventually did venture out from my stateroom I recognized on the faces of countless fellow passengers the pale—nearly green—complexion that I saw in my own looking glass. My indisposition occupied me for a good long time, and it was all I could do to summon the energy to read one of the novels I'd thought to bring with me, never mind opening my sketch book or putting pen to this diary. (And, if my aunt had taken note of the sort of novels I packed, all gifts from R., I am sure she would have confiscated them, but I can see that Mr. David Herbert Lawrence will be a most agreeable companion on this voyage.)

After ages at sea, I began to feel more myself, which is to say I could scarcely contain my anger over my enforced confinement in this floating gaol, my punishment for I know not what misdeeds. Why must I be banished to the ends of the earth while the rest of England rides out the storm of war at home? And what purpose does my exile serve when I might be called upon to contribute to the empire's defense in some way? I am treated as a child or, worse, as damaged goods, discarded without reason. Is what I did so terrible as to warrant such cruelty?

Having mostly recovered, then, I at once made it my business to get to know my fellow inmates, and it arose that they were, to my surprise, a colorful, and I daresay memorable, lot. One who stands out is Mr. Edmund Preston, a novelist whose name I recognized immediately upon being introduced to him. (I asked him if he knew Mr. Lawrence, and he claimed that indeed they were intimates. I shall have to inquire further.) He seems a jolly fellow, and my first impression is that he could be the source of much amusement both here and, ultimately, in Singapore, where he is also bound. Another passenger is Miss Lydia Spencer, a schoolteacher from Manchester. Such a clever girl, able to recite from memory dozens of sonnets, and blessed with a lovely singing voice. I am sad to learn that she is traveling only as far as Bombay to join her fiancé, a young man in the Civil Service there, but for now she makes a delightful partner for the whist table and as we sit alongside one another on deck to watch the dreary waves.

Despite the enjoyable prospect of sharing the voyage with Miss Spencer and Mr. Preston, I continued to find my situation intolerable. Why should I have no say in my own destiny? And so, as we were to drop anchor at Cape Town for a matter of some days before resuming our trip, I resolved to make my escape. If I was expected to arrive in the East, and there to continue my captivity under the sharp eyes of my uncle, a virtual stranger to me, all the more reason to stop in South Africa instead, examine its charms, which I had heard were considerable, and, perhaps, to make it my new home, far from the meddling relations. How I might support myself there I hadn't a clue, but surely there would be among the Europeans in residence a need for a governess or tutor with training in art and music.

Fully myself again, I emerged more frequently from confinement in my stale, dank cabin and spent a great deal of time on deck, where the air was fresher, if just as damp and also laden with salt. At least it was possible to breathe there, and to imagine my freedom. I sketched in my pad—portraits of Lydia, our fellow passengers, the hard-working sailors, even Mr. Preston—and when at long last we did come within sight of the coastline, I drew its shapes and contours.

All the while, however, I was formulating a plan. Upon our arrival at Cape Town, I would inform the captain of my intention to remain in the settlement there and he would have no choice but to put me ashore as I requested. I began to pack my belongings into my trunk and made my farewells. Both Lydia and Mr. Preston did try valiantly to dissuade me, but I had made my decision.

And then, one morning, we arrived, alerted by the shrieks of birds we had not heard in some time and, too, there was a change in the air, unfamiliar scents on the breeze, smoke now mingled with the salt. Shouts of "Land, ho!" rang out on deck and there was much scurrying in the passage as the boys made ready for our anchorage. From the ship we could see an odd-shaped mountain that seemed as if it had been sawed off at the top to make a flat surface, and there was a great deal of activity evident in the town as our appearance must have generated much excitement.

I had imagined Cape Town to be something like London, a place I had visited only once, with R., or at least Liverpool, but in this I was sorely mistaken. It looked from the ship more like a rustic sort of village, with muddy lanes and natives running half naked along the shore. I confess that this impression did somewhat diminish my enthusiasm for the course I had chosen. Nonetheless, I located the captain and informed him of my plan to disembark, in response to which he laughed. Laughed out loud, in fact, his mouth agape and revealing the disgraceful condition of his teeth.

"No, Miss," he said, once his laughter had subsided. "I think not, Miss."

When I protested, he summoned one of the sailors, a rough-looking fellow with leathery skin who looked as though he might have been at sea his entire life. "Tell the young lady," said the captain, with a nod in my direction, "why it's not a good idea for her to go ashore here in Cape Town."

The sailor took on a deeply grave expression and stroked the scruffy beard on his chin. "Oh, no, Miss, begging your pardon, Miss, you mustn't go into that cesspool," he said, with a dripping accent I could not place—Newcastle, perhaps? Northumberland?—and scarcely understood.

"Cesspool?" I asked. "Whatever do you mean?"

Bowing slightly, he said, "Begging your pardon, Miss, but 'tis not safe for the likes of you, a refined lady such as yourself."

If he only knew.

"Tell her about Braxton," urged the captain, who crossed his arms smugly to await the story.

"Well, Braxton. That's a sorry tale I hate to tell, but it happened on our last voyage. Aye, Captain, Braxton was as fine a galley-swab as ever rode the waves, and that's a fact."

"What happened to this Braxton fellow?" I asked.

"It wasn't pretty, Miss, and if you don't mind my saying—"

"What happened?" I said, perhaps too tartly, as I was hoping to spur him onward. I like deference to one's betters just fine in the proper circumstances, but I have no patience when a man is trying to shield me from something "for my own protection" or some such nonsense. I'm afraid I may have frightened the poor fool with the sharpness of my inquiry.

"Yes, Miss. Begging your pardon, Miss. Braxton was warned that we were all to stay together. In a pack, you might say, like animals. For safety, Miss, because we sailors all know what can happen in these primitive ports o' call. And we did all gather inside a tavern, every one of us, not a very nice establishment mind you, but suitable for rough fellows such as we are, and the ale was fine enough, and they served a kind of stew made from some wild beast like I've never before in my life tasted."

He seemed to be savoring the recollection of the stew, and I swear he smacked his lips at the thought of it. I gave him an impatient look then and I might even have tapped my foot to hurry him along because in response he nodded, swallowed, and took a deep gulp of air as if he were now prepared, at long last, to get to the point.

"At any rate, when it was time for us to return to the ship, one of the lads noticed Braxton was missing. I know for a fact he was with us when we began the evening, owing to a wee wager we had made about certain young—yes, well, never mind about the wager, but as we were heading back to the ship, there was no doubting that he was no longer among our company. Well, Miss, it turned out Braxton was no longer among anybody's company, if you get my meaning, because his corpse turned up with a bloody knife in his back."

"Oh, my. Someone from the ship? A quarrel of some kind?"

"Not on your life, Miss. This was a native sword, an evil-looking dagger with a carved black handle and a curved blade that's just the thing for—well, I don't want to say, Miss."

"For God's sake, just tell me, man."

"Yes, Miss. Begging your pardon, Miss. The curved blade is just the thing for disemboweling a bloke, Miss, which is, more or less, what happened to Braxton. No, Miss, the Town is no place for a young lady such as yourself, Miss."

And then the captain dismissed the sailor, who seemed most relieved to be on his way, returning to some mind-numbing chore below decks, I'm sure.

The point was certainly made, and I now realized that perhaps I was not fully prepared to strike out on my own in a place that was not terribly civilized, with no one of my acquaintance to even look for me if I should run afoul of some "native sword." I offered my thanks to the captain and returned chastened to my cabin.

And so, we sail on to Singapore.

· · · · ·

18 August 1914

We have arrived at the port of Bombay, but I no longer desire to disembark. I am resigned to my fate. I shall continue to Singapore to be imprisoned in my uncle's house like a common criminal, perhaps to be put to work as a servant to him, for what do I know of the ways of these men of the colonies who set out to earn their fortunes and tame the local savages. Is it civilization they spread, or mere domination and control?

I bade a tearful farewell to Lydia Spencer and urged her to visit us, but I know how unlikely that is, as the two settlements are still so distant from one another. The rest of the voyage will be terribly lonely without her.

I suppose I was a bit curious about the port, but all indications are that it is a dirty city, with every manner of filth on the streets and floating in the river. At table last night in the dining saloon, I overheard a gentleman say that women engaged in the same sorts of manual labor as the men, laying brick, mixing cement, and so on. It strikes me as marvelously egalitarian, to employ men and women equally so, even in such backbreaking tasks. Still, while I am as interested as ever in earning my freedom, I do not think I would be at all suited for such a life.

I continue to sketch daily. While we are in port, I considered breaking out my paints, but it will only be for a short time, and I thought it better to wait until we arrive at our final destination, where I can work on terra firma, if my uncle will give me leave to do so in his house. I am so anxious to work with brush and canvas again. Mrs. Olivia Judson, a lovely Lancastrian widow who is traveling to visit a cousin in Penang, one of the other communities that, together with Malacca and Singapore, make up the Straits Settlements, sat with me this morning and allowed me to sketch her. It felt so good to exercise those muscles, and I truly think that I was able to capture her image. What character! An aquiline nose—not a compliment for a woman, I know, but on her it was positively majestic. Full lips. Eyes that in the sun shone bright, like gems. High cheekbones, narrow brows, and long lashes. A brooch of epic proportions that constantly drew my eye and also reflected the brilliant light. It was so kind of her to sit for me, and the experience was refreshing.

I am encouraged by the prospects for my new home. Art can make all the difference in how we see the world—one of the many important life lessons R. imparted to me.

· · · · ·

I confess that until the incident at Cape Town, when I thought I might leave the ship and settle there, I had paid little attention to the men employed on board. But now, without the companionship of Miss Spencer to amuse me, I am intrigued by these rough and tumble specimens. For the most part, I gather, they are sailors based in Liverpool, as English as I am, despite the uncouth accents I can barely decipher. And these men, bearded, each of them, boast skin bronzed by the sun, some of them as leathery and tough as old sea chests.

There is one man, however, darker and more compact than all the rest, with an angular face and thick black hair, handsome in his way, who is certainly not English. Like the other men, he does his work diligently, if without haste, but unlike the English sailors, who sing and chatter as they go about their tasks, he is taciturn and somber. I have yet to see the man smile or even speak, and I wonder what language he would utter if the need arose.

It was devilish of me, but I contrived to find out. Shortly before we left the port of Bombay, I took my place on a deck chair, sketch pad in hand, and from the shadow afforded by my wide-brimmed hat, watched him coil ropes the thickness of my arms. I pretended to draw, but I could scarcely move my eyes from the sight of him: his skin the color of damp earth, glistening with sweat, the cords of his muscular shoulders swelling and twisting with the strain, his face partially hidden behind a thick black tangle of a beard.

I set aside my pad and swung my legs to the deck, beginning to stand, then allowing my knees to fold beneath me as I sank, emitting a muffled cry. As I intended, the sailor's attention turned to me. I thought I saw in his eyes some puzzlement, as if he had never seen such a sight before in his life. It wasn't simply hesitation. He truly did not know what to do.

"Please help me," I said feebly, perhaps overplaying my part. "Please?"

I doubted that he understood my words, although he could not help but know my meaning. He set aside the rope and came to me, unhurried, his face still expressionless, and offered his hand, the underside of which was as pink as a sunset, yet rough and scarred. With his help, I stood and settled back onto the chair.

"Thank you so very much," I said, and still his expression did not change. "I'm terribly sorry to interrupt your work." Nothing yet.

"What is your name? So that I might give a good report to the captain?"

He turned to look over his shoulder, as if he had been forbidden to speak to the passengers, or at least the female passengers, and wished not to be seen doing so. He looked back to me and nodded, acknowledging, at least, his understanding.

"I am Samir," he said.

"What a lovely name," I said. "Well then, Samir, I am Elizabeth Pennington, and I thank you for your gallant rescue."

Samir nodded again and backed away from me, anxious, I'm sure, to be out of the mad Englishwoman's presence.

It occurred to me then—how could it have escaped me until that moment?—that Singapore was no doubt full of such exotic specimens. I had assumed the colony was populated entirely by Englishmen and their wives and families. Had I not seen for myself that Cape Town, which I had once imagined to be akin to London, was no more than a village, filled with a veritable stew of races? And had I not seen the same in Bombay, with the dark-skinned laborers, both men and women, thronging on the shore? Surely Singapore, being at the Eastern edge of the Empire, would be an even greater hotchpot.

How naïve I have been and how terribly incurious about my new home. I must open my eyes to what the world has to offer.

What will become of me in Singapore?

24 August 1914

Now we have come to Ceylon, the port of Colombo, and I am frightfully weary of The Duchess and all on board, even Mr. Preston, who has grown exceedingly tiresome.

From the deck, the city looks white and pure, glistering in the summer sun like a polished stone. On the quay, a group of bald-headed men in lovely orange robes bow towards us—or maybe it is to their ocean gods, or to whomever they pray—and toss petals on the waves. Behind the city, radiant green hills rise majestically, and all along the coast are marvelous sandy beaches. I detect wood smoke on the breeze, a fragrant scent that is at once new and familiar, sandalwood, according to Mr. Preston, and I do wish that I could stop here for a time to rest, to walk on solid ground and breathe something other than the salt air. But my fate is sealed. The end is near (oh, how absurdly dramatic that must sound!) and I must go on.

I continue to watch for the handsome Samir, the dark sailor I have come to understand after making inquiries is Indian, but he seems to have disappeared. I feel terrible that I have frightened the poor wretch so! Did he fling himself into the turbulent waters between Bombay and Ceylon? Or did he volunteer to be a galley slave in the bowels of the ship in order to avoid me? For his sake, I am glad we will soon arrive in Singapore, and he will be rid of me, once again permitted to enjoy the light of day.

The news from Europe is grim. We are, it seems, officially at war with Germany. Who knows if I shall ever be able to go home? At least my poor brother is spared the horrors of battle, although in his confinement at the asylum, I imagine he faces his own horrors. And my father, who saw the conflict coming and considered returning to duty, brought down by his own son's madness. I cannot imagine what it must be like to find oneself in the center of such a conflagration. I am not even sure why we are fighting, or against whom. Are there not close ties between the English and Germans? And what is it we hope to settle?

My only consolation is that in the East I shall be far from the hostilities and the repercussions of my own family's tragedies.

In the meantime, I must make do. I draw. I make polite conversation with the other passengers, no matter how they bore me. I tolerate Mr. Preston's stories, ever more fantastical and unbelievable, about his exploits in the far reaches of the empire. And I bide my time until the glorious day when we at long last arrive.

30 August 1914
I am a foolish girl. My thoughts on the long days and nights of this voyage have been only of myself and how resentful I am to have been sent away from the verdant hills of England against my will. But the conditions in Europe might merit more concern than my own plight, as there is talk—it is only talk, as far as I can tell, but perhaps with a kernel of truth—of Germany's army occupying Brussels and the war spreading, much like a virulent fever, throughout the continent and, indeed, beyond. We have heard of a great battle that engulfed the French army and killed tens of thousands of soldiers. I pray it is not true, merely the idle exaggeration of travelers with little else to do but traffic in gossip. Another rumor is that scores of brave women have volunteered to help the cause, as nurses and ambulance drivers or in some other vital capacity. I am filled with admiration, but I am ashamed to say I do not have such courage. Perhaps, after all, I am more fortunate than I had imagined.

It is time, then, for me to look forward to my new life in the Far East. While it is not of my choosing, as I have said in these pages repeatedly, I must make the best of it. Mr. Preston, for all his foibles, made an endearing attempt to offer me comfort this morning. I believe he noticed me alone on deck, gazing despondently at the endless, brooding sea.

"Do not despair, Miss Pennington," said Preston, guessing correctly at my conflicted emotions. "There is much in life that comes along to alter one's expected course and against which it is pointless to resist. From what little I know of your circumstances, I believe this may be one of those moments for you. Perhaps the words of Marcus Aurelius can provide guidance. He said, 'Accept the things to which fate binds you, and love the people with whom fate brings you together, but do so with all your heart.' In other words, my dear, you may be moving to the ends of the Earth, but it is not the end of the world. Think of it as a grand adventure. Imagine the people you will meet, the wonders you will see. Embrace it!"

The dear man then left me alone to think about what he had said, and I felt instantly cheered. Improbably, the sun broke through dense clouds and the waves, glinting brightly, no longer appeared as dreary as they had only a moment before. Mr. Preston—and Marcus Aurelius, whom I confess not to have read—are right. Within the limits of my circumstances, I must make my way. I must embrace my path and find joy in it. I will have my pencil and my paints. I hope to locate a piano so that I can make music. I will discover a circle of friends. And I shall find life in Singapore to be a joy.

31 August 1914

This morning I sought out Mr. Preston to thank him for his words of wisdom yesterday. They have altogether changed the complexion of my outlook. I still have my moments of doubt, of course, and I long for England, but as my former home is now out of reach, I begin to have thoughts of my new situation.

I do not generally share my work with others, at least not until I consider a piece complete, but Mr. Preston had put me in such a mood that when he asked to see the sketch in my pad, I reluctantly turned it in his direction.

"Why, Miss Pennington, this is stunning!" he said, and I am sure I blushed to hear him say it. Truthfully, the drawing pleased me. It had begun in its earliest stage as a realistic portrait of Mrs. Judson, she of the aquiline nose, but had become something rather different as I allowed my imagination to break free. Inspired by dear Mrs. Judson's most prominent feature, now the figure soared, eagle-like, as if hunting for prey.

"How did you learn to draw like this?" Preston asked.

How, indeed. To such a question there is no simple answer. I drew from an early age, captivated by the natural world around me, the plants and flowers in our garden, the trees in the copse beyond the village. I drew and drew and drew and became adept at creating on the page what I saw with my eye, in effect bringing it to life anew. My parents, Father, especially, praised me for my skill, and their praise encouraged me to continue. It was a refuge from the turmoil in our home, the constant bickering, an escape more than a mere pastime.

One day Father took me by the hand, and we walked a great distance, such a distance that at some point he lifted me onto his shoulders so that I might ride him like a pony, although I was already much too old for such a game. At last, we came to a lane, and down that lane we walked until, over a hillock that had hidden it from view, there appeared a house. It wasn't a grand house such as one might find on one of the manors of the county, but it was a good deal larger than our own cottage. Approaching the house, Father hallooed, and we were met at the door by a woman, the housekeeper it appeared from her apron and mobcap, who scowled, or so it seemed to me, and directed us to follow a stone path along the side of the house.

Which we did, Father taking me by the hand to pull me along, and there saw a kind of shed or barn, with great windows in the roof the likes of which I had never seen. I was frightened of the place, particularly because I did not know why we were there. I knew that a chum of mine, a girl we all knew by the name of Pretty, had been sent away to enter service, to become a maid, that is, because her family could no longer afford to keep her. It occurred to me in a blink that this was also to be my fate, and that somehow this odd barn was tied up with my future. As it developed, I was not entirely wrong.

Father pushed open the door to the shed and we entered. It was a magical moment. Perhaps it was the light from above that made the shed seem otherworldly, but in any event, I was transported. What was this place?

A man stood at an easel before a large canvas, his face twisted in concentration. A painter! The reason for our outing dawned on me. As he worked, I was able to study him, fascinated by every aspect of his appearance. His hair was full and bounteous, a great brown shock of it thrust back over his head, threatening to fall into his eyes whenever he leaned too far forward. Beneath his smock, which was stained beautifully with smears of paint in every color imaginable, he wore an open-collared shirt that I thought must at one time have been white but was now dull and grey. His face was not properly bearded, but coarsely hidden by stubble. I was perhaps most taken by his height, as he was a good deal taller than my father, and his movements before the canvas were like those of an athlete—bold, assured, powerful.

The man finally felt our presence, apparently, for he turned to us. Reluctantly at first, I thought, but then his face melted into a welcome, and he reached out his hand to Father and beamed at me.

"So this is little Lizzie, the budding artist!" And with those words, I fell a little bit in love.

I told Mr. Preston this story, more or less, leaving out my childish infatuation with the man, and hurriedly went on to explain how my father had met the artist in a pub and had shown him one of my drawings. How the artist had swooned over my talent, how I became the pupil of one of England's great painters, Richard Thompson Bromley.

"Bromley?" Preston asked. "Richard Bromley, you say?"

I nodded. "He kept a house in the country."

"Remarkable," he said. "Richard Bromley, indeed."

It was. It truly was, more than Preston could imagine.

1 September 1914

The journey is nearing its end. It has at times seemed interminable, as if I had arrived in my own special inferno in which I am tormented not by fire and brimstone but by a foul odor as of rotting meat, the arrogance of biting flies, the monotony of the waves, and the incessant (and largely unwanted) attentions of Mr. Preston.

The man is, it seems, everywhere. It was endearing at first, and he can be pleasant enough, but now I cannot stroll on the deck at any hour of the day without being accosted by him. This morning I left my cabin before the first light. I stood at the railing, gazing out into the blackness of the water, lost in my reveries, when I felt a presence at my elbow as if some dark spirit had appeared, perhaps conjured by my own funereal thoughts.

"Good morning, Miss Pennington," Preston said. "Up early?"

I was taken aback, to say the least, and I don't recall my response, although surely I said something clever, even in my state. Preston offered a cigarette from a silver case, I accepted, and as the sun rose, the two of us watched the coast—the island of Sumatra, Preston informed me, part of the Dutch East Indies—materialize, as if it were a leviathan rising to the surface. And then there were others about, passengers and crew both, and the solitude I had sought on the deck was lost.

Mr. Preston is, as I have before mentioned in these pages, a writer, a rather successful writer, or so I am led to believe. (I believe I have this impression from Preston himself, as I am quite certain I have not read his work previously, although his name was known to me, perhaps from a volume in R.'s own library.) Indeed, he is rarely without a little leather-bound notebook in which he scribbles with the nub of a pencil. I have seen him take it from his pocket during meals, in the middle of a conversation when, presumably, his partner has said something memorable. I have even seen him writing in it during a most unfortunate incident when a cabin boy found himself entangled in a rope and was accidentally flung overboard. While some of the passengers sought to assist the crew with the rescue, Mr. Preston was more interested in recording the details of the near tragedy for, presumably, later incorporation into a story.

As I make that notation, I wonder if I myself might one day appear in one of his stories. I am both appalled and strangely excited at the prospect. What might the man have to say about me? Now I regret divulging to him my acquaintance with Richard Bromley, not to mention my former determination to disembark at Cape Town, which surely seemed foolish in his eyes and would make for fertile, if comic, subject matter for his pen.

While somewhat repulsive—he has a disconcerting habit, or else a medical condition, that causes him to belch loudly without warning—Mr. Preston does have his charms. He is mostly very considerate when it comes to the crew of the vessel, who are remarkably hard-working men, including the comely boy who serves our meals in the dining room. I have noted the way the writer's eyes follow the boy as he completes his tasks, and I wonder if this is more research for a future piece concerning a steamship server. I think, probably, not, and although I will not record specifics here, I have heard gossip in this regard from more than one of my fellow passengers, Mrs. Judson included. I am disinclined to believe such tales and disinterested in any case. Who am I to judge?

And yet Mr. Preston is full of his own stories: of his exploits on previous journeys to Singapore and elsewhere in the Orient, the young women he has known and kept company, the various sheiks and rajahs whom he has befriended, etc. He is most interested in my reasons for traveling during these difficult times, but I am not sure that I shall confide in him the sum of my personal woes more than I have done already. As amused as I might be to discover myself in his writings in the future, I would not wish to recognize anyone resembling my late father, God rest him, my absconded mother, or my poor, mad brother, who is beyond help and must be forgotten.

After I told him that I had studied with Bromley—and that was all I disclosed of our relationship—Preston said he believed he had made Bromley's acquaintance, as well as having dined on numerous occasions with various other well-known painters in Paris and London, names I recognized from my time with R. Whether I can credit these outlandish claims I do not know, but my impression of the man has not been burnished by them. If anything, they make me doubt all the tales he has told up to now. I certainly do not think R. would have put up with him.

. . . . .

Having now thoroughly resigned myself (how often must I say this, as if still, after all this time, seeking to be convinced?), I have grown increasingly curious about my new home. Given Mr. Preston's vast experience and his previous visit to the settlement, I thought to ask his impressions, although I wasn't sure how much stock to put in them.

"Singapore?" he responded. "The pearl of the Orient. Mark me, one day it will be the most important city in the world. It is truly the jewel in the empire's crown. It sits at the junction of—"

"But I do not care about geography, Mr. Preston," I said with the impatience for which my father often chided me as a girl. "What is it like to *live* there?"

"Yes. Well. Living. I have found it a most pleasant environment for my purposes, Miss Pennington. Affable companions and hosts. Thriving society. Friendly natives. Frightfully hot, of course, but one grows accustomed."

"One does, I suppose." Does one? "Is it like Cape Town? Or Bombay?" I fear that I winced at the prospect.

"Oh, my dear, no. It is far more civilized. Singapore was nothing but a native fishing village when the English arrived and built the city. It's not London, I'm afraid, but it's perfectly safe for us. A bit provincial, of course, but cultured enough."

And what sort of culture, I wondered, might I encounter in this civilized Singapore?

My conversations with Mr. Preston have led me to reflect on my time with R., and all that he taught me. Being only a child when we met, there was much to be learned, and he opened my eyes in so many ways. Most importantly—at least where the art is concerned, although in so many other matters as well—he taught me to see differently, to feel the movement in my surroundings and my subject. After R., the world never stood still for me again.

7 September 1914, morning
We have passed so many small islands since we left the coast of Sumatra, each time raising my expectations that this was the one, that we had reached our destination, but always we steamed past, leaving the land once again, with its dense covering of jungle, to fade away into the water like a sinking stone.

At long last, though, I recognized the flurry of activity among the crew as they prepared for arrival in port, and now I am delighted to record that after five long weeks at sea, the ship is anchored off Singapore Island. The clouds over the settlement are thick and dark, but they do not appear to threaten. They are like smoke and seem to roll in plumes across the lush landscape. What a place this is! So green, with glistening white buildings, including an impressive church steeple, rising up the low hills some distance from the port. No, this is not Cape Town or Bombay. It is no wonder that my uncle has made it his home. And now, owing to his generosity, I suppose it is mine as well. (You see? I have wholly embraced the adventure to which I have been delivered by my circumstances. Carpe diem.)

7 September 1914, later
Farewell to The Duchess! We have arrived at last. We were ferried from ship to shore in rickety little vessels the men called "junks," which seemed a name both appropriate and frightening, but the word is apparently derived from the local language and has nothing to do with the dilapidated condition of the boats. These junks were operated by nimble little Chinamen in cone hats, who Preston tells me perform most of the manual work here. Where on earth did they all come from? Another wonder to behold and completely beyond my experience.

When I stepped foot again on solid ground, it seemed yet to sway and buck as if I were still on the ship. I could barely stand without holding onto a railing or the nearest arm. It must have appeared as if I might be intoxicated. Soon, though, as I continued to walk toward a row of carriages on the harbor's main thoroughfare, I regained my balance well enough. Still, it's a wonder I did not fall flat on my face.

And now I had the opportunity to take in my surroundings. With the sea at my back, I gazed up at a row of somber buildings, unmistakably the seat of local government or, at any rate, the manifestation of imperial might. There was a bustle on the street that ran along the quay, horse-drawn carriages and little two-wheeled carts pulled by more Chinamen, as if they were somehow competing with the animals for custom!

After such a long time at sea in the tropics, I had become, as Mr. Preston had assured me I would, more or less accustomed to the heat, but here on land I missed the sea breezes, and the moist heat grew uncomfortable. I would have to learn how the ladies dressed in order to tolerate the oppression. I longed for the shade of the exotic trees that grew along the shore, and wondered where I was to go, how I was to find my uncle.

At last, however, a small, rotund gentleman approached me, removed his hat, and bowed.

"Lizzie, my dear, I am your Uncle Cyril," the man said, and I all but wept with joy. My fellow passengers had become a family of sorts over the long journey, especially dear Lydia, but here was actual family, my mother's brother, and it made me realize how much I longed for home, my poor mother and father and brother, despite all our troubles. I startled him, I'm sure, but I nearly leapt into his grasp and willed his arms to encircle me. It felt so good to be held! And then the moment passed, and my uncle, with all appropriate reticence, extracted himself from my embrace.

"Yes, well, I'm sure," he said, flustered by my display. "Welcome to Singapore, my dear."

Now I studied him as he regained his composure and looked about us to see if we had been observed. He was no taller than I, but as round about the middle as a prize gourd. A handsome man, with a full head of dark hair streaked with grey and a thick mustache, he wore a rumpled linen suit with a vest that strained to contain his belly, and gripped in one hand a straw boater while the other held a gnarled walking stick. What a delightful image he presented, and I had the urge to locate my sketchbook and preserve him forever on the spot. There would be time for that enough, I soon realized, perhaps endless days.

I did not ask how Uncle Cyril knew the ship had come to port, but it was apparent our arrival was common knowledge, as half the town now seemed to throng the waterfront, seeking out relations or goods or collecting bits of news and gossip from Europe. Uncle replaced his hat on his head and offered his arm to lead me away from the crowd, lest it topple us back into the sea.

The ship's captain, without a word of my attempted Cape Town misadventure, had assured me that my trunk and other belongings would be delivered to my uncle's residence, and so we were free to depart. As the carriage pulled away, I turned for a last look at my home for the past weeks, wondering what awaited me in this remotest of outposts.

"Tell me about your voyage, my dear," said Uncle Cyril, grasping my hand as our carriage trotted inland. I accommodated him as best I could although I very much desired to take in the sights on this, the final leg of my journey, amazed by the startling busyness of the commercial center of the town, anticipating all the wonders that might next appear, as if turning the pages in a storybook. But I complied and described my views of Cape Town, Bombay, Ceylon, and the rest, and told him about Lydia and Mr. Preston and the others, my impressions of the sailors, my attempts to sketch on board and how I longed to break out my paints and properly set to work with oils, or watercolors if oils were not to hand. I told him I had letters for him from home, and he practically swelled in anticipation of them.

"It's marvelous to have you here," he said, patting my knee as if I were still the child he knew as Lizzie. But I suppose that is how he thinks of me, for the last I saw him, on some long ago visit to England, I was indeed a child. Before Richard Bromley. Before my mother vanished and my brother went mad. Before the world fell apart.

He grew distracted as we progressed up a macadam road, past more official looking buildings, some of them exceedingly grand, as well as shophouses and teeming markets, then past orchards or plantations of some kind, until we entered a part of the city that seemed engulfed by jungle, and ultimately arrived at a glorious house in a forest clearing, where the carriage stopped. It was like nothing I had ever seen, and yet it did look familiar, almost like an English cottage, with its black planks set into white plaster, topped by a cheerful, red-tiled roof.

"Here we are, my dear," said Uncle Cyril. "Our little paradise."

4

Aislinn didn't feel like celebrating Independence Day, no matter what the calendar said. Fourth of July? What difference did it make? At home they might have had plans to watch fireworks from someone's rooftop terrace—gaudy, defiant bombs bursting in the air over New York's skyline, the altered skyline, the first July without the Twin Towers. But here? No such celebration in Singapore. Just another Thursday, even in the American community, although the American Club had decorated the place with red, white, and blue bunting, and little flags adorned the tables in the coffee shop. Besides, if she were truly independent, she wouldn't be on this tiny island at the edge of the world, trailing after her husband. She'd be home, in New York, advancing her own career, doing what she was trained to do.

But here she was. By May, they'd sold the townhouse and put what they couldn't bring with them, like her piano, in storage. The flight—she hadn't flown since before 9/11 and leaned on first one pill and then another to manage her terror—seemed interminable, from JFK to Tokyo and then on to Singapore.

All she remembered of the trip was arriving near midnight at Singapore's Changi Airport and marveling, even in her stupor and resentment, at its cleanliness and efficiency. They stood in the immigration line with a dazzling assortment of fellow-travelers: a young Chinese couple carrying exhausted toddlers; a pair of briefcase-toting Japanese businessmen in rumpled suits; stout older women in headscarves, huddled together, Muslims, she supposed; an extremely tall African man in a multi-colored dashiki; men of various dark complexions with scruffy beards, wearing mud-spattered jeans and work boots, as if they'd come directly from a construction site. New York City was the most diverse place she'd ever lived, but this was another magnitude of multiculturalism. Why had she assumed that everyone would look and sound like that artist she'd met?

The line had moved fast. An unsmiling clerk, a brown-skinned man in a blue uniform, waved them forward, and Liam slid both their passports across the counter. The clerk, whose feathery mustache looked like tentative pencil strokes, studied Liam's face and then the photo on the page. Why did they do that? Did they memorize unusual features to see if they could find them in the picture? The barely noticeable scar above his upper lip? One ear slightly higher than the other? What were they looking for, exactly? Terrorists? Her husband—tall, handsome, white—hardly fit the profile, did he? Then it was Aislinn's turn. The clerk looked up, looked back at the photo, looked up again, and she wondered what he'd missed on the first glance. Her hair was different, long and blond in the passport photo, shorter now, against Liam's wishes, prepared for the tropical heat. Should she take her glasses off to match the picture? Or explain that she really was married to Liam, even though they had different last names? It occurred to her that terrorists weren't the only category of villains they were screening for. Singapore had a reputation for harsh treatment of drug traffickers, and who could say what a smuggler looked like? Like her, with her stash of buttons tucked away in her checked bag, wrapped in lingerie. She hadn't thought to be worried about that until now.

Passports stamped, luggage collected, customs cleared, they'd been met by a driver who whisked them into the city along an empty expressway that soared between high-rises and the bobbing lights of ships in the harbor. At which point she must have fallen asleep, because the next thing she knew she was being escorted through the cavernous lobby of the Shangri-La Hotel, past a freakishly large display of alien flowers, and into an elevator that delivered them to a wide, carpeted corridor and their suite, home for a week or two until they moved into a furnished corporate flat while looking for a more permanent home.

The suite was grand, including a spacious sitting room just inside the entry with a loveseat upholstered in soothing gray, accented with red pillows. A red lacquer cabinet held a television and minibar, and another arrangement of unfamiliar tropical flowers in orange, yellow, and red graced a glass coffee table. Beyond that was the bedroom, dominated by an inviting, king-size bed, two armchairs, and curtains that opened to a balcony overlooking the hotel's lush gardens. It was the most beautiful hotel room she'd ever seen.

The next morning, while Liam was getting settled in his new office, wasting no time to establish himself, Aislinn explored the hotel's grounds and its spectacular array of orchids and unfamiliar flowering shrubs. In the afternoon she sipped juice by the pool and was lulled to sleep by the chittering of mynas and parakeets. She didn't want to be there, she wanted to be home in New York, but she couldn't help feeling as if she'd landed in paradise.

• • • • •

The last six weeks had passed in a blur of activity: meeting Liam's colleagues and a few other American expats; finding a place to live; the disheartening search for a job; taking delivery of their household shipment from New York; unpacking and making the apartment feel more or less like home; shopping for what they hadn't been able to bring with them, like appliances that would run on Singapore's higher voltage electricity.

Now, while Liam was in the bathroom getting ready for work, Aislinn put on her robe, the white silk peignoir he gave her last Christmas when they were still in the city, still recovering from the 9/11 horrors, and went to the kitchen. She missed her own morning rituals: brushing her hair, still long then; applying her makeup, not that she used much, lipstick and a little blush; picking the right outfit for whatever was happening in the office that day, a rare court appearance, a negotiation, a closing, a client lunch. She hadn't given up on the idea of getting work here—she couldn't give up—but the prospects were looking dim. Despite her impeccable credentials, so far none of the American or English law firms in town had even wanted to talk to her, much less give her a job.

For now, her routine was making coffee for Liam before he headed to his office to concoct multi-million-dollar deals for his bank, the same kinds of deals she used to work on when she was assisting Frank on the SJ Freeman account at Morrow, Dunn. In the kitchen, her feet bare on the cool travertine floor, she spooned the grounds into the filter, filled the reservoir with water, and flipped the switch. She hated to disturb the maid, whose tiny room was just off the kitchen, and she did her best—setting the cups gently on the granite counter, easing the silverware drawer open without jostling the spoons—but it wasn't possible to be completely silent. The gurgling of the coffeemaker made her wince every morning, and every morning, without success, she willed it mute.

Of all the strange things about Singapore that would take time getting used to—and the list was long—having a live-in maid, an *amah*, was the strangest. She had resisted the idea at first, but some of the other expat wives she'd met had convinced her she would need help taking care of the apartment, not to mention the inevitable entertaining she and Liam would do for his customers, as if somehow that would be *her* responsibility. In Brooklyn they'd had a Dominican cleaning woman who came in once a week, but they never saw her, and Aislinn only knew she'd been there by the lemony scent in the air when she came home from work.

She tried to picture Cecilia in her room, a space barely large enough to contain a twin bed and the tiny television she'd brought with her. Aislinn had never in her life lived in a room so small—not growing up on the farm in Virginia, not in her college dorm, not in her Cambridge apartment during law school. Even the virtual closet she occupied in a Manhattan sublet she shared with Jessica when she first started working at Morrow, Dunn was bigger than the maid's windowless cell. Aislinn was still getting to know the woman, but so far she had learned that Cecilia was from the Philippines, like many of Singapore's *amahs*, had left behind three young children, two girls and a boy, or the other way around, to be raised by her husband's parents in a village far from Manila, and that her husband was also working overseas—in Dubai, Aislinn thought, or at any rate somewhere in the Middle East—because there were so few jobs at home. How could she abandon her children like that? She needed to earn a living, of course, everyone did, and maybe it meant a better life for them down the road, but still. And when Aislinn thought of how little they were paying the woman, it made her shudder. She'd asked the other expat wives if they felt guilty about it, because how could they not, and only got blank stares in return.

Waiting for the coffee to brew, she retreated to the living room and gazed out the floor-to-ceiling windows at their surroundings, the dawn indistinct, just a promise, streetlights still glowing down below, windows ablaze in neighboring apartment blocks. At home, the early summer sun would have been long up at this hour, but here, just north of the equator, the light came and went with monotonous regularity. Up at seven, give or take a few minutes, down at seven, all year long. One more item on her list of things to get used to.

Although she'd grown wary of high-rise buildings after the attack on the World Trade Center and couldn't step too close to the windows without trembling, the view from their twentieth-floor flat was spectacular. From this angle she couldn't see the congested downtown skyline, the one part of Singapore that bore a passing resemblance to New York, but to the north and east was a verdant expanse stretching all the way from the center of the island toward the South China Sea. Here and there apartment blocks and hotels broke through the rainforest canopy, and even in the faint light she could make out a church steeple and a minaret from a small mosque. Somewhere hidden in the trees was a Buddhist shrine, too, she knew, and on one of her jogs around the neighborhood she'd passed a Hindu temple. She had resisted leaving New York to move here for Liam's promotion, forfeiting her job and friends, her career, but she had to admit it was a beautiful city, a metropolis in the jungle and a fascinating mix of cultures, one that had not yet stopped surprising her.

Because of her new fear of heights, she'd asked the property agent Liam's office had retained if there weren't some rental houses she might see instead of high-rise apartment buildings. She had heard from her new acquaintances, primarily Jenny Morelock, the wife of Liam's new boss, about the Black and Whites, houses that dated from the colonial era, often on stately pieces of property with private gardens, and the agent reluctantly showed her one that was massive and filled with antiques on two floors. It was far bigger than they needed, would have required a gardener and at least one maid, maybe two, and Aislinn couldn't imagine having servants, plural, but she regretted that Liam had vetoed it as an option. It reminded locals of a dark period in their history before independence and would be bad for business, he'd insisted. She had to admit the apartment they'd taken instead was beautiful, larger than their townhouse in Brooklyn and more luxurious than she was accustomed to. There were other advantages of the apartment, too. The Fullerton, named after the first Governor of the Straits Settlements that included Singapore, comprised two blocks of flats and a large pool, was close to shopping and the American Club, and was walking distance to the subway. Plus, Jenny lived in the other tower in the same complex, which made Aislinn feel a little less isolated and lonely.

Because he was keen to prove himself in his new position and so was working long hours, Liam had left the furnishings entirely to her. When he put it that way, she felt another stab of resentment, for herself and on behalf of wives everywhere. Was that going to be her role now? Housewife and interior decorator? She had little else to do, though, so the pain dissipated quickly, and she found she enjoyed the process of filling the large apartment, an outlet for long-lost artistic dreams. What she'd assembled so far pleased her, a combination of the chrome and glass pieces they'd shipped from New York and the oddities she'd acquired here that added local and, to her eye, exotic flavor—an antique

Chinese chest with delicate ink paintings on the doors, Persian carpets she'd bought from a mysterious Iranian rug merchant, and house plants in barrel-sized pots that helped fill the expanse and also brought the tropics inside, without bringing the heat in with them.

The most astonishing finds, though, were the three paintings she'd hung in the dining room. The extravagant purchase from a small shop called Orientalia was an impulse buy, but the paintings, done in the early part of the last century by an English artist, enchanted her. She'd gone with Jenny Morelock to a small shopping center specializing in home decor, where she'd found the Chinese antiques and the rugs, and Orientalia was their last stop.

Before examining any of the store's wares, however, she noticed the shopkeeper, a tall man who welcomed them with a warm smile. "I'm Martin Roy," he said. "Please let me know if I can be of any help." He was close to her in age, she guessed, and had a complexion the color of wet sand, his long, black hair swept up and back in a thick wave. He wasn't from any of the main Singaporean ethnic groups as far as she could tell, and his accent was another variation on what she'd heard in the country so far. Not British, but maybe Australian? His surname, Roy, was possibly Indian, she thought, but he looked and sounded nothing like the Indians she'd encountered in the restaurants she and Liam had sampled. She had loved the fancy, Mughal-style places that served creamy North Indian dishes, and Liam preferred the humbler South Indian establishments down on Race Course Road in Little India that served spicy fish-head curry and pepper chicken. But this man, this Martin, looked only vaguely like the people who ran those places.

While the shopkeeper busied himself with another customer, Aislinn browsed through bins of antique prints, lush scenes from throughout Southeast Asia depicting town and country as they once existed under the domination of the European colonial powers, as well as a variety of colorful maps of the region from that era. She occasionally looked up from the prints, observing Roy with his customer, the way he moved awkwardly around the shop, as if he'd only just started working there, unfamiliar with the inventory.

As her gaze followed him, she noticed a group of paintings on the shop wall, and she froze. One of them, a scene of people in some sort of temple, seemed to move, like the paintings she'd seen at that gallery in New York, telling her a story. She turned to Jenny and pointed at the paintings, but the older woman shrugged and looked at her watch. Now the movement had stopped.

"There are more shops to see on the second floor," Jenny said, moving toward the door, and Aislinn reluctantly followed.

On a second visit, Aislinn stood before the paintings again. There were three of them, each alive in its own way. At the center of the largest of the three, the temple scene, was a woman who was looking right at her, or at the artist, as if daring her to come closer. As she watched, smoke rose from a cauldron next to the woman and the scent of sandalwood drifted toward her. A trio of children danced across the temple courtyard. They laughed and pointed at her, shouting words she didn't understand.

"Fascinating, isn't it?" said the shopkeeper, startling Aislinn out of her reverie. The painting's movement ceased. She shook her head as if to erase what she'd imagined.

"Yes, it's hard to look away. What can you tell me about the artist?"

"Not much, I'm afraid. Still learning my way around the shop. I only know that the artist was a woman by the name of Elizabeth Pennington, presumably English, although I don't know that for sure either, and these paintings are from 1915 or so. The temple in the largest picture is a local landmark."

"A woman? I wouldn't have guessed that. I wonder what she was doing here."

"Couldn't tell you, I'm afraid. A bit before my time." They both laughed.

Aislinn didn't hesitate. They were pricey, but she bought the temple painting and the two portraits that had flanked it in the shop and mounted them on the long wall in their dining room, where they were illuminated by spotlights.

The result of her efforts in the apartment was an eclectic look, far different from the sleek, all-modern decor of their townhouse in New York, but she thought it worked. Liam said he loved what she'd done, and he sounded sincere, although he'd made it clear that he didn't much like the paintings—amateurish and pedestrian, he'd called them—and didn't understand why she'd bought them. Still, if she had to be here in civilization's most distant outpost, at least she was comfortable, and the apartment was beginning to feel, almost, like home. If they'd been able to bring her piano, she might even be content.

In the kitchen again, the coffeemaker now silent, she listened for evidence that Cecilia was awake. Hearing nothing, she was tempted to drop a cup or a spoon to make enough noise that she could stop this walking on eggshells, this absurd politesse in her own home. The woman was a maid, for God's sake, not a guest. Yes, it would take getting used to. Aislinn reined herself in, poured the coffee quietly, and took her cup and one for Liam into the bedroom.

The bathroom door was open now, and she watched Liam shaving at the sink, one of their plush towels wrapped around his waist. Although his days as a competitive swimmer at Boston College were long behind him, Liam maintained his lithe body through tennis and regular visits to the gym. Since they'd moved to Singapore, he had returned to outdoor pools, both in their apartment complex and in the lap pool at the American Club, which accounted for the lovely tan that had been missing in New York. She joined him in the bathroom, set down the coffee cups, pressed her lips to his shoulder, still damp and minty from the shower, and ran her fingers over the fuzz that coated his chest, mostly dark but augmented now with a hint of gray. She moved her hand lower, over his firm stomach, her fingertips dipping beneath the towel, brushing his cock.

"Do you have to go?" Her fingers were having the effect she'd hoped for, and she pressed harder.

"Love, you know I do. It's going to be another busy day." He eased her hand from the towel, took her in his arms, and kissed her, shaving cream and all. "You're a temptress, Aislinn Givens. Let me finish up here." He wiped the cream from her face and shooed her out of the bathroom, but she was satisfied. Her husband wanted her, and she'd be on his mind all day.

She returned to the living room and pulled open the sliding glass door to their terrace, determined to face her fear of heights. Back home, she'd considered seeing a therapist about it, although many of her friends were experiencing the same thing, discomfort in tall buildings, airplanes, on bridges. Here, it just seemed like a character flaw, something to overcome, something she couldn't even mention to people who hadn't been in New York on 9/11. Every morning it was a struggle to be out there, so far above the ground and close to the edge, but when she was seated at the patio table, forced to look up and over the magenta bougainvillea that grew along the railing, as if in a sunken garden, it was tolerable. And maybe she was getting better. She sipped her coffee and savored the dawn breeze and cooler air she knew would soon give way to blistering heat.

Liam joined her, looking sharp, his keen fashion sense learned, according to his daughter, from his ex-wife, a former model. He wore a favorite gray pinstripe suit from Brooks Brothers, a crisp, white shirt, and a robin's egg blue tie that was only a shade lighter than his eyes. The jacket made no sense in this overheated climate, and she'd seen plenty of local businessmen who went without, but Liam's office hadn't bowed to that reality, apparently, at least not for the expats who called the shots and needed to project—something. Superiority? Domination? She wasn't sure what. It was hot in New York now, too, summer in full swing, but this was ridiculous.

He leaned over and kissed her. "Forgot to tell you," he said. "I'm bringing a couple of business associates home to dinner tonight."

"You're joking. We just moved in, Liam. We're not ready to host dinner parties."

"The place looks fantastic, love. You've done a great job with it. And anyway, it's not a dinner party. It's just a couple of colleagues, TJ Kwan and the fellow from New York I told you about, Stephens. They won't be taking a tour of the bedrooms. Tell Cecilia to make extra of whatever she's cooking. It'll be fine." And he was off.

They'd met TJ Kwan at a reception hosted by the Morelocks on their first full day in Singapore. Aislinn had begged off, blaming jet lag, but Liam wouldn't hear of it. "It's a whole different environment here," he'd argued. "We're a package deal when it comes to socializing with clients. All for the greater good." "Of the bank," she'd said. "Can't you tell them I'm not feeling well?" But no, he couldn't do that, and insisted she wear her new tennis bracelet, part of making a good first impression. So she did, and they went.

Jenny Morelock greeted them at the door of their apartment. A large woman, grandmotherly, she seemed to relish her hostess duties, serving hors d'oeuvres and filling wineglasses and generally attending to her guests. Aislinn instantly took a liking to her. Then there was Jenny's husband, Bruce, Liam's boss, a stout fellow with thinning blond hair and a mustache that needed trimming, an amiable smile and a bellowing laugh. At one point during the party, Aislinn saw that Liam and Bruce were on the balcony with another man. Despite her fear of heights, she dragged open the heavy sliding glass door and closed it behind her, already sorry to abandon the cool apartment for the sticky evening. The men were all smoking, which she detested. Her father had been a heavy smoker until the early stages of emphysema had forced him to quit, and as far as she knew, her mother still smoked. Liam never smoked unless he was around other smokers, as if he was keeping them company, indulging them, pretending to be one of them. He didn't even look convincing when he smoked, holding the cigarette awkwardly, blowing the smoke skyward too deliberately. Or was that, too, part of the act?

It was Bruce who introduced her to TJ Kwan, the Chairman of the Board of SJ Freeman's joint venture in Singapore. "TJ knows everyone in these parts," Bruce said. "It's a pleasure to meet you, Aislinn," Kwan said. Late 50s, Aislinn guessed, with fleshy jowls, neatly trimmed salt-and-pepper hair combed straight back. Immaculately put together, wearing a bright pink tie—no jacket—and stylish wire-rimmed glasses, a flashy ring. There was something about his eyes, though. They were small and dark, like stones in a pool. Although she understood from his name and features that Kwan was of Chinese ancestry—Singapore's history and diverse racial makeup had begun to fascinate her as she learned more—he had an accent she couldn't identify, almost but not quite British, just like that artist she'd met in New York.

When Liam made it clear they were in the middle of a business discussion, she took her cue and returned to the cooler air of the apartment, where Jenny now introduced her to Shirley Lim, TJ's wife. Tall, with permed, coal-black hair—dyed, Aislinn thought—she wore black slacks and an elegant red silk blouse. Thick makeup failed to hide the lines on her brow. Gaudy rings glittered on both hands. "Welcome, Aislinn," Shirley said. "Your first time in Singapore?" Aislinn nodded, noticing that the woman's gaze was fixed on Aislinn's bracelet. "What's your first impression?" Tell the truth? Or be polite with people who might be important to Liam? "Too soon to say," she'd said.

· · · · ·

Enough bravery for one day. There was too much to do now to linger on the terrace. She retreated to the living room and uncovered Mack's cage, liberating him from total darkness. Mack was a young military macaw she had acquired from an American couple in the building who were moving home and had anticipated difficulties getting him into the country, as he was technically an endangered species, or at least threatened. Aislinn wasn't sure what the rules were, but she was delighted to have him. With a scarlet forehead resembling a beret and the rest of his body covered in emerald and teal feathers, making him look like some sort of banana-republic dictator, he was the most beautiful bird she'd ever seen, even after years of helping her father care for hundreds of parrots and other exotics in his veterinary practice.

Liam was less thrilled with Mack's presence, at least at first. He had made it clear that he didn't want the bird in the apartment, but if it would make Aislinn happy, then fine, he could stay. They warmed to each other, though, Aislinn was sure of it, and Liam seemed to enjoy taking him out of his cage and working to enlarge his vocabulary. Now, out of the darkness, Mack opened one eye, blinked, and seemed unsure where he was. Aislinn knew the feeling well. She'd get ready to start her own day and would wait to interact with Mack later, when he was more awake and ready to be sociable.

When she returned, Mack was squawking for attention, calling for "Bub," which, Aislinn had determined, was his name for Liam, the source of grapes and the yummy fruits Mack preferred.

"Bub's not here, my friend," Aislinn said. "You're stuck with me." She brought a carrot from the kitchen, opened the cage, and lifted Mack to her shoulder. "Apron," Mack said, for no apparent reason, although she wondered if that wasn't his attempt at saying her name, something Liam had tried to teach him. Close enough. Mack nuzzled her neck before gnawing on the carrot and settled back onto his perch.

· · · · ·

During the day, Aislinn helped Cecilia make the apartment presentable to guests, even though Liam had instructed her not to go to any trouble. Together they worked out the menu, shopped for groceries, and then, in the afternoon, realizing that dinner was under control, Aislinn returned to the shopping center where she'd bought most of the furnishings for the apartment. She remembered seeing a lacquer serving tray in one of the shops there and decided it would be perfect for the evening. And, while she was there, she could stop into Orientalia, the source of her dining room paintings, to see what else she might find to make herself happier about being marooned on this island.

The young Chinese clerk in the antique store seemed to have no recollection that Aislinn had been in the shop numerous times, or perhaps white foreigners all looked alike to her, tourists who would soon be gone, never to return. Her wrapping of the serving tray was all business and no chatter, and Aislinn decided she liked it that way. Next was Orientalia, and Martin Roy smiled when she entered.

"You're back," he said. He was wearing a black V-neck T-shirt that accentuated his broad shoulders and chest.

"In the neighborhood," she said, and held up the shopping bag from the antique store as evidence.

"I'm glad you stopped by," he said. "Let me know if I can help you find anything."

She strolled among the tables and shelves, glancing at the crowded walls, waiting for something to catch her eye, although she looked up frequently to watch Martin. She decided he reminded her of Clark, the man she'd loved and nearly married in law school and who had died when the South Tower collapsed. Physically imposing. Self-assured, unassuming. The thought of Clark now made her long for home, her old life. Unlike the antique store clerk, Martin at least recognized her, but Aislinn supposed she was still just another customer to him. She was in need of a friend, but this man, attractive as he was, made an unlikely candidate. A local who couldn't understand what she was feeling, a shopkeeper at that, and what did she know about him?

The shop had filled the space where her paintings had been with less intriguing prints of waterfront scenes and landscapes. Aislinn browsed through the old books on one shelf, wondering if the woman who had painted her pictures might have kept a diary. It would be thrilling to read about her life at a time when Singapore must have been so different. What had brought her here? Probably some man, like other expat wives, dragged to the other side of the world for her husband's career, part of the colonial invasion and exploitation. Maybe not so interesting after all.

She stiffened when she sensed Martin approach.

"Looking for anything in particular?"

"Not really, no. But I'm curious about these old books. Where did they come from?"

"Various places. Some of them my father acquired from collectors, but I think most of the books we have in the shop are from his personal library. He was quite a reader. Since he died last year, my sister and I have been going through them and bringing into the store those we think customers might find of interest."

She pulled one volume off the shelf and saw that it was a collection of short stories by a writer named Edmund Preston. Aislinn thought she recognized the name from a college literature course, an obscure English writer, but remembered nothing about the man or his work except that she thought he'd written about his travels in Asia, and that sounded intriguing. The book was musty, with yellowed pages and no inscription or writing in it, but a publication date of 1920. Aislinn bought it, if only to spend a bit more time with Martin.

• • • • •

A little before eight, an hour after they were expected, Liam entered the flat with TJ Kwan and another man, an older gentleman with a ruddy complexion and thinning gray hair who was a head taller than TJ and stooped as if in compensation. TJ greeted her with a broad smile, and she detected gold rimming several of his teeth. She hadn't noticed that when they'd met at the Morelocks' reception, but she was reminded what a charming man he was. All three men were disheveled, although the American visitor seemed especially rumpled, as if he had just stepped off the long flight from JFK. They had loosened their ties and carried their suit jackets over their arms, sensibly, Aislinn thought, bowing to the reality of the tropics. Liam introduced the visitor to Aislinn as Harold Stephens from the bank's New York office.

"I used to do legal work for the bank when I was at Morrow, Dunn & O'Brien," Aislinn said. Meaning, because she doubted Liam had told him, I'm a professional and not merely a banker's wife. She was determined not to let her present situation erase her identity, and if she had to keep reminding people, and herself, sobeit.

"That's Frank McKee's outfit, isn't it?" asked Stephens. "Fine firm." The mention of her old boss made her long for her former life all the more, but at least Stephens had heard the message.

Aislinn knew better than to comment on Liam's lateness, especially in front of his colleagues. It was almost as if he'd done this on purpose to get a rise out of her, or to show her she hadn't quite tamed him. Or to show the other men who was in charge in Liam Connolly's household. He'd done the same thing in New York occasionally, claiming pressing business matters, even if, as tonight, it was evident he'd been drinking.

She showed the guests to the dining table, pleased with the vibrant floral arrangement on the side table and the way the room's overhead spotlights illuminated the antique paintings. The entire apartment, in fact, was lovely, although none of them had commented on it.

Liam made drinks for Kwan and Stephens. Aislinn poured a glass of wine for herself, then checked on dinner. She was annoyed with Liam for being late and not calling to let her know, but Cecilia was unfazed, launching into action as soon as the men had arrived. There was rice that had been kept warm in the rice-cooker, a soup that needed only to be reheated, and three stir-fry dishes for which the ingredients were all chopped and ready for the wok. While Aislinn offered to help finalize the meal and serve, Cecilia, anxious no doubt to be done for the day, shook her head and urged her out of the kitchen.

"I hope the meal is to your liking, gentlemen," Aislinn said. "Of course, Cecilia has had to keep it warm for some time." She looked at Liam, who returned her glare. But didn't she have a right to be angry?

"I'm sure she'll get over it, love," Liam said. "And if not, we'll find someone else."

"I'm afraid it's my fault we're late," Stephens said. "I insisted on visiting the famous Long Bar at the Raffles Hotel to try their Singapore Sling, and we may have had more than one. I'm only here until tomorrow afternoon and I've never been. You see, your husband is blameless."

"Mr. Stephens, my husband is many wonderful things, but he's never blameless."

"We had business to discuss, Aislinn."

"I'm sure you did." She didn't mean to be this annoyed, did she? Be good, Aislinn.

"Bub! Apron!" squawked Mack from the living room.

"How charming," said Stephens.

"Aislinn, can't you shut the damn bird up for one evening?" Liam asked.

"Your wish is my command." She rose from the table and covered Mack's cage. She heard him shuffle on his roost, but the darkness put him quickly into sleep mode.

Cecilia brought out the first course, a ginger and garlic soup that filled the dining room with its complex aroma, on the lacquer tray Aislinn had bought that afternoon. No one commented on the tray, but it reminded her of the paintings, which she gazed at now, and also that she had something to look forward to, the old book she'd bought at Orientalia. Tomorrow she was going to dive into Edmund Preston's stories about his travels in the region, transported, she hoped, to the world Elizabeth Pennington knew. The men focused on the soup, but her appetite was gone.

Next came the first stir-fry course, a spicy chicken dish with mushrooms and red peppers, along with the steaming rice, and Liam poured another round of drinks.

"TJ, what do you think of the paintings I bought?" Aislinn asked. She had hoped he would notice them without prompting. She pointed over his shoulder, and he twisted to look. "An Englishwoman did them here in Singapore almost a century ago."

"I don't know about these portraits," TJ began, "because they're barely even recognizable as faces." Then he pointed to the picture of the temple. "But I recognize this place."

"I've told her they're amateurish crap," Liam said. "There are fine galleries in the city where we could support young local artists and make a smart investment at the same time. Instead—"

"But these are historically significant, I'm sure of it, Liam. TJ, what can you tell us about the building?"

"It's a Hokkien temple," TJ said. "There has been some kind of waystation on that site ever since the English began bringing Chinese workers here as coolies, and other immigrants followed along with merchants and Chinese seamen. It was a house of refuge in those days, taking in laborers and others in dire straits. Now it functions as a Buddhist shrine and something of a community center in Chinatown."

"Mr. Stephens, what do you think?" she asked.

"Quaint. A curiosity. But I would think that outside of Singapore they would have very little value."

He'd given them only a cursory glance, and between his jet lag and the booze he'd been guzzling, he could barely focus. Just like a banker, she thought, to treat art as a commodity instead of a thing of beauty with a story to tell, valuable for that reason alone.

Aislinn excused herself to help Cecilia in the kitchen and returned with a full glass of wine for herself, although she'd gone through most of a bottle already, keeping up with the men.

"As I was saying," Liam said, "I don't mean to be uncharitable, but Bruce Morelock is an impediment to our progress here." He looked toward TJ. "Kwan and I agree."

TJ nodded. Guardedly, Aislinn thought, as if uncertain how far Liam would go, and how far Stephens would let him.

"Yes," Stephens said, "I read your report."

"Let me be blunt," Liam said. "There was more I didn't think I could say in writing. Morelock was a mistake from the beginning. I know he's an old-timer with the bank. But he came from the mortgage unit, didn't he? Or one of the regional outfits we picked up? A money-loser. Not what a bank of our stature should be dabbling in, and certainly not the least bit relevant to the merchant banking business overseas, especially in a sophisticated market like Singapore, where we're doing cutting-edge work with innovative financial instruments. If you'd been in charge, the bank never would have brought him here. He belongs in Cincinnati or Charlotte, not Asia. That's one thing."

"But I thought Bruce *did* have international experience," Aislinn said. "Peace Corps, wasn't it? Something like that?" Jenny had mentioned that Bruce had been overseas for a couple of years as a young man, she was sure of it.

"Probably an English teacher, although God help the poor African kids he was teaching." Liam laughed and TJ joined him, although without enthusiasm. Stephens's face remained stony.

"No, there was more to it than that. His MBA, I think. Yes, Jenny told me. It's in international finance. From Thunderbird. It's the mortgage work that's the aberration, and I don't think it was a big part of what he did."

"And Jenny is who?" Stephens asked.

"His wife," Liam said. "Another part of the problem."

"In what way is Jenny a problem?" Aislinn asked. "She's been perfectly nice to me. Extremely helpful, in fact. I like her."

"She's just not very bright, Aislinn, and you've seen what she looks like. It's the wrong image. But why don't you let us discuss this among ourselves. Does Cecilia need help?"

"No, Cecilia does not need help. But since you asked so nicely, I'll be sure to keep my mouth shut."

"Aislinn."

She sipped her wine.

"Moreover," Liam said, "Morelock has an alcohol problem." He looked at Aislinn as if to warn her not to contradict him on this point. "Obviously I'm not going to criticize him about drinking at home in the evening, not while I've got a glass of Scotch in my hand, but it's more than that. Drinking at lunch, being virtually incapacitated in the office in the afternoon. And more than once, I swear I smelled it on his breath in the morning. It's a problem. A serious problem."

"Forgive me for interrupting," Aislinn said, "but if that's the case, shouldn't you be trying to help him deal with it?"

"That's not our concern," Liam said. "This is business."

"Your husband's right," Stephens said. "We're a compassionate organization. Always have been. And if we were back in New York or—where did you suggest, Connolly, Cincinnati?—we might have more options. Temporary leave of absence, that sort of thing. But this is a high-profile joint venture. We have obligations to our partners." He glanced at TJ. "It's a reputational risk. We don't have much flexibility, I'm afraid."

"And that's not even the biggest problem," Liam said. "Basic competency. He simply doesn't have the skills we need." Now Liam looked directly at TJ, who had been silent during the discussion, cuing him up. This was a routine they'd plotted in advance, apparently. Bad cop, bad cop? "We've heard this from clients, especially Singaporean firms who are interested in US-bound investments, and he just doesn't know what he's talking about. Tell him what you told me, TJ."

"Unfortunately, it's true. My contacts tell me they have no confidence in Morelock. Take the Singco deal. When that fell through—a completely avoidable collapse—word spread around town that Bruce was responsible. That he'd overlooked a critical regulatory matter. That sort of reputation is hard to overcome."

Aislinn remembered Liam talking about Singco. Hadn't he told her that the backers of the deal decided it was too risky? He'd never said anything about a problem with Bruce. And wouldn't the lawyers have been responsible for regulatory issues? She wondered if Jenny knew about it, or if she'd discuss it if Aislinn asked.

Aislinn stood and helped Cecilia clear the table when it seemed the men had concluded their business, with Liam having made his case to Stephens. The visitors said their goodbyes, left unsteadily, and Liam headed to the bedroom to change.

Aislinn had the feeling that Bruce's fate was sealed, but she didn't understand why. Both Jenny and Bruce had been welcoming and generous to them, and she had come to depend on Jenny for a million things, from finding the best dry cleaners in the neighborhood to which hole-in-the-wall restaurant had the tastiest chicken satay. True, they were stolid Midwesterners and maybe a little out of their element here, just as they would have been in New York, but did that matter so much? She'd never seen this side of Liam before, and now he was full of these schemes. It sounded as if he was plotting a coup to take over the office he'd only just settled into. And what did TJ think of all this? He'd agreed with what Liam had been telling Stephens, but he seemed hesitant, letting Liam step out front, and she wasn't sure she believed him.

She wondered if she should warn Jenny. Friend to friend? Or maybe an anonymous note? No, saying anything to her at this point was probably out of the question. For one thing, Stephens might find a different way to deal with Bruce. He might see through Liam's self-serving allegations, or, even if he believed Liam, it was possible he'd do nothing at all once he'd spoken with Bruce and convinced himself that the problem was not as dire as Liam claimed. And if that was the case, and Aislinn said something to Jenny, she'd be creating a problem where none existed. Even if they did fire him, or send him to Cincinnati, if Aislinn revealed that she knew it was coming, Jenny would still be angry with her. She'd done nothing to stop it, after all. She'd made a feeble attempt to argue with Liam, to elicit facts where it seemed Liam had none, as any good lawyer would, but it was clear that with TJ in his camp, Liam believed he had all the weapons he needed. The only question was what Stephens would do with the information.

She lingered in the dining room, woozy from all the wine she'd had, and looked at her new pictures, gripping the back of a chair to steady herself when the larger painting began to move. The smoke of incense drifted across the temple courtyard as a man in black trousers and grimy singlet bowed before the shrine, muttering his devotions, indifferent to the observer, Aislinn or the artist. She smelled burning sandalwood as the man dropped to his knees. From inside the temple came the drone of chanted prayer. The painting to the left, a portrait, looked directly at her, his eyes following her. TJ was right that the style, usually, made the portrait indistinct, as if the artist meant to disguise the subject's identity, but now it came into focus. It was a portrait of an English officer. The man had kind eyes, or at least the artist saw them that way. But it was the way he looked at her that moved Aislinn. His gaze was alive. He loved this woman, the painter, or longed for her. And didn't that amount to the same thing? There was a connection there. Lovers? She was sure of it.

She didn't care that Liam hated the paintings or that he'd belittled her in front of his colleagues for having bought them. They showed a clear vision of what Singapore was like back then, through the eyes of a European, a woman no less, who had been as much a stranger here as Aislinn was. Liam couldn't see that because he felt he belonged here, that he was entitled to rule this new kingdom he'd found. For all his talk of wanting to get out of New York, though, he seemed to be stuck there, or had brought his New York mindset with him, his eyes closed to their new environment, this vibrant jungle with a deep history. The paintings spoke to Aislinn in a deeper way than she could explain, and that was far more important to her than technique or some hypothetical market value.

Who was this woman who had come to Singapore almost a century ago? The more Aislinn looked at the paintings, the more she felt connected to her. Why was she here? Had she come with her husband, some British colonial official, because wasn't that why most of the foreigners were here? And where did they live? One of those Black and Whites, maybe, the houses she'd heard were for the colonialists. What was her relationship with the British officer in the portrait? She wondered again if there was a diary, some place she could learn more about the woman and what her life was like. If there was one, what might have become of it? She imagined it tucked in between the old books at Orientalia, or on Martin's father's shelves at home. Martin had mentioned that he'd come back to Singapore when his father became ill and still lived in his house, even after the older man's death. Maybe there was more to find that he and the sister had yet to uncover.

Cecilia had finished in the kitchen and was preparing to shut herself into her tiny room for the evening. Aislinn apologized for the lateness of the hour, but Cecilia barely blinked in response. She closed her door. Aislinn heard the maid's television come on, laughter and applause from some distant studio audience.

Although the kitchen was spotless, Aislinn took a damp cloth to the counter. She rinsed her wineglass and left it in the drying rack. She opened the refrigerator door and absently wondered about dinner the next night and the night after. She was stalling, and she knew it. She'd gone too far in her defense of the Morelocks and was sure to hear about it from Liam. She hated when they argued and hoped he'd be asleep by the time she went to bed. In the morning, the argument wouldn't seem so important and would be forgotten.

She could wait no longer. She turned off the lights in the kitchen, took a last look at her paintings before turning off the spotlights in the dining room, checked to see that the apartment door was locked, listened for movement in Mack's cage, and went into the bedroom.

Liam lay on the bed, reading *The Economist*.

"I thought you'd be asleep by now," she said.

He put the magazine aside. He stood, came to her, raised his hand as if to slap her and instead grabbed her arms and threw her onto the bed.

"Liam!" She shrank from him, edged further away.

"Don't *ever* do that again," he shouted. "*Never* contradict me in front of my colleagues."

She was too startled to respond. Liam had never struck her before, and the sight of his raised hand had shocked her. But it was a distraction, she realized, so he could lift her off her feet.

"I didn't contradict you, Liam. I was asking questions. That's my training, you know. What you're alleging is serious, and it's going to have serious consequences for Bruce and Jenny."

"And if we don't do something about him, it will have serious consequences for the bank. And for us."

Aislinn stood, but when Liam approached again, she moved out of his reach.

"Did you hear me? *Never* do that again."

He went into the bathroom and slammed the door.

She was afraid to move. He hadn't struck her, but tossing her on the bed was as violent as if he had. He wouldn't hit her, though, would he? That would leave a mark. People would see that. She'd have to explain it. She would be reminded of it when she looked at her face in the mirror. She'd witnessed his temper before, but not like this. What the hell was she supposed to do now?

Trembling, she retrieved the box she kept in her lingerie drawer, heart-shaped, stamped silver with an inlaid turquoise cross, opened it, and pinched a single white pill that she popped into her mouth. She'd kept away from the buttons since they'd come here, knowing that she couldn't continue to keep them hidden. How many were left, and what would she do when they were gone? She returned to the kitchen and poured the last of the evening's wine into a glass. She knew better, but if the wine made it work faster, so much the better, and if it killed her right now, that would be all right, too.

She'd waited for relief, pacing the living room, her arms tight across her chest to keep from shaking, angry with the world, angry with Liam for taking from her everything she'd loved, until finally she began to feel it. The warmth spread through her, igniting in her chest, seeping outward to her arms and legs. She felt it in her fingers last, watched them swell and grow, reaching for purchase, like tendrils of a jungle vine. She sat at the dining table and gazed at the paintings. The portraits came into focus and the faces watched her, both the British soldier and the turbaned Indian, their eyes full of love and concern, both of them. The worshipers at the temple turned toward her, as well, the smoke of incense drifting between them, inviting her to join them at the altar, to pray for salvation.

When the trembling had stopped and she knew Liam was asleep, she slipped into their guest room and sank into bed.

5

Aislinn had thought, briefly, that she'd landed in paradise. She hated giving up her job, hated leaving New York and all that it offered despite the recent trauma, but Singapore was stunningly beautiful in a way that no other city she'd ever visited could match: lush and vibrant, trees and flowers everywhere, exotic but with a touch of the familiar, modern and immaculate yet with pockets of historic charm and grit.

Now, though, now that Liam had frightened her so, she knew it had all been a colossal mistake. Could she stay with Liam? She knew countless women had faced this dilemma, many who had suffered far more than the scare she'd had. Still, it was unacceptable, wasn't it? No man should treat any woman that way. Could she unwind these last few months? Admit defeat, pack her bags, and go home? Home to what?

She questioned now why she had even married Liam. He had been loving and attentive, not just during the secretive, early days of their affair, the anonymous cards and flowers sent to her office, the furtive romantic getaways when they would travel separately to some distant city and rendezvous at a hotel, but even after they were married. He'd been solicitous over every imposition, however slight, every sign of illness, however minor. He'd worried that she was working too hard, that the firm wasn't treating her right. What had happened to that Liam? Or was the real Liam now emerging? The one her mother had warned her about.

Her parents had argued from time to time, especially in the last year of their marriage, before her mother fled and regained her independence, but Aislinn didn't remember her father ever touching her mother in anger, or even raising his voice. It was her mother who had done the yelling, even throwing a plate or a cup against a wall during some of those disputes. She could understand arguing and live with it. But now? Now she was frightened.

On the morning after the dinner party, after a night in which she slept in the guest room, Aislinn made coffee while Liam dressed for work. He joined her on the terrace with the local newspaper and they ate croissants she had warmed. There was a breeze, and light clouds floated over the distant harbor. They needed to talk about it, she knew, but she didn't want to disturb this moment of tranquility, fearful it was the last. She couldn't pretend the night before hadn't happened or excuse Liam's behavior. He'd been drunk. He was under a lot of pressure at work. He wasn't himself. She'd pushed him too far. None of which justified what he'd done.

He pointed to a story in the paper about the expected American invasion of Iraq and shook his head. "It's only going to cause more trouble," he said.

"I think you're right," she said, although she wasn't sure he was. Was she allowed to disagree? "Isn't that the sort of thing the terrorists are mad about in the first place?"

He nodded. He took a last sip of his coffee and stood, kissing her on the cheek. Did he notice her flinch at his approach?

"I have to run. Stephens is still with us this morning. He'll see for himself what's going on. I'll probably take him to the airport this afternoon and be home early."

With that, he was gone. She stayed at the table, gazing out at the murky sky, and felt the breeze grow warmer. It wouldn't be long before the heat chased her inside. She thought about Jenny—poor Jenny, who was about to have her world turned upside down—who had said you could get used to the heat. What drove her mad were the monsoons, winter and summer rainy seasons when mold grew everywhere, practically overnight, and you couldn't go outside without the risk of getting drenched. And that wasn't the half of it. Sometimes the rains would come and stay for days, a week, she said, and then it was best just to wait it out. It didn't stop the locals or the more intrepid expats, but Jenny hated it. From the look on Stephens's face last night after Liam and TJ had stated their case, she didn't think Jenny was going to need to worry about another monsoon.

As much as she felt sorry for Jenny, Aislinn had her own worries.

On top of the argument with Liam, she felt awful, not just from the fierce hangover, the result, she assumed, of taking the pill with wine, or just too much wine, but also with regret. She had hoped moving to Singapore would help her end the reliance on the pills. Because what would she do when they were gone? She must stop. She must. From now on, whether it was knee pain or the strain of being in Singapore or whatever was happening between her and Liam, she would work through it on her own.

She removed her silver case from the dresser drawer and opened it, planning to flush the remaining pills down the toilet, but as she gazed at them, her precious buttons, she felt grateful for the relief they'd given her for so long. When the next wave of pain washed over her, what would she do if she didn't have them? That, just then, was more troubling than her worry about being dependent on them. She would be stronger, she decided, if she kept the pills but refrained from taking them unless she absolutely had to. She replaced the lid on the case and slipped it back into the drawer.

Once she had recovered from her knee surgery in college, although she never played competitive lacrosse again, she ran regularly. That kept her sane through law school, but the crushing hours of being a junior associate in the law firm and the stress of her affair with Liam had disrupted her routine. She hadn't run at all since they'd arrived in Singapore, but maybe that was just the thing to help her adapt, to tolerate her new life without the pharmaceutical crutch. To cope with Liam's transformation.

Now, with nothing else to do, she laced on her Nikes and set out.

· · · · ·

The secrecy of their affair—out-of-town rendezvous, trysts in borrowed apartments—though romantic and thrilling, had been a strain and had threatened to affect Aislinn's work. After a few months, when Liam showed no sign of leaving his wife, she ended it. She stopped returning his calls. She began seeing Clark again now that he had completed his clerkship for an Appellate Court judge and was working for a firm downtown. Their relationship in law school had been intense, constantly together, but now that they were established in important law firms, living independent lives, they were both more casual, less demanding. She had time again, and so she'd resumed running.

It helped that her roommate, Jessica, was a runner, too. One morning, they rose with the sun and headed out to Riverside Park from their Morningside Heights apartment. As much as Aislinn appreciated Jessica's constant chatter—she was considering a job change, she was worried about her younger sister, she thought the time was right to come out to her parents so she could introduce them to her girlfriend—Aislinn had nothing to say in response and would rather have been alone with her thoughts.

How could she be so foolish to fall for a married man? He would never leave Janice, and why should he? He had the best of it all: a pretty, suburban wife to manage the kids, plus Aislinn to fuck on the side. Did she even want him to leave Janice? Did she want to be responsible for a divorce and what that would do to his family? Although Aislinn's mother had certainly done the best thing for herself by leaving Aislinn's father, and could not have foreseen that he would turn a hunting rifle on himself, she was going to bear the guilt over what she'd done for the rest of her life. Who knew what impact a divorce would have on Liam's kids? And then there was Clark, who was sweet and gentle and endlessly sincere, brilliant and sensitive. They'd been in love once, but was he someone she could be with long term?

They reached the north end of the park and then turned back. For her first run in ages, Aislinn was feeling good. She'd pay later, she suspected, but for now she pushed herself, matching strides with Jessica, controlling her breath, letting her mind wander.

What was she going to do about Liam? Should she just forget about him? Get on with her life and focus on the work she loved? Frank had surely noticed she'd been slacking off, not staying as late in the evenings, not working as many weekends. It couldn't be good for her future, so it was just as well that the affair was over. For the best. A relief.

Now they sprinted back to their apartment building. Jessica let Aislinn have the shower first and, for the first time in weeks, she was looking forward to starting her day at the office. The run was exhilarating, and so was her decision to forget about Liam.

And yet. Another live orchid came to the office. That was followed by a signed first edition of Atwood's *The Handmaid's Tale*, which made her laugh out loud because she was certain Liam had no idea what the book was about. The calls didn't stop, and eventually she relented. She talked to him. She agreed to see him. They made love in a hotel in Newark. She broke it off with Clark a second time.

· · · · ·

Running in Singapore was a challenge because of the heat. From the apartment complex, Aislinn made her way to Orchard Road, then dodged meandering tourists on the promenade as she jogged toward the Botanic Gardens. At this early hour, although the air was thick with humidity, the temperature was almost bearable. She crossed Orange Grove Road—a narrow street that wound past the Shangri-La Hotel—and soon enough turned onto Nassim Road, not far from the historic Black and White she'd hoped to rent for them, that Liam had vetoed. Her knee felt fine.

She ran under a canopy of trees and was grateful for the leafy shade, slowed past a series of gated mansions, wondered briefly who lived behind those walls, whether government ministers or wealthy businesspeople, made another turn and came to the park entrance. The Gardens were, so far, her favorite thing about Singapore. Established in the mid-nineteenth century, they covered more than 200 acres and showcased every conceivable kind of tree, bush, and flower that grew in the tropics, and even some more recognizable species transplanted from temperate climes, not to mention one of the most extensive collections of orchids anywhere on the planet.

At this hour there were few visitors, but a small army of men and women swept leaves and branches from walkways. She passed a tourist group that moved together in a swarm led by a young woman holding an orange pennant aloft—Japanese? Korean? She wasn't sure—ran up a hill past soaring palms and flowering bushes, then down another hill toward a placid lake. She had learned the names of some of the plants on previous visits, a variety of hibiscus, flame tree, an assortment of bougainvillea in shades of red and orange, like the one that grew on their balcony, but she could never know them all. Jogging along the lakeside path, her gaze drawn by a pair of luminous swans gliding across the green surface that reminded her of the sailing ships in her Miro print, now hanging in the apartment's spare bedroom—*her* bedroom for the moment—she fell into pace behind another jogger. Blond hair in a ponytail—another American perhaps, maybe someone she could be friends with. She'd missed having a running buddy, those long runs with Jessica, someone to pace her, to push her, someone to commiserate with.

The woman veered onto a narrow path back up the hill, and Aislinn continued beside the lake, feeling an odd sense of loss at this missed opportunity. What might have been? Ahead of her on the path, a man and a woman walked arm in arm. From behind, the man seemed familiar, but that was ridiculous. Black hair slicked back. A white dress shirt and suit pants, black shoes, overdressed for the park. Familiar, but he could be anyone, and she didn't yet *know* anyone. The woman, nearly as tall as the man, with black hair almost to her shoulders, wore a red dress, sleeveless. She looked familiar, too, which was more absurd. The only women she'd met were expat wives and her maid. As the gap closed between her and the couple, she realized who they were: Liam's colleague, TJ Kwan and, improbably, the Singaporean artist she'd encountered in New York, Shan Lee, back when she was still struggling with her dilemma.

She diverted her gaze and accelerated to pass them, hoping they wouldn't recognize her. She was embarrassed by Liam's behavior the night before, and her own, and TJ was the last person she wanted to talk to just now. She was tempted to turn as she passed, to be sure it was them, but that would have drawn attention to herself. She continued around the lake, glanced across the water at the couple, then forced herself to look away. Ahead of her was another group of tourists. She navigated through the crowd, worked her way back to the gate, and ran back to the apartment.

• • • • •

The run helped to clear her head. If she were advising a friend in this situation, a friend whose husband had just assaulted her, she would tell her to get out, to stay somewhere else until she felt comfortable enough to return or could move on. It was her own life she was dealing with, though, her own husband, and logic didn't apply. She was angry with Liam, but if he apologized, if he was genuinely sorry for what he'd done, she knew she would forgive him. Was that a mistake? Was she deluding herself? Had she ceded so much power in their relationship that she didn't have a choice? They would have to talk about it, and he would need to make amends for what he'd done, but, at least for now, she would stay. If, that is, she could find something productive to do.

Her efforts to find a job had so far not borne fruit, but a job was the only thing that would keep her from going crazy—or going home. It had occurred to her on her run that she might write something. She would prefer paid employment, especially given her precarious relationship with Liam, but publishing an article in a law review or even a popular legal magazine like *The American Lawyer* might be a start. Her preoccupation with the Pennington paintings had made her curious about Singapore's colonial period, so what if she combined that with her own legal experience? Many American and English law firms had offices here, but she'd come across a slew of local firms while plotting her job hunt, some established over a century earlier. It could be a fascinating story to tell. At the very least, the research would give her something to do.

Aislinn took a taxi to Stamford Road near Fort Canning Park and found the red brick building that housed the National Library. She'd read online that the shabby structure had been slated for demolition for some time, and certainly it looked nothing like either the imposing colonial-era government buildings or the modern office towers of downtown. The card catalog for the library's collection was all digital, however, and within seconds the reference librarian had printed out a list of the books and microfilm Aislinn would need to begin her search—histories of the island, court records that mentioned the local law firms and their lawyers, newspaper reports, even memoirs of some of the legal pioneers from the early days of the colony.

At a broad table in the reading room, she opened the first musty volume, excited to be back at work. She wasn't being paid, she wasn't serving a client, there were no deadlines or billable hours, and there was no partnership brass ring, but she felt this was the beginning of something important, a project that could ultimately be rewarding. Starting with the general histories, she read about Sir Stamford Raffles's tragic story—his establishment of the settlement at Singapura in 1819, the delight he took in it, and then the illnesses that devastated his family. That very early history wasn't what she needed, though, and she turned pages until she found what she was looking for—the arrival in 1880 of Archibald Alexander, his tenure as Queen's Advocate, and the establishment, with William Gladstone, of one of the earliest law firms in the city.

Aislinn took furious notes on all the lawyers named who were associated with the firm, and with other firms that also arose in Singapore in the early days. The description of one case in particular enchanted her. It seems that Mr. Alexander represented a man who was suing to recover a loan to a brothel owner whose defense was that the man knew the loan was to be repaid out of immoral earnings and was therefore unenforceable. Alexander's client prevailed in the end, but apparently it was no sure thing. In a more recent case, this one from the early twentieth century, a lawyer named Cyril Stratton had successfully defended the owner of a rubber plantation against claims by a nutmeg grower that the rubber trees had somehow caused the blight that was destroying the nutmeg plantation. There were so many avenues to pursue and peculiar cases to study, she could see the project would take a long time and might make for a fascinating article, or even a book.

In another volume she read about the rise of the Chinese merchant class and the great trading houses that grew as Singapore became a natural entrepot situated where the Straits of Malacca, the all-important route between India and the Far East, joined the South China Sea. She came across the name Kwan and wondered if there was any connection to TJ, but she knew most Chinese names were from widespread clans, so it might have been a distant relation, or none at all. Still, she was curious about this TJ, upon whom Liam had already come to rely so heavily. She supposed she could simply ask him what his family background was. If that was a cultural mistake—it probably was—she could use the excuse that she was an ignorant American who didn't know any better. The question might mortify Liam, and Shirley would be haughty and stare at her with disbelief that she had committed such a faux pas, but TJ would forgive her.

Although she was enjoying her research and had convinced herself that it was an acceptable and even productive use of her time and skills, she wondered again if TJ's connections wouldn't be a way for her to land a job, if not with a US law firm, then maybe with one of these old-line Singapore firms. She probably couldn't dangle the promise of business from Liam's bank, as that would be wading into murky ethical waters, but TJ might help. She was still on good terms with Jenny and Bruce, whatever the friction was between Bruce and Liam, so there was that possibility, too. Might Bruce put in a good word with one of his contacts? Despite Liam's predictions of imminent regime change at the bank, it was still Bruce who called the shots, at least for now. And these old firms, from what she'd been reading, had once upon a time been made up entirely of foreigners when the Brits ran the show here. Maybe they wouldn't mind having a New York lawyer on their payroll. She couldn't advise on Singapore law, of course, just as she couldn't practice in California or any state other than New York, but she was a damn good negotiator, having learned from Frank, who was a master, and she knew the ins and outs of New York law, the most important legal system in the world for cross-border commercial transactions. A local firm could steal a page from the foreign law firm playbook and offer advice out of their jurisdiction without writing opinions that would get them into hot water. It was worth a try.

She exhausted the obvious sources at the National Library. The helpful young reference librarian—she was Malay, Aislinn guessed from her features and rich brown coloring and coffee-colored headscarf—explained how she could get permission to use the National Archives and the University library, although she doubted they'd have much of significance beyond what Aislinn had already examined. She also suggested that one of the book dealers in the city might have antique volumes that would be of interest. She'd already found the Preston story collection at Orientalia, but she'd need to take a closer look at Martin's books with this new focus in mind.

When she got home, an enormous flower arrangement occupied the center of the console table in the foyer. It reminded her of the arrangement they'd found in their Shangri-La suite the night they arrived, but now she was able to name some of the tropical varieties—bird of paradise, anthurium, heliconia, and a large purple orchid. She opened the attached card, which read "I'm sorry, Love, Margaret Atwood." It made her smile, remembering how her affair with Liam had begun.

So, he was sorry. That was a start. She hadn't forgotten what he'd done, but maybe she could file it away, like a promissory note to be called in when needed. One time was an anomaly. But if he ever did it again, she was done. In the meantime, she would make the best of her situation. She was going to write about Singapore's legal history and find a way to use her legal training. She would run. She would make friends. She would not take another button.

• • • • •

"Say, I understand you've been spending time with Jenny Morelock," Liam said over dinner. "Did you see her today?"

Her day's work at the library had satisfied her, and, provisionally, so had Liam's apology. Still, she was on guard. "Not today, no. But we met for coffee at the club the other day. Why?"

"I told you not to get too chummy with her, didn't I? It will only make it harder when they leave."

"I can't very well avoid her, Liam. She's practically the only person I know here. And anyway, they have no intention of leaving. They love it here."

"So Bruce told me. He also told me you two have been shopping and having a grand old time together."

"Someone had to show me where the shops are. When we moved into the apartment, there were all kinds of things we needed, and Jenny knew where to find them."

"Just...make new friends."

• • • • •

That night, she lay in bed reading the volume of stories by Edmund Preston, transported to a very different Southeast Asia than the one she was experiencing—colonial society, steamships, pirates, cannibals. Liam was in their living room on the phone to his New York office, twelve hours behind them, but his voice carried down the hallway to the bedroom.

"You should have seen him, Ben."

Aislinn knew Ben Mitchell, Liam's occasional golfing buddy, and they had gone out to dinner a few times with Ben and his wife, Anne

Marie, although it was awkward because Anne Marie was friends with Liam's ex-wife. Ben worked in a different department, but he was keeping Liam informed of the goings-on in the head office. From the sound of it, Liam was making sure word got back to New York about what was happening in Singapore, reinforcing what he'd already told Harold Stephens.

"Drunk as a skunk," Liam said.

She still found these stories about Bruce unsettling. On the several occasions she'd seen Bruce Morelock in their brief tenure in Singapore, he'd been completely sober, even at social functions where everyone else was drinking. Not that she doubted her husband, but it seemed completely out of character for Bruce to be drunk at work.

"Totally blew it," Liam said. "We had that fish on the fucking line, and it was if he reached out and cut it with a knife. It was like he didn't even want the business. Suicide, really."

She had no idea what Liam was talking about. He'd said nothing to her about a deal gone bad. She marked her page and put the book down to concentrate on Liam's conversation, but his voice grew muffled and distant, and she felt herself drifting into sleep.

• • • • •

Aislinn and Liam were the guests of TJ Kwan and his wife at Min Jiang, the stylish Szechuan restaurant in the Goodwood Park Hotel. Aislinn had been surprised to learn that most Chinese women kept their own family name, rather than taking their husband's, a discovery that added to her growing admiration for the culture. Shirley's red and gold cheongsam, with its high collar and short sleeves, fairly glowed in the flickering candlelight. Crowned by stiffly permed black hair, she sat erect, imperious, as if disdainful of her husband's foreign business associates. Aislinn's first impression of the woman, that she was a cold-hearted aristocrat, formed at the Morelocks' cocktail reception when Shirley had uttered barely two words to her, was reinforced.

"This hotel," Shirley said, "was once upon a time the German Club of Singapore."

"German? Really?" Aislinn lifted her gaze to the vaulted ceilings, the vaguely castle-like walls, tried to imagine a crowd of Germans dining on beer and schnitzel but instead saw only Chinese faces on the diners and servers alike.

"But that was a long time ago, in the years before the First World War, when the city had a thriving German community. No more. It's part of our colorful history."

"Courtesy," TJ said, "of our former colonial masters."

When a waiter appeared, TJ placed their order in Chinese, barely glancing at the menu that ran for a dozen or more pages. While they waited for their food, Shirley asked—perfunctorily, Aislinn thought, her gaze fixed on diners at another table—about her life in New York, the transition to Singapore, and finding a suitable apartment. Aislinn answered, but Shirley's focus was now on her fingernails, and she knew the woman wasn't listening. As TJ's wife, she had a role to play, just as Aislinn had her part, and she was speaking her lines. But that was the extent of it, and she was making no more than the minimum effort. TJ, though, was different. As Aislinn talked about her work at her law firm, he kept his eyes on her, appearing rapt. Whether he was truly listening or was simply a better actor than his wife was almost beside the point.

A squadron of servers delivered bowls of steaming white rice and platters of food. Aislinn recognized a beef dish with Chinese broccoli, a platter of something that looked like an assortment of mushrooms, and a whole snapper, steamed, complete with its head and a beady eye that appeared to be blaming her for its predicament. One particularly tantalizing dish was a cast-iron skillet filled to overflowing with sizzling plump shrimp and glistening red peppers.

"Be cautious with the shrimp," Shirley said. "Between the sesame oil and the Tien Tsin peppers, it's been known to kill." Indeed, the cloud of steam and smoke from the burning oil drifted Aislinn's way, pungent with spice, launching her into a coughing fit that a long swallow of beer only exacerbated. The condescension in Shirley's voice made Aislinn more determined not to embarrass herself.

She'd been practicing with chopsticks—how had she gone so long, a frequent visitor to New York's Asian restaurants, without mastering this skill?—and lifted a strip of beef from the platter, gripping it firmly until she was able to let it fall onto her rice. She was proud to get it that far without soiling the tablecloth, but was that a look of disapproval on Shirley's face? Should she have risked ferrying it directly into her mouth?

Liam, clumsily but unselfconsciously, reached for a shrimp, which he devoured in two bites, and then grabbed a red pepper with his chopsticks.

"Try one of these, Aislinn," he said. "This food is so much better than we get in New York."

It was delicious, the beef tender and flavorful, but they'd eaten in fabulous Chinese restaurants in New York that were every bit as good as this. Still, TJ beamed proudly, and she saw what Liam was doing. This was business, after all. Honesty and sincerity weren't what mattered. He'd been the same at home, she realized, stoking the egos of clients and colleagues, or anyone who could help him get ahead. Had she been any different? Probably not.

All right, then. She understood the game. She'd play along. "It's wonderful," she said. "The best I've ever had." She reached for a pepper, hesitated.

"I dare you," Liam said, then popped his into his mouth. His entire face turned crimson, nearly the color of their macaw's crown, and she almost laughed at his obvious distress. But he sipped tea, took a long pull on his beer, and soon returned to normal. With his chopsticks, he reached for another pepper and lifted it toward Aislinn.

When she opened her mouth to protest, he dropped the pepper on her tongue. Caught off guard, she bit down, felt the crunch of the pepper, and then swallowed, thinking at first it wasn't so bad. Then the sensation grew, the fire spreading inside her mouth, burning her tongue, her gums, her lips. There was no flavor to it, just the acrid oil that invaded her throat, choking her, the charred flakes of pepper like metal filings. She could no longer feel her mouth. She couldn't breathe, and Liam, the bastard, was laughing. TJ and his wife didn't join him, although Shirley's I-told-you-so smirk was evident. Aislinn reached for her tea, nearly knocking the cup over in the process, and swallowed. She couldn't speak. The waiter refilled her cup. She drank again.

"Well," she said, when she had recovered, "that was an experience." She was furious with Liam but couldn't berate him in front of Kwan. She couldn't toss the dregs of her tea in his face, which she'd considered briefly. She couldn't storm off or yell at her husband in public, which would confirm Shirley's suspicions that this American woman was an inferior being, unfit for Singapore society. All she could do, all that was left to her, was to play the fool. Exactly what Liam wanted, she guessed, showing off for his new mentor, displaying his dominance over his mate.

From that point on, she avoided the shrimp and the fish with its accusatory stare, the slippery mushrooms, and stuck with the milder, manageable beef. The small talk had evaporated, Liam had not yet brought up business, and she saw her opportunity.

"Tell me, TJ," she said, "what do you know about the local law firms?" Liam had said that TJ knew everyone in the region. He seemed an obvious choice to help her get a job, but she was also still curious about the history of the local firms.

"You'll have to forgive Aislinn," Liam said. "She's obsessed with law firms. I've heard she's been running around town, handing out her résumé to all the foreign lawyers in the city. It's a wonder she hasn't been arrested for solicitation."

Aislinn felt the heat rise in her cheeks, this time without the peppers, but she smiled, as if sharing in Liam's joke. It's not as if she hadn't told him she'd approached those firms, so if he'd heard about it from anyone, it was from her.

"What would you like to know?" TJ asked. He was a gracious host and now filled her empty glass from one of the large bottles of Tsingtao beer that occupied the center of the table. Despite the tea and beef and rice, there was a residual burning sensation from the red pepper, and she sipped her beer in hopes of washing it away.

"In the course of finding out what foreign firms have offices here," she said, looking from TJ to Liam and back, "I discovered there are dozens of local firms, some of which have English names. I know Singapore used to be under British rule, but that seemed strange to me."

"It is something of an oddity, I suppose," TJ said. "But not so surprising, really. As in the US, some of these firms were founded in the early days of the city's existence, long before we became, with Malaya, an independent country. In fact, it's a bit like this beer. Europeans established the Tsingtao Brewery Company more than one hundred years ago in the foreign concession of Shanghai. It eventually passed into the hands of the Japanese during the war and then the Chinese took over when the foreigners left."

"I'm sure Aislinn's not interested in ancient history," Shirley said.

"Oh, but I am! I have so much to learn. Please start from the beginning."

TJ sipped his beer, and Aislinn saw he enjoyed the role of teacher to these ignorant foreign guests. She doubted he'd be able to tell her anything she hadn't already read in the histories she'd been studying, but it wouldn't hurt to stroke his ego. She glanced at Liam, who nodded approvingly.

"When Stamford Raffles, a bureaucrat with the British East India Company, came ashore, close to 200 years ago, Singapura as it was then known was little more than a Malay fishing village, the vestige of a thriving kingdom that had collapsed for reasons that still are not entirely clear. But now, suddenly, the British were here, subjugating the natives, building a city that reflected themselves and their own heritage, plus their experience as a colonial power in India and elsewhere. Along with the early arrivals came the trappings of government—administrators, law enforcement, and courts. And of course, where there are courts, there are also lawyers. Lawyers joined together and developed law firms, following the model of London. At first, they employed only their own, white men who trained in London and came here seeking to make their fortunes, so naturally the firms bore their British names. As the Chinese and Indian boys became educated—a surprising number were sent off to England for schooling—they entered the profession and joined the ranks of the law firms. A few established their own chambers, bearing their own names, but others simply survived the eventual mortality of the colonial founders. Now, you might expect them to change the names of the firms, but most were content to preserve the venerable names and character of their practices, and I suppose that explains the names. Alexander & Gladstone is still Alexander & Gladstone, long after Mister Alexander and Mister Gladstone have met their maker."

"Fascinating," Aislinn said. "And is that the oldest? Or the best? What are the other old firms?"

Liam took Aislinn's hand. "Easy there, kitten. Let TJ take a breath, will you?"

"Yes, of course," she said, sitting back. "I'm sorry to pick your brain like this, TJ. It's just that I'm so used to the New York way of doing things. I have a lot to learn—and it amazes me that many of these Singapore firms are every bit as old as the foreign firms. Older, in many cases."

"Changing the subject," Liam said, lowering his voice, "I wanted to talk to TJ about the lunch I had with Bruce today."

"Yes," Aislinn said. "I suppose we've had enough fun for one dinner. Time to talk business." Severed from her own professional obligations, she felt momentary guilt at forgetting that Liam was still employed, and TJ Kwan was an important part of his business, as was Bruce Morelock.

"Bruce popped into my office this morning and invited me to join him at the Cricket Club for lunch. Speaking of colonial vestiges." He winked at Aislinn. She'd learned from her reading about Singapore that the Cricket Club, a dining and athletic facility attached to the cricket pitch on prime real estate in the heart of downtown, was another sore spot with some locals, a point of pride with others. "Anyway, I suppose the pressure to succeed in this assignment was getting to the guy."

"What do you mean?" TJ asked.

"Yes, what *do* you mean, Liam? He seemed fine to me last time I saw him, and Jenny hasn't said a word."

"She wouldn't, though, would she? But how else to explain stumbling back to the office drunk?"

"You're not serious."

"And it's not the first time, from what the staff tell me. I don't suppose it's my place to report this latest incident to Stephens, having already spelled it out for him, but it seems like something management should know, following up on his visit."

So he's passing the buck to Kwan. Let TJ be the bad guy here? Backstabbing was so unlike Liam.

"Are you sure?" Aislinn asked. "Maybe he's been ill? What makes you think he was drunk?"

"I was there, Aislinn. I know what I saw."

• • • • •

The next morning, after Liam left for work, she stayed on the balcony, despite the heat that seemed to rise around her like a bath, reading the Edmund Preston stories. Inside, Cecilia vacuumed, and Mack squawked. Aislinn tried to focus on the page, but she felt a bead of sweat rolling down her neck, the taste of the red pepper from dinner with Kwan and his wife still haunted her mouth, and she couldn't silence the voice in her head that said she was not the kind of woman who lounged on her balcony reading while her maid cleaned her house and the rest of the world marched on pursuing their productive endeavors.

At which point, there was a tap on the sliding door and Cecilia gestured that there was a phone call.

"I asked TJ if there wasn't something we could do to help with your job search," Liam said, "and he's got a lead for you."

"I've tried all the foreign firms already, and no one is hiring."

"Not a foreign firm. He spoke to the managing partner of one of the oldest firms in town and he thinks they might hire you, or at least talk to you about the possibility. No promises, but it's a start, right?"

"That's great, Liam. Thank TJ for me, please."

More than the flower arrangement and his note, this was Liam trying to make amends. It was no more than he'd promised to do before they left New York, but it was a welcome development.

· · · · ·

She walked the ten minutes from their apartment to Orchard Road and was already damp from the heat and humidity when she entered the MRT station. The train, usually comfortable, was stuffy and hot today, all the riders fanning themselves with whatever they had on hand. By the time she reached Raffles Place, she could barely breathe. She was early, though, so she ambled through the station, took the escalator to the exit, strolled toward the Overseas Union Bank Building, where Bradford & Co. had their offices, and rode the lift to the firm's floor.

The air conditioning in the reception area allowed her to recover a bit from the heat, but she didn't have to wait long. Shortly after the receptionist called to announce her arrival, an Indian gentleman with unruly white hair materialized. His bushy eyebrows made him appear to be peering at her through a mask. Shorter than Aislinn, he wore a crisp white shirt and a narrow, black tie.

"Mrs. Givens, good morning. I'm Selvadurai." He extended his hand. They shook, and he led the way to a conference room. After they were served tea by a uniformed attendant, a tiny Chinese woman who crept around them like a cat, he said, "Please tell me how I may be of service to you."

His accent differed from TJ Kwan's, less clipped, more melodic, but was far from the caricatured Indian lilt she'd been expecting. It was different, too, from Martin Roy's accent, although she understood now that Martin was at least part Indian. This Singapore was a genuine melting pot, she thought, not for the first time.

She was in Singapore with her expat husband, she explained, and had left a position with a New York law firm to come. But it was an adventure in a part of the world she knew little about, and she was excited to be living in a city so vibrant and different from what she was accustomed to. He was looking directly into her eyes when she said that, and she wondered if he could see that she was lying. Perhaps a little more honesty was called for.

"To be frank, I had hoped to find employment with one of the American law firms here, but that hasn't worked out. I love the law, worked very hard for my firm in New York, and was on the verge of partnership." Was that true? An embellishment, perhaps, but it should have been true. She took a copy of her résumé out of her briefcase and slid it across the table to him.

While he studied it, she looked around the conference room: windowless, paneled in an oppressive dark wood, brightened with a trio of colorful lithographs, not unlike her own Miro print. Whereas hers suggested sailboats setting out on a voyage, this group seemed to speak of the arrival.

Selvadurai excused himself and returned with two other lawyers, one an older Chinese man and the other a young Chinese woman, whom he introduced to Aislinn as his partners. The four of them talked about what they understood the history of the firm to be, from its founding in the late nineteenth century by an English barrister, and its continuation under the current name beginning in 1915, when Avery Bradford took over. Aislinn mentioned that she'd been doing some reading about the earliest law firms in the country and found their origins intriguing. The young Chinese lawyer was especially interested in Aislinn's experience in New York and the kinds of transactions she'd worked on there. They took her on a tour of the office that ended at the elevator, where Selvadurai shook her hand and promised to be in touch soon.

· · · · ·

Selvadurai called the next morning.

"Mrs. Givens," he said, "my partners and I enjoyed meeting you yesterday."

"And I enjoyed meeting you, as well," she said. "It's very kind of you to call."

"I must say, we were impressed with you, not only with your experience in New York but also your sincere interest in the history of Singapore, which is not frequently the case with foreigners, especially Americans."

"It's a fascinating country."

"And so, to the point. We were wondering if you would be interested in working for Bradford & Company as a consultant. There are sensitive issues of licensing, and the firm does not want to be seen as attempting to practice American law, which would be a violation of our Law Society's rules, but we have clients with investments in the States and they often have questions about US law that the Singapore lawyers can't answer with confidence. Most local companies are reluctant to seek out advice from the American firms, however, because it's so expensive to do so and viewed by some as unpatriotic. Then, too, we have American clients who can be uncomfortable dealing solely with Singaporean lawyers. They might also appreciate being able to consult with a lawyer who understands them."

The irony of the proposal was not lost on her. The firm began as a colonial institution that eventually, and probably reluctantly, employed locals. They, in turn, gradually took over, and now they were in a position to hire a foreign lawyer to work for them.

"Mr. Selvadurai, I'm flattered, and I love the idea. But won't I face a work visa problem? That's what some of the foreign law firms said."

"No promises, but I think we might have a better chance with the Immigration Authority in arranging a work visa than a foreign firm would. Also, the position would probably only be part time, at least at first, because most of our work is purely domestic. Is that something you'd be interested in?"

Aislinn was thrilled. Failing to find a position with the American firms had been devastating. It was the first time she'd experienced failure of that kind, and it made her long for New York even more. She'd been admitted to every college and law school she'd applied to. She never received lower than a B in college, and that was in calculus, for Christ's sake, a subject that neither appealed nor mattered to her, but checked off one of the arcane boxes required for her liberal arts degree. In law school, she'd missed being *summa cum laude* by one tenth of a point in her grade point average, and she blamed that on the randy old goat who taught criminal procedure. She'd had half a dozen offers from New York law firms, and a few from the mega-firms in Chicago and Los Angeles. Being unable to find a job in Singapore had, to say the least, shaken her confidence.

This, though, was validation—a position with one of the oldest law firms in the country. It wasn't perfect. It was doubtful that any deal she'd work on would be as complex or as interesting as the projects she'd handled in New York, but it was something. And the fact that it was part time would make it more palatable to Liam, who thought she didn't need to work at all. The job would fill this void she had feared would turn into something permanent, inexplicable to potential future employers back home, but she'd still have time to play hostess for Liam's bank, an obligation that would presumably expand given the Morelocks' imminent departure. Now, when she went back to New York, her résumé would be solid, no gaps, and she'd have this unique experience besides. Even if her old firm wouldn't take her back on the partnership track, as Frank had implied, she'd be more likely to find a place in another firm that valued international experience.

And, to top it off, her days in Singapore would not be stretching before her, long and empty.

* * * * *

On the following Monday, she arrived at the firm's offices in the Overseas Union Bank Building and was greeted by name by the pretty young receptionist, a slim Chinese girl wearing a plain black shift. A long-stemmed, purple orchid decorated the girl's desk. She stood and showed Aislinn to Selvadurai's office.

Selvadurai then took her to another office, small, but with a window that had a view of the Raffles Place Plaza and the harbor beyond visible between two other office towers. On the desk was a stack of files.

"This is the nicest of our vacant offices," Selvadurai said. "By tomorrow, there should be a phone and we'll get your name on the door."

He summoned a clerk who would give her instructions on how to keep her time sheets—they'd recently gone to an intranet system not unlike her New York firm's—and her first task was to review the files on the desk concerning an American company that purchased a minority stake in a local manufacturer. He'd be back at the end of the day to get her impressions.

As she was settling into the office, the receptionist tapped on her door.

"This just came for you, Mrs. Givens," she said, placing a vibrant purple orchid with five large blooms on her desk. The attached card read, "Happy First Day of Work, Love, Margaret Atwood."

Aislinn was in heaven. All right, not heaven, but for the moment, she was at peace. Liam had made sure she understood that Selvadurai had hired her as a favor to TJ and, probably, in hopes of snagging some of the bank's legal work. Even if he was right, this was real work, and a real opportunity to accomplish something. She'd get her article on the history of Singapore's law firms done on her own time, and meanwhile she'd keep her legal skills sharp. And she'd still have time to be Mrs. Liam Connolly when the occasion called for a hostess.

At four o'clock, Selvadurai's secretary appeared and asked Aislinn to join him in the conference room. She gathered up the files and followed the young woman, a slender Chinese girl who introduced herself as Serene, to a different room from the one she'd seen before. While she waited for her new boss to arrive, she examined the artwork on the walls. One painting grabbed her attention immediately. It was a square oil painting of a bird of paradise flower. The style looked just like the pictures she'd bought at Orientalia—impressionist brush strokes, an illusion of movement and a similar frame. Another Pennington? The frame obscured the signature, but the tops of the letters were visible, and they looked right. There was a date—1915. How did Pennington's work come to be in this office?

Selvadurai entered and closed the door. She wanted to ask him about the painting, but it wasn't relevant to their purpose, and it seemed unlikely that the managing partner of the firm would know the details of every piece of art in their collection. There was business to conduct first, and she was reminded of her early days in New York and the tasks assigned to her by Frank McKee.

"So, Mrs. Givens," Selvadurai said, "what did you learn?"

When she was a younger associate, being quizzed by a senior partner would have made her heart race, no matter how sure she was of the answer. She remembered a moment in a department meeting in her first year when Byron Morrow, then the head of the firm, quizzed another associate on the Packers and Stockyards Act, a law she had at that time never heard of. When the young lawyer flubbed the answer, admitting that he was unfamiliar with the Packers and Stockyards Act, Morrow was furious and called upon a junior partner to educate the associates about this important aspect of commercial law. It was worse than being a 1-L at Harvard and having to endure a Socratic interrogation on an arcane common law tradition. Now, though, Aislinn knew her stuff and responded calmly and with confidence.

"Your client is being purchased by a small Texas-based holding company, the parent to numerous manufacturing subsidiaries. It's privately held, with two investors being the principal owners of the company, both involved in management. But the investors are apparently more interested in buying existing companies, repackaging them—reducing payrolls and taking other steps to improve the balance sheet—and then selling as quickly as possible for a nice profit than they are in growing the acquired company's business. They've done that repeatedly. Good for the investors, but rarely good for the companies they acquire, or their employees."

Aislinn looked at Selvadurai to gauge his reaction so far. He nodded and she continued. She added details about the investors and their holding company that she'd garnered from the internet, including ongoing litigation and a pending regulatory action that would likely be settled with a significant fine. "Also, the principals appear to be involved in other companies in which they're more directly engaged. It seems unlikely they would give this acquisition their full attention." She removed from the file a document she'd found online that contained disturbing background information on one of the owners and explained why his personal troubles added a layer of risk to the proposed transaction.

"That's exactly what we suspected, but without these additional details for confirmation," Selvadurai said. He then asked about contracts that were in the files, and Aislinn pointed out several provisions that she would have handled differently if she had been counsel to the company. Everything else, though, appeared to be in order.

"Thank you," Selvadurai said. "I'll be passing along your observations to our client. It's obvious you are a thorough lawyer. I think this is going to work out nicely for both of us. This file review was routine, but tomorrow afternoon you'll find something a little more challenging on your desk. Good night."

He was gone so quickly that she didn't have a chance to ask about the painting, but she'd talk to the office manager, who was more likely to know its provenance. She might even ask to have it moved into her office, although there was no rush. It felt as though she'd found a new home, and she wasn't planning to leave anytime soon.

When she looked at her watch, though, she realized she needed to hurry back to the apartment. Liam was bringing TJ by for dinner—more conniving and plotting, she assumed—and if she wasn't there when they arrived, she'd hear about it from Liam.

• • • • •

"You're looking lovely tonight, Aislinn," TJ said when he and Liam came in.

"Thank you, TJ. You're always such a gentleman."

Kwan joined Liam, who was pouring drinks for them both.

"So, I gather this is going to be a working dinner," Aislinn said. "Although I would think you'd be able to conduct all your business in the office during the day."

"TJ isn't there much, love. He has his own offices down on Shenton Way."

"That's right. The bank's office here is a joint venture, and we—the local partners and I—leave management to SJ Freeman. I don't interfere, and I don't often visit so that we don't confuse the staff as to who is in charge."

But who *is* in charge, Aislinn wondered. She wondered, too, if TJ spent this much time with Bruce, who was, after all, still the boss.

While Cecilia served the meal—chicken adobo, a Filipino dish Liam had complimented her on—they engaged in small talk. There had been an anti-government demonstration earlier in the day, but it hadn't amounted to much. Aislinn was curious about that, but felt uncomfortable asking for more details. There had been a plane crash in Sumatra, just the latest involving one of the low-cost Indonesian airlines. No survivors, apparently. And a typhoon was closing in on Hong Kong and southern China.

Finally, Liam asked TJ to brief him on the Thailand deal he was brewing.

"I wouldn't want to bore Aislinn," TJ said.

"Please, I'm interested in hearing about Thailand."

"All right then. A company in Bangkok is looking to expand one of its lines of business throughout the country. It finances automobiles and motorbikes by taking title documents to the vehicles. The proposal is for a syndicate of banks to provide a loan based on a percentage of these leases. That capital will allow the company to quadruple its business in the first year, more than enough to service the loan."

"What's the security for the loan?" Aislinn asked. She half-expected Liam to tell her to help Cecilia in the kitchen, but he was silent. It seemed a reasonable question, one that he should have asked.

"The titles. Through an agent, whom we pay from the loan initiation fee, we hold the documents in batches, releasing them back to the company as the leases are fully paid or as our loan is paid down."

"I don't suppose Thailand has a lien registration system like we do in the US."

TJ shook his head.

"Physical possession of the titles is probably even better security," she said, "although it would be hell to enforce payment by repossessing a million motorbikes scattered all over the country."

"But it wouldn't come to that, of course," Liam said. "TJ tells me this company has an excellent reputation. Isn't that right?"

"First rate," said TJ. "I've known the CEO, Khun Anuwat, for many years."

"I told you," Liam said, "TJ knows everyone."

"Did you bring this deal to Bruce?" Aislinn asked.

"Bruce is history, love," Liam said.

"I did," TJ said. "Mr. Morelock thinks he's still a missionary. This project will make the bank a great deal of money. Bruce could not see the benefits."

6

8 September 1914

I thought the voyage might never end, but I thank the heavens that it has. No doubt it will take some time to settle in here, and I am still, stubbornly, resentful to have been banished so, but I must be optimistic. It will do me no good to dwell on the calamities of the past.

For one thing, I am most fortunate that Uncle Cyril has taken me in, and my fears of being placed in servitude were unfounded. Instead, it seems, I am to be like his own daughter, filling a familial void and creating an atmosphere he has never had the pleasure to experience. Furthermore, this house is truly a marvel. He says when he first arrived in Singapore as a young lawyer, having been accepted as a clerk in one of the local firms, he stayed for a time at the Raffles Hotel, eventually taking rooms in a lodging house until such time as he rose in esteem in the legal community, established his own firm, and could afford to build a bungalow.

He calls it Heatherleigh, a name he has had carved into a stone at the entrance gate, after a cottage he remembered in Sussex where he spent time as a young man. It reminds me of nothing I've seen in England, not even Richard Bromley's house, although Uncle tells me it is based on English designs that have been modified for the tropics. It is never cold here (I am sure come winter I shall miss sitting by the stove on a brisk evening), so exterior walls serve only to hold up the roof and not to keep out the chill. In most rooms we have broad windows, or no covering at all except shutters to protect from the occasional blowing rainstorm and to serve the dictates of modesty. Under a portico, broad steps lead up to the front veranda and the entry hall, with the drawing room to the left and dining room to the right. So much space! Compared to our modest cottage at home, this seems a palace, although neither electricity nor telephone lines have yet reached it, lending the house an even more rustic and remote character.

The bedrooms, which are generously proportioned, are upstairs and equipped with what I initially mistook for sheer curtains around the beds. Uncle informs me that this fine cotton netting is protection against mosquitoes, which apparently carry a deadly disease. It has taken me some time to grow accustomed to sleeping inside the netting, which at first made me feel as though I had been wrapped in a shroud. Now, though, the enclosed space gives me some comfort, providing at least the illusion of security in this unfamiliar land.

Then there are spaces out of doors. It is such a joy to take tea on the veranda, which wraps around three-quarters of the house, with the jungle only yards away. So lush! I have not yet ventured close to examine the varieties of trees, shrubs, and flowers, but I am excited to paint it all. Incredible colors: reds and oranges and yellows, and every shade of green. So vibrant!

Uncle employs a man just to look after the garden. This morning I listened to Uncle berate the man, a native of Malaya, in his own tongue. I was shocked to hear him use the language so fluently, its lovely singsong rhythm rolling from him as if he had been speaking it his entire life. Of course, I had no idea what he was saying, or what the poor man had done to deserve the lashing, as the garden looks lovely to me. It is my hope to learn at least a few words, so I might not feel so foreign here.

I have thus begun my exile, but it is far from the prison I had envisioned. Primarily in these first days, I have spent my time acclimating to the house and stagnant heat, but Uncle says he will soon be introducing me around. I have hopes that there will be interesting people to meet. And young men, perhaps? While I am determined to create an independent life for myself, there is no reason why I should be entirely cloistered, is there?

10 September 1914
Mr. Preston called upon us today. It turns out that Uncle Cyril and Mr. Preston are acquainted, which should not have surprised me, as each seems to know everyone of significance in the settlement—or professes to.

Although the novelist on this occasion has been here no longer than I, he is a font of gossip and rumor, having paid calls on all his familiars from previous sojourns. Mrs. Pettigrew has taken ill, it seems. I do not know Mrs. Pettigrew, but Uncle was most concerned to hear it, as the fevers that come upon the residents and natives alike can be deadly and spread. Mr. Gledhill was heard in a shouting match with his law partner, Mr. Allen, at the bar of the Raffles Hotel. Mr. Preston wasn't certain if the altercation was about a lady or money or both. Given that the gentlemen in question are Uncle's competitors, he took an unseemly interest in this titbit. Whether we can credit Mr. Preston's tales remains to be seen, but he does provide a pleasant afternoon's entertainment, and I shall look forward to his future visits. I prayed that he would not mention Richard Bromley, as I do not know to what extent Uncle Cyril was made aware of the circumstances at home and the fullest of reasons for my banishment, and thankfully he did not. Perhaps he has forgotten I mentioned the name, and we can allow R. to fade into the past. That saddens me, but it is for the best, I'm sure.

And the news from Europe is ever more frightening. A civilian passenger ship has been sunk in the Mediterranean, with many casualties, confirming the wisdom of my aunt's booking my passage around the Cape instead of through Suez. I am horrified by the senseless loss of life. There is no rational explanation for this war, nothing to be gained. Now that it has begun, I fear it will not be stopped. Once again, I feel some shame that I am given refuge so far from the conflict and have done nothing to offer aid, as so many of my countrywomen have. Might there be something I could do yet?

12 September 1914
At tea today in the home of Mrs. Antonia Burke with a number of other ladies of the settlement, all at least twice or three times my age, I began to learn something about colonial life. For one thing, it is as shallow as a puddle. Like Mr. Preston, these women have nothing better to do than spread lies about each other. One wonders what they will have to say about me when I am not in their company. Mrs. Pettigrew's illness is better than it was, no she's taken a turn for the worse, no it isn't the fever at all, it's a feminine complaint, and the poor woman unable to defend herself. They are all acquainted with Mr. Preston, of course, who has made the rounds, and his proclivities, of which I first learned on board the Duchess, are well known, though spoken of ever so obliquely. He has moved from the Grand Hotel, it is reported, to a high-class rooming house, but has been seen in unsavory company, whatever that might suggest. They all nod their heads, ambiguously but knowingly. Truly, I must read the man's novels!

Mrs. Burke mentioned, without derision and so I believe she meant the remark admiringly, that a Mrs. Hoyt, whose husband I gather is engaged in the P&O Shipping Company, has begun volunteering at St. Mary's Home, an orphanage that is in great need. I wonder if I might be able to contribute in some way, if the children might need lessons I could provide, or simply comfort? It would not be helping the war effort directly, but I feel I must do something!

Much discussion also was made of the 5th Light Infantry Regiment, which has recently arrived from India to help defend the settlement from the Germans: who has been disciplined, who promoted, who departed. Captain such-and-such is from a fine family, Colonel someone is well connected in London, and so on. Most tedious, I am sure. (But the mention of the men of the Regiment did stir my interest, I must admit, and I hope to learn more in due course.)

I tried to steer the conversation to the arts, as that is my primary interest, and the ladies were horrified to hear of my enjoyment of the novels of Mr. Lawrence. In retrospect, I probably should have kept that to myself. And I am afraid I shocked them all off their chairs when I said I intended never to marry and to support myself with my painting and drawing. The poor dears.

Fortunately, the subject then turned to music, and in that we are in agreement. Mrs. Burke's daughter, Daisy, was summoned to play for us, and she did a creditable job with a bit of Chopin on a lovely vertical piano that was only slightly out of tune. I took a turn and played a Beethoven sonata I learned long ago, although I am terribly rusty. I wonder if I might prevail upon Uncle to acquire an instrument so I can resume regular playing. I'm afraid that life here will be most insipid, if this afternoon is any proof, and I shall need all the distractions I can find. Still, it is pleasant to have made the acquaintance of these ladies, as they are, I gather, pillars of the community.

Speaking of distractions, I have learned that an art club of some kind has been functioning for as long as wives have been present in the colony (or at least for as long as any of my new acquaintances can remember) and that its members put on exhibitions once or twice a year. Mrs. Burke promised to introduce me to Mrs. Barker, the wife of the gentleman who is in charge of the prison, who organizes these events. Apparently, she is a talented painter herself, although Mrs. Withers barely suppressed laughter when Mrs. Burke said as much, and so I suppose Mrs. Burke might have been giving Mrs. Barker too much credit. Of course, I am no bright light either, despite my tutoring with R., but I fancy that I do have an eye and a way of expressing myself on a canvas that is somehow profound and something of a mystery, even to myself. Whether others will be similarly moved I cannot say, and of course painting is the most subjective of the arts. In any case, the prospect of a group exhibition certainly gives me something to look forward to, and I am more resolved than ever to refine my craft.

14 September 1914

I met the most charming gentleman this afternoon. Or, rather, I did not meet him but glimpsed him from afar at a Government House reception. I suppose I am no different from other women who say a man in uniform is more attractive than other men, which must reveal something superficial in ourselves, perhaps a desire to be commanded, although that is far from the conception I have of myself. Whatever norms society has prescribed, I have no wish to be subservient to any man.

Still, there he was in glittering white, beribboned for honor in service to the empire, and my gaze was drawn to him. His chin, at an angle, seemed too sharp, but when he turned toward me, I saw that it was square and strong. I looked away quickly lest he notice I was staring, but I could not help myself. In conversation with Mrs. Burke or any of the other ladies in attendance, I would let my eyes seek him out and then force myself to return my attention to my interlocutor. Eventually, inevitably, our eyes met, and I felt such a shiver in my body, despite the heat.

I'm afraid I am no good at discretion. Just as my emotions reveal themselves on canvas, so do they read plainly in my face. When I asked Uncle about the officer, he raised his eyebrows, and a vulgar smirk grew on his lips. He recovered himself and warned me to stay clear of the Regiment. In the end, though, after my unseemly wheedling, he assured me he would make inquiries. I wondered again how much Uncle knew about my history with R.

"I will ask," he said. "And perhaps we can arrange an introduction. But you will comport yourself as a young lady. My station here is most public, and it would not do to have my reputation besmirched."

I nearly laughed out loud at his pomposity, but I feigned offense instead. "Well, I would never," I spluttered, and then fled around a corner into the ballroom where my amusement would not be observed.

The Regiment and its handsome officers aside, Government House is a most impressive edifice. The grounds were once, I was told, part of a nutmeg plantation. When a blight destroyed the trees, the land was acquired and turned into something of a park and a home for the Straits Settlements' offices. Uncle says it is designed after a traditional Malay house, and while I know nothing of such things, I could see for myself that it featured open verandas and louvred windows, much like Uncle's own bungalow. But I also observed classic columns and arches on the façade, which I doubt very much are elements of the home of any native in this part of the world. The grounds, though, are lovely, perfect for strolling and watching. And being watched. Even during the short time we were there, the light changed dramatically as clouds came and went, and it occurred to me that a series of paintings of the building at different times of day or year might convey something of its vibrancy, a breathing organism with a life of its own.

Wherever my gaze turned, however, it soon sought out the officer. I longed to know more about him and, without waiting for Uncle to make inquiries, took it upon myself to ask Mrs. Burke if she knew what the officer was called. Oh, I am a forward child, ever have been, and I care not of raised eyebrows and twisted lewd grins and other such warnings that I am treading where I ought not.

With evident reluctance and after some hesitation, Mrs. Burke offered the intelligence I sought: Captain Charles Bingham.

15 September 1914

From the looks of things, the rain that began overnight will not let up today. I have settled on the veranda with my sketchbook, but I find myself working dreamily or not at all. The face that appears on the page is, more or less, the young officer from yesterday's reception. I can think of little else, I'm afraid. Such a foolish woman I am. I have no need of a man to be fulfilled. I have my art. At least he has supplanted R. in my dreams.

But, oh, how I long to return to England. The oppressive heat. The strictures of society. The ever-watchful and wary eye of Uncle Cyril.

The rain makes me dizzy with sadness, I think. Nothing moves, except water dripping from the eaves and from the trees in the garden. The sky is thick with clouds that threaten to smother me.

I must shake off this feeling. I must strengthen my resolve. Tomorrow, at first light, if the rain has ended, I shall set up my easel and break out the paints. Determination!

17 September 1914

At tea this afternoon, Uncle Cyril said something most peculiar, and it made me wonder if he doesn't know more about what happened back home than he has thus far let on.

He said, "Your mother would be thrilled to know you are thriving, my dear."

How should I respond? How *could* my mother know? Unless Uncle is in touch with her, which would mean that he knows where she is.

"You have heard from my mother?" I asked.

He looked terribly alarmed and vigorously shook his head, as if he might be draining water from his ears.

"No, Lizzie, no. I know no more of your mother's whereabouts than you do, I assure you. I only meant if she could know, she would be pleased."

We said no more then, but I suspect Uncle is withholding something from me and that he may not know exactly where Mother is at this moment, making the words he spoke technically true, but that he has a way of communicating with her. I wonder. Has he received letters from her, and might they not be hidden somewhere in this house? Is there some dark corner where he has stashed away his secret treasures? He did warn me when I first arrived that the servants are not to be trusted, and so there must be such a hiding place.

The realization that he surely knows where my mother is made me think of my poor brother, James, and I was immediately struck with a wave of guilt because I have not given him even a moment's thought in days. How I wish he'd been able to come with me, despite all his troubles. But perhaps what I really wish is that we were still children, gamboling in the fields near our home, racing down the village high street, our parents in frolicking pursuit.

An image comes to me of the very last time I saw my mother. One afternoon, the four of us had settled onto the grass of the village green. Mother and Father were engaged in some urgent discussion, a not infrequent occurrence, hushed so I could not hear their words, although I had heard her complain often enough of her drudgery, and how she longed for the glamorous life to which she thought she was entitled. A book lay open on my lap, the lovely pictures drawing me in, mountains and rivers such as I had never seen in real life. And my brother, only a year older, lay on his stomach, studying the ground intently, eyes fixed on I knew not what.

"What is it, Jamie? What are you looking at?"

"It's a worm, Lizzie," he said. "See how it twists and turns?"

I had no interest in a worm and instead gazed into my picture book. My parents took no notice at all.

My father's voice grew louder, angry, I thought. I hated it when they quarreled. They were constantly quarreling.

"Mummy," Jamie called, "look at the worm."

Instead of joining Jamie on the grass, Mother stood abruptly and marched across the green, out of sight, and, as it developed, out of our lives. Despite my pleading, my father would never speak of her again. Her things, the pretty dresses and shoes, the glittering bits of jewelry I so admired, the books of poetry she favored, they all vanished from our cottage. It was as if she had never existed, and in all this time, after Jamie's troubles and Father's death, there has been no word of her.

Does Uncle know what happened to my mother? Why has he said nothing?

18 September 1914

A stormy morning that would recall England, if it weren't for the heat, and Jamie is on my mind again today.

His troubles began not long after my mother's disappearance, which, of course, we did not understand.

"Where's Mummy?" we both asked our father, begging to know when she would come home.

Stony silence.

We muddled along with the help of a village woman, Mrs. Gowan, who cooked and cleaned, but she was no substitute for our mother. She offered no comfort when Jamie skinned a knee, or I misplaced a hair ribbon. When I ran to her in tears, I was met with crossed arms and a scowl, so that I knew my efforts were wasted, a lesson I remember to this day. What is the point of tears when our comfort must come from within?

Jamie, though, responded differently to Mrs. Gowan's coolness towards us. Instead of turning inward to books and pictures as I did, he acted out. I will never forget the Manx cat that visited our cottage door on occasion. I suspected my mother of feeding the cat, over my father's objections, inducing its visits, and so perhaps Jamie associated the animal with her. Not long after our mother went away and Mrs. Gowan started her work with us, I realized I hadn't seen the cat in some time. She didn't feed it, I surmised, so it had taken its attentions elsewhere.

One morning Jamie ran toward me, cradling something in his hands.

"Lizzie, come see," he shouted. He so loved nature and all its mysteries.

"What is it, Jamie?" I asked, peering into his cupped hands. At first, I thought he held a blossom, and I wondered why his hands were wet and red.

"It's the cat, Lizzie. Look! She has a heart!"

19 September 1914

After the rains of recent days, the air is surprisingly fresh. I have set up my easel in Uncle Cyril's garden and begun to paint. No single image has come to my mind, and it is the jungle wall, the verdant tangle of undifferentiated green that grows on the canvas, plants I still do not know by name, only by their shapes and texture. As I wield my brush, my eyes adjust to what I see: the sharp spears of giant grasses near the ground; at eye-level, broad oval leaves the color of moss, flapping noiselessly in the morning breeze; the flag-like fronds of the banana trees, spouting tiny yellow clusters of delicious fruit; and soaring palms, as straight and tall as masts on a sailing ship. I seek to capture not just the movement in the air, but the very being of these plants, as if they were living, breathing animals.

And then the wall fades again into unbroken green as the young officer intrudes on my concentration.

I did not imagine as I sailed from England that I might meet someone like him, a dashing military man. I felt as though I had been shipped off into exile, to be hidden from life and all its complications and perils. To forget my mother and poor brother, to mourn for my father, and of course to be kept apart from R. Instead, I wonder if my life is only now beginning. Is this my rebirth? I have yet to speak to the man and still there is a warmth that rises inside me when I think of him.

And now I begin to contrive how I might see him again.

It is not as though I have entirely forgotten Richard Bromley, nor could I. After father showed the famous man my drawings, he agreed to take me on as his pupil and assistant, a most unusual arrangement, not only because I was so young but also, mostly, because I was a girl. From Richard, I learned so much—about materials and surfaces, yes, but also about seeing, imagining, understanding both the surface and what goes on beneath. Richard said, frequently, that he painted not for the casual observer who might glance at the work in an exhibition, but for the participant, the man or woman who willingly entered the world of the painting and truly felt its movement and emotion. Despite all that has passed between us, this is what I remember.

7

Aislinn woke when she felt Liam sit up in bed. She hadn't heard his alarm, but she watched him lift the sheet, in slow motion, as if sneaking away. He padded to the bathroom, eased the door shut, and turned on the shower. It was early yet, no light showing through the bedroom blinds. Why was he up? Was something wrong? She began to tremble as all the anxiety of the past few months flooded back: the nightmare New York had become, wrestling with the decision to come to Singapore for Liam's promotion, the struggle to find work and rebuild her life in a new city, a new country, the change that had come over Liam. But why was he up so early?

Now she remembered: he had an early flight to Bangkok for TJ's motorbike deal, and he'd booked a pre-dawn cab to Changi Airport. She appreciated his efforts not to wake her, even though she'd told him she didn't mind. She knew this trip was important to him, still new in his position, still looking to make a name for himself, and she wanted to see him off, wish him safe travels, tell him she loved him and would miss him terribly. The truth was more complicated than that, though, and she was looking forward to having a little time to herself, to process what had changed between them, and what the future might hold.

The flight worried her. When she was younger, traveling with her parents or during breaks from college and law school and even as a junior associate in the law firm new to the experience of business travel, she loved flying. There was something about being above the clouds, watching the world pass below her, that was both comforting and exhilarating. But lately—since 9/11, which had changed everything—she dreaded it, for herself and loved ones. She used to think it was perfectly safe, statistically, at least, but she now knew anything could happen. Flying had become dangerous. Their flight from JFK a few months ago had been ungodly, interminable, and she'd been quivering with panic until the Xanax kicked in. Just the thought of flying now made her nervous. How long was Liam's flight to Bangkok? Two hours? Three? She wasn't sure she could do it. Liam had promised vacations in all the exotic locales in Southeast Asia, most within just a few hours of Singapore—Bali, Chiang Mai, Angkor Wat, Vietnam—but the prospect terrified her.

• • • • •

After Liam left for the airport, Aislinn took her own shower and got ready for work. Although her part-time job as a foreign legal consultant at Bradford & Co. was nowhere close to the ideal situation, it was, she kept telling herself, better than nothing. Besides being one of the oldest firms in Singapore, Bradford had, from what she'd been able to learn from TJ Kwan and others, a stellar reputation. Selvadurai, the genial managing partner, was a former Law Minister of Singapore, and exceedingly well connected in the legal community and beyond. She'd been flattered when he had offered her a job and was keen to turn it into more than just a way to fill her days.

By the time Aislinn was ready to go into the office, Cecilia had emerged to begin the day's dusting and cleaning, chatting with Mack as she moved around the living room. The bird squawked in reply, with occasional calls for Bub and Apron. Leaving the apartment, Aislinn let Cecilia know that Mr. Connolly would not be home for dinner, so there was no need to cook tonight. Closing the door behind her, she wondered what Cecilia really did when she was gone, whether the closing of the door might be all the signal she needed to put her feet up and turn on the television. Or was she too mistrustful of the woman? Had she learned that prejudice from the other expat wives who carped constantly about the failings of their maids? Really, though, she had no complaints about Cecilia's performance and considered herself lucky to have her. She still felt guilty about the arrangement, but didn't Cecilia and her family benefit, too? It's not as if she was forcing the woman to work for her.

She had the lift to herself, not counting her infinite mirrored replicas, descended the twenty floors, and greeted the security guard, Mr. Wong, the nearly hairless retiree who worked mornings. Stooped and gaunt, the old man flashed a smile in return. Pushing outside through the lobby's heavy glass doors, she prepared herself for the assault of Singapore's heat and humidity.

· · · · ·

She surveyed the sky—the white blue she'd noticed on that first day in the country, exploring the lush grounds of their hotel—but she knew the absence of clouds meant next to nothing. Rainstorms seemed to materialize out of nowhere, and by the end of the day there might be a downpour. Someone had told her—probably Jenny Morelock, the source of most of her knowledge about Singapore—that there were two monsoon seasons, one when the rains came from the Northeast and one when they came from the Southwest, but she still hadn't figured out which was which. She'd already been caught in one torrential rainstorm, drenched one afternoon when she went out for lunch with people from the office to the charming Telok Ayer Market, a historic covered food court with a dozen or so purveyors of local dishes, and now never left home without an umbrella. Not that an umbrella offered much protection when the storms raced through the city accompanied by ferocious winds, driving the rain horizontal.

Their apartment complex was in something of an expatriate enclave, a forest of high-rises on a hill near both the American Club and the largely British Tanglin Club, not far from several five-star hotels and the luxury shops and department stores of Orchard Road. There were locals here, too, wealthy Singaporeans, but she saw more foreigners in this neighborhood than anywhere else in the city. She headed down the hill, past a Starbucks, past the tacky Texas Roadhouse steak joint, weaving through bewildered tourists on the wide sidewalks of Orchard Road, past the hotel with the garish yellow roof, making her way to the subway station. She noticed an odd atmosphere in the air today, charged, as if for a holiday or a momentous event. There were so many holidays in Singapore she knew nothing about, part of the multicultural foundation of the country—Deepavali, Vesak Day, Ramadan, Hungry Ghosts. Was this one that had escaped her attention?

But there was something else. Two fierce-looking policemen, in their maroon berets and intimidating dark blue uniforms topped by bulky black Kevlar vests, submachine guns at the ready, stood sentry at the subway entrance. She rode the MRT almost every day now—it was the cleanest, quietest, and most efficient transit system she'd ever used, if not quite as ubiquitous or convenient as New York City's or London's—and she hadn't noticed this police presence before. On the occasions she *had* seen police officers, they were far more benign, more like school crossing guards than riot police. Did they even carry guns? She hadn't noticed.

Usually, teens loitered outside this entrance—it seemed to be a great meeting spot for them thanks to its proximity to countless shopping malls and a broad plaza ideal for skateboarding—but today there was no one. Riders lowered their eyes and slipped past the two policemen, careful not to draw attention to themselves. She considered asking one of the cops what was going on, but thought better of displaying her American ignorance and followed the example of the other passengers. She took the escalator down into the normally bustling station that today was virtually deserted, bought her ticket, and rode down another level to the platform.

The train arrived, nearly empty. The doors whooshed open, and she concluded that it *must* be a holiday. How odd, she thought, that there had been no mention of it at the office yesterday. She studied faces, but no one made eye contact. They saw her watching and turned their heads. The usual passenger chatter was absent.

At Raffles Place, she exited the train. Here, inside the cavernous station where two subway lines crossed deep below the surface, there were a dozen or more police in riot gear. Arriving and departing passengers steered clear and hurried through the station. She rode the escalator to the surface and emerged into the suffocating heat, puzzled by what she'd seen.

• • • • •

At Bradford & Co., the mood was somber. Although venerable, it was a small firm and quieter than her New York office had been, but it seemed especially so today.

"What's going on?" she asked Serene, a normally outgoing young Chinese woman with her hair in short braids. "Is there something happening I don't know about? Did someone die?"

In a near-whisper, Serene said, "It's a demonstration."

"Of what?" And then she realized it wasn't *that* kind of demonstration. "Who's demonstrating? And what are they demonstrating about?" Was this the reason for the visible presence of the riot police? She remembered there had been a small protest a few weeks earlier, but the response then had been barely noticeable.

Serene shook her head, almost imperceptibly, and returned to her desk. She didn't know? Or didn't want to talk about it? In New York, Tawnisha would have been keen to broadcast whatever gossip or speculation was current in the office, and had no compunction about sharing her opinions, political, personal, or otherwise. This woman, though, seemed afraid to speak.

Aislinn settled into her office. Her desk was an antique solid oak table that, she liked to imagine, might have been Avery Bradford's own, shipped to the colony from England, back in the days of slow steamers and rubber plantations. She'd picked out a philodendron for the desktop, adding that to the orchid Liam had given her to create a miniature tropical garden in her office. On the wall opposite her desk was the stunning painting of a bird of paradise flower that she'd first seen in a conference room, another Pennington. She'd given up trying to find out where the painting had come from—it had been part of the firm so long that there were no records of when or how it had been acquired—but when she'd quizzed the office manager about it a second time, he'd offered to move it into her office. Now, its orange flame-like bloom drew her attention whenever she lifted her eyes from her work.

Chun-po, the Tea Lady—such a demeaning job title, Aislinn thought, although Liam said every office had one, even the bank—now brought Aislinn a coffee. The poor woman, drowning inside a smock much too large for her, seemed so nervous, on the verge of tears most days, that Aislinn was afraid anything she said might drive the woman over the edge, and so she nodded and smiled her thanks. Serene had told Aislinn, although she hadn't asked, that Chun-po's name meant Spring Bud in Hokkien, the dialect of her village in China's Fujian province, from which she had recently arrived. Another immigrant woman, Aislinn realized, like Cecilia, willing to work for slave wages at the bottom of Singapore's capitalist machine, like thousands of laborers who toiled at countless construction sites across the city, and millions of migrants in the US from Mexico and Central America. As Chun-po left her office, Aislinn took a sip of the coffee, knowing it would be dreadful, and it was. Maybe it was time, she thought, to join the firm's majority and switch to tea. Either that or slip out to the Starbucks around the corner.

She pushed the coffee aside and began the contract review Selvadurai had asked her to do. This was largely what her job consisted of now, offering an American law perspective for American clients doing business in Singapore and Singaporean companies doing business in the US. It was a delicate balance and a gamble for the firm, as she was not qualified to give Singapore law advice, and the firm could not be seen to be practicing US law, either of which would be a violation of the Singapore Law Society's rules. In addition to being a former Law

Minister, Selvadurai was also a former president of the Singapore Law Society, however, and seemed unconcerned. If he wasn't worried, she certainly wasn't. In this case, she identified several clauses that might create problems for the local partner of a joint venture with an American company, and proposed alternatives that would be more favorable. It was work a competent second-year associate could have done in her old firm, and she longed for more challenging projects. Could she do this for the two or three years they'd be in Singapore?

· · · · ·

During the lunch hour, Aislinn donned her suit jacket—Liam had convinced her it made her look more professional—and left the building, heading toward Hong Lim Park, several humid blocks away. This was the site, she'd learned from one of the younger lawyers in the firm, of the Speaker's Corner, the one place where anti-government demonstrators were permitted to assemble. She'd received a quick and shocking course on Singapore politics: how the People's Action Party was dominant in the country and had been since the island gained its independence first from Britain and then from Malaysia; how the government didn't tolerate dissent and used the legal system—via defamation lawsuits and colonial-era detention laws—to suppress opposition voices; how the PAP used patronage in the various neighborhood constituencies to ensure loyalty. Occasionally, though, anger and frustration bubbled to the surface, and the result was a demonstration like the one planned for today. Licensed, neatly contained where the authorities could keep an eye on it, and ultimately impotent, but the closest Singapore came to freedom of speech.

The farther she walked, the more she regretted her decision to indulge her curiosity. It was just too hot. How did people live in this climate? Sweat seemed to pour from her skin, and she'd barely gone three blocks when she felt wilted and defeated, ready to turn around, ready, in fact, to go back to New York. But no, she couldn't give up yet, not on this little lunchtime adventure and not on her commitment to

Liam to give Singapore a shot. She removed her jacket and draped it over her arm. She'd keep going.

As she neared the park, which was not much more than a green strip between Canal Road and Upper Pickering Street, the sidewalks grew thicker with pedestrians, and a raspy loudspeaker blared a voice, although Aislinn couldn't make out what was being said, or even what language was being used. When she'd heard about the demonstration, she'd imagined something like Central Park overflowing with thousands of people, a real happening, masses of citizens making their voices heard, but Hong Lim didn't come close, reminding her more of the urban playground near their Brooklyn townhouse. At least there was shade. Only a few dozen people occupied the small park itself, and they were virtually surrounded by a cordon of police.

She knew that few countries in the world had the same standards of free speech that she was used to in the United States, but this was blatant intimidation. It was the opposite of free speech, wasn't it? The speakers, it seemed to her, were either extremely brave or very stupid for exposing themselves like this. She didn't yet know enough about the country to understand or assess their grievances, but surely citizens should feel free to speak their minds. How else would the politicians learn what the people wanted? Apparently, though, the politicians here believed they knew what was best for the people and didn't want to hear what they had to say. From what her colleague at the office had told her, if the government wanted to crack down, if it didn't like what the speakers demanded, lives would be ruined.

Aislinn hovered at the edge of the demonstration, partly because she felt, as a foreigner, she had no right to become involved in domestic politics, but partly because she was afraid. Even in the US these things could turn violent with little or no provocation, and hadn't there been massacres of pro-democracy demonstrators in China and Korea in the recent past? Could that happen here? She had no idea and didn't even know what the protest was about. Was it something that would make the government angry enough to respond violently?

When she was a second year at the University of Virginia, there had been a demonstration on the campus against something the first President Bush had done, she no longer remembered what. The war in Kuwait, maybe. It had begun tamely enough but had devolved into a rock-throwing melee in sight of the famous Rotunda, resulting in several injuries. The world had changed so much in the past decade that she could imagine a far more calamitous outcome now, even an overzealous police force responding brutally, maybe lethally, to protests over the war the current President Bush had begun in Afghanistan and threatened in Iraq.

With one eye on the cops in their riot gear, she crept along Hong Lim Park's periphery, looking at the faces of the demonstrators, who seemed to be as diverse as the country as a whole—many Chinese, fewer Indians and Malays. Some wore masks to hide their identities, and she wondered if that alone would raise the government's hackles. Many seemed to be mere spectators like her, watching from the sidewalk, but others were crowded closer to the speakers, listening intently, applauding and cheering.

Scanning the crowd, she spotted one face she recognized: Martin Roy from Orientalia. She took a step toward him to say hello, then thought better of it. He wasn't hiding, obviously, but was it better or worse for him if he was recognized? Might she be causing him trouble? Or causing trouble for herself? She drifted away from him, occasionally glancing in his direction, observing that his attention remained focused on the speakers.

A cheer arose from the demonstrators near the stage as a new speaker took the microphone. Aislinn strained to hear what this man was saying, but only detected that he was angry, shouting, stirring up his listeners who responded to his shouts with loud whoops, culminating in an indecipherable chant. This was nothing like the joyful cheers at a football game at UVA's Scott Stadium, but it was just as boisterous. The speaker raised a fist in the air and the crowd answered with an even more furious shout. From what she'd seen in her short time as an expat here, the country was prosperous and efficient. It was clean and seemed safe. The citizenry looked well fed. What were these people so angry about?

Some bystanders closer to the speaker rushed away from the center, all at once and in the same direction, as if there had been a signal Aislinn had missed. Then she saw why: a sleek white bus with blacked-out windows had disgorged another phalanx of police that marched toward the speaker, while the original force spread out to encircle the demonstrators at the center of the park. As they muscled their way through the crowd, they wielded clubs, sending some demonstrators shrieking to the ground. Aislinn looked on, helpless and horrified. This had been a peaceful demonstration. Why were the police doing this? She hadn't even understood what the speakers were saying—how dangerous could they be? Not far from her, a young man rushed a policeman, apparently trying to wrest the club from his grip, and was met with a blow to the head that Aislinn heard, the sickening crack of wood against bone that dropped the man to the dirt. The speaker, still shouting into his microphone, exhorting his followers to resist, made no attempt to evade the police, who, once they reached him, seized the microphone, yanked him off the stage, and dragged him to a police van. Now the most ardent demonstrators fled, few making it past the police barrier.

Aislinn couldn't move. What was she supposed to do? Someone grabbed her arm roughly, and she instantly had a vision of spending time in a Singapore jail, caught in the roundup of the protesters.

"Come with me," said a voice, and she turned to see that it was Martin Roy who had grabbed her. "We need to get out of here."

"Thank God," she said.

They ran across Canal Road along with a horde of other onlookers, but the attention of the police was not on the fleeing spectators. Once they were a block away, close to the promenade along the Singapore River, Martin took her arm again and they slowed.

"Time to blend in," he said. "Running will only draw attention to us."

Aislinn nodded, breathless, and walked beside him. She'd become aware again of the heat and sun, even more oppressive when they slowed to a walk. She studied an islet of debris floating in the almost-still water of the muddy river and pondered what she'd just witnessed. A peaceful protest that the riot police had turned into a pitched battle for no reason she could discern, with multiple injuries and arrests. What the hell was the point?

"Thank you for getting me out of there," she said. "But why did the police do that? I still don't know how Singapore works, but it seemed so senseless."

"Why do fascist governments do anything they do? It's about power. It's about the perception of invincibility and making sure there are no cracks in the wall. It's been that way here since day one. Allowing dissent is seen as a sign of weakness. That was true in colonial times, and despite the promise of independence, it's even more true now. Our new rulers learned well from their former masters. God forbid they might actually listen to what the opposition has to say."

"But what *were* they saying? What was the demonstration even about?"

"Who knows? A little of everything, honestly, and not enough to make a damn bit of difference. What passes for political expression here is a joke. One of the hallmarks of the opposition groups—to call them political parties is too grand—is that they lack cohesion. Mostly they want more of a say in Parliament. For some, labor rights are paramount. Some think the country is too crowded and the government's immigration laws too liberal. For others, it's about access to education and opposition to policies they think favor the Chinese over the other races. Still others insist on property rights or wealth-sharing or lowering prices for essential services, like water. The minorities want favorable treatment, or at any rate, equal treatment. And then there are the Eurasians. My people—the mutts of Singapore—feel neglected altogether. The surface is smooth as silk, but you don't have to dig far to find the tensions. It's ridiculous. Everyone needs to wake up to what's happening here—what has *always* been happening here—before it's too late. The real problem is the country is one big corporation that wants to enslave us all. It's all about power—those who have it and plan to keep it and those who don't. If the opposition groups ever joined forces and came up with a coherent message, they might have a stronger voice, but not when they get suckered into useless conflicts like the fiasco we saw today. Now the government is going to use this to crack down again. Played right into their hands. It's a major setback, I'm afraid."

They turned off the quay just past the Overseas Union Bank Building, and Martin jumped back into shadow.

"What is it?" she asked. "What did you see?"

"The police are still all over Raffles Place, probably watching people going into the MRT station."

"Do you think they're looking for you? Or us?"

"Probably not. The government already knows who the troublemakers are, like that idiot they went after back at the park. He knew exactly what he was doing, begging to be taken down, earning his martyrdom. For the rest of us, we're probably safe. I'm sure there was someone snapping pictures, though I doubt they can match faces to names. But I'll tell you, it makes me long for Australia, where we have real freedom of speech. Just like the US."

"We were only watching. Surely that's not illegal."

"I'm sure you're fine, Aislinn. They won't bother you. Being white has its advantages here, like most places. But I think I'll avoid getting too close to the jacks just now."

"Oh, God," she said.

"What? What is it?"

"My jacket. I must have dropped it back at the park in the mad dash."

"Shit," Martin said. "Was anything in it? Anything valuable?"

"My work ID badge was in a pocket," she said, now feeling utterly lost. "Name, address, ID number. So much for being anonymous."

"Look, don't worry, I'm sure it's not a problem," he said with a glance toward the station. "I'd better go."

Aislinn watched Martin cross the river on the old pedestrian bridge and vanish, circumventing the police surveillance of the MRT station. She felt terribly alone. How could she have been so careless to leave her jacket behind? Despite his assurances that she wasn't in danger, she didn't head directly to her office. Instead, she returned to the quay and walked along the river past the Standard Chartered Bank Building, avoiding the station, entering her building from the opposite direction. She passed the security guard in the lobby, who nodded and didn't ask for her ID, to her relief, and rode the elevator to the firm's floor. She peeked into the hall when the doors opened, fully expecting to be confronted there by the police, but she saw no one, not even the receptionist, and slipped into her office unnoticed. She closed the door and sagged into her desk chair. New York may have become a nightmare, but how was this better?

Her eyes rested on the Pennington painting of the bird of paradise. As she watched, the flower rose and unfurled its magnificent blossom, like an elaborate headdress. The brilliant orange of it soothed her, reassured her. Martin had said she was in no trouble. She had to believe him. She thought of calling Liam in Bangkok to tell him what had happened, to hear his voice, but, no, she was calmer now, and she could deal with this on her own. She'd only been watching. She'd done nothing wrong.

On her journey home after work, the police were gone, the normal bustle had returned to the subway, the hum of idle conversations and laughter. The gloomy tension was missing from the air, as well. But was that the end of it? What was going to happen to that fellow they'd dragged off, and to the others who had been arrested or hurt? Martin seemed unconcerned for his own safety, although it sounded as if he sided with the protesters and even knew some of them. And what kind of trouble had Aislinn created for herself?

. . . . .

When she entered the apartment, pungent smells emanating from the kitchen greeted her. Going to investigate, she dropped her briefcase on the dining table and found three pots bubbling on the stove: rice, chicken adobo, and the *kangkong* greens Cecilia often made.

"Cecilia?" No answer. "Cecilia," she said again, louder.

The maid's door opened, and her tiny figure emerged.

"What's this? Didn't I tell you no dinner tonight?"

"Yes, missus." She edged back toward her room.

Aislinn picked up the pan with the chicken and slammed it back down on the stove, splattering sauce onto the surface and the other pots, a loud hiss erupting from the burner. "Then what the hell is all this?" She already regretted this outburst, her raised voice and the childish saber-rattling. Cecilia looked terrified, and Aislinn realized the woman had probably only been making dinner for herself.

"Oh, God, Cecilia, I'm so, so sorry. I don't know what…I just had a very bad day. I'm so sorry." She yanked on the refrigerator door, relieved to find an open bottle of chardonnay there, and retreated with it to her bedroom.

Shaking, barely able to pour the wine, she swallowed one button from her dwindling supply. Maybe she couldn't deal with it on her own, after all. She wished she had someone to talk to about the demonstration, and the more she fretted the angrier she became that she was here, in Singapore, in this fascist little country, and that she'd sacrificed her career to take a shit job in a shit country, all for a man who wasn't even here to comfort her. How the hell did this happen? How had she made such a terrible mistake?

8

25 September 1914

Uncle Cyril this morning apologized profusely that he has thus far not properly shown me around the settlement, so that I might have a better understanding and appreciation of my new home. I confess that I do not yet think of it as a permanent home, although I suppose I ought to begin to do so, for who knows when I shall be able to return to England? Nothing remains for me there, and if the war does not end soon, will England itself survive?

To that end, he proposed a grand tour in his carriage, and I apparently clapped my hands together in delight at the prospect because his grin consumed his entire face, reflecting my own pleasure.

We traversed Orchard Road, the aptly named thoroughfare I had seen on the day of my arrival and once or twice since as Uncle had taken me around to introduce me to some of his acquaintances. He pointed out the Chinese Burial Ground, Tai Suah Ting, that he said had been used by the Teochew community for over fifty years, the Teochew being a group of Chinese from the far southeast in China. A little beyond Tai Suah Ting was another burial ground, this one for the Malay people. I found it so interesting, and I wanted to take it all in, to study it and understand the significance. Uncle told me there are also a few cemeteries for the Europeans, some affiliated with various churches, another for Jews, one for Armenians, at least one for Mohammedans. How odd that these different peoples, none native to this place, have found their way to this small island, to live and work side by side, to be forever separated in the earth. As much as I would have liked to linger there, we drove on.

Next was Emerald Hill, a lovely row of terrace houses stretching up and away from the main road and shops. Our immediate destination, however, was the Esplanade, the wide expanse of land that was both a pleasure ground and a buffer between the sea and various government buildings. I am no expert on architecture, but I found these grand edifices to be a harmonious blend of styles, a bit of French here, Spanish there, and of course English, including the Gothic spires of St. Andrew's Cathedral. We passed by the elegant Raffles Hotel, Uncle explaining that it was named for Sir Stamford Raffles, the fellow who acquired the island for the empire from some local prince or other nearly a century ago. I was curious about the hotel as I had heard about it from Mr. Preston and others.

"Might we stop at Raffles, Uncle?" I asked.

"No, my dear, not today," he responded, as if I were a child, although I suppose my request was in the nature of a child's. "But one day soon we shall return for tiffin, I promise."

"Tiffin?" I asked.

And so I learned another peculiar word of the colonies, this one meaning a meal that might be tea, or dinner, or whatever the speaker wishes it to be.

"Tiffin," I said. "I shall like that."

From the Esplanade we made our way into the commercial district, where Uncle had his chambers not far from the quay where I had come ashore just a few weeks earlier. This part of the settlement was something of a shock to me, as it bustled with activity, a great contrast to the idyllic life I had been leading. There were crowds of horse-drawn carriages like Uncle's, but also many of the man-powered carts. Some of the buildings at Fullerton Square and Battery Road were most impressive, and signs proclaimed their custom: Medical Hall, Jeweler, and a marvelous establishment I plan to return to called John Little &

Company, which Uncle described as an emporium offering all manner of goods for sale.

I began to suspect that Uncle was keen to demonstrate to me that Singapore was far from the uncivilized outpost that I deemed it to be. Indeed, our carriage had to navigate a modern-looking electric tramway, and although he was not convinced that they would catch on, we saw a number of automobiles on the roads of the commercial district as well. I didn't tell him they were already common at home, and that Richard had owned one for some years.

Next, Uncle took us past the Telok Ayer Market, a smaller version of which I had visited closer to our bungalow, along a road that was home to a spectacular Chinese temple Uncle called Thian Hock Keng, and I asked if I might return to draw its marvelous façade.

"My dear, if you come here, I must insist that you be accompanied. It is not safe for a proper Englishwoman in this district. Please respect my wishes in this."

Despite this warning, I resolved to return. The building's elaborate ornamentation was irresistible, and I could already envision the drawing I might make.

We next drove along South Bridge Road into what Uncle called China Town. Although less grand, this area was just as busy, if not busier, than the English commercial district from which we had come, crowded with the man-powered carts—I now know to call them rickshaws, a Chinese word with the same meaning—and boxy carriages, which Uncle called gharries, but far fewer automobiles. The shops here were colorful and spilling into the street, and, despite the pervasive odor of sewage, I longed to get out and walk to view their wares more closely. Uncle would not hear of it, of course. Still, from our carriage I saw many odd-looking fruits and vegetables and signs written in their peculiar language—as a painter I am intrigued by the way each word appears to be a little drawing—so that I could not begin to make out what was being sold. I was reminded in any event that we were in their part of the world, and that it was English that was the foreign tongue here, not Chinese.

Uncle pointed out a pair of peculiar buildings as we passed. Although the area was known as China Town and was home to most of the Chinese on the island, many of them living in crowded tenement buildings, these structures were a mosque, that is, a house of worship for Mohammedans, and an ornate Hindu temple. Outside both structures, dozens of people swarmed in a riot of colors and fashions such as I had never seen. I know so little of these religions and the people who are drawn to them and long to learn. I must find a way to return.

Then we headed back inland past Fort Canning, a military post that commands a fantastic spot atop a hill that must give it a view of the entire island and so early warning of any potential invaders.

Uncle wanted to make one more stop before we arrived back at the bungalow, and that was the Botanic Gardens. To get there, we again drove past the orchards, but we went beyond to the edge of the Tanglin Barracks, another military post. Here, the land was predominantly raw jungle, and fragrant with all manner of blossoms and vegetation.

We passed through a gate into a land that I could scarcely imagine. It was much like Uncle's garden, but on such a scale as to make it nearly unbelievable. I had visited gardens in England, of course, but nothing like this. We drove beneath a canopy of trees that felt very much like we had entered a tunnel, so devoid of light that the bits of sunlight peeking through the leaves seemed like stars in the night sky. On and on the grounds went, with everywhere something more spectacular to see, flowers in every color of the rainbow, and yet to call them flowers seems wholly inadequate. They were like an entirely new variety of vegetation. Passing beneath the trees, we were accompanied by the most colorful birds I could imagine, orange and red and green creatures that seemed to follow us. Their shrill calls sounded almost like words, and I wondered what they might say if they could speak. What secrets might they tell? They made me think of poor Jamie, who so loved nature and its mysteries.

We paused by a small lake, where varieties of waterfowl swam in tranquil waters and several European couples strolled along the shore.

It seemed that Uncle was saving the best for last. He meant to show off to me the home he had found in the remotest of places and to assure me, I think, that I would find it to my liking as well. And he has succeeded. There is so much to see and do in this city, and I am fortunate, if still tentative, to call it home.

27 September 1914

Uncle and I took our breakfast on the veranda as we usually do. While he pored over a London newspaper—some weeks old, as it had arrived on board a steamer recently come to port—I gazed towards the garden and imagined myself stepping into the jungle. As I did, the garden came alive, the solid green wall parting to allow me in and then closing behind me.

Without a word to Uncle, who scarcely took his eyes from the page, I stood and retrieved my sketchbook from my room and attempted to draw what I had just felt, that I had been swallowed alive. It was not an unpleasurable sensation. To the contrary, it was entirely agreeable, almost carnal, as if I had become one with the jungle, consumed and consumer, and the feeling shuddered through me in a fashion I know I was unable to hide.

Indeed, looking up from the paper, Uncle said, "Are you all right, Lizzie?"

I'm sure my face had flushed, and I did feel the warmth rise to my cheeks. "I'm fine, Uncle. Just…feeling a bit warm, is all."

"I hope it isn't the fevers, my dear. We must be on guard against the fevers."

"Is there news, Uncle? Has the war been won or lost?"

"You shouldn't make light of it, Lizzie. It's serious business. Imagine if the Germans captured the entire continent of Europe and then began chipping away at the empire. England would be nothing without its possessions."

"Were we nothing before, Uncle? Before we set about seizing control of half the globe?"

"It's not a matter of seizing, Lizzie," he spluttered. "We are civilizing the world. We bring knowledge and industry. We create markets and jobs and opportunities."

I thought of the Chinese coolies who work like animals pulling carts through the streets because there is no other work they can do here. What opportunities do they have? But I had heard this all from Uncle Cyril before, and knew better than to repeat my arguments, which would fall on ears that if not deaf were entirely shut. He would never concede that the motive for civilizing the natives was to earn gargantuan profits from their labors in the mines and the plantations.

He laid the newspaper aside. "You know, Lizzie, it might do us both good to take a trip up to see the Feddersons at Butterworth." The Feddersons are our cousins by marriage, or at any rate, the Strattons and the Feddersons were connected in some fashion. Uncle had told me they operated a rubber estate in Malaya, but that Mrs. Fedderson kept their house in Butterworth, a town on the coast just across the strait from the island of Penang. "You could see for yourself the results of the investments we are making for the betterment of the local people. And I'm told that it is possible to travel into the mountains above the town, where the air is considerably cooler. It would do you wonders, I'm sure."

Despite the lesson in economics he meant for me to learn, the notion of a visit to a cooler climate did sound appealing, and I would not be opposed to such an adventure, although having only just arrived I have had enough travel for the time being.

1 October 1914

Breathless. I am not sure I will ever again experience the like of it. After Uncle's tour of the settlement the other day, I took it into my head that I should return to some of the most unusual sites to sketch and to reinforce my memory of the colors and the sheer emotions I felt at first glance. The enormity of the Chinese settlement filled me with wonder, but not only in its size. It is a district that spans the ages and races of all mankind, a portal to another world, and will not easily be brought to life on canvas.

I knew Uncle would not approve of my plan to return on my own to the temple he showed me, and so I waited until he had departed for the day in his carriage before I approached Lao Po, the older woman who runs our household.

"I want to go to the Tian Hock Keng temple and would like to hire a carriage to take me there," I said to her.

She looked at me with the eyes of a blind person, not seeing, not understanding, and without responding went back to her work, the endless task of sweeping the floors.

I repeated myself, more insistently, and finally she looked at me, shook her head, and spoke in Chinese words that conveyed their meaning clearly enough: It is forbidden. I understood that Uncle had left instructions to this effect, but I was not to be so easily deterred.

"Very well," I said. "I shall make my way there myself."

I had no idea how I would accomplish such a trip, but I gathered my sketch pad and my hat, and set off down the bungalow's steps toward the road. That bit of bluster had the desired effect, and soon Lao Po was right behind me, muttering, calling out to one of the other servants.

"Wait," she commanded, and so I stopped, curious as to what solution was to be found to our standoff.

Soon, a boy appeared. I say "boy," but he must have been sixteen or seventeen, a strapping fellow, and I came to understand that he would accompany me and look after my safety on this most dangerous errand. I was also made to understand that the boy, who was called Ching, was Lao Po's grandson, and so could be trusted. Pleased with the outcome of this negotiation, I set off with my escort.

I know not how, but Ching arranged a gharry for us, as Lao Po deemed a rickshaw unsuitable for the likes of me. Off we went, with Ching chattering away about nothing in particular, keen, it seemed, to practice his English, and happy also to be relieved of whatever tedium that might otherwise have occupied him.

When we arrived, he helped me down from the carriage and procured from one of the shops a stool where I sat, first in front of the temple and later inside the courtyard where I was able to properly observe visitors and worshipers.

From the very moment I passed through its gate, and despite the unwelcoming stares my presence attracted, the temple's power entered my spirit and fostered within me a sense of peace, of safety. It is nearly impossible to describe in words, but I hope to be able to do it justice on the canvas.

On the way home, I did not want to speak, so I took out my sketchbook again, the sight of which silenced Ching, and in gratitude I quickly drew his handsome, guileless face, presenting it to him when we arrived at the bungalow. His face glowed in wonder, as if he believed he had witnessed a miracle.

9

By Saturday, the shock of the demonstration had diminished, but like a faded bruise still sensitive to the touch, it hadn't left her entirely. At least Aislinn no longer trembled when she thought of what had happened, and the police hadn't come to arrest her as she'd feared. No doubt interference in local political matters was a serious offense in Singapore, and they had only to present her lost jacket and ID as evidence.

She had apologized to Cecilia, who seemed to have no idea what she was talking about, and Aislinn realized the poor woman was used to being berated by her employers, in perhaps far worse a fashion. No one should have to become used to something like that, and Aislinn felt even more ashamed for what she'd done. She resolved to be kinder to the woman. That wasn't enough to make up for her servitude, but what else could she do? She'd heard stories of expat men abusing their maids, demanding sex, threatening to send them home if they didn't comply, and the thought of it horrified her.

The city atmosphere had returned to normal, the subway bustling and filled with chatter, the office its usual happy, if deceptively sedate, place. But she was still desperate to talk about what she'd seen, and she longed for Liam's return. She had considered visiting Orientalia to talk to Martin about the demonstration, but she was embarrassed by having to be rescued by him, and worried that being seen together might endanger them both. Was that irrational? Was she worried about nothing?

The worst part of being in Singapore, even worse than not having a demanding job, was that Aislinn was lonely. She missed Jessica, her teammate and best friend, who could be counted on to meet for coffee or a drink and to commiserate over their respective love lives, their families, and their jobs. At work, she used to pop in to see Hannah Boseman from time to time, just to reassure herself that she was on course in the firm, that there were other women who had succeeded there. And she saw old law school classmates now and then in the city, usually in groups at a bar or restaurant, never for intimate conversations, but somehow that was comforting enough because they were all experiencing more or less the same pressures. Here, she had no one. If seeing Jenny was forbidden—although she had no intention of strictly adhering to that particular edict—what was she supposed to do for friends? In truth, because she and Jenny had little in common, and Jenny was so much older, Aislinn couldn't see them spending that much time together, anyway. She needed a friend her own age.

She could join organizations where she might meet other women. She wasn't a churchgoer and hadn't been since middle school, but that was an option. It might even be interesting to attend services at St. Andrew's Cathedral, the Anglican church downtown she'd admired. It was a Gothic presence that drew the eye, one that had stood for nearly 150 years. Beautiful and historic, but probably not the place to meet the kind of friends she needed. Was there a Harvard Club in Singapore? Likely there was, and now she wished she'd thought of that sooner. She'd heard of the American Business Council, and she resolved to join, although Liam had been nearly as dismissive of the ABC as he'd been of the American Club. In any case, she was impatient and wanted someone to talk to now.

In her office at Bradford & Co., she gazed at the painting of the bird of paradise. The artist was presumably long dead, but Aislinn wished she could talk to her. She knew nothing about the woman, but sensed— from what, the subject matter, the brush strokes, the expressions on the faces of the people in the other paintings?—that they shared a great deal. Both strangers here, both lonely, both learning to live in a place they didn't belong. So, if not Elizabeth Pennington, what about Shan Lee, another painter whose work spoke to her? Aislinn had once imagined them becoming friends. And why not? They were about the same age and had an interest in art. The more she thought about it, the more she convinced herself that she must find Shan Lee, that Lee was exactly the person she needed in her life. The artist apparently knew TJ, but Aislinn couldn't ask him without revealing that she'd seen them together. How to find her?

She started with one of the younger lawyers in the firm who seemed to know about the art scene in Singapore and had been responsible for the acquisition of a few pieces that hung in one of the conference rooms. He didn't recognize Shan Lee's name, but on his recommendation, Aislinn set out to visit a cluster of galleries and studios at Robertson Quay along the Singapore River in a stretch of old warehouses, or godowns, as he called them. From her office, she followed the Riverwalk inland, thinking there might be a cooling breeze off the water, but the sun's reflection on the surface made the heat even more oppressive, and the walk was much longer than she'd anticipated. She crossed Bridge Road, surprised to see bars and restaurants crowded with tourists. The river itself was muddy, marred by floating trash and oil slicks. Beyond the bars, she came to the gallery district and marveled at the quaint structures with their mixed colonial architecture—whitewashed walls and sloped tile roofs. She had no idea where to start.

Unless she happened to stumble onto Shan Lee's studio, she thought she'd have better success in one of the galleries. The first one she came to was a long narrow space with large canvasses hung on three walls. A woman sat at a desk in the far corner of the space, not looking up when Aislinn entered. She strolled through the gallery, but none of the paintings, hyper-realistic renderings of laborers—dark-skinned construction workers, shirtless boatmen, a uniformed street-sweeper—attracted her. Well done, and an interesting commentary on

Singapore's hierarchical race and class structure, but not to Aislinn's taste. And not Shan Lee's work.

When she reached the back of the gallery, she approached the woman at the desk, who looked up when Aislinn cleared her throat. The woman, Indian, Aislinn assumed, with black hair done in an unstylish flip, was wearing a high-collared black dress and a gaudy gold necklace with a starburst medallion. She appeared to be waiting for Aislinn to speak, but Aislinn wasn't sure what to ask.

"I was wondering," Aislinn said, "if you know an artist named Shan Lee."

"Not here," the woman said.

"Yes, I can see that, but I'm curious about her work. And her. I mean, I'd like to meet her."

The woman handed Aislinn a brochure with glossy photos of the paintings on the gallery walls, with the artist's name in bold: Ramachandran. Aislinn returned the brochure, thanked the woman for her help, and left, barely able to contain her laughter. Did the woman not understand English? Or was she just obtuse?

She strolled through the district, gazing in gallery windows, hoping she might spot Lee's work, which she thought she'd easily recognize. But there were other galleries in this complex, other studios, and many more scattered around the city. The chance she'd stumbled onto the right area was, she knew, slim, but it was fun to explore. After all, it was in part the lure of the city's art scene that had prompted her to agree to the move.

She came to a café, which gave her the opportunity to sit and rethink her plan. She ordered an iced latte and sat at one of the outdoor tables under an umbrella. Two young Chinese men sat at the next table, one of them wearing a paint-streaked T-shirt. Artists? It would be a ridiculous coincidence in a city of five million people, but maybe they knew Lee?

"Excuse me," she said to the men. "Do either of you know an artist named Shan Lee?"

They looked at each other and laughed. Paint-streaks pulled out a cell phone, scrolled through his contacts, wrote a number on a napkin, and handed it to Aislinn.

• • • • •

The address Shan Lee gave her on the phone was near the Botanic Gardens, too far from the apartment to walk if she didn't want to arrive drenched with sweat, and in any case the skies threatened rain. She took a taxi and was pleased when the driver pulled up in front of a colonial bungalow similar to the house she'd hoped to rent. A local in a Black and White? Hadn't Liam and the expat ladies told her that wasn't done? That just made her more curious about the woman.

She passed through the open gate between brick pillars on either side of the driveway and a curious boulder that had something etched into it, too worn to read. The house was not as large as some she'd seen, but it had a red-tiled roof, which was apparently customary, and the standard white façade with black trim around windows and doors.

She climbed the steps to the veranda, and Lee came out to meet her wearing jeans and a red scoop-neck pullover.

"Now I remember you," Lee said. When she'd called, Aislinn had described their meeting in the SoHo gallery, but the artist couldn't place her. "Your hair was longer."

Aislinn ran her hand through her hair, self-conscious now. "It seemed the right thing to do for the climate."

"It's perfect," said Lee, grabbing her own shoulder-length cut. "I've been thinking of doing something radical myself, like shaving it all off. But there are, well, obstacles to being too radical."

Aislinn wondered if TJ was one of those obstacles, and she realized this might have been a mistake. Would Lee tell TJ about their meeting? Not that there was anything wrong with seeking her out. They'd made contact in New York long before she'd even heard of TJ Kwan. It had nothing to do with him and, besides, he didn't know she'd seen them together in the Botanic Gardens.

Lee showed her to the sitting room that opened onto the back garden, and then left to bring tea. The room was not what Aislinn expected, but it did fit Lee's personality. The other house she'd seen when she was looking for a place to rent overflowed with antiques—heavy cabinets and sofas, chairs and lamps. Their property agent had explained the house and décor were in the Peranakan style, derived from the grand, old families who were the first wave of Chinese immigrants to the Malay Peninsula, not strictly one of the British colonial houses but from the same era. Lee's house, though, was sparsely decorated with modern furnishings—a long, sleek couch and matching chairs, a glass and chrome coffee table, a torchiere that was as much sculpture as lamp. Instead of intricate Persian carpets on the dark, wide-planked wood floor, Lee had chosen plush rugs with vibrant, modern designs, reminiscent of Klee and Miro.

Paintings of various sizes, a mix of modern and older works, crowded the inside walls of the space. Aislinn recognized nothing that might be Lee's style, but she supposed it made sense that she wouldn't display her own pieces here. Aislinn liked one that reminded her of the German expressionists and another that looked like an imitation of a Frida Kahlo self-portrait, with the same vibrant, contrasting colors and mysterious eyes. One that really drew her in, though, was an oil that she thought might be another Pennington. The more she looked at it, the more certain she was. It was darker than the one in her dining room and from a different perspective, and it depicted not the temple but a shophouse with piles of fruits and vegetables on display. Here, the curious face of a woman was looking directly at the viewer, or the artist. As Aislinn gazed at the woman in the painting, a cloud of smoke rose behind her, a fire that Aislinn could almost smell. The woman shook her head as if to ward off the artist. "No," she seemed to be saying. "You should not be here."

Lee returned with a tray of tea and cookies—biscuits, she called them—and they sat at a table on the veranda overlooking the garden. Before she left the wall, though, Aislinn looked back at the painting, which had ceased to move.

"Your garden makes me think of the painting I saw at your show in New York," Aislinn said. "The trees, the flowers. It's beautiful. Inspiring."

"My studio is upstairs, and I often paint on the upper veranda. The garden is a patient model, and the elevation gives me a different perspective, as if I'm a bird perched in a tree."

"Your work is one of the reasons I'm in Singapore," Aislinn said, and then explained how her move had come about.

Lee seemed flattered by Aislinn's visit and shared her life story—schoolteacher parents, attracted to painting at a young age, studies abroad, intentions to stay in Paris or New York, her return.

"Singapore used to be so dull, as if it existed under a wet blanket. Fun restaurants and nightclubs, or any place lively that popped up got suppressed by Lee Kuan Yew, who was nearly our Prime Minister for Life. Authoritarian. Paternalistic. Not evil, but inflexible. It seemed like there was nothing to do here when I was younger, but it's really come alive in the last decade. Music in every vein, better restaurants, galleries, and art programs. Still sanitized, still restrictive in many ways, but far more interesting than it was. I went away to study because it was such a dead zone, but now we have world-class schools. I'm able to teach drawing and show my work. There's a thriving community of artists, including foreigners who find Singapore a congenial place for creativity. It's hard to explain what a colossal shift that is. It feels revolutionary."

"I'm intrigued by your collection." Aislinn pointed inside toward the sitting room wall. "So diverse."

Lee laughed. "A 'hodge-podge,' isn't that what you Americans say? Yes, and isn't that the wonderful thing about art? How boring to look at nothing but paintings of haystacks or parliament buildings all the time, as exciting as Monet makes them. These painters aren't even famous, but each piece speaks to me in a different way, and I love them all. The faux-Kahlo, for example. That's by a friend of mine who fancies herself a Chinese Frida, oppressed by both her environment and her lovers. If you look closely, you'll see the eyes are altered and there are a dozen or so variances from the original—the necklace is a dragon carved into a piece of jade, the wings of the butterflies in her hair are decorated with the Chinese character for happiness, and so on. Really imaginative."

"The one of the Chinese vegetable seller is puzzling," Aislinn said. "The expression on the woman's face, startled as if she'd seen a ghost and was warning the artist. And the shop itself seems almost alive." She was too embarrassed to say she thought she owned paintings by the same artist and that another decorated her office at Bradford & Co., although she had no idea where that one had come from.

"Yes, exactly! I'm so glad you feel that way. I love it, and it's not even mine. I mean, I didn't buy it. It was in this house when I moved in, tucked away in a bedroom. Covered in dust. I don't know anything about the artist. Just a date—1915—and her name. It's so typical of colonial times, though. This foreign artist, white no doubt, is taking something that doesn't belong to her, telling this voiceless woman's story. And I can almost hear that woman's voice, can't you?"

"I'm curious about the artist," Aislinn said. "I mean, 1915, you said? What was she doing here? What did she see when she looked at that market?"

"If I had to guess, I'd say she was married to some Brit, part of their empire, doing what the Brits did best—exploiting, extracting, brutalizing the brown and yellow people. That's what that face says to me. The woman is telling the artist she doesn't belong here."

"Did the people really hate the English? Do they still?"

"Of course they did, and to a certain extent, they still do. I mean, independence came before I was born, so I don't personally feel it, although, I mean, honestly, have things changed all that much? No offense, but here you still are—white people, Americans now mostly, but Europeans too—showing up to make as much money as possible from Asians. But it's the same all over the world, isn't it? America has done the same thing everywhere, and it's not hard to understand the resentment. And I'm no expert on American history, but didn't your settlers basically wipe out the native people and bring over African slaves to do their work for them?"

Lee's rebuke stung, and Aislinn wondered if she should even try to defend America. Hadn't the country also helped lift countless people out of poverty by stimulating trade, by providing jobs all over the world? Where would they be if Americans hadn't built factories or invested in industry? But she knew there was an element of truth in what Lee had said. It was capitalism, not altruism, that was America's guiding star, and how much pain and suffering had been inflicted in the name of progress and profit?

"You know," Aislinn said, not sure what she was going to say or how to say it, only wishing to change the subject, "I think I saw you in the Botanic Gardens last week." She hadn't meant to be so blunt. Was it just curiosity that was driving her? She didn't need to know what Lee's connection to TJ was, did she?

"Oh?"

"I was jogging, and I thought I recognized a business associate of my husband's, and when I got closer, I realized he was with you."

Lee's gaze narrowed, a darker expression clouding her face. Aislinn noticed for the first time that her eyes had a flush of color to them, almost hazel instead of the black eyes of most Chinese. Lee dug out a cigarette from her purse and lit it, exhaling toward the garden. "TJ Kwan works with your husband?"

"Yes. I know it's a small world, but I'm surprised you know each other. I mean, the banking and art circles rarely overlap."

"TJ is a patron of the arts."

And, Aislinn wondered, do you frequently take early morning strolls through the park with patrons? But why would this woman tell her the truth, even if Aislinn had the nerve to ask? They barely knew each other.

"I'm pleased to hear that," Aislinn said. "I've only known the man a short time, of course, and he's very charming, but I wouldn't have guessed that about him."

Lee stubbed out her cigarette, and Aislinn took it to mean that the visit was over. She'd gone too far.

"If you'll excuse me, I should get back to work," Lee said. "I've got a show coming up at a posh gallery and there's loads to be done."

"Of course," Aislinn said. "I'm sorry to intrude, but it was a pleasure to meet you and see your beautiful home."

On the way out, Aislinn lingered at the painting of the shophouse. What was the woman looking at? What was she saying to the artist? Was Lee right and she was just wishing the Brits away? Or was there something personal to Pennington? Was it a warning to her alone?

· · · · ·

Martin looked up from his desk when she entered the shop, a smile spreading across his face that she thought was genuine, not a shopkeeper's standard welcome to a customer.

"I'm happy to see you," he said.

"I wanted to thank you. For the other day at Hong Lim Park."

The shop was small, and they were certainly the only ones there, but he looked around to be sure they were alone.

"Are you all right? You seemed shaken up when I left you."

"No, I'm fine. It's just that…I don't know what to make of it. I don't know what I'm doing here. In Singapore, I mean."

"If you're worried about the jacket, I'm sure a sweeper picked it up and is either wearing it right now or it's at the bottom of a dustbin somewhere."

"You're probably right."

"You don't seem convinced."

"I'm not."

A couple wandered into the shop, older, portly. Americans, Aislinn thought. Martin busied himself straightening prints on the wall. The couple wandered out again, but the moment had passed.

"How are those paintings?" he asked. "Not having buyer's remorse, are we?"

"No, I still love all three. Despite my husband's dismissal of them, I think the painter had real talent. I see something new every time I focus on the scene and the faces. A new detail I'd missed before, an expression that begins to make sense. I feel as though I'm getting to know her."

"Isn't that the way of the world? We're too busy to see what's really there. We see only what we assume we're looking at and never have the time, or take the time, to look closely. At paintings, at people." As he said this, his gaze, fixed on her, held steady. She knew what he was doing, and she was flattered. It was what she wanted, wasn't it? The real reason she'd come? She'd offended Shan Lee by asking about TJ, but there was still Martin, a potential friend.

She moved further into the shop, looking away from him, scanning the walls for new pieces. "I wanted to tell you, though, about another of her paintings. At Bradford & Co., where I'm working, there's a painting of a flower she did, a bird of paradise. It's stunning and just as evocative as the others."

"Amazing. I wonder how they came to have it. Have you asked?"

"To the point of being annoying, yes. The office manager deliberately avoids me now. It seems I have to accept the fact that he doesn't know where it came from, only that it predates the records they have of art acquisitions. His guess, and it's just a guess, is that long ago some partner of the firm brought it into the office and it's been there ever since. No idea who that might have been or when."

"A bit like your paintings, then? We don't know how my father came to have them, either."

"Yes. And there's another one. I'd almost forgotten. I was visiting a friend, and she had one similar to the temple scene I got from you." She hesitated to describe it more, to suggest that she found the expression on the subject's face to be disturbing, a warning of some kind. The more she'd thought about it, the more foolish it had seemed.

"I think I've learned more about her, though. The artist, I mean. I bought a book from you, stories by Edmund Preston, who wrote about his travels in the region. And I think one of the characters he wrote about is her. Or some version of her, anyway." Aislinn pulled the book from her bag. "Listen to this passage: 'Mary Katherine was a delicate girl when she first arrived, a hothouse flower prone to fits of melancholy. She longed for her home in England and confided in no one the circumstances of her removal to Singapore, her banishment, as she termed it. There could have been any number of reasons. The war raging in Europe. The death of her parents, leaving only her uncle to look after her. A sweet affair gone sour. We all had our reasons for coming to Singapore, of course. We all had our secrets.' And then later he says this: 'Indeed, as the months passed, Mary Katherine, whom we all called Molly, grew radiant, even in the monsoon. She was often seen at Boat Quay or in the public gardens with her sketchbook or her paints. She was ever cheerful, greeting passersby with a smile and a wave. Life in the Straits agreed with her, it was plain to see.' It's her, don't you think? He must be describing Elizabeth Pennington!"

Martin grinned.

"Are you laughing at me?" she asked.

"No, of course not, but it's a bit of a leap, isn't it? And it's fiction, after all."

"Yes, but there's more. He goes on to describe a captain in the Army or British Navy or something who this Molly character is smitten with. Don't you remember the portrait I bought? One of the paintings is of a military man. That's him, I'm convinced. Plus, Preston hints that Molly had an affair with an Indian soldier—that's the other portrait!"

"All right. I believe you. What else did you learn about her from Mr. Preston?"

"That's it, I'm afraid. In that story, she's a minor character. It mostly deals with a traveler, a man I take to be Preston himself, and his escapades. But I'm going to keep reading, find other books by him, and maybe she'll pop up again."

Another couple entered the shop, Japanese tourists this time, and she busied herself by looking again through the old books, still hoping to find some connection to Elizabeth Pennington, perhaps another volume by Preston. When the tourists were gone, Martin approached.

"Now, where were we?" he asked.

Yes, where were they? What was she really doing here?

"What do you do for fun, Martin? I see you here in the shop and shadowing demonstrations—"

"Just the one, thanks. I hope I don't have a reputation for prowling around with the lunatic fringe."

"Is that what they are? Fringe? All right then, just the one demonstration. But that still raises the question: what else is there? What does Martin do in his time off?" And now she was embarrassed. Was she being too forward with this man, this shopkeeper, whom she barely knew?

Martin stepped into the alcove that passed for his office and returned with a framed photograph. Aislinn expected to see a picture of the woman who occupied his free time, or a child, but instead he showed her a snapshot of a sailboat.

"A boat?" she asked.

"Some people play golf or tennis. I sail. I'm not sure how my father got interested in it, but I practically grew up on a boat, crewing for him on the old wreck he used to own. It was a wonder that tub didn't sink. When I was in Australia, it was the only thing I missed about Singapore, although I managed to get out on the water now and then down there, crewing for a friend. Pop bought this newer boat a few years before he died, from some Yank who was going home. Not sure what possessed him, because he wasn't exactly bougie. More of a blue-collar guy with a penchant for old stuff. Technically, it's my sister's boat now, inherited from Pop, but Isabel's husband isn't much of a sailor, so it's up to me to take care of it."

Aislinn handed the picture back to him. "I had a friend who sailed a lot. We spent some lovely days on the water." Clark had been an expert sailor, whisking her off to his family's boat every chance he got during law school. Thinking of Clark now made her miss home even more. It was on the boat where they'd been careless about birth control, overtaken in the moment, leading to the predictable result.

"You should come with me some time," Martin said. "I could use an experienced crew. This boat is a handful for a solo sailor."

"I'd love that," she said.

· · · · ·

Liam and TJ had gone back to Bangkok to finalize their motorbike deal with the mysterious Khun Anuwat. It sounded too good to be true to Aislinn, but she was still learning how business was done in this part of the world, and Liam assured her there was a Thai lawyer helping them to structure the project.

At loose ends, Aislinn was delighted when Shan Lee invited her to a wine bar in the Riverwalk gallery district. Given their last encounter, and the blunder she'd made by mentioning TJ, Lee was the last person she'd expected to hear from. After work, she walked from her office along the river. It was September, and Aislinn kept thinking the air should be cooler, that there might be a hint of color in the trees, but in Singapore the only thing that changed was the calendar, not the weather. Lee was waiting for her when she arrived, seated at a table by the water. She stood and greeted Aislinn with a kiss, as if they were old friends.

"I wanted to apologize for the other day at my house," Lee said. "And to explain."

"You don't need to explain anything to me," Aislinn said.

"I think I do. And maybe it won't be easy for you to understand. Our culture is a bit different from what you're accustomed to. You said you'd seen me with TJ Kwan?"

Aislinn nodded.

"So. While he was born here in Singapore, his is a very traditional family from Fujian. That's a province in southern China where a lot of Singaporeans have their roots. And the customs there…I'm only trying to say that it's not so unusual in that environment, and other cultures around the world, of course, it's not so unusual that is for a man, a certain kind of Chinese man…to take a second wife."

"A second wife? Like a mistress?" That's what Aislinn suspected, after all, and it was what it had looked like to her in the park. So, Shan Lee was not so very different from herself, having a relationship with a married man.

"No. Or, yes, but not exactly. The second wife, the *er nai,* is something more than a mistress. You saw my house. It's actually TJ's house. The government was going to demolish the house and redevelop the property, but then he bought it. For me. We…share it."

"Does Shirley know?" As soon as she asked the question, she knew how naïve it was. Unlike Aislinn's affair with Liam, that they tried desperately to hide from Janice and everyone else, Lee's relationship with TJ was obviously more public. A house where he came and went. A stroll through the very public Botanic Gardens.

"Of course. Everyone knows. That's how it works. There's no scandal in it, at least not among the Chinese. I'm not sure how your husband would react if he knew, or other Americans. I mean no offense, but some of you can be awfully judgmental when things don't fit your preconceived ideas. Here, though, it's more or less accepted. If TJ were poor, it would not be possible."

"But he isn't poor."

"No. He's very rich and powerful and can do pretty much as he pleases."

"I see. But where does that leave you? Are you happy?"

"Happy? I don't even know what that means anymore. When I was still a student, he saw my work. Or maybe it's more accurate to say he saw me, but either way, I was giddy at the attention he showed me. And the glamor of it all. Did you know he has a private jet? We would fly off to Koh Samui or Langkawi for the weekend and stay at a beach villa. Or we would dine at the house—the house he maintains just for me—and the finest restaurants on the island would cater for us, with the most expensive wines. Or he would send me to Paris for a week because there was a show I wanted to see at the Pompidou. But now…."

"Now?"

"I feel trapped."

• • • • •

Aislinn had agreed to meet Martin at the Changi Sailing Club, where his boat was moored, instead of driving together, because he wanted to do some work on it before they went out. She had her reason, too. Being alone with him in his car seemed too intimate, and she was more comfortable with this arrangement.

With Liam away, she drove his car, the farthest she'd ventured on Singapore's roads since their arrival in May. Driving here made her nervous, with the unfamiliar roundabouts and crowded highways, not to mention being on the wrong side of the road. Still, she managed to find her way on the Pan-Island Expressway, past endless clusters of housing blocks and factories, many of which had familiar names, big multinational brands. She had no idea they had presences in Singapore, or that the country was such a center for high-tech manufacturing. Was this more of the global exploitation Shan Lee had bemoaned? Martin had mentioned labor practices as being one of the opposition's complaints, and she wondered if these factories were like the sweatshops she'd heard about in Vietnam and Indonesia. Would the local people be better off without this pervasive foreign presence? She had no idea.

She arrived at the sailing club long after the time Martin had indicated and pulled into the parking lot, the car park as she remembered to think of it. She made her way down to the dock, admiring the dozens of boats in a variety of sizes bobbing in the water, from dinghies to catamarans and a ketch that resembled Clark's boat, all moored to buoys spaced at neat intervals. Martin had said to look for a sloop with a blue hull, and that made it easy to spot, as almost all the others were white. As he'd told her to expect, there was a young man in a dinghy waiting to ferry her out to the boat, and with barely a moment's wait, she was on the water.

"Welcome to the good ship Lizzie," Martin called as Aislinn climbed aboard.

"Lizzie?"

"That's her name. Pop never told us where the name came from. I thought it might have been the previous owner who'd named it, but the title records show he changed the name when he bought it."

"She's beautiful," Aislinn said, taking in the spacious deck and what looked like a roomy cabin below. It was smaller than Clark's boat—his family's boat—but with plenty of room to maneuver. Liam had never shown an interest in sailing, but she felt a twinge of guilt for having an adventure she couldn't share with him. One, in fact, she might have a hard time telling him about.

"I'm sorry I'm late," she said.

"I thought maybe you'd changed your mind."

She very nearly had. Since she'd been married, she'd gone out for drinks with Jessica and other girlfriends, or with mixed groups of friends and colleagues, but never with a man alone, not even Frank. It felt like cheating, but of course it wasn't. It was just sailing. It was something to pass the time. She'd thought of letting Liam know what her plans were, so if he somehow learned of it later, he wouldn't think she'd been hiding it from him, but she suspected he wouldn't have reacted well. He'd never been the jealous type, but he would have told her not to go, or he would have asked her not to go, and the fact was that she wanted to do it. She'd been looking forward to it for days. She'd have to decide later if she'd tell him.

They motored out of the harbor and into the channel before Martin hoisted the sails, heading west in light winds into the Johor Straits. He pointed out features of the coastline, the beaches of Pasir Ris on the Singapore side of the strait, the jungle on the Malaysian side. They tacked toward the east, passing Pulau Ubin, an island that was home, Martin said, to a restaurant with some of the finest fresh seafood on the planet, until they passed the sailing club again, then the sprawling Changi Airport, and were moving into the open water of the South China Sea.

"This is my favorite part," Martin said. "We come out of the Straits into the vast nothingness of the ocean, a bit like launching into outer space. It frightens me and calms me at the same time. No limits, nothing to stop us."

Aislinn felt the sun and spray on her face and followed Martin's gaze. Nothing to stop them at all. They could just keep going, leave Singapore behind.

Martin stood and pulled his T-shirt over his head, revealing broad shoulders and a more muscular chest than Aislinn had suspected. He popped down to the cabin and returned with two cold cans of Tiger beer, offering one to Aislinn and opening it for her when she nodded.

"It occurs to me I know next to nothing at all about you, Martin, and I've probably told you far more than you wanted to hear about my situation."

"What do you want to know? There's not much to tell, really."

"Well, to start, how do you fit into the picture here? I've learned a lot about the Chinese and the Malays, the British colony, but what about you? Why is your family here?"

"I ask myself that all the time. But it's not that complicated. My father arrived from India before World War II, for reasons that were never clear to me or my sister, but as a Muslim, I suppose he thought he would find more religious tolerance here. Both India and Singapore were Crown Colonies at the time, and there was some fluidity between them back then, and you've no doubt noticed there's a large Indian population here. A lot of them are Tamils, though, and occupy a different stratum than my father, but there are Punjabis, too, and immigrants from all over India. He had some minor clerical position in the government until he opened the shop. He once told me he'd been curious about Singapore as a boy because his father had served here during the First World War."

"Your grandfather lived here, too? You have a long connection with the country then. Did you know him?"

"No. In fact, he died in the war, as I understand it. As a toddler, my father barely knew him before he was conscripted by the Brits, so he couldn't tell me much about him."

"What about your mother? She was from England?"

"Australia. Another colony, although she was at least part of the dominant race there."

"But she ended up here, somehow. Why?"

"The same reason as my father, oddly enough. She had some relative who lived here ages ago—probably some colonial nabob, I guess I don't remember or never knew—and she was curious about the place. Anyway, she trained as a nurse in Melbourne, came here to work back in the sixties, right around the time Singapore and Malaya broke away from the Brits. And Pop was a patient. He never really recovered from the second war. The Japanese did a number on him and everyone else they interned at Changi Prison, so he was for years in and out of hospital. But he fell hard for the pretty young nurse from Oz, and the rest is history."

"Oh my gosh, he was a prisoner of war here? I guess he was older than she was?"

"He had a good two decades on her. And still managed to outlive her, too."

The breeze was light, barely filling the boat's sails or softening the blows of the equatorial sun. Martin handed her another beer.

"Perfect," she said when she'd swallowed her first gulp. "What a beautiful day this is!"

"Yes," he said, his gaze lingering on her. "Perfect."

Aislinn pulled her own T-shirt off, revealing the bikini top she'd decided to wear. She returned his gaze and thought of that day with Clark on his boat, how they'd made love in the cabin. What, exactly, was she going to tell Liam about today?

"I think," Martin said, "we'd better get Lizzie back to the club before that gets us into trouble." He pointed behind Aislinn and when she turned, she saw what he meant—a foreboding line of fierce black clouds.

10

1 January 1915

What a pleasure it is to start afresh in the new year! It is time to begin again after letting my attention to these pages lapse in recent weeks, and I shall ignore completely what I have written in last year's diary, about that horrid war in Europe and being banished (for that is what has happened, although my dear Aunt Margaret would not have used such a word) to the East.

I have long since recovered from the tedious voyage and have settled rather comfortably into the home of my uncle, who, from all appearances, has become a prosperous and respected gentleman of the law in these parts. With his sponsorship, I shall have access to the best this remote society has to offer and have already encountered a good many of its most prominent citizens. While it seemed odd to celebrate Christmas when the weather was so frightfully warm, the community still managed to be festive, with services at St. Andrew and small gatherings with Uncle's familiars that we both enjoyed. We also attended a smashing dinner dance at the Raffles Hotel on Christmas Eve, and I dare say I have not enjoyed myself so in many months.

Although I was escorted to the affair by Uncle, I was pleased that Captain Bingham, looking most handsome in his formal attire, was present, as I suspected he would be. Since our first meeting at Government House, we had on a few occasions exchanged greetings at public gatherings, but despite my earnest wish that he would do so, he made no effort to further our acquaintance. Having lost patience with his inattention, I attempted by force of will to cause the good captain to turn his gaze towards our table, towards me, and I nearly fell out of my chair when he did so in that instant. I had no idea I possessed such power!

In short order, he approached and, most decorously, asked Uncle if he would very much mind if Miss Elizabeth joined him for a dance. Stunned by this success, I failed to note that he had not asked me this question and instead had asked my keeper, but gladly, and without a word, took his hand to rise when it was offered. It was only one dance, and little was said except for the eloquence of our mutual gaze, but I observed the captain dancing with no other women that evening. As Uncle and I departed for home, I was content that perhaps the holiday had delivered what I had wished for.

· · · · ·

And so, on this grand new day of the new year, I find myself in a glorious mood, lounging in the garden of our Heatherleigh, the home Uncle has erected for himself in the jungle. Everyone of my acquaintance here has told me of Uncle's considerable good name and reputation on which he has built his legal firm. And though the house is not as lavish as some, and is not attached to a great piece of land as he might wish, even a plantation such as our Butterworth relations manage, it is nonetheless a fine house, finer than ever I was accustomed to in England, and I do not complain.

It is a pity, though, that Uncle is not married, for his life here must be a solitary one. It is perhaps one reason he readily accepted the suggestion that I come under his protection, for a house such as this needs a woman's touch, I think, and I have begun to make minor improvements, which Uncle has said he appreciates. In addition to the hideous artifacts Uncle had collected before my arrival, we now have some charming native crafts in the parlor, as well as fragrant wood cabinets imported from China. And, if I may be so bold, I have in mind hanging one or two of my own paintings on the wall in the future. Yet, life here cannot be easy for Uncle without a wife, and I wonder what might be done to remedy this deficiency.

The maid has just served tea. The household is in something of an uproar this morning, although I do not know exactly what is the matter. I have listened to them muttering—for it sounds to me like muttering, in their language that I shall never understand—and rushing about the house and garden as if they were a hive that had discovered some intruder in the nest. But it seems the opposite is true. They seem to be one *fewer* in number this morning, and the girl who would normally attend to my breakfast is, apparently, absent. In that this is something of a holiday for us, although not for the staff, for whom the Chinese New Year, some weeks hence, is, I am told, the one time of year they are allowed off, more or less en masse, leaving us to our own devices, I was inclined to attribute the girl's absence to some celebration of which I was not aware. It seems this is not the case, however, as I have now been made to understand, and the girl, I'm told by the housekeeper, is simply gone.

I do not know if my uncle will be very much bothered by this news, for I think he was rather fond of this particular girl. He seemed to smile more broadly in her presence when she attended on us. And when he puts in his appearance this morning, which I expect him to do at any moment, he may soon fall into a surly mood if he discovers that she is absent. Perhaps he will be able to get to the bottom of the matter, though, as he has managed to learn a good deal more of their language than I ever shall.

If my uncle is not in too foul a mood, he may accompany me to a gathering the Governor General will host this afternoon at the residence. I expect to see Charles there, and if so, that would certainly be an auspicious beginning to the new year.

Now here comes Uncle Cyril, and from the scowl he wears, I fear there will be little celebration today.

2 January 1915

I was in all regards mistaken about yesterday.

Uncle did seem in an awful mood, but to my surprise, the absence of the girl was not the cause. In fact, when another servant brought tea, he seemed puzzled for a moment, asked where May was, for that is the name she goes by, and was told that she had left. Far from propelling him into a deeper funk, the news seemed to buoy him. He immediately reminded me of the affair we were to attend that afternoon, and it was he who suggested that we might see Captain Bingham there. I had thought that Uncle did not approve of Captain Bingham's attentions, although I could not understand why. My own father had once aspired to a career in the Royal Navy and most certainly would have found Charles Bingham a suitable match for his daughter. Uncle had appeared to prefer his own law clerk, Mr. Avery Bradford, as a candidate for my hand, whether I found the man to my liking or not. In any event, perhaps since the Christmas Eve dance, Uncle appears to have changed his mind about Charles, and so now was eager for me to renew what could only be described as a courtship.

In the end, it came to naught, for Charles was nowhere to be found at Government House. Indeed, the entire officer corps was absent, which many of us remarked was most peculiar, and engendered a kind of foreboding that rather spoiled what was meant to be a celebratory occasion. It was, I suppose, a reminder that, although our life in Singapore is calm and peaceful, the situation in Europe is anything but that, and we understand there are sacrifices to be made even here. And yet, Governor Young, addressing the assemblage, remarked that he was confident the war would soon be over and that the German miscreants would be punished for their crimes. His speech was so stirring, in fact, that a chorus of hoorahs erupted. The Governor is a distinguished gentleman, nearly as portly as Uncle, with a bulbous nose, a thick, graying mustache, and expressive eyebrows that seemed to rise and fall with the intensity of his words.

I was oddly morose when he had concluded, but soon found myself in the company of Mrs. Framingham, wife of the assistant councilor in

Penang, who was visiting for the Christmas and New Year holidays, and Mrs. Craddock, whose husband, Andrew, a familiar of Uncle's, is something important in our own administration in Singapore, although I don't know quite what and am not sure that anyone has adequately explained it to me. Mrs. Craddock asked where Charles Bingham was and winked at me in a peculiar way, as if there were some vile confidence we both shared. I said, of course, that I had no idea, but that I knew military men had responsibilities that mere civil servants did not, and that their time was rarely their own. I meant it to be rude, and it seems it was taken exactly as I intended, as Mrs. Craddock dropped her arm from around my waist and expelled the grin from her lips. Mrs. Framingham, however, did not notice that anything was amiss and continued to chatter away about the voyage from Penang, about the social season in Georgetown, and about other matters that were wholly inconsequential or, in any case, of no interest to me.

"My dear," said Mrs. Framingham, "Polly here tells me you are an artist and that you do the most marvelous drawings."

Recovering somewhat from her affront, Mrs. Craddock said, with a warmth that I appreciated, "They really are lovely, dear."

"I wonder if Mr. Craddock could arrange an exhibition," Mrs. Framingham said. "Wouldn't that be just the thing to keep our minds off the unpleasantness in Europe?"

I am afraid I was rather noncommittal about the idea of an exhibition, although in truth, the thought of it sent a chill through me. Until now, I have only shown my work to a few people in this world other than Richard Bromley, and Mrs. Craddock only knows of my avocation because of a visit she and her husband paid to Uncle's house during which she stumbled upon me toiling at my easel in the room Uncle has allowed me to use as a studio. I had moved to cover the painting, which was far from finished—a simple scene of the garden surrounding my uncle's house—but I was too slow, and Mrs. Craddock expressed her admiration for it. I had no reason to doubt her sincerity, but I was greatly embarrassed by the attention and hoped she would soon forget what she had seen.

Apparently, she had not. I mumbled something about "Thanks," and "Perhaps," and "We shall see," and excused myself to find Uncle Cyril.

Uncle and I returned to Heatherleigh, which seemed oddly quiet and devoid of life, and I was left to wonder when I would again see Captain Bingham.

3 January 1915

Captain Bingham has been here. We sat together in the parlor, along with Uncle Cyril as chaperone, and drank tea. He apologized for his absence at the Governor's reception and Uncle quizzed him on what was happening with the war, what plans were being made for the island's defense, and what was being done about the sizable German community that makes Singapore its home. Matters that I barely listened to, honestly, and cared about not at all. Occasionally, Charles's eyes would shift from Uncle to me, and that at least provided the spark that kept my mind from wandering too far away. I longed to tell Charles about the exhibition that Mrs. Framingham had proposed and that Mrs. Craddock had seemed to endorse, but there was no opportunity to do so.

"And so, Captain Bingham," Uncle Cyril said, "I hear that the Regiment is bound for Hong Kong."

"That is what we hear, as well, sir. But then we have also heard we're bound for Africa to fight the Turks. I don't suppose we'll know for certain until we set sail."

At this, I must have perked up. I hadn't realized that Charles would be leaving.

"And when is this mysterious voyage expected to commence?" I asked.

"In one month's time," Captain Bingham said. "Or so I gather."

"That's awfully soon," I said. "Why did you not say something earlier, Captain?" I tried not to reveal too much in my questioning, but I'm certain my worry was transparent to Uncle.

"Indeed, it is soon, Miss Pennington. That is why I've come today. We have only just learned of our orders. We had expected to be here for some time. It is now all but certain that we are leaving. Only our destination is unknown."

"I had hoped," I said, but then I wasn't sure what I had hoped and said nothing more. "Will you be returning?" I asked.

He shook his head. "Only God knows. Wars by their nature are unpredictable, as your good uncle will attest. They are like wild animals that move in ways man cannot understand or predict. Once they are cornered, they have a tendency to escape, reappearing where we least expect. I hope to return, but I'm afraid I cannot say when."

I stood, as it was clear that Uncle Cyril wanted to continue interrogating Charles, and I had already heard all I could bear. I excused myself to stroll in the garden.

As I was certain he would, Charles soon joined me there. I had no doubt that Uncle watched from the house, but at least we were alone and could speak our minds.

"I'm desperate to be with you," Charles whispered, although there was no one on the grounds who might hear us. His urgency was unexpected, as we had spent so little time together until then, but it was not unwelcome.

I could only nod, as I was instantly breathless. "Do you really think it will be over soon?" I managed to say.

He stood between me and the house, effectively blocking Uncle's view if he still watched. Charles took my hand and raised it to his lips. "We must find a way," he said. And then we heard Uncle Cyril approaching, clearing his throat, giving us fair warning. Charles dropped my hand, turned on his heel like the soldier he was, and marched off.

4 January 1915

I have heard from Mrs. Craddock that Mrs. Framingham is most serious about mounting an exhibition of my paintings, and I find myself in the position of having to work to a deadline. Mrs. Framingham will be returning to Penang shortly after the Chinese New Year, which is little more than a month from now, and would like to host a grand soiree in my honor before she leaves. I must say that I am enormously flattered by the attention and am aware that such an exhibition is rather unusual and will almost certainly offend the ladies of the painting club who are not granted such solo outings. I have not informed Uncle, as he believes my painting to be nothing more than a woman's diversion, and a silly one at that, although the one painting he has seen of mine, that I gave him as a gift for Christmas, he expressed much delight in. The painting was of a monkey that likes to visit our garden. Not that the merry little fellow holds still for his portrait, but he does come quite close, especially if he thinks there is a possibility of a bit of crust from the table or a piece of fruit, and so his image was fixed in my brain. Enough, anyway, to make a small painting that Uncle enjoyed.

"Very talented, my dear," he said. "I had no idea."

Does he really not know about Richard?

And so, I must assemble the canvasses and the paper for new paintings, although where these might be found I do not know, and must see to the framing of several pieces that have accumulated in the studio since my arrival, that I did on materials I brought with me. I think I need just a few more, and am keen for the added pressure, as of late I had grown too lethargic. Perhaps John Little & Co. can supply my needs.

There is, however, the further matter of Captain Bingham, who has sent two messages since he was here yesterday afternoon. The second was in case the first had been intercepted by Uncle, which it might well have been except that I was in the garden, pondering the subjects of the new paintings I might create, when the messenger arrived.

Charles begged me to meet him. He would be waiting for me, and he gave the location of a particular place in the Chinese settlement, an area where I had been only once on my own with the boy Ching as an escort, but that, I must be honest, frightened me. Captain Bingham's note itself unsettled me with its demands upon me. I wondered if he had learned of an earlier-than-anticipated departure from Singapore, or perhaps some other dire news that he could not share in a letter.

I resolved to meet him, as ill-advised as I knew such a rendezvous must be. While I previously had no doubt of Captain Bingham's honorable intentions, he seemed to have taken leave of his senses and manners to make such a request of me, and I was uncertain of how I should react. When the second messenger arrived, with a missive that was even more fervent than the first, I wrote my own note, saying only, "Yes," and sent it back. To what I was agreeing, exactly, I could not be sure.

5 January 1915
It was my good fortune that Uncle was to be away at Courts all day, and so I had no need to use my excuse of meeting Mrs. Craddock to discuss my forthcoming exhibition in order to have a plausible reason for leaving the house at the appointed hour. It seems that whenever I go out when Uncle is present, I must inevitably testify, as if a witness in some dispute, as to where I should be and whom I would be seeing and how long I expected to be away and so on. While I am loath to lie to the old boy, who has been so good to me, I had taken it into my head that it was the most important thing in the world for me to meet Charles, and I was prepared to enact any subterfuge in order to keep the appointment. Furthermore, I chafe at Uncle's monitoring of my whereabouts, as if I were one of the servants or, worse, his prisoner, as I once expected I would be. Which, perhaps, is exactly what I am, prisoner and servant both. As it was, I did need to deceive Lao Po so that she would not insist again that her grandson accompany me.

Given that I am writing about it, I have obviously survived to tell the story, but it is one that I am not sure I have the stomach to relate. And so, perhaps, I shall keep it to myself for another day.

10 January 1915

This morning, in the garden, I painted. It was a lovely morning, after an evening rain that washed some of the heat out of the air, and although the grass was wet, I walked along the stone path. I set up my easel next to a brilliant plant that Uncle calls the bird of paradise, because, I suppose, of its passing resemblance to a flamboyant variety of bird, perhaps one of the exotic creatures that frequent the jungle around us. I believe, after the events of the last few days, that I might like to *be* a bird of paradise, majestic and arrogant, independent, unafraid to speak my mind. The fronds sway so gently in the morning breeze that I might think they beckon, and indeed they do. "Come look at me and touch me if you dare," they seem to say, with good reason. The large orange flowers are almost indescribable, like the head of a bird, yes, but also like a flame held in the palm of one's hand.

I am not accustomed to the painting of still life scenes, but I could not resist painting this amazing flower that seemed to have a personality, more like an animal than a plant. It held me rapt for the better part of the morning trying to capture both its stillness and its vibrancy at the same moment, and I only broke off because of the arrival of Lieutenant Raj, with a message from Charles.

It was the Lieutenant who brought the first messages last week, and I scarcely noted him then because of the startling contents of the missives. But now he has come several times, and I should remark on this unusual specimen. He reminds me of the only other Indian man I have closely encountered, that being Samir, the handsome sailor on board the ship. Both men are taciturn and horribly inscrutable. But Raj is an officer of a unit of the Regiment made up entirely of Indians, sepoys, they are called, under the command of Captain Bingham and his superiors. He is rather tall, compared to his compatriots, and I would say sinister if his eyes did not convey a kind of warmth that suggests not ill-intent but, rather, longing. At least until the Regiment departs, I expect I will be seeing much of Raj.

And now I must write of Captain Bingham, as I have not come to these pages in several days. But first—yes, I am finding every excuse to avoid the subject—I must tell of the girl from our household staff who went missing on New Year's Day. May returned on Sunday, briefly. It was early, and I sat on the veranda alone, drinking tea. Uncle was not yet out of bed, as the girl would have known. She came to see me, distraught, hands trembling, her entire body trembling, it seemed.

"Miss," she said, and that was the last word out of her mouth that I truly understood. She spoke in her own tongue, and I could make no sense of it. What I did understand, though, was that she was deeply troubled. I begged her to sit down, but instead she knelt at my feet and clutched the hem of my dress. When I suggested I might waken my Uncle to see if he could assist in whatever it was that had disturbed her, she jumped to her feet, shook her head, and then raced off, through the house, down the front stairs, which I don't suppose she was accustomed to using as I have never seen any of the servants come or go that way, and straight into the road. The entire incident passed so quickly that I thought I might have dreamt it, except that she left behind a lovely embroidered handkerchief she had been torturing in her hands. I picked it up and stuffed it into my pocket. When Uncle emerged, I thought of mentioning the visitation to him, but something in the girl's reaction to the mention of Uncle Cyril, as if I had offered to summon the devil himself, made me stop.

And so now, I suppose, I am able to write about Charles. On the day he begged me to meet him in the Chinese settlement, I went. Despite Uncle's objections and Lao Po's interventions, I had grown somewhat accustomed to traveling about on my own, with neither escort nor servant to accompany me. I would simply let one of the ladies know that I wished to leave and she would—I know not how—arrange for one of the two-wheeled carts pulled by a man, or one of the boxy carriages they call a gharry, and one would appear at the house. Singapore, in this regard, strikes me as far safer than a city such as London, where the occupation of cutpurse seems to have thrived like no other, or at least that is the impression I had from Richard Bromley and the gentlemen who would visit him from the city on occasion. I must admit, however, my trepidation, for as I have said, I had seldom been in the part of the settlement where Charles had bade me come, and only once on my own with Ching. I could not imagine why he had chosen that particular location, nor why he had been so secretive. So secretive, in fact, that on this occasion he sent a carriage for me so that my destination would not be made known to our servants by a confederate cart puller.

Of course, I should have understood the secrecy. And if I had known what Charles had in mind, would I have gone to him? I suppose I might well have, because in truth it was nothing more than I had myself imagined and wished. Still, I resented Captain Bingham's presumption that I would come to him, that I was an object to which he was entitled. He is perhaps accustomed to women who would not object to being treated so. You see, I am sorely conflicted. As much as I consider myself truly an independent woman, in need of no man, I long for the comfort to be found in submission to his will. I long for him and want to be with him.

I have no idea how Charles arranged it, but the place I was to meet him was immediately adjacent to the joss house, the temple that I had sketched on my one other visit to the area, not far from the waterfront. When I stepped down from the carriage, I was met by a stooped Chinese woman who, smiling and bowing, indicated that I should follow. I entered a gate, which she closed behind me, and then hurried on ahead once again through a narrow passage. It seemed to be some sort of inn, although nothing at all like the lodgings with which I am acquainted in England. The woman came to a closed door and spoke in short, crisp syllables. The door opened, and there was Charles. I was dumbfounded. The woman bowed and disappeared. Charles took my hand and pulled me inside.

I cannot possibly write about what happened next, but it began with a gentle kiss, followed by one far more urgent. And while I did not encourage Charles's advances, I did not resist, either, because he was but fulfilling the very fantasy I had previously fashioned.

I was like the bird of paradise flower, the flame burning in my breast, begging to be touched, and I opened myself to him eagerly. I can say no more.

11 January 1915
I have returned to the Chinese settlement. Charles is a drug I cannot resist, but he is not the only magnet that pulls me there. The joss house, too, is powerful, and I go to draw. I draw the children who gambol in the courtyard. I draw the women who light incense and burn scraps of paper in the ovens that flank the great chapel of this place. I draw the men who come, fresh off their boats from China, with nothing to their names—one assumes they have names, but even that is not certain—except their own ragged clothing and, perhaps, a jute sack slung over their shoulders in which they guard their meager possessions. They are destined to toil for the good of the settlement, working the junks and bumboats and pulling the carts, backbreaking labors that few Englishmen would undertake, and I wonder if they resent their lowly condition. Is that resignation I see in their faces? Or determination?

I draw the fruit stand near the temple, with its cornucopia of exotic varieties, the lychee and rambutan, jackfruit and malodorous spiked melons for which I have no name. I draw the woman who tends the stand, who scowls at me as I draw, and urges me away. Perhaps she knows of my scandalous behavior, or perhaps she thinks I am bad for her business.

The pencil marks appear on the paper of my pad as if by themselves. When I paint, I feel as though I am an instrument, united with the brush, through which another creates the image. I am not so devout as to believe that "other" is God, although surely there is a divine force at work. The pencil strokes are rather different. I do not feel present in their creation. Like a photograph, they simply appear.

At home, in the studio, I apply the paint, the oils that I favor, and I cannot fathom what I have done. How did this likeness come to be? It is not, as some have complained, a replica of the subject. It is, instead, an image that contains all my thoughts and emotions as well as my vision and the life of the depicted, and my own life as well. In the painting, I see not just a man, but the village he has come from, the family he has left and hopes one day to rejoin, the toil he has abandoned, traded for unimaginable travails, the master he now serves. And so I see myself.

12 January 1915
Charles has visited again, at Uncle's invitation.

"You two have not seen enough of each other of late," he said at breakfast, and of course I could not contradict him. "Captain Bingham is a good man, despite his profession. I have asked about him in the Regiment, you know. A highly regarded fellow. Even Preston, that writer, who has nothing good to say about anyone, expresses his admiration for Charles."

And so Captain Bingham came to tea. At the hour appointed for his arrival, I was nearly faint. I could not bear the thought of being in the same room with him without being able to touch him or to be touched by him. Uncle did not know, of course, but what he had devised so thoughtfully was simply torture to me, and I presume also to Charles.

We sat on the veranda, which, although beastly, was at least moderated by an occasional breeze. From there I could see the bird of paradise flower, and I imagined holding the flame in my hand.

"Any news of the war, Captain Bingham?" Uncle asked.

It may sound peculiar to say it, but I had nearly forgotten about the war. Despite the recent developments locally—a German ship had been captured in the straits and its notorious commander imprisoned at Tanglin, not far from Uncle's house—it all seemed so distant.

"We have heard that the battle against the Turks in Africa rages on, but there is little news, I'm afraid, from France," Charles said. "It is difficult for us to be so far away from the action, as you can appreciate."

"And yet you have an important role to play here, do you not? Singapore and Hong Kong must be protected, and not just from the

Germans. Our allies the Japanese do not seem to be as cooperative as they once were. Nor do the Dutch. And there are far more Russians about than I find advisable."

If Charles found Uncle's concerns absurd, he did not show it, and in fact he nodded gravely. But as much as I wished to be with him, I could not bear to look at him for long. What we had done...what we were doing...I could only feel the warmth spread to my face, certain that I had given myself away.

Secretly, of course, we were betrothed. It had happened without prelude, but naturally, as if it were the obvious and inevitable outcome of our attraction to one another. Charles asked me on that first night together and I accepted. And in that way, I felt married and also felt that what we were doing was not wrong. But if Uncle knew? I would be sent back to London, I expect, or, more likely, on to Australia, land of convicts and outcasts. After Richard, after being sent to the Far East, I had no intention of marrying. I was determined to live as an independent woman, to break the chains men have used to restrain women for millennia. But intentions must bow to reality and fall at the feet of desire.

I listened to Charles speak at length to Uncle about the war, about the condition of the troops he commanded—the Regiment was made up almost entirely of Indians such as Lieutenant Raj—and about the challenges of maintaining discipline. Half the men spoke little English, he said, and had difficulty communicating amongst themselves since their native tongues were also varied. Even though they believed they would be sent into battle, Charles was privately relieved that their orders would more likely take them to Hong Kong to defend that colony, as he could not imagine these particular men in combat.

In the main, I merely listened to the sound of his voice, the same drone that comforted me as I drowsed in his arms. When I closed my eyes, transported to the room in the Chinese settlement, I grew warmer, a heat that was at least the match of the heat of the day. I felt myself drift away on a cloud, reliving our last rendezvous.

"Elizabeth?" Uncle said. "Lizzie, are you all right?"

I composed myself, sipped tea. And soon made excuses. I could not bear to be in the presence of Captain Bingham any longer.

14 January 1915

The painting of the joss house has become three, and there may be more. It continues to haunt me, this house of refuge for newcomers. It is, in a very real sense, my own house of refuge. I am not free to be with Charles, and yet I cannot be without him, so I go when he bids.

I thought of painting a portrait, to expand my repertoire, but the only face that comes to mind is Charles's, and I am afraid of what I might do to his face on canvas. What ecstasies would the brush reveal? I am certain that Uncle would recognize our secret if he were to see it, as would anyone with a discerning eye, and so it is best if I leave the face undrawn for now.

With Charles's departure imminent, I do not know what I shall do. We cannot marry, and yet we are married. We cannot be together, and yet we are together. He sent a message again today, and I must go to him.

15 January 1915

Uncle Cyril and I dined with the Craddocks last evening. Mrs. Craddock has made all the arrangements for my exhibition, and I cannot thank her enough, although in these last weeks since the idea was proposed I have done little new work. There are the birds of paradise, and the views of the joss house, which I am not sure I can show to anyone because they reveal too much, I think. And there is the portrait of Charles that I have painted only in my head.

At supper we talked about the war, which is only natural, but Mrs. Craddock and I found it horribly tedious—for different reasons, perhaps—and I was grateful when she guided the conversation to other topics. She discussed an entertainment we are told will soon appear. In these times it is most unusual, but there are traveling musicians expected, and a concert will be held in February. It made me long again to find a piano on which I might practice regularly, but they are a rare commodity here, it seems. We discussed the coming Chinese New Year festival, which Mrs. Craddock reminded me repeatedly I have not previously experienced. She says it is among the loudest of holidays because of the Chinese fondness for crackers, some of which are as deafening as cannons, she says. I doubted this, but she insisted it was so.

When the men had excused themselves to smoke on the veranda, leaving us to ourselves while the servants cleared the meal, I wanted to ask Mrs. Craddock about marriage. Why should Captain Bingham and I not be married? What is the impediment? He will soon set sail for Hong Kong, but could I not accompany him? I suppose I am thought too young, though Mrs. Craddock herself was no older than I am now when she married. I cannot bring myself to ask these questions because I am certain she would not understand me. She would think I am concerned with intimacy, but what I am more concerned with, what I fear losing most in the world, is freedom.

Does a wife not subjugate herself to her husband? I was once subject to my father's rule. As Richard's pupil and assistant, I was expected to obey him. Now I am dependent on Uncle Cyril. Should I trade one dependency for another? When does a woman emancipate? This is the question with which I struggle, and I fear that Mrs. Craddock would have no clear answer, for it is surely beyond her reckoning.

11

Selvadurai asked Aislinn to help one of his younger partners understand the convoluted corporate structure of a US company his client planned to acquire, a fish processing conglomerate based in the Pacific Northwest with multiple subsidiaries and facilities. Eventually, the Singapore-based holding company was going to need lawyers in the US to complete the purchase, but at this stage, they only needed to know the basics. Reviewing the investment proposal brought back memories of the complex projects she'd worked on with Frank. It seemed like an interesting transaction, one she'd love to handle if it moved forward, maybe associating with the American law firm to bring the deal to a close, a possible steppingstone to a more satisfying job.

She looked up when there was a loud knock on her open office door, surprised to see TJ Kwan.

"Good afternoon, Aislinn."

"TJ, what a nice surprise. To what do I owe the pleasure?"

TJ held out to her the jacket she'd lost at the Hong Lim Park demonstration. "I thought you might like to have this."

She considered denying it was hers, but she remembered that her office ID had been in the pocket.

"Where did you find this, TJ? I thought it was lost forever. I think I left it at the Telok Ayer Market one day at lunch."

"The police found it, Aislinn. In a most unusual place. Not the market. And that's not where you lost it, is it? At any rate, the propriety of interfering in our local political matters aside, the Commissioner of Police is an old school friend of mine and he dropped this by my office, knowing that we are acquainted. And now I'm returning it to you."

She couldn't move and felt the familiar ache spreading from her knee. Her hands trembled. It was disconcerting that the police were aware of her attendance at the demonstration and of her connection to TJ. In New York she'd often felt invisible, but here, apparently, that wasn't the case.

"I appreciate the return of the jacket, TJ, but I'm not sure I know what you're talking about."

"Oh, Aislinn, I think you do. And just let me add that you should select your friends more carefully, even if they do have sailboats."

The trembling grew worse. She slipped her hands beneath the desk and gripped her legs. He knew about Martin? Most likely, then, he also knew she'd been spending time with Shan Lee. Was he warning her to stay away from them? Or was he just sending a message that she was being watched?

· · · · ·

On Saturday, Liam was due to return from Bangkok. Mid-morning, Aislinn left the apartment and headed toward the small supermarket that catered to the neighborhood expats and carried more imported and luxury items than the Cold Storage stores did. The intense heat—so incongruous for October—made it difficult to breathe, and although the walk was short, she was wilted and damp by the time she entered the store, supremely grateful for its supercharged air conditioning. She strolled the store's aisles, smiled and nodded at other shoppers, some of whom were beginning to look familiar, and found ingredients for a welcome-home dinner, shrimp scampi and a salad, a loaf of French bread, a nice bottle of wine. Laden with a plastic bag in each hand, she trudged up the hill back to the apartment.

In the afternoon, Aislinn worked with Cecilia to fix dinner, trying to be as gentle and thoughtful as possible. Did Cecilia notice her efforts, or care? Even after four months, she still wasn't used to having Cecilia living with them, especially in that inhumane space, although every day it seemed like an impossible luxury to be freed of the cleaning and most of the cooking. Still, it felt like slavery to basically own a woman from the Philippines who was living next to the kitchen and available at all hours to do her bidding.

• • • • •

Cecilia served dinner and then disappeared into her tiny room. Liam nodded approvingly when he tasted the pasta.

"Tell me all about Bangkok," Aislinn said. "It sounds so exotic."

"We were in endless meetings. I didn't see much of the city."

"Surely you saw something. Isn't it supposed to be full of canals and temples?" Other expat wives had told her that Bangkok was notorious for the sex trade, and that some men saw nothing wrong in visiting the local massage parlors, despite their ties to human trafficking and prostitution. Was that the sort of man Liam had become? She didn't suppose he would tell her if he'd done that, even if she asked. And maybe she didn't really want to know.

"I saw the river. Does that count? We stayed at a hotel right on the river, in fact, another Shangri-La, pretty much like the one you and I stayed in here that first week. Elegant lobby, beautiful suite. TJ came back here early, and the client did have someone take me to a temple one afternoon, an amazing, ridiculously ornate place. Gold statues encrusted with jewels. Wat something. I've forgotten the name of it already."

She thought she should tell Liam about the demonstration, about the ridiculous behavior of the police, and also TJ's visit to her office, but he was still wound up from the trip and kept talking about the bank, the idiots who worked for him and for whom he worked.

"Bruce is in way over his head. It's only been a couple of months since we arrived, and I've saved his bacon more than once. Don't think I didn't let Robinson and Stephens know about it." Robinson, Aislinn remembered, was the Regional Managing Partner, based in Hong Kong. Stephens was the guy from New York who'd visited the apartment with TJ. She thought she had that right, but maybe it was the other way around. Liam was amazed they hadn't yet sent Bruce packing.

"And the rest of the people aren't any better. We've got vice presidents who should never have been hired in the first place. Or at least should never have been sent overseas. They have no clue." On the Bangkok trip, TJ had filled him in on the history of the joint venture bank, how the global organization Liam worked for relied heavily on the local Board for area business contacts. It gave them the ability to invest in opportunities that purely foreign banks would not be welcome in, but some of the hidebound Americans, like Bruce, didn't get it.

"TJ is a dim bulb, too, frankly, but he'll be useful to have on our side. He's connected. Very connected. Knows everyone, and where the bodies are buried. You should have seen him operate in Bangkok. He's not big on details or number-crunching, but he's slick as hell. TJ is the key. He came back Thursday so I could get down to brass tacks with their numbers guy."

She could tell he was thinking aloud, plotting. She hadn't seen this side of Liam in New York, where he'd seemed more of a team player, still making a name for himself but basically just doing a job. And it was a far cry from how morose he'd been after the World Trade Center attack.

"What was the deal TJ had in mind in Bangkok? The same people as the motorbike deal?" she asked. "Must be interesting."

Liam hesitated. "It's complicated," he said.

"Try me. I've worked on complicated deals before."

"I know, love. It's just…we're still working out the details."

• • • • •

Early Sunday morning in bed, the sky still dark, Liam's cell phone rang. He reached for it on the nightstand, simultaneously climbing out of bed and moving toward the living room. Now that Aislinn was awake, she strained to hear what he was saying. He wasn't speaking, though, or at least nothing she could hear, and she drifted back to sleep.

She woke again, still in darkness, and Liam hadn't returned to bed. Now she was worried. A problem with his children? She got up and slipped on her robe. When she entered the living room, she saw him sitting in the dark. There was enough reflected light from outside that she could see him lift a drink, sip, and she heard the clink of ice.

"Liam, what is it?" She switched on a lamp, and he turned to her. Tears streamed down his face. "Oh, my God. What's happened?"

"Rebecca called."

"Is she all right? Jason?"

Liam shook his head. "It's in Bali this time. A bomb. Some fucker just blew up a bunch of kids at a nightclub."

Bali, an Indonesian island only two hours from Singapore, was a favorite tourist destination in the region. Beautiful beaches, a majestic volcano at the island's heart, an arts village called Ubud that she was keen to visit, a surfer's paradise. Jenny had mentioned spending the Christmas holiday there at one of the beach resorts, and Aislinn assumed she and Liam would travel there eventually, too, her fear of flying notwithstanding. It sounded like an idyllic getaway. Until now. She knelt in front of him, wrapped her arms around him. He was trembling.

She looked up at him and saw the pain in his eyes. "Rebecca wasn't there, was she?"

"She wasn't sure where Bali was," he said. "She thought it might be closer to us."

He picked up the remote, turned on the television, and found CNN, where they were reporting on the story, complete with live footage from the scene. There'd been multiple bombs, including one at a popular nightclub in Kuta Beach. At least a hundred dead, most of them Australian tourists, dozens more wounded. No one had claimed responsibility yet, but an Islamist group linked with al-Qaeda had been active in the region and was suspected.

Aislinn brought Liam tissues, and he wiped his eyes and cheeks, then held her close on the sofa. She thought of her brother, who had entered the army to join the fight against terrorism after 9/11. What did this mean for him? How can you fight an enemy like this, one with no scruples?

"I thought we were safe here," he said. "I really did. But nowhere is safe."

. . . . .

New York, a little over a year ago. Light filtered into the bedroom through the plantation blinds, and they both stirred, anticipating the alarm. It was an extraordinary time of day, lush and muted, before the hurry and rush that would follow. She was still mired in sleep, on the edge of consciousness, and aware, vaguely, of being alive, of looking forward to something, not sure what. It was a gauzy, womb-like sensation, and she savored it.

Liam's leg pressed against hers, rousing her. There was a distant hum, unidentifiable—the refrigerator downstairs, maybe, or a streetlight, a car idling out front—and the combined rank scent of their bodies. Then the noise faded, the odor vanished, both lost to the overload of her awakening senses and the touch of Liam's hands on her thighs. His lips brushed the nape of her neck, his tongue dabbed at her ear. She heard his breath. She felt his warmth against her back, the fine hair of his chest, the beating of his heart, his growing hardness. His arm snaked under the sheet, across her hips, between her legs.

· · · · ·

While Liam showered, Aislinn closed her eyes and dreamed, reliving their dawn lovemaking. Buried under the sheet, she was still with him, breathing him in, feeling him move inside her.

Her marriage wasn't perfect. He wasn't as attentive as he'd been at first, when their relationship was still new. Now they quarreled about little things, about groceries and housekeeping, about her long hours in the office, about his children, about his ex-wife, especially about his ex-wife, who seemed to grow needier by the day, about his desire for Aislinn to have a baby and start a new family. But on mornings like this, when he took her, when he whispered how beautiful she was, how much he loved her and wanted her, all the rest receded. She couldn't expect more. Perfection was unrealistic and unattainable.

After Liam had dressed and gone off to an early meeting, Aislinn luxuriated in the steamy bathroom and turned her attention to the day ahead. There was a recruiting lunch with a 2L from Harvard, a meeting with Frank about a potential new project, drinks later with a law school friend visiting from Paris, a late dinner with Liam. It promised to be a slow day, though, and that worried her. At this stage in her career, the billable hours were crucial, all fuel for her progress toward partnership, but despite Liam's complaints about her long hours, her workload at the moment was light. The new deal should help, but she'd have to ask Frank if there wasn't yet another project she could take on, maybe another partner she could assist. Liam wouldn't be happy about it, but she was convinced her future depended on it.

· · · · ·

On the way into the city, despite the nagging work concerns, she couldn't help but smile. The sky spread wide and deep blue above her, unreal, like a painting, gorgeous, invigorating, as she walked the two blocks from their brownstone to the station. The crisp air held the faint scent of fall, her favorite season, and there was no hint of last night's storm except for damp leaves on the sidewalk. She stepped onto the platform just as the train arrived, further evidence that the day was going to be grand.

Her smile broadened, and she didn't care if everyone on the B-train thought she was a lunatic. In reality, though, no one would notice. That's the way New Yorkers were. It was a cliché, but true nevertheless. She could collapse and die on a street corner and pedestrians would jump over her to get wherever they were going. They wouldn't yell at her for being in the way. They certainly wouldn't stop to help. They'd simply keep going, and to hell with everyone else in the city. To hell with the rest of the world. But not even the indifference of her fellow New Yorkers could keep the smile from her face this morning.

She held onto the pole near the door and smiled again, studying faces: the secretaries, who were no longer called secretaries, in their short skirts and the sneakers they'd trade for high heels when they arrived at their desks; the college students in all shapes and sizes and colors headed downtown or uptown, to universities and institutes and conservatories; the bankers, on their way to Wall Street or Midtown offices to make deals and negotiate deals and close deals; the cashiers and clerks, on their way to shops; the waitresses heading for their shifts in restaurants and cafés and bars; and lawyers, like herself, none of them with smiles on their faces, headed into their tiny offices at their mega-firms or their boutique firms or their courtrooms.

When the train lurched and the man next to her tumbled against her shoulder, mumbling his apology, she smiled again. It wasn't his fault; she knew it and wanted him to know she knew it. New York was the greatest city in the world, teeming with the most amazing people, of which this man was one and she was another, and there was nothing to apologize for if, for this one instant, the energy of the city thrust them together. She smiled at him, wondering who this man was and where in the world he might be going on this beautiful morning. He looked away, but she smiled at him again.

At Bryant Park, she pushed out the door and followed the flow up the escalators to the street. The sky was still that impossible blue, cloudless and deep, and she smiled again, and thinking about her silly smile only made her smile widen. She stopped at the Starbucks in the lobby of her building, nodded to the barista, splurged on a venti latte to celebrate the glorious morning sex with her husband and the cloudless sky and her clear path to a spectacular future, a world-beating future, and when she approached the bank of elevators she was rewarded with opening doors. A crowd flooded in. Here there were faces she recognized, most of the men and women her colleagues in the law firm, few she knew well, but she nodded and smiled as she turned to gaze forward. And when the doors opened on the 47th floor she bounced out, greeted the receptionist, "Good morning, Paulette, isn't it a glorious day?" and hurried down the hall toward her office, anxious to tackle whatever the morning might bring.

Her firm occupied several floors of the building, but space was tight. In her first year she'd shared a tiny, dark interior room with three other new associates, but she'd survived those early tribulations and had been compensated, eventually, with sunlight. She loved her little office with its narrow window. Her view was of the tower across 7th Avenue, but she could still see glimpses of the amazing blue sky, and sunlight reflected in the tower's glass façade, and that's all she cared about.

She sipped her coffee. Her computer hummed, signaling the arrival of an email, and the message light on her phone blinked. In the center of her desk was a thick accordion file and a Post-it Note with her name on it—she recognized Frank's precise handwriting. The phone rang, identifying Frank as the caller. He wanted to discuss the file, the new project she'd been assigned. Her day was already galloping ahead. Maybe she'd worried for nothing.

There was a loud gasp outside her door, shrieks down the hall, and it seemed as if the air in the office had disappeared. Something terrible had happened and she couldn't breathe. The blare of sirens rose from the street below and she thought she heard voices rising as well, but surely that was impossible this high up. A man rushed past her door—

she didn't see who it was—and then a woman. An emergency. A heart attack, she thought. Someone should call a doctor. She put her hand on the phone, as if she might be needed to do just that.

And finally, someone stopped, stuck her head into Aislinn's office, and told her that a plane had crashed into the World Trade Center.

• • • •

It was a small plane, they told each other. A bizarre accident. But how could a small plane make such an impact? The truth nagged at them as more information came in. Not a small plane. Not an accident. And then the second plane hit.

Frank told her to go home, but she was torn. She called Liam but couldn't get through to his cell phone. His meeting was downtown somewhere, she didn't know where, but she told herself it wasn't at the World Trade Center. Near there, maybe, but not in the Towers themselves. She stayed in her office for a while, expecting her phone to ring, but it was agony. Everyone crowded into conference rooms or senior partners' offices, anywhere there was a television, and they watched. She joined a group in Frank's office. Most of the women were crying, as were some of the men. No one spoke. When someone did utter something, a hypothesis or a rumor or a curse, he was shushed. When the Towers fell, someone shrieked as if she'd been shot. Others shouted that it couldn't be real. It was impossible. Then the room fell silent, except for muffled sobs.

How many people had died? Five thousand? Ten? It was no accident, obviously, but what exactly had happened? Who did this? What monsters? And where was Liam?

She couldn't watch anymore. She was worried about Liam, of course, but so many others, too. Several of her law school classmates worked in law firms in the Towers, including Clark, dear, gentle, Clark, and wasn't there an associate from her firm who had just left to join another outfit on the top floor? He'd been so excited about the move downtown. Where the action was, he'd said, where cutting-edge law was happening. And the planes. Where was her mother just then? Her brother? Jessica? Were they traveling? Might they have been on the planes?

Aislinn returned to her desk but couldn't focus on the papers before her, the new file. She gazed out the window, and the sky looked just as it had before. There might have been smoke, and something floated in the air like snow. Was that ash? This far north? Was she imagining it? There was wailing in the hall. She left her office, tried to comfort the woman, a paralegal who said something about her son, a broker in the South Tower, but Aislinn couldn't understand. Was he dead? Did he get out? Had she heard something?

Aislinn said, "My husband…," but she didn't know what else to say. She called Liam's cell again and still couldn't get a line. Her call to his office wouldn't go through, either—no ringing, no voice mail, nothing. One of the assistants was on her phone, an international call. Her family in Australia had just heard and was checking on her. How odd that they could get the overseas line, but up in Midtown they didn't know what was happening at the tip of the island.

If Liam was okay, she reasoned, he would go home. That was simple enough. If he couldn't get through to her on the phone, he would know she'd be worried, so he'd go home to wait for her there. Wasn't that what she would do? She found Frank in his office.

"I don't know where Liam is," she said, unable to say more. She had sensed Frank's disapproval of her marriage to a client they had both worked with, one who was married to someone else when they met, but he'd never spoken to her about it. He would only bring it up if it affected her performance, and she'd made sure that it had not. Now, he rose behind his desk and came to her, his arms spread wide. She gladly let him fold himself around her.

"Go home," he said.

She extracted herself from his embrace, nodded, and wiped away the tears that had begun to flow.

She went back to her office, called Liam's cell one more time, picked up her briefcase, and joined the exodus. Past the sobbing receptionist, into the elevator, through the lobby of the building, and out into the disbelieving world beneath the sky that would never be the same.

· · · · ·

On the street, she learned that the subways had been halted, so she began to walk. Already she saw survivors, some covered in ash, moving north, trudging like the living dead, focused on their feet, on the sidewalk, on getting home. She couldn't look at them. She couldn't think about who they were or what they'd lost. What had she lost?

At first, she was walking against the flow, so many grim, stooped people tramping north, away from the Towers. Most were silent, but some couldn't stifle their anguish, which escaped in deep moans or high-pitched yowls. Sirens and the smell of smoke filled the air. She had thought she could walk all the way downtown to the Brooklyn Bridge, but she saw now that might not be possible. She headed east, through the Bowery, and was relieved to join the throng heading toward the Williamsburg Bridge. There was less smoke here, above the river, and her back was to the city, the billowing tower of ash. She didn't have to look behind her to see what was no longer there, that symbol of New York, of America.

It took hours, but she made it home. Stepping inside the townhouse, she realized she was barefoot, that her feet were leaving bloody tracks, but she couldn't remember at what point she'd abandoned her shoes. She couldn't feel her feet.

She didn't have to call Liam's name. She knew he wasn't there. The house was deathly silent, and dark, her piano a hulking shadow. She stripped off her clothes. Did they smell of smoke? She couldn't tell, but they were repulsive to her. She left them in a pile on the floor of their bedroom. When she returned from the shower, she put on her robe. She checked her cell phone, but there was still no service. She looked at the television in the bedroom's corner and considered turning it on, to find out what had happened, exactly, or why. There would be time for that later. For now, she didn't want to know.

Where was Liam?

She poured herself a Scotch and retreated to the sofa in the living room to wait. His meeting wasn't in the Towers, was it?

· · · · ·

As the hours passed, she grew more certain he'd been in the Towers, that he was one of the thousands who had died, and she wondered if she should try to tell someone he was missing, if someone somewhere was compiling a list. And what about his children? How could she reach them? Should she call his ex-wife? But she couldn't call anyone. She didn't know what to do. How could she be prepared for something like this? How could anyone?

She gave in and turned on the television, watching the horrific images of the bodies falling from the sky, of the Towers crumbling like castles of sand. Smoke and ash and debris ran through the canyons of Wall Street in roiling clouds, and the images played again and again and again. It looked like a Third World disaster, not something that could happen here in her city. She turned it off, unable to watch any longer, learning only what she already knew, that this was no accident, this catastrophe. Deliberate. Murder.

Closing her eyes, her mind floated back to the morning, the beautiful morning, the lovemaking, the sky filled with such promise, the day like every other day except that it was better, fresher, hopeful.

She heard steps at the door, a key turning in the lock, and Liam appeared, his face and hair covered in ash and soot, his jacket missing along with his tie, and he stood there in the vestibule, gazing in at her. Their city had suffered an unthinkable calamity, but here they were, together. She didn't run to him, but rose and moved, deliberately, barely aware of her feet on the cold floor, the blisters on her heels, the gash on her instep, and slipped her arms around him, pressed her face into his chest, breathed in the sweat and smoke.

They spoke in urgent whispers, telling their stories. He'd been in his meeting—not in the Towers, but in an office around the corner on

Fulton. They'd heard the first crash, unimaginable discord of ripping metal and an explosion, a bomb, they thought, and saw the sky change instantly, the air filled with screams and clouds of smoke. They ran to see, and then watched, helpless, when the second plane hit, slamming into the South Tower. But no, not exactly helpless. They did help. Evacuees streamed by, some with injuries, and Liam and his colleagues did what they could to treat them, a makeshift clinic growing in the lobby of the building on Fulton. When the Towers fell, they were overwhelmed, and the victims kept coming and kept coming, the injuries beyond what they could handle. But then the flow of survivors stopped. There were only the dead, and there was nothing more he could do.

• • • • •

She eventually reached her mother in DC, who had feared the worst when Aislinn didn't call right away. From her, Aislinn learned about the attack on the Pentagon and the other plane that had gone down in Pennsylvania. And on the phone her brother, who had found work in a Miami marketing firm after college, could barely speak, choked with rage and thirsty for retribution for whoever had done this.

• • • • •

It seemed impossible, but the world edged forward. Aislinn's office reopened, and she went back to work. Liam did the same. They cleaned the house; they shopped for groceries; they ate dinner at home in silence. When they did talk, they spoke of anything other than the attack. But it was never far from Aislinn's mind, and she knew it weighed heavily on Liam, too. How could it not?

When she learned from a friend that Clark was missing, presumed dead, she didn't think she could go on. Not Clark. A colleague of Liam's had been on one of the planes, a man whose son had just started college. So many others missing, dead.

It was hard to fathom. How could these murderers have done what they did? The story slowly emerged. She didn't blame them for hating America, which had behaved egregiously abroad, exploiting people and natural resources around the world for at least a century. But terrorism worked against their purpose, didn't it? It only hardened the hearts of people like Aislinn and Liam, good people who wanted their country to do the right thing. Now, though, she was angry, and she wanted to fight back. Her brother made plans to enlist, to join the war against whoever the enemy was. He wasn't the only one.

And when would it all end? She wasn't alone in the suspicion she felt toward Muslims now, or brown people generally who might be Muslims for all she knew. The taxi driver with the name that sounded Arabic, the grocery clerk wearing a headscarf, the turbaned waiter. These people weren't terrorists. She shouldn't be suspicious just because of their accents, or their names, or the color of their skin, or their religion. They were her neighbors, people she saw all the time. And yet, after what had happened, how could she be sure?

At work, she joined the crowd floating through the lobby of her office building. They carried briefcases and wore scarves around their necks as cooler weather settled in, suits under their overcoats, and they looked like they had always looked, as if nothing had happened. Some even smiled, which most people she knew didn't do anymore. The wound was too fresh. They'd all lost friends or family or lovers, and some mornings she thought she'd never smile again. She worked, she went home, she had forgettable sex with her husband, and that was all she did. She didn't want to think, because if she thought, if she looked into anyone's eyes and saw their sadness, she'd remember. And if she remembered, she might cry.

But she did remember, and she did cry, often. She tried to hide it, staring forward into the emptiness of the elevator doors, hoping no one noticed. Burnished metal, almost a mirror, reflected her image, as blurred and distorted as she felt. Her consolation—she wasn't alone. She focused to distract herself: a sweet fragrance, too much, from the woman to her left; hip-hop from the earphones of the delivery man to her right; a cough and a sniffle behind her. It helped, but only for an instant.

• • • • •

And now, a year later and on the other side of the planet, Bali. They had tried to get away from it, but nowhere was safe.

• • • • •

Liam had, for Aislinn's benefit, agreed to join the American Club, after arguing for membership at the posh Tanglin Club, where many of the Brits and the more cosmopolitan locals spent their time, and both clubs were close to their apartment. "Tanglin is where the business is, according to TJ," Liam had said.

She liked the American Club. It wasn't New York, certainly—most of the women she'd met there were from Houston or New Orleans and their husbands worked in the oil industry, spending long stretches in Indonesia and other nearby oil fields in Malaysia, Brunei, and Vietnam—but it was a slice of America, a way to escape for a bit. She enjoyed spending time there, taking advantage of the gym and the lending library, and before she'd landed the job with Bradford & Co. there had been little else to do.

When she arrived to meet Jenny and her friend Pamela for lunch, the club had beefed up security in response to the Bali bombing. A burly policewoman inspected her handbag and guided her through a metal detector, then a club employee studied her membership card, which caused further inquiries as she'd been issued a temporary card that didn't include a photo. Past that hurdle, she made her way to the café and found Jenny and Pamela already seated. Neither was smiling.

"I thought about canceling," Jenny said. "The bombing was just so horrible. But life has to go on, you know?"

"I couldn't stand to look at the news," Pamela said. "What's the latest?"

"Liam was obsessed with it," Aislinn said. "He watched CNN all day yesterday. Two hundred confirmed dead, scores injured. They're saying now there were three bombs, all targeting places popular with foreigners." She wanted to remind her new friends that she was in New York when the World Trade Center was attacked. Liam had thought they'd gotten away from it by moving here. And now, would they even stay?

"My husband…," she began, but she couldn't tell them how this had affected him, how he'd cried. Aislinn couldn't talk about her own loss. She'd given so much thought to the reasons for these attacks, and yet she still didn't understand what the terrorists hoped to gain. Was it simply hatred? Retaliation for decades, centuries, of exploitation and subjugation? Maybe that was it. But where would it end?

"On a lighter note," Pamela said, "I have some news."

"What is it?" Jenny asked.

"Yes, tell us," Aislinn said. "Are you moving?"

Pamela frowned. "No, silly, I'm pregnant!"

"That's wonderful," Aislinn said, trying to muster the appropriate level of enthusiasm. "You must be thrilled."

Aislinn couldn't imagine. This would be Pamela's third. The oldest was enrolled in the American School and the little girl would be headed that way in a year or two, but now Pamela, with a newborn on the way, was sentenced to another five years at home. Even with the full time help Pamela's husband could afford, the burden seemed too much. Not to mention the horror of bringing a child into the world now.

The bombing had only made her career more important to her, not less. The world was falling apart, but her place in that world was the only thing that gave her comfort. And was there a place for children? Before Bali, Liam had been urging her to get pregnant so they could have a family of their own, and she'd almost been convinced. "It's the perfect time," he said. "You have help at home. Your job is only part time. Let's do it."

But now? Did it make sense anymore?

She couldn't say that to Pamela and Jenny, though. They'd seen each other nearly every week since her arrival, and Aislinn had come to understand that Jenny didn't want to hear about Aislinn's life before coming to Singapore, or the importance to her of her legal career. Jenny had gone to college at a teachers' college in Illinois and enjoyed her elementary education studies and her sorority life. She and Bruce married right after graduation, and she'd never put her degree to use, had never worked outside the home at all. Their kids had come right away, just two years apart, she and Bruce both had elderly parents, and there was so much to do, especially when Bruce was studying for his MBA. Then one transfer after another, or a new job, packing and unpacking and setting up new households, the grandchildren, the move to Singapore. Working had never been part of her plans, and Aislinn understood that professional women made her uncomfortable. So she didn't bring up her professional life. Or, when stories from her law firm days sprang forth, as they tended to do, she stifled them in order not to unsettle Jenny.

She felt sorry for Jenny. Did that make her a snob? If so, she couldn't help it. She felt sorry for any woman who was trapped the way Jenny was. Smart and capable, but totally dependent on her husband, and entirely defined by her role as wife and mother. Aislinn found it hard to believe it was enough for anyone. Ultimately, it hadn't been enough for her own mother, and it would never be enough for her. Liam seemed to think it could be if she gave it a chance, and Jenny apparently was content. Unless she wasn't and kept it well hidden.

On the other hand, maybe Liam was right. She had a job, but it wasn't demanding. She had Cecilia to help at home. She'd said she wanted children eventually. Maybe now was the time.

12

On a Friday afternoon, the Bradford & Co. receptionist reminded Aislinn that the office would be closed on Monday for a public holiday, Deepavali. The young woman giggled when Aislinn asked what that was, her mouth covered by fingers tipped with glittery, pink nails, but she explained that it was a Hindu festival of lights celebrated by the Indians. She confessed, again through a mask of fingers, that being Chinese, she knew little more than that.

Aislinn understood, vaguely, having learned as much from Martin, that there were both Muslim and Hindu Indians—it was what led to the partition of the Indian subcontinent into separate countries, Pakistan and India, after the UK ended its colonial rule there, as well as much of the sectarian violence that had erupted since then—and that both, along with other Indian religious groups, were represented in Singapore. As a New Yorker, she'd made a point of learning more about Islam after 9/11, dispelling most of the vicious smears that hyper-nationalists in the US spread equating Islam with terrorism, but Hinduism was still a mystery to her.

They'd made one foray to a banana leaf restaurant on Race Course Road on the edge of Little India shortly after they arrived, enjoying the spicy southern Indian curries that were unfamiliar to them, although they ate off the banana leaf with a fork and spoon instead of using their fingers as the locals did. Because Indians made up the third largest ethnic group in Singapore with almost ten percent of the population, she'd been wanting to visit that district again, to learn more about them. Even Liam was eager to see what the festival was all about and agreed to go with her.

Selvadurai had advised her not to drive there, as parking would be a nightmare. The subway line that might get them close was still under construction, so they called a taxi, and that at least took them to the outskirts of Little India before the crowds made car passage impossible. They joined the throng on Serangoon Road that flowed loudly in both directions, like a raging river crashing in on itself. Under beaming strands of lights that hung between buildings on both sides of the street, they made their way among the crush of festivalgoers. Gaudy, she thought, worse than a shopping mall decked out for Christmas, but it was, after all, their festival of lights.

Aislinn had never been terribly bothered by the crowds of New York, or even the human jumble at rock concerts she'd gone to when she was younger, which at the time reminded her of swarms of ants, but this was another magnitude of congestion. There were hundreds of bodies, or thousands, she supposed, packed tightly together, shoulder to shoulder. Being with Liam gave her some comfort, and she held his hand as they made their way, carried forward by the pack, deeper into the morass, but she wished she'd thought to take a button before they left the apartment. It was so loud, with shouts of the revelers, the families and couples, young and old, and music blaring from the shops along the road, the resonant twang of a sitar, the high-pitched warble of a woman's voice in a language beyond her comprehension.

The people around her were Indian, most of the women and girls draped in colorful saris. The sari of the woman directly in front of her was a rich blue, the color of a crisp autumn sky back home, printed with a pattern of gold emblems, flowers maybe, and a border of gold at the neck and sleeves. As they moved forward, toward what Aislinn didn't know, the space between her and the blue sari closed, until her face was pressed nearly into the woman's cascade of lustrous black hair.

198 | THE LAST BIRD OF PARADISE

"Liam," Aislinn said, feeling the panic in her own voice, uncertain if she'd spoken his name aloud. This must be what drowning is like, she thought, the certainty that another breath would not come, that the end was upon her. She dropped Liam's hand and pulled to the right, knifing her arm in front of the man there to claim an opening, shouldering him aside. "Sorry, sorry," she said, and pushed, determined to get to the edge of the crowd.

"Aislinn!" Liam shouted, and she sensed him following in her wake as she plowed ahead.

"Sorry, sorry, sorry," she said again, bolder now, pushing, shuffling, and at last reached the sidewalk. The people nearby, perhaps seeing her panic, parted.

They waited there, Liam deflecting the crush away from her, until the horde thinned. She desperately wanted to sit, to drink something, to be back in the apartment or, better yet, back in New York.

· · · · ·

Although the celebration in Little India had taken place on Sunday, Monday was the official public holiday, and Aislinn's office was closed. Liam's was, too, but he still went into work and was gone most of the day, which was fine with Aislinn. She gave Cecilia the day off, spent part of the day by the pool, and went for a run to shake off the sense of panic from the day before.

On Tuesday morning, they were on the balcony drinking coffee before heading off to work. It felt almost like the old days in New York, except that it was almost November and bloody hot.

"You might want to avoid Jenny Morelock," Liam said.

"I don't see her much as it is now that I'm working," Aislinn said. "But why?"

"You don't want to talk to her just now. Leave it at that."

"But I want to know why." She struggled to keep her voice calm. When Liam made commands like this, which he'd been doing increasingly, it was hard to be around him. He'd talked big about their partnership, but by now she'd recognized that it was just that—talk.

"I'm late." Liam stood, slurping down the rest of his coffee. "I won't be home for dinner," he said without explanation. And then he was gone.

She had no plans to see Jenny Morelock, but now she was curious. What was different today? Had Liam learned something when he was at the office over the holiday, probably by himself? He had already advised her not to get too close to the Morelocks because he didn't expect Bruce to be around much longer, so this must be the day when whatever that was all about came to a head. Fine, she'd avoid Jenny.

· · · · ·

Aislinn spent the morning at the office, but by early afternoon she'd finished the project she was working on—another review of contracts between a Singaporean investor and a US company—and headed home. She was grateful to have the work, but worried that it wasn't enough. She missed the pressure of bigger deals and complex structures and longed for a real job, in an American firm, with a clear career path.

She was at the pool when Liam called. "TJ and I are going out to celebrate. Come join us."

"What are we celebrating?" she asked.

"I'll tell you at dinner."

· · · · ·

The restaurant was in a historic district of Singapore called Emerald Hill that had undergone extensive rehabilitation and repurposing instead of the demolition and rebuilding that had happened in other parts of the city. La Chine was an elegant room in a converted shophouse, and she recognized immediately that it was a French and Chinese fusion restaurant like the one Liam loved in New York. She preferred one or the other, but Liam admired the sort of innovative chef who could create a wild dish that was neither European nor Asian and get away with it.

TJ and Liam were at a table in a quiet corner, a bottle of champagne on ice between them.

"Ah, at last," Liam said, although it was exactly the time he'd given her.

He stood to kiss her cheek and hold her chair.

"Doesn't my wife look stunning?" he asked TJ while the waiter poured the champagne. She was wearing a sleeveless black cocktail dress with a red scarf, a combination she knew Liam loved.

"Radiant," TJ said.

"Thank you, gentlemen."

Liam lifted his glass, first toward TJ's and then Aislinn's. "To success." He drank his glass down and poured another.

After taking a sip, Aislinn said, "Now, will someone tell me what this is all about?"

"This is about meteoric climbs. Rising up against the overlords. This is about friends in high places. This is about replacing fools with men who know what they're doing and how to get things done."

Aislinn now understood that whatever Liam had been planning to do to Bruce had been accomplished. She hated that Liam was taking such delight in what must be a painful situation for the Morelocks.

"What happened?"

"The call came in this morning. Frankly, I was surprised they didn't do it last night. Morelock was told that he was being moved to a subsidiary outfit in Cleveland—even worse than Cincinnati, which is what I originally thought would be appropriate for him. Effective immediately. He's to pack up and go as soon as he can, and he's relieved of duties in the office. I got a call right after that informing me I would be assuming Bruce's responsibilities on an interim basis, but I imagine they'll make that permanent before long. Bruce was out of his office by midafternoon, and I've already moved in."

He poured more champagne for them all.

"I saw Jenny this morning—"

"I told you to avoid her, goddamn it."

"Calm yourself, Liam. I didn't talk to her. I was coming out of our building on my way to work and saw her from a distance. She waved. I don't think she knew then. She was smiling."

"Is their apartment bigger than ours? It's on a higher floor, right? I wonder if we could move into it."

"I think it's exactly the same size and layout. And we've just gotten settled. I'm not moving."

"No, I don't suppose there's anything to be gained. Just a thought."

"I should call her to see how she's doing. She loves it here, you know. I suppose for Bruce it's just a job, but for her it's different."

"Were you not listening? I told you not to talk to her."

"Fine. No talking. But can you tell me something? What was your role in all this?"

"Me? I had nothing to do with it, really, beyond letting Stephens know what was happening. Part of the job was to report what I saw back to New York. TJ here is in regular contact with them, too. They respect him, listen to him. We both made sure they understood what a liability Bruce was. He can't do much damage to the bank in Cleveland, but the decision to move him was all theirs. Frankly, though, I would have fired his pathetic ass."

"They're our friends, Liam."

"Not anymore, they're not."

"Now that it's settled," TJ said, "I think we have an opportunity."

"I like the sound of that," Liam said.

"A deal," TJ said. "A very lucrative deal for the bank."

And why, Aislinn wondered but didn't dare say, did the bank have to wait for Bruce to be out of the way for this very lucrative deal to move forward? She opened her mouth to ask, but sensed Liam's eagerness, his hunger for the carrot TJ had just dangled before him, and stopped herself. Liam used to value her opinion. When did that change? Was it when she gave in to him and sacrificed her own career for his?

"Sounds great," Liam said. "What's the deal?"

"A loan," TJ said. "Short term, high interest. We can discuss the details tomorrow."

"To tomorrow," Liam said, and toasted TJ again.

• • • •

In the morning, the image of Jenny and Bruce making sudden plans to move to Cleveland came back to her. She couldn't ignore them, although that was what Liam had commanded her to do. That may be how Liam dealt with his friends, but it would never be Aislinn's style. After he'd left for work, she plucked up her courage, took the elevator down, walked across the compound to the Morelocks' building, went up in their elevator, and knocked on their door.

Bruce answered.

Although she'd been thinking while walking the short distance between buildings of what to say to Jenny, she hadn't thought of what she might say to Bruce himself. His eyes were filled with suspicion and hurt and anger.

"What do you want?"

"I heard what happened," Aislinn said.

"You have some nerve coming here," Bruce said.

"I'm so sorry, Bruce," she said.

"Who is it?" Jenny called from the kitchen.

"It's Connolly's wife," he said over his shoulder. "Come to gloat, I suppose."

"No, it's not like that at all," Aislinn said.

Jenny appeared at Bruce's side.

"I hope you're proud of what your husband has done," Jenny said. "Or did you two plan this together? 'Let's get rid of the Morelocks?'"

"You've got the wrong idea, both of you."

"You are so fucking naïve," Bruce said. "Or stupid. You must know that your husband orchestrated the whole thing, had his eye on my job from the minute he set foot in the place."

"You're wrong, Bruce. You're our friends."

"No, we're not," Bruce said, and closed the door.

She couldn't blame them for being angry, but none of it had been her doing. Even if this was something Liam planned and executed, which she didn't want to believe, she'd certainly had no part in it. She felt sorry for them, that was all. And maybe a little sorry for herself, too. Jenny had been her only friend here. She felt completely alone.

• • • • •

Before heading into the office, Aislinn stopped by Orientalia. Martin was there, sorting antique maps. She told him she'd been studying the Pennington painting in her office, and she felt she knew the artist, felt a connection to her as if she were present in the woman's garden while she painted.

"I can't get this woman and her pictures out of my head. Are you sure you don't know more about her? Or maybe your father had books that were somehow linked to her?"

"I've been through most of them," Martin said. "But I can't say I was looking for connections to Pennington, so I may have overlooked something. You're welcome to come by the house to have a look. In fact, I'd like that very much."

Liam was heading back to Bangkok, something about the new deal TJ had proposed, so after work, Aislinn went to Martin's house, not far from the Botanic Gardens. It was tidy and well-maintained, with neatly trimmed bushes and a red-tiled roof, in a row of nearly identical bungalows. She knocked on his door and he opened it almost immediately. He dressed casually at the shop, but now he was in a different mode altogether, a tight-fitting T-shirt and jeans. Barefoot, he led the way to the back of the house to a small ground-floor bedroom lined with bookshelves.

"This is it," Martin said. "If there are clues, they're here, somewhere."

Aislinn pulled a book off the shelf. "I asked you this before, but do you have any idea how your father acquired the paintings?"

Martin shook his head. "I figure he bought them somewhere, an estate sale or the like. My guess is that's where a lot of the books and prints in the shop came from, but I don't know that for sure. Maybe they were his personal pieces. But I wasn't here, and I never asked."

She put the book back on the shelf and gazed at the wall, hundreds of volumes, some bound in leather.

"And the books in here I confess I haven't looked at closely. The ones Isabel and I took into the shop were in boxes. These in his bedroom I thought meant more to him for some reason. Silly, I suppose."

"No, I understand completely. When my father died, it was painful to deal with his house and all his things. My brother and I did it all. I thought my mother would come, but they had separated at that point, headed toward a divorce, and I'm sure she felt guilty."

"Guilty?"

"Long story." Aislinn rarely talked about the circumstances of her father's death. Of course, her mother felt guilty. Aislinn's father would not have killed himself if her mother hadn't left him the way she did. She couldn't have known, but she would forever feel responsible. "So, will you take these into the shop as well?"

"I suppose I will. It seems foolish not to. I'm not sure what I was thinking."

Aislinn now took in the rest of the room, the faded curtains, the rumpled bedspread, as if nothing had changed here since his father's death. A small portrait above the bed caught Aislinn's eye and she moved closer. It was the face of a monkey, gazing expectantly at the viewer. Perhaps waiting for the artist to hand over a treat?

"Martin, I think that's another Pennington painting. The colors and the brush strokes, they're the same. I'm sure of it."

"Damn. Can't believe I've never noticed that before."

"Where did it come from?"

"Maybe I was wrong about the estate sale. He must have brought it from the old house, the books too."

"You haven't always lived here?"

"No. We moved here in about 1980, I think. I was a kid, five maybe, but I think that's right."

"And where did you live before that?"

"We were in an old colonial house, a real run-down place. My father had lived there for a long time, before my mother came along. Sorry, I guess I should know that, but I barely remember it."

"So, you used to live in an old house? A Black and White?"

"Yes, I hated it."

She clapped her hands at this new development, feeling as childish as she must have looked. "That's marvelous! Do you know where that house is? Maybe we—or you, I suppose—could get access to it? I looked at one of the restored Black and Whites when we were house hunting. They're amazing."

"Why would you want to get inside our old house?"

"I don't know, just a hunch, really, but I wonder if there isn't some connection between your father and the painter. It just seems odd that he would have this picture here and the ones in the shop. I'm dying to know what it is."

Martin shook his head.

"What's wrong?"

"It's gone, I think. That's why we moved here. The government hated the old houses—colonial remnants of the despised British empire, you know. In a nationalistic rampage they managed to take a lot of the old houses from people and tear them down, then sold the land to developers or built public housing projects on the land. We were assigned to one of those flats for a while, but my parents hated it and somehow found this house."

Aislinn turned back to look at the books. She'd imagined Pennington's diary before, and was it too much to expect she might find it here?

"What are you thinking, Aislinn?"

"I'm still wondering if she kept a diary, something that would help me understand what she was doing here, what she was feeling when she did the paintings." Her fingers trailed across the spines of the books on the nearest shelf.

"If there's a diary," Martin said, "I don't think it's here."

She felt Martin's hand on the small of her back and froze, still facing the books. Now his whole body pressed against her, his arms folded around her. She wanted him, didn't she? Since the day on his sailboat, hadn't she imagined something like this moment? Every day, her relationship with Liam grew more strained, but was she ready to do this to him?

Aislinn shrugged out of Martin's arms, shook her head, unable to speak, to say no, and left his house.

• • • • •

They received next to no mail—everyone she corresponded with in the US used email, and more substantial items, like books or magazines, came through the weekly FedEx parcel from Liam's New York office—but she dutifully checked the box in the apartment building's lobby every day. One afternoon she was rewarded with an invitation to an opening of a gallery showing of Shan Lee's latest work in the Riverwalk gallery district. It pleased her that Lee thought enough of her to invite them, and she was also excited by the prospect of a social engagement that had nothing to do with Liam and his bank.

On the day of the opening reception for the show, she met Liam at his office after work and they took a taxi together. Entering, Aislinn remembered the intimate SoHo gallery where she'd first seen Lee's work, the large paintings of the jungle and the city. This space, though, was immense, and there were far more pieces on display. Guests milled through the old warehouse, studying the work, and a crowd clustered around Lee in the back. As she and Liam strolled, wineglasses in hand, Aislinn admired the new paintings. The jungle was still prevalent, but it seemed populated now by humans as well as animals. And the city paintings were more focused on individual buildings instead of the skyline, textures instead of mere shapes. She remembered how she'd been drawn into the painting in New York and hesitated now to look too closely, but she was pleased to see Liam study several of the pieces. She wondered what he would think if he knew about TJ Kwan's relationship with Lee.

She looked back at the huddle around Lee and caught the artist's eye. Lee waved and broke free of the men who had surrounded her.

"Aislinn!" she called, hurrying toward her. "Thank you so much for coming." And then, in a whisper, "And thank you for giving me an excuse to escape from those philistines."

"I'm honored you invited us." She took Liam's arm. "Shan, this is my husband, Liam Connolly. Liam, Shan Lee."

Liam shook her hand. "It's the philistines who have the money to buy art, I think."

Lee laughed. "Indeed. That's why they're here! Speaking of which, let me greet some new arrivals." She dashed off to shake more hands.

When she was gone, Liam and Aislinn drifted in different directions. Liam seemed particularly drawn to a painting of a skyscraper sprouting leaves and branches, but Aislinn found herself fascinated by a picture of a setting she recognized as the garden behind Lee's house. The picture, in realistic detail, less impressionistic than Lee's customary style, portrayed a nude woman lying in the grass, surrounded by a jungle that was closing in on her. Tendrils reached out from the dense growth and seemed to be alive, growing closer to the woman as Aislinn watched. She had difficulty pulling away from the painting, fearful as she was for what she knew was going to happen to the woman. Did Lee feel threatened by something? Did she feel the jungle closing in?

Aislinn looked for Liam and saw him seated in front of a desk, engaged in conversation with a gray-haired gentleman in a batik shirt. Now they were both standing and shaking hands, as if some kind of deal had been struck.

"We are now the proud owners of a Shan Lee original," Liam said when he rejoined her, and guided her by the elbow to the painting of the skyscraper he'd been admiring.

Aislinn stood before the painting, taking it all in. It was over-sized, nearly six feet square, like most of Lee's work. The building was a glass tower—no actual edifice she recognized—with roiling black clouds behind it. At ground level, the skyscraper was surrounded by growth, the seething jungle that was ever-present in Lee's paintings. What was striking, though, was the vine snaking out of the ground that wrapped itself around the building, spreading branches that climbed in all directions, including one that seemed to be reaching out to the viewer. Like the garden painting Aislinn had admired, this one felt threatening.

"It's stunning, Liam. For your office? Or our living room? You might have consulted me, but I do like it. Whatever possessed you?"

"A tip from TJ. I mentioned you were dragging me to this opening, and he said he knew the artist, that a piece with her name on it was a great investment."

"An investment."

"Well, sure, I mean, I like the thing, too, but it's a bonus if it makes sense financially, isn't it?"

"And did TJ say how he knew the artist?"

"Not that I recall. Why?"

A figure moved behind Liam then, his back to them, but she was sure it was Martin. As he turned, her smile rose involuntarily, which caused Liam to turn. But it wasn't Martin, and the man moved on, studying the paintings.

"Who was that?"

"No one," she said. "Just someone I thought I knew."

· · · · ·

On Sunday night, with Cecilia on her one day off, they were having a quiet dinner at home. Aislinn had made spaghetti, garlic bread, and salad. She'd uncorked a nice red wine, an expensive Bordeaux that Liam liked, and they sat down in the dining room under the Pennington paintings.

Liam was in an expansive mood, filled with the exhilaration of moving into the corner office that had been Bruce's, discovering more and more flaws in Bruce's management of the joint venture, even the people he had hired.

"I fired his secretary Friday," Liam said. "The way the labor laws work here, it's going to cost us to get rid of her, but I just couldn't have her around anymore. She actually cried when Bruce left the office, and she didn't look happy the next morning to see me in his chair."

"You fired her for not looking happy?"

"It was more than that, obviously. But I just couldn't trust that she'd be loyal."

"It sounds to me like she's very loyal."

"Yeah, but to the wrong guy."

• • • • •

The following Saturday, while Liam was in Bangkok again, Aislinn was surprised by a knock on the apartment door. It was Jenny.

"Would you like coffee, Jenny?"

"I can't stay. This isn't a social call."

"Please don't be angry with me, Jenny. I told you, I—we—had nothing to do with what happened."

"I believe *you* didn't, Aislinn, and that's why I'm here. For your sake. I think you should know what Liam has been doing behind your back."

"Oh, Jenny. Don't start that. It's so transparent. You claimed Liam lied about Bruce, and now you're going to do the same thing to get back at him."

"A friend of ours saw him. In Hong Kong. Last night. With a woman."

"That's ridiculous," Aislinn said, although she knew it wasn't ridiculous at all. She knew all too well that Liam was capable of cheating. "Liam's not even in Hong Kong. He's in Bangkok with TJ."

"I'm sure that's what he told you. But my source—this is someone from the bank's Hong Kong office we've known for a long time—spoke with him. It was Liam, all right."

"Then there's an explanation. It's beneath you to gossip like this, Jenny. Liam told me to stay away from you, but I thought we could be friends."

"I don't even blame Liam for the trouble he caused. TJ's behind it all, I'm sure. Bruce never trusted the man. And you and Liam better watch your backs."

When Jenny left, Aislinn closed the door and sank against it. Was Liam really having an affair? What did she expect? That's who he was, after all, and it probably wasn't the first time. Had he been faithful in New York? She wondered. And what did Jenny's warning about TJ mean? He'd seemed charming at first, but she'd had an uneasy feeling about TJ for some time. What kind of danger might he pose? She hadn't told Liam about the jacket or TJ's visit to her office, the warning he'd delivered, but what exactly could TJ do to her? Or to them?

· · · · ·

Liam was due back from Bangkok. Aislinn sat in their living room, reading a novel, a luxury she had rarely indulged in when she lived in New York. There was never enough time, and when she did have time, she was too exhausted, mentally and physically, to engage in some writer's fantasy, no matter how realistic it was. The real world was strange enough. But now, she didn't know what to do with her time, and so she'd picked up this book by D. H. Lawrence at Martin's shop, one published around the time Pennington was in Singapore. She had hoped to find another collection of stories by Preston, to see if he'd written more about the girl he called Molly, but nothing had turned up at Orientalia. She sipped wine and turned the page.

Footsteps outside, a key in the lock, and the door opened. Liam entered, dropping his suit bag on the floor. She got up and kissed him.

"That was nice," he said. "Do that again."

She did. "I missed you," she said. "How was Bangkok?" She almost said, "Hong Kong," knowing that Jenny's accusation was possibly true.

"Crowded," he said. "You've never seen traffic jams like they have there. We're lucky to be in Singapore."

"There's wine open. Want some?"

"Sure. Let me take a quick shower first."

"Want me to join you?"

"That sounds wonderful. But I'm beat. Rain check?" He kissed her on the cheek and headed toward their bedroom.

She picked up his suit bag, followed him to the bedroom, and laid the bag on the bed. He stripped off his jacket and tie, the shirt. He pulled off his pants, and she watched his broad back and firm ass disappear into the bathroom. The water ran in the shower.

"What did you do while I was away?" he called over the splash of water. "Anything exciting?"

"Not really. Just investigated that painter."

"What painter?" He was inside the shower now and she imagined his body, the fine hair on his chest, water running down his flat stomach and streaming off his penis. She rarely initiated sex with Liam because she didn't have to, but now she slipped out of her clothes, entered the bathroom, and pulled the shower open.

"What are you doing, Aislinn?"

"I need a shower, too." She stretched to kiss him and reached for his cock.

"I'm tired, Aislinn."

"Too tired to fuck your wife?" She was angry, thinking that Liam was cheating on her, and she wanted him to prove her wrong.

He returned her kisses and responded to the attention of her hand. He turned off the water, and they stood in the shower, kissing, groping.

They toweled each other off and moved to the bed. He pressed into her, and she closed her eyes.

• • • • •

The next day, she promised herself she wouldn't give another thought to Jenny's accusation. And yet, she did think of it. Had Liam been with someone in Hong Kong? She remembered the secret rendezvous they'd had when their affair began. He would plan business trips and invite her to meet him in Chicago or Miami or wherever. They would be booked into separate hotels but would generally stay in hers. They'd make love in the king-sized bed and order room service or dine out in dark and obscure restaurants and come back to make love again. Did he ever return to his wife and tell her he was too tired for sex? Probably Janice hadn't climbed into the shower with him when he got home, and probably she hadn't asked him to make love to her or hadn't expected it. If she had, would he have had such vigor as he'd had last night? If Aislinn and Liam had made love in the afternoon before his flight home, would he have begged off at first with Janice and then, if compelled, lasted twice as long as usual, unable to reach his climax a second time so soon?

Liam was a handsome man, with a body he kept toned through tennis and swimming and regular visits to the gym. He could have other women. Probably she hadn't been the first woman he'd cheated on Janice with. His daughter had suspected as much, and Aislinn had heard rumors at the firm. A senior associate had hinted that she'd slept with Liam when she'd worked on an earlier project for the bank, before Aislinn arrived on the scene. They'd had fun, she'd said, and both had moved on. That woman had advised Aislinn to get out while she could, but Aislinn hadn't believed her. She thought she was in love. She *was* in love, and she was still in love. Nothing had changed, really. She wasn't particularly happy with her life in Singapore right now, and she still wanted to revive her career, but their relationship was salvageable. He had a temper, and had frightened her when it became physical, but that was under control most of the time. Probably it was the result of the stress he was under to produce business for the bank. He was more domineering now than he used to be, but that could be stress, too. Or was she still making excuses for him?

She didn't want to believe he was cheating on her, but maybe he was. How could she know?

· · · · ·

Shan Lee called to propose an outing.

"I'm planning to do a little plein air sketching and thought you might want to come along. We have this odd thing in Singapore called the Bird Park. It's way out in Jurong and terribly touristy, but it's one of those places you have to see to believe."

"I love birds!" Aislinn said, looking into Mack's cage, where he returned her gaze as if he knew she was talking about him. "We have a macaw here, and my father had birds at home when I was growing up. It sounds fun!"

She made her way to the bungalow, and Shan bounded down the front steps to meet her. Aislinn put her hand to her hair, acknowledging that Lee's hair was now cut short, a garden of spikes. "I know!" Shan said. "What do you think? TJ hates it."

"I love it."

Lee drove them out to the Bird Park in her green MGB, a cute two-seater, with the top down. Aislinn hadn't been in one of these since college, when one of her sorority sisters had a red model she loved. She imagined her hair flowing in the wind behind them as they raced down the highway, except her hair was so short now, and Lee's was even shorter.

As they pulled into the parking lot, a tour bus disgorged a small army of Koreans, led by a short man in a yellow hat bearing a yellow flag.

"As I said," Shan said, "it's a tourist's Mecca." She grabbed Aislinn's hand, and they hurried to the entrance to beat the Koreans into the park.

Aislinn had never been anywhere like this place. Even the zoos she'd visited in America kept their bird specimens caged, but here the birds flew freely in wide-open spaces. Lee found a bench and opened her sketch pad while Aislinn wandered. When she was a girl, her father had fostered a rotating menagerie of parrots, and she'd grown fond of having Mack around in their apartment here, but this was a unique experience. As she passed into an area dense with trees, a flame-red bird nearly the size of a wild turkey flew over her head and squawked. At her? Had she disturbed it? But no, there was another large red bird, a scarlet macaw, she thought, in a nearby tree. Then a green bird she couldn't identify swooped from one tree to another, and a feeling of guilt stabbed Aislinn for keeping Mack confined. Wouldn't he be much happier in an environment like this? Next, she came to a pool and waterfall where dozens of flamingos waded, a sea of pink birds.

She continued to wander through the park, dodging the swarms of tourists. Some bird specimens were caged, she discovered, with signs that explained they were rare or, in some cases, new acquisitions being acclimated. She could relate and wondered how long it would be before these beautiful creatures would earn their freedom. In one exhibit she saw a bird with almost unbelievable plumage, orange feathers draped behind like a train. She nodded in recognition when she read the sign that identified this magnificent specimen as a bird of paradise, which made her think of the painting in her office.

She found a refreshment stand, bought two bottles of water, then joined Lee on her bench with her sketch pad.

"Perfect," Lee said. "That's exactly what I needed. You're an angel."

"Or some variety of winged thing, anyway. This place is amazing. I've never seen so many birds before, and so many exotic species. Just now, I saw an incredible creature called a bird of paradise. I've seen the flower with that name, but the bird itself is something from another world."

Lee laughed. "I love that bird so much, and the flower, too. When I was a girl and had really long hair, I gave myself a secret name—Niao Hua, which means Bird Flower."

"I love that," Aislinn said. "Niao Hua. And I love this place."

"I like to complain about the government—it's a favorite pastime of my generation of Singaporeans—but they've done some things extraordinarily well. The Bird Park is unique as an attraction—the walk-in aviary, where the birds fly free, is astonishing—and they also do amazing conservation work, rescuing birds, protecting endangered species, and so on. If I ever left Singapore, this is the one place I would miss."

"And now you're going to be painting birds?"

"That's kind of embarrassing. I feel like a sellout. But TJ got me a commission from Singapore Airlines to do a series of aviation related paintings. I couldn't bring myself to paint pictures of jumbo jets, but I had this idea to do birds instead. I pitched the idea, and they loved it.

I'll try to do a decent job of it while pocketing the filthy lucre. And then I can get back to doing more meaningful work."

They laughed. Aislinn wasn't surprised that TJ had connections with the airline and probably with every other big company in the city.

When Lee had done what she needed to do, they left the park and returned to Orchard Road in the MGB.

"I have an idea," Aislinn said as they pulled into her apartment complex. "Come up for a glass of wine. Let me show you where we're planning to put the painting of yours my husband bought."

"A lovely way to end the day. I accept."

With glasses of chardonnay in hand, they toured the flat. Aislinn first introduced Lee to Mack, who squawked something unintelligible. Then she led the way to the bedrooms, including the master suite where she'd hung her Miro lithograph and the O'Keeffe poster. Lee nodded appreciatively, but Aislinn could tell she wasn't impressed. It all seemed trite to her now, seeing it through the eyes of this artist. In the living room, they paused before the blank wall where Lee's painting would go.

"That's perfect," Lee said. "I love this spot, with the large potted palm almost in reach, a virtual extension of the jungle in the painting. I'm honored. Really. Please thank your husband for me."

What Aislinn really wanted to show her, though, were the Pennington paintings, so she steered Lee toward the dining room.

"I know these," she said. "The style, at any rate. Like the one you saw at my place. How odd to see them here!"

"That's right. I'd bought them at Orientalia and made the connection when I saw the one you have. I can't explain it, but they really speak to me."

"The shop at Tanglin? I haven't been there in years. Curious that they'd have these paintings."

"I'm trying to find out more about the artist. Apparently, she was an Englishwoman who lived here during the First World War. That's not much to go on, I know, and Martin—that's the owner of the shop—didn't know more."

Aislinn noticed—or thought she noticed—Lee flinch at the mention of Martin's name. She poured more wine for them both.

"I should tell you, I suppose. I know Martin. Knew him. When we were younger, in school."

"Classmates?"

"More than classmates."

"I see."

"I'm not sure what happened, exactly, but we were from different worlds. I got serious about art, and he did his mandatory national service and then went off to Australia, and, well, life went on."

Aislinn tried to imagine Martin and Shan together and realized that what she was feeling was jealousy. What did it matter that this man, nothing more than a friend, if she could even call him that, had been Lee's lover?

When they were on their second bottle, they sat in the light reflected by the blank living room wall where Lee's painting would hang. They both gazed at the wall as if the picture were already there, and then Aislinn looked at Shan, grateful at last to have made a friend. She saw again there was color in Lee's eyes, not the typical dark Chinese eyes. What could cause that, she wondered.

"What are you staring at?" Lee asked.

"I'm so sorry," Aislinn said. "It's the wine, I'm afraid, and now I'm going to embarrass myself further. Your eyes are beautiful."

Lee lifted her hand to her eyes as if to shield them from Aislinn's view, but when she lowered her hand, she was smiling.

"Most people don't have the grit to say anything about them. I like that about you. I used to be so self-conscious about my eyes, so different from everyone else I grew up with. I even got brown contacts for a while to hide the color, but that was just annoying. My parents didn't have an explanation or claimed they didn't. But when my grandmother died, I learned the truth, or what I now understand is the truth. Her husband, who died before I was born, had a white father. No one knew who he was, apparently, and so that was the end of it. Not uncommon in the colonial period. Other Chinese get it by looking at me, even if to the rest of the world I'm just another Chinese girl. Eventually I came to appreciate that I was different, my own woman, not like everyone else. I guess that's why I've always had a rebellious streak in me."

They stared at the wall again, and Aislinn saw the painting—which wasn't yet there—come alive, the jungle reaching for the city.

"It was TJ who suggested to my husband that he buy your work," Aislinn said. "As an investment."

Lee had been slumping on the sofa, the wine apparently getting to her, but now she seemed to gather herself. She got to her feet, stumbling, but kept her balance.

"I have to go," she said.

"I'm sorry," Aislinn said. "Did I say something wrong?"

Lee grabbed her purse from the coffee table, nearly knocking over the wine bottle in the process. Was she crying?

"Shan," Aislinn said, "what's the matter?"

"I don't know what to do," she said, and collapsed onto the sofa again. "I tried to end it. I tried to tell him I couldn't live like this anymore. He can't leave his wife, even if he wanted to. Even if I wanted him to. I'm not sure what I want anymore. But I feel trapped."

"I think I know the feeling."

"I don't know what to do."

"Leave. Can't you? You're a successful artist. You're established. You can be on your own."

"You don't know TJ," Lee said. "He would never allow it."

· · · · ·

She had come to Martin's house, she said, to search his father's bookshelves, looking again for any trace of Elizabeth Pennington, or Edmund Preston, or anything that would shed light on the painter and the paintings. She no longer knew why she cared or why she was interested in them but couldn't stop now. What had she overlooked? She'd found nothing in the father's bedroom, other than the portrait of the monkey that seemed to watch her as she worked, touching each volume, examining it for clues, replacing it on the shelf.

Now back in the living room, Aislinn took another look at the books on the shelf there but saw nothing that appeared to be tied to Pennington.

"Would you join me in a glass of wine?" Martin asked. He was being cautious, she thought, after she'd rebuffed him on her last visit. And now she wondered what had happened between him and Shan Lee.

"That would be lovely," she said. "It seems I'm in no great hurry to get home."

Martin went to the kitchen and returned with a bottle of chardonnay. Aislinn sat on the sofa, and she thought he might join her there, but he settled into an armchair opposite. Cautious, yes.

"I've been thinking about the families that have lived in Singapore for generations," Aislinn said. "Like yours, and the gentleman who runs the law firm I work for. And maybe the artist, for all we know. Might her descendants be here still?" And TJ Kwan, she thought. He and Martin were from very different social strata, but might there be a connection?

"What do you know about TJ Kwan?" she asked.

"Kwan? Not much. One of the richest men in Singapore, I think. Why do you ask?" There was an edge to his response, as if she'd raised a painful topic, and she remembered Shan Lee's similar reaction when they'd first talked about TJ.

"My husband works with Kwan, and…I don't trust him."

"You have good instincts."

"Why do you say that? Is there something about Kwan I should know?"

Martin set down his wineglass and went upstairs, returning with a framed photograph.

"This is my mother, a snap taken in, I don't know, maybe '78?" The woman in the picture was in a white nurse's uniform and cap, a tired smile on her face. "I was still an ankle-biter. From what I understand from my father, Kwan was briefly a patient at the hospital where Mum worked. He set his sights on her, and he was already back then used to getting what he wanted. When she gave him the cold shoulder, he made life hell for my father, trying to break down her resistance. It's the main reason she started spending more and more time in Melbourne."

"Did that work? He gave up?"

"He found a new target, someone younger, and eventually left us alone. It didn't stop my father from doing some digging in his spare time, though. Just in case Kwan tried to cause trouble. Insurance, you might say."

"Digging?"

"For dirt. He built quite a file of information about Kwan's activities, some legit, some questionable. He called it his 'dossier.' Insurance."

"Questionable? Really? And do you have this 'dossier' now?"

Martin shook his head. "It might still be here, somewhere, but I haven't come across it. My guess is he let it go after Mum died. It didn't seem to matter anymore."

If there was dirt to be found, maybe she should do her own digging. Jenny had warned her TJ was dangerous. If that was true, Liam needed to know. She put her wineglass down. "I should be going." She stood.

"Don't go," he said. "I mean, unless you want to. I was going to make supper, nothing fancy, but I'd like it if you stayed."

"That's tempting," she said, honestly. She wanted to stay. "But I really should go. Liam calls, you know, and I should be home when he does." Sheer nonsense, of course. Liam hardly ever called when he was traveling, and if he did, he'd try her cell phone, which was in the purse she clutched now.

Martin followed her to the door. She had her fingers on the knob when she felt his hand on her shoulder. She turned, electrified by his touch, and found his face coming toward hers. He kissed her, and because she wanted nothing more than to be kissed by him, she let him. She felt his arms wrap firmly around her, as if he could not let her go. Her entire body shook, reacting as it had not done since the early days of her affair with Liam.

She couldn't be doing this. She was married. It wasn't right. She lifted her arms and gently pushed Martin away.

"Don't," she said.

"I haven't felt this way in a long time," Martin said. "And I know you feel something, too."

"I'm married," she said. That hadn't mattered to Liam, of course, back in New York, and maybe now.

"Since when does that stop anyone? If it did, we'd all be dried up and dead. It's what we want. It's why you came here tonight, isn't it?"

"No. The painter—"

"I don't believe you."

"I'm a married woman who can't give you what you want." And, she wanted to say, a married woman who knew exactly what it was like to be in his place. Wasn't he making the same rationalization she had made just a few years ago? She didn't give a damn about Liam's wife at the time, not really, despite her protests to the contrary. The only thing that mattered then was what she wanted, and that was Liam.

"If this wasn't what you were after, Aislinn, why did you come?" He reached for her hand and this time she let him take it. He pulled her back into his arms and kissed her again. "Your husband doesn't have to know. No one needs to know. This is what we both want."

He led her to the stairs. She knew it was a mistake, but she'd already made too many mistakes. Too many. She shouldn't have come to Singapore. She shouldn't have excused Liam's behavior when he threw her on the bed when he was angry. And yet, there was no one waiting for her at home and here was a man who wanted her.

In his bedroom, there was only dim light. He unbuttoned her blouse, her skirt. He pulled off his T-shirt. Her hands reached for his warm skin and felt the soft covering of hair. She felt his chest rise and fall and heard his breath.

"I've wanted you since the first day in the shop," he said into her ear as he unclasped her bra.

He pulled her onto the bed. She wrapped her arms around his shoulders, and he kissed her. Now his hand was between her legs, gently caressing her. He lifted one leg over hers, and then his jeans came off, they were both naked on the bed, and he rolled on top of her, his erection easing into her, in no rush now, she was his, they could take their time, there was no reason to hurry.

· · · · ·

It was fully dark when Aislinn left Martin's. He offered to drive her home or call a taxi, but she said no. She didn't say there shouldn't be a record of a cab picking her up there, at the home of this man. The truth was, she knew too well how to avoid detection by a suspicious spouse. She'd walk out to Bukit Timah, a major thoroughfare, and get a cab there. He wanted to go with her, but she vetoed that, too. No, she said. They shouldn't be seen together.

On Martin's street there was no traffic, but on the main road, the cars streamed past. She found a streetlight and a taxi stand, and soon there was a cab and it stopped. She nearly sent it on its way and turned around to go back, to spend the night with Martin, but she knew she couldn't. She could never go back to that house.

13

16 January 1915

A message has come from Charles, canceling our plan to meet at the joss house. I am stricken with the news, and not a little angry. We have not been together in days, and the change in plans injects into me a poison. Does Charles have another woman he sees when he is not with me? One of the Japanese women I have heard about, or maybe one of the pretty Chinese girls I have seen in the vicinity of the temple?

Lt. Raj, the loyal messenger, waited for my reply.

"Lieutenant," I asked, "do you have a wife at home?"

"I do," he said, after a moment's hesitation in which he seemed to ponder why I had asked and how much about himself to divulge.

"Are you faithful to her?"

"Miss?"

"No, that's unfair of me to ask. But is she faithful to you?" I knew I had confounded the poor man, but I pressed on.

"Miss?"

"But of course she is. You are Mohammedan, are you not?"

"Miss?"

"Don't move," I said, and ran to get my sketch pad.

Although he was waiting for my reply to return to Captain Bingham, I found that I could not take my eyes from this dark man's face. His black eyebrows, the brown lips that held his mouth together in a gentle oval, the high, tight collar that seemed to stretch his neck to impossible lengths. He had been carrying messages between Charles and me for some time, but this was perhaps the first time I had ever really looked at him. A married man, far from home, far from his children and wife. In need of comfort. A young white woman, perhaps. The lover of his superior officer. Is that desire I saw in those black eyes? Should I fear this man?

"What are you thinking, Lieutenant?"

"Do you have a message for Captain Bingham, Miss? I must be returning to the barracks."

"How do you feel about carrying these messages for your captain? Are you not curious? Do you know what your captain says to me in these messages? Would you be shocked by what he says?"

"I only carry the messages, Miss. I do not read them."

"No, of course not. He is your captain. But perhaps you would be shocked after all."

I sketched. I reached out and touched his chin, intending only to turn his face to catch the light, but he recoiled as if an electric current had jolted him. And so perhaps it had, because now he looked at me differently. Just as I had not seen him, he had not truly seen me before, I think. His eyes were open wide.

"Now what are you thinking, Lieutenant?" He had the most beautiful eyes. Foreboding, dark, beautiful eyes.

"I cannot say," he said.

I put down my pad and pencil, took up the note he had carried from Captain Bingham, and wrote my reply.

18 January 1915

Captain Bingham has not summoned me now in some days. I am not sure what to think of this, but I fear it is the case that he believes he has won me, and having won me, has no need of me. Or, perhaps, as I have guessed before, there is another woman, or he finds his comfort in one of the settlement's brothels. I am tempted, I am not ashamed to admit, to visit unannounced to see what I might learn.

No doubt I am being silly, and altogether too dependent on the good captain. After all, I was not coerced, and I did not act against my will. With Richard Bromley I was much younger and did not fully understand what was happening. With Charles, though, I freely submitted to his desires and, in truth, returned them in full. In short, I also obtained what I wanted. But is that all? He will soon be gone, and so perhaps it is just as well that our imaginary marriage was only that.

Still, I have conceived of a plan. I have taken the notion that I will go to him at the barracks, not the hideaway next to the joss house. If he will not come to me or send for me, then I shall go to him. We will profess our love in public or he will refuse me, and either way, the matter will be resolved.

Between the declaration of my intention and the performance of the deed lies a great distance. I may reconsider. Or I may not.

19 January 1915

Uncle had gone to Courts early this morning, and I was at home when Lieutenant Raj appeared. At last, I thought, a message from Captain Bingham.

In fact, though, it was not. Raj had brought his own enigmatic message.

"Miss," he said, "I would like to suggest that you make plans to visit Penang for the coming holiday. I believe you have relations there."

"Penang? For the Chinese New Year?"

"Yes, Miss."

"Why on earth would I want to do that?"

"I cannot say, Miss." And with that, he left.

He cannot say? It immediately crossed my mind that I should like to discuss the matter with Charles. But Charles has chosen to ignore me, it seems, and, besides, it might not do to tell him that his lieutenant had come to our house unbidden and not on Charles's command. For the same reason, I thought I could not speak of the matter to Uncle Cyril. Such a mystery are these men. What shall I do?

We do have relations in Penang or in nearby Butterworth, the Feddersons, and so a visit might not be questioned, but why now? And then I remembered the exhibition that was to open on the holiday, so of course my absence would be impossible. Still, what was I to make of the suggestion? Mrs. Craddock was perhaps the only person in whom I might confide, and so I resolved to call on her in the afternoon.

20 January 1915
When I visited with Mrs. Craddock yesterday afternoon, I was not surprised to find Mrs. Framingham also in attendance. And, given the latter's residence in Penang, that suited my purposes well.

We first spoke about the painting work, and I did not admit that it had come along slowly.

"I have been painting the most marvelous flowers in the garden," I said. "The bird of paradise is like nothing I have ever seen. And while the canvas does not compare to the thing itself, the colors are glorious." What I did not say is that I have completed little else in the last two weeks, only sketches in my pad or unfinished paintings on my easel.

"We are more than keen to see what you have done, Elizabeth," Mrs. Framingham said.

"And speaking of the coming holiday," I said, laughing at the perplexed looks on the faces of my hosts, who had said nothing about the holiday, "I wonder if now would be a good time to visit Penang?"

"Is there any particular reason you would want to go to Penang now, my dear? Although the notorious Emden has been captured, we've heard reports of other German vessels wreaking havoc on shipping lanes. I wonder if such a voyage would even be safe. Don't you think it would be best to wait? Surely the war cannot last much longer, and then we can all get back to normal."

"Yes, of course, that is a concern," I said, although honestly I had not thought at all about the trip being dangerous, and now I wondered if Mrs. Framingham intended to remain in Singapore until the war was concluded. Naturally, I knew about the capture of the Emden—that ship's crew were held at the Tanglin prison along with all German males previously resident in the settlement under suspicion of espionage—but I suppose I thought the danger had passed along with the capture. There was a train, though, was there not? "What about rail?" I asked.

Both women laughed heartily. I was naïve, but I was determined to learn if it would even be possible to get to Penang for the holiday if I wanted to, which I was by no means certain that I did.

"We are laughing, my dear, at the thought of an unaccompanied woman traveling by train through the jungles of Malaya. I dare say there is no wilder corner of the empire and a terrain that would put off even the bravest souls. It would be ill-advised, to put it mildly."

I was rather offended by the dismissive tone. Had I not recently traveled alone from England, thousands of miles through dangerous waters in the company of rough and tumble sailors? But perhaps the ladies were right. I could not disclose the reason for my inquiry, but it now appeared that the options available to me would not be undertaken easily. I resolved to learn more from Lieutenant Raj—or perhaps Charles—the cause of his advice.

I did not have to wait long, for Raj was on the veranda when I returned to Uncle's house.

"Lieutenant Raj," I said, "just the man I wanted to see."

He must not have observed the grin on my face because he turned to me in all seriousness and said, "You wanted to see me, Miss?"

"Yes, to ask about what you said earlier. But first, do you have a message from Captain Bingham?"

He did. He handed an envelope to me. I excused myself to read it inside the house, so as not to reveal too much of myself to Raj, which was wiser than I knew, because from the moment I opened the letter I felt the heat rise, and I thought I might have turned the color of the Chinese paper lanterns hanging in our garden. Let me say here only that the silly thoughts of Charles abandoning me vanished instantly and my longing for him returned. How could I have doubted dear Charles? He wanted me to come to him at our usual place.

But how could I? He had left me hanging for days. Wasn't this the perfect opportunity to make my own needs known to him? That he durst not take me for granted as he had done? And so I wrote a message to him for Raj to carry.

When I returned to the veranda, Raj waited. I handed him the note, but the look of puzzlement that sprang to his face made me laugh, since I was once again in the mood to laugh.

"What's wrong?" I asked.

"No reply," he said.

"I beg your pardon?"

"Captain Bingham, Miss. He does not expect a reply."

"No, I don't suppose he does. But then why have you waited?"

He took my hand.

• • • • •

Well, no, of course he didn't take my hand. That would have been nonsense. He did nothing of the kind. He did not gaze longingly into my eyes, although he did have deep, dark eyes that expressed—not longing, exactly, but sympathy, perhaps. We were both commanded by Captain Bingham, ruled by him, in our ways, and so there was a kind of solidarity between us.

But, no, not that either. He was waiting to be dismissed. Nothing more.

"Miss, you said you had wanted to ask me a question."

"Did I? I suppose I did." But something had changed. Penang was impossible, and I knew that now. "I seem to have forgotten. Perhaps it will come back to me another time. Thank you, Raj." He turned at heel and left.

Just then, Uncle arrived, encountering Raj in the drive.

"The lieutenant said he carried a message from Captain Bingham," Uncle harrumphed when he had climbed the steps to the veranda. He was nearly out of breath, which gave me time to consider the question and to concoct a suitable response.

"Charles has invited us to tea at the mess," I said, a patently absurd lie. "But I know you are especially busy at this time of year, and I sent our regrets."

"A pity. I should like to have visited the barracks, but you are quite right, my dear. Another time perhaps."

"Uncle," I said, "Can you think of any reason I—or we—should visit Penang for the Chinese New Year?"

"Why, no, Lizzie. Unnecessary travel is not recommended these days. The Germans are afoot, you know. It may be safer here than in Europe just now, but we're better off within the city walls, so to speak."

So, no trip to Penang. I do wonder what Raj might have been thinking, and perhaps I should have pressed him on the matter, but I do not believe he was inclined to tell me in any event.

21 January 1915

The painting of Lieutenant Raj is progressing nicely. I am not much for portraiture, I must confess, and yet this likeness of him—although perhaps "likeness" is not the right word, because I have allowed myself liberties—does please me. I have captured the rich, dark skin that is almond in color, and the nose that is much more prominent than the Chinese nose and somewhat akin to the Greeks and Romans. His brown-black mysterious eyes come through, as well, although I have not quite got his look of sympathy, or pity, or whatever it is he may be feeling towards me.

Truly, though, what can I do with this painting? I certainly cannot include it in the exhibition. What if Charles should see it, which he most certainly will. I'm afraid the portrait shows far more affection for my subject than the good captain would appreciate. But why should I not be fond of his messenger? Did Pauline not feel kindly toward Cyrano? Charles would not understand, I fear. Or perhaps he would understand too well. And so it is best that I keep this little picture to myself.

It gives me the notion, however, of doing another portrait, one of Charles. I could invite him here for that purpose, on a Sunday when I would expect Uncle to be present as well, believing he was providing us with a rare opportunity to be together. They could chatter about the war, or whatever they chose, and I could paint. Perhaps I would paint them both. And why not? Whereas at one time my father and Richard Bromley were the most important men in my life, their places have been supplanted by Uncle Cyril and Captain Bingham. It is only fitting that I should render them together in this way, to be remembered for posterity.

22 January 1915

If only I could dismiss this as a dream, but neither is it real. I cannot get Lieutenant Raj out of my mind, and that is the oddest thing of all. Each time I dismiss him from my thoughts, he returns. Captain Bingham is not far off in my thinking, either, which makes the fascination with his dark-skinned junior officer all the more perplexing and, even for me, shameful. I do not think women have such thoughts as I have had, about either Charles or Raj, much less both men. And worse, Richard Bromley appears, while I had all but forgotten him with the healing passage of time. Because now they all blend together and, in my fantasy, I am not sure which of them is in my arms. I am not sure in whose bed I wish to lie. It is most troubling.

Perhaps this is the reason for Raj's warning to me to leave for Penang. He has bewitched me, it seems, and he bade me slip beyond his spell before it is too late. What other explanation can there be? But it is already too late. His magic, whatever magic these Mohammedans work, has its grasp on me and will not easily be undone. It is I who may be undone.

Just in time, Charles has summoned me. The messenger is another man, not Raj, not an officer. He handed me the envelope with a sharp bow and immediately withdrew, but only after sneaking a glance at me, his superior officer's lover. What stories would he tell? This time, instead of being vexed at Captain Bingham's presumptuousness, I had no choice but to comply, for it was all that I wished.

22 January, Evening

It is late now, and I have returned from seeing Charles. We did not speak. We were together, but we could not utter a word. I did not dream of Raj.

When Uncle asks where I have been, I shall have to tell him something—that I had imposed upon Mrs. Burke so that I might play her piano and lost track of the time, or I was asked to give drawing lessons to her daughter Daisy. Any lie I tell him is sure to be found out, but what option do I have?

23 January 1915

The girl May has reappeared. Her absence for these three weeks remains unexplained. I have not attempted to interrogate her, and when I asked Lao Po where the girl had been, she shrugged as if she did not know the answer, but I believe it is far more likely that she did not respond because she did not wish to tell me a lie, and she would not tell the truth. Uncle is aware of the girl's return, but I can detect no interest one way or the other. She serves my breakfast, but by the time Uncle has emerged, she has moved on to other chores around the house. I will get to the bottom of this mystery.

The light this morning was exceptional, and I put it to good use, capturing the likeness of a second bird of paradise, smaller and more delicate than the first. On the canvass, the flower took on a new life, as if generating its own light. It is all but unrecognizable, but I can see the passion in it, the stem and the heart of the flower, the carnality, and I pour into it my soul. It will be my secret, I think, but perhaps Charles alone will take my meaning.

24 January 1915

We have been to Government House. Uncle was summoned along with other senior residents of the settlement, and he took me along, although

I protested. I did not much want to hear what the Governor had to say, and because I was not invited, I felt that I did not belong, although I found that irksome enough. In the event, though, several of the men brought their wives with them, and I did not feel so out of place after all. I left Uncle's side and joined Mrs. Craddock and Mrs. Framingham while we waited for the Governor to emerge and make whatever announcement was to be made. I doubted it had any connection to me, unless—and when the thought occurred to me, I stood straighter, more attuned to my surroundings—unless he was going to tell us that the war was won, that troop movements were a thing of the past, that life as we once knew it could resume. I scanned the crowd searching for Charles, for if that were the news, surely he would be there as a senior officer of the Regiment. But I searched in vain. He was not present.

After some delay, Governor Young stood before us and fairly shouted to be heard.

"Gentlemen," he said, ignoring the fact that there were half a dozen ladies in attendance, "thank you for coming." There were murmurs of "get on with it" and "what in bloody hell is this all about?"

"We have received word that there may be German spies on the island. Although, as you all know, we have interned adult males from the former German community in Singapore, it has come to our attention that some merchants of the local population may be harboring those who were not known to us when the war broke out. Consequently, we urge each of you to be vigilant in your dealings with Europeans of unknown origin and with certain local people who may be sympathetic to the German cause, which is nothing less, we believe, than to challenge our empire throughout the world."

Or something along those lines. It was hardly a memorable speech. When the Governor had concluded, I felt a hand at my elbow and knew at once whose hand it was. Indeed, Charles was with us, after all. As we stood in the middle of a crowd, I turned to him, smiled, and said, "Oh, Captain Bingham, I am so concerned about these German spies." I could scarcely contain my mirth, and I dare say Charles was similarly amused, if only by my performance.

I excused myself from the ladies and walked with Charles to a table where Uncle Cyril was seated with a law colleague whom he detested.

"Captain Bingham," said Uncle, punctuating his greeting with a vigorous nod of his head.

To my relief, we did not join the two men who were, I suppose, debating the Governor's warning, and instead continued walking out of Government House and into the lush garden.

"What will we do?" Charles said. "How will I live without you? You must find a way to come to Hong Kong."

"Uncle will not even allow me to travel to Penang," I said, "so I am certain Hong Kong would be out of the question."

"Penang? What on earth made you think of going to Penang? With the Hun's interests in Siam, I'm afraid travel to Penang is even more fraught with danger than Singapore or Hong Kong these days. No, I would not be planning a voyage to Penang anytime soon."

If Charles saw no reason for me to go to Penang, whatever did Lieutenant Raj mean by his warning?

14

From her position in the greeting area just outside customs at Changi Airport, Aislinn first saw Rebecca. A tall girl, her blond hair wild, she looked dazed as she stood in line to pass through the checkpoint. And there, behind her, was her brother, Jason, pushing a luggage cart. Jason was as handsome as Liam, but with little of the aggressiveness, having inherited—or learned—from Janice, a different way of dealing with the world. Not that Aislinn saw that as an advantage, necessarily, and she knew Liam considered his son weak, but she thought he'd be all right. He was a good kid.

Hugs all around.

"Where's Dad?" Jason asked. Rebecca spun around, as if expecting to see him in the crowd meeting their flight.

"He couldn't come," Aislinn said. "He really wanted to, but he had a meeting he couldn't get out of. You'll have a chance to get rested back at the apartment, and then your father will be home tonight for a nice dinner."

"It's so *hot* here," Rebecca said. "How can you stand it?"

· · · · ·

At the apartment, Aislinn got them settled into their rooms, grateful now for the large apartment and the extravagant amount of space they had. Exhaustion struck both of them, and they were ready for naps.

She was looking forward to having them around for a few weeks, which would make the holidays seem more festive, even without the cold weather and traditions they were accustomed to at home. From what she'd seen of them, they were both decent human beings, without the sort of angst she knew the children of divorced parents often exhibited. Rebecca was already a senior at Dartmouth, self-assured, thinking about her next steps. Jason was a little more fragile, but he was beginning to look at colleges, and that move would be good for him. He'd been on his high school swim team for three years, mostly to please his father, Aislinn guessed, and Liam was proud of him. If she thought a child of her own might turn out as well as Liam's kids had, maybe starting a family would be a good thing.

Rebecca was first to emerge in the late afternoon. When Jason made his appearance, Aislinn introduced them to Cecilia, who served them tea on the balcony. As they talked about the tourist sites they might visit—the Botanic Gardens, the Bird Park, Chinatown, Little India—Aislinn realized she'd grown accustomed to being on the balcony, her fear having dissipated.

Liam got home just as dinner was ready. He hugged the kids—Aislinn watched, hoping he'd show more warmth toward them than he usually did, but she detected the familiar stiffness, unsure what to do with them once he had them in his arms, releasing them a little too quickly from his embrace. It was more than reticence, though. He seemed preoccupied.

Now that they were rested, both Rebecca and Jason were full of stories about the trip from New York on their Turkish Airlines flight. The food on the flight had been unfamiliar, the stopover in Istanbul confusing. Their seats had been near the back of the plane on the first leg, surrounded by families with young children who made a lot of noise. While both had been to Europe in the past—before the divorce, Janice had taken them—this was their first trip to Asia. They'd now only been in the country a few hours and were eager to share their impressions, beginning with how fancy the Singapore airport was, and then the trip into town past gleaming office towers and lush greenery.

• • • • •

The next day, Liam left early for work, leaving Aislinn to entertain Rebecca and Jason. When they got up, they joined her on the terrace for coffee. Rebecca eyed the pool from the balcony; Jason shrugged and said at least he'd be able to get his workout in. Aislinn had to go into her office in the afternoon but would spend the morning with them walking around the area to help them get their bearings, so they wouldn't feel confined to the compound. It occurred to her they could drop into Orientalia on the pretext of finding a unique gift for their mother there. She could see Martin without being tempted by him, as long as the children were with her.

She led the way into the shop and Martin hurried toward her, stopping abruptly when he saw that she wasn't alone.

"Martin," she said, "these are my husband's children, Rebecca and Jason." Both teens stared at Martin until Aislinn drew their attention to the antique maps she thought Janice might like.

"Let me show you something I just got in," Martin said, taking Aislinn's elbow and guiding her away from her stepchildren.

"I've got to see you," he whispered. "Where have you been?"

"I can't do it," she said. "It's impossible." And she pulled away, occupying herself with the maps again, employing Rebecca as a shield.

She shouldn't have come to the shop. Not only did it reawaken her feelings for Martin, she was certain that Rebecca and Jason had both seen the attraction between them. She hurried them out of the store.

"But I think you were right," Rebecca said. "Mom would like one of those maps."

"Plenty of time for that later, if you want to come back. It's not going anywhere."

• • • • •

On Saturday, Aislinn took Rebecca and Jason to the American Club. Liam said he had to work—he and TJ were finalizing a deal that was sure to solidify his position with the bank and remove the "interim" from his title, he said—so the three of them sat around the pool there. It wasn't much different from being at their apartment complex, but it was a change of scenery, among other people. They baked in the sun when back home an early snowstorm was threatening New York.

Aislinn marveled at Jason's firm young body, and he seemed to love showing off his swimmer's physique, walking around the pool, diving in with such grace that it was hard not to watch, and then turning in an impressive number of laps, knifing through the water with barely any wake. Aislinn was pleased to see that he was now seated on the edge of the pool, talking to another boy who looked like he might be about Jason's age.

"What do you know about that guy at the map store?" Rebecca asked.

"Not much," Aislinn lied. "Why?"

"Why? Because he's hot as hell, that's why. I was thinking of swinging by there again sometime, maybe see if he's busy later."

"He's too old for you, Becca. And besides, your father's taking us all out to dinner tonight."

"I meant later, later. After dinner. Or another night. And he's not that much older. I bet he's no older than Daddy is to you, is he?"

Touché. Aislinn realized she was probably right. "That's different," she said.

"How is it different?"

"I just don't think you should go out with him."

"I hate to break it to you, but you're not my mother. And my father doesn't give a damn what I do."

"No, I'm not your mother." She watched as two girls in bikinis walked by Jason, turned and walk by again. He didn't seem to notice, and she thought she saw them nodding to each other, understanding the problem. Liam had told her, early in their marriage, that Jason was gay. He said he was OK with it, that the revelation when it had come out was no great surprise, but she sensed that he felt he had somehow failed his son.

"Anyway," Rebecca said, "it looks like Jason is all set."

· · · · ·

On Monday, Aislinn left for work early, leaving Rebecca and Jason to entertain themselves. On her way home, she stopped by Orientalia. She'd sworn to herself that she wouldn't see him again, but her reaction to Rebecca's interest made her realize she had to.

There were other customers in the shop, tourists, browsing. She made eye contact with Martin, who stood from his desk when she entered. He moved toward the other customers, hovered near them, and asked if he could help them, then asked again, until finally they left.

"Where have you been? Why haven't I seen you?" His voice was low but urgent.

"Because this is impossible. What we did was a mistake. A huge mistake."

"Then why are you here now? If it was a mistake, you wouldn't have come."

"I shouldn't have come, but—"

"Your stepdaughter was here today."

"She was?"

"I think she was flirting."

"She thinks you're hot and wants you to ask her out."

"Maybe I should."

"Don't you dare."

"When can I see you again?"

"I told you, I can't. We can't."

"When?" He kissed her neck.

"I don't know. When they're gone." She stepped away from him. She moved behind one of the low shelves, unable to look at him, and when a customer entered the shop, she left.

· · · · ·

Dinner that night was pizza that Rebecca and Jason insisted on making together. Aislinn opened a bottle of red wine, and even let both the kids have some. If Liam noticed they were drinking wine, he said nothing about it. Aislinn opened a second bottle.

"This is fantastic pizza," Aislinn said. "You guys did a great job! Didn't they, Liam?"

"Yeah, it's good. For pizza."

"Jason did most of it," Rebecca said.

"Are you keeping up with your laps?" Liam asked his son. "You don't want to be out of shape when you get back to school. The season starts soon, doesn't it?"

"January. But you know I never swim in the meets, Dad. I'm not even sure why Coach let me on the team."

"You might swim in meets if you applied yourself, son. Nobody gets better by whining."

"Jason wasn't whining, Liam," Aislinn said.

"That's what it sounded like to me. And it's no way to get ahead. You win by making yourself better, and making the other guy lose."

"That's your philosophy of life? You win if the other guy loses? Is that what happened with Bruce Morelock? I guess Jenny was right."

"Who's Jenny?" Rebecca asked.

"I warned you not to talk to her. But what did she tell you?"

"She told me—but that's all past. Jason and Rebecca don't want to hear about the Morelocks, do you guys? People you never even met?" She poured more wine. "Let's talk about something else, shall we?"

Rebecca looked at her brother. "Jason?"

Jason took a sip from his glass.

"Is that wine you're drinking?" Liam asked.

"Dad, Aislinn, there's something I wanted to tell you."

Aislinn watched Liam and wondered what might be coming. Jason had already come out to his father, so what new revelation could there be?

"The thing is," Jason said, taking a deep breath, "I think I'm going to quit the swim team."

"You want to quit?"

"I sort of already did."

"Why? I thought you enjoyed being on the swim team."

"I do. I did. But you haven't been to a meet in a while, Dad. We've got a really strong team. Even if I work hard and get better, I'll never be as good as those guys. It's just not possible. I'm wasting my time. And theirs."

Liam drank the rest of his wine. When Aislinn tried to pour more in his glass, he waved her off. He got up and took the Scotch out of his liquor cabinet.

"So you quit. You just decided it was too hard and quit." Liam drank his Scotch and leaned against the wall. "You've been lying to us these last few days about your laps at the pool?"

"No, of course not," Jason said. "I'm doing laps because it's a great workout. I don't want to swim on a team is all."

"I'm disappointed, son. I didn't take you to be a quitter." He drank down the rest of his Scotch. He pushed his dining chair under the table and headed toward the bedroom.

· · · · ·

The trip had not been planned, but Liam announced that he needed to go to Hong Kong for business. Since Jason's announcement that he had quit the swim team, Liam had barely spoken to the boy, although Jason didn't seem terribly upset by that.

Aislinn watched from the terrace as Jason did laps in the pool, then joined him poolside.

"It was brave of you to tell your father face to face," she said.

"Honestly," he said, "I knew Dad wouldn't take it well."

"I think he appreciates that you came all this way, at least."

"Maybe. But I doubt it. He's not a bad father, in his own way. I've got friends whose dads are way worse."

Rebecca joined them at the pool, and Jason resumed his laps.

"I can't believe Daddy ran away like that," Rebecca said. "He can't deal with Jason, so he flies to Hong Kong?"

"No, not his finest moment," Aislinn said.

"Does he go there a lot? Hong Kong?"

"A fair amount. The bank's regional headquarters is there."

"The thing is," Rebecca said, "when we were little, he didn't travel so much." She was spreading sunscreen on her shoulders and arms. "He didn't start traveling until a few years ago. But I guess you know about those trips."

Rebecca was a smart girl, and apparently knew that Aislinn had been seeing her father long before Janice found out, and that they'd often met out of town to avoid being seen together in New York. Was she implying that the same thing was happening again? Did she know something, or merely suspect? Aislinn still didn't want to believe it. If it was true, though, what was she going to do about it?

Was it time to admit defeat and go home? She'd fallen too easily for Martin. Life with Liam had become a struggle—over her work, over the apartment, over his kids, over his pressure for her to give him a second family—and nothing was the way it should have been. She was miserable. She should be back in New York, preparing to become a partner in her law firm.

"Speaking of which," Rebecca said, "I have a date."

"Oh? With whom?" Rebecca had been spending a lot of time at the American Club, and Aislinn assumed she'd met someone her own age there.

"That guy from the antique map store."

"Really? I thought—"

"Yes, he's older than I am. You told me. But it's just a date, *Mom*. It's not like I'm going to marry the guy."

"He asked you out?"

"No. It's a brave new world. I asked him." Rebecca stood and jumped into the pool.

· · · · ·

Liam returned from Hong Kong, and nothing further was said about Jason's announcement, either with Jason or privately in the bedroom.

She knew that while Liam was away, Jason had been spending time with the boy he'd met at the American Club, but it didn't seem necessary, or wise, to mention that.

On Sunday, though, Rebecca asked her father if she could bring someone to dinner. Liam raised an eyebrow, but agreed.

When Rebecca told Aislinn that Martin was coming to dinner, she said, "I know you don't approve, but that's too bad, because it's none of your business."

Martin appeared at 6:30, after he'd closed the shop for the day. When Liam saw him, Aislinn thought he might react as badly as he had with Jason's news. Not only was Martin significantly older than Rebecca, he was dark-skinned, and while Aislinn had not witnessed overt racism in her husband, this was his daughter's date, and she knew from her own experience that a father's true feelings emerge where his daughter was concerned. Liam shook Martin's hand and offered him a drink.

"White wine, if you've got it."

"You like Australian wine? My wife seems to have developed a taste for it, although at home we drank French or Californian."

"Yes, Aussie wine is just fine."

"I'll have some, too, Rebecca said."

"No, sweet, I don't think so. You're too young, remember?"

"I'll be twenty-one next month!"

"And next month, we'll celebrate. Tonight, you're too young."

As much as it pained Aislinn to see Rebecca at odds with her father, that was well played, she thought. Let's drive home to Martin that Rebecca is too young. Not that Rebecca's age mattered to Martin. He was using her to get to Aislinn.

"Martin—it's Martin, is it?—do I detect a bit of an Aussie accent?"

"I thought I'd done a good job of burying that," Martin said, "but I guess not."

Liam handed him the wine.

"Actually, I grew up here, went to school in Melbourne after my compulsory military service, and came back last year."

"In school all that time?"

"No, I was working there. I came back to help my father with his shop."

"A shopkeeper, then." Martin turned to Rebecca. "Sweet, you didn't tell me you were seeing a shopkeeper. Were all the garbage men busy?"

"Liam," Aislinn said sharply. "Martin runs the shop where I bought the paintings."

"That's all right, Aislinn," Martin said. "I'm sure your husband has higher hopes for his daughter."

"On the other hand," Liam said, "I have to admire your salesmanship." He raised his glass in Martin's direction. "Somehow you convinced my wife here to buy the trash hanging in the dining room. I can barely hold down my food."

"I like them, Daddy," Rebecca said.

"As an art historian—that's the class you've been wasting your time on, isn't it?—is that your considered opinion? That you like them?"

"Aislinn," Rebecca said, "how do you put up with him?"

"The question," Jason chimed in, "is how did Mom put up with him all those years."

"Martin, have you met my son? The quitter?"

"Liam, that's enough. What has gotten into you? Please stop."

Martin stood up. Aislinn thought, since he was a bit bigger than Liam, that he might be planning to throw a punch. But he didn't. Instead, he put down his wineglass, looked at Rebecca, and shrugged.

"Thank you for inviting me to dinner, but I really must be going," he said, and headed toward the door, pausing briefly when he noticed the large Shan Lee painting above the sofa. He opened the door without looking back and closed it behind him.

No one spoke. Aislinn stared at the door for a moment before turning to her husband. "Liam, what in hell got into you?" she asked. "You owe us all an apology."

"I don't think so," he said. "I'm protecting my daughter. That guy is bad news. I could smell it on him. I don't want him anywhere near

Rebecca." He turned to his daughter. "Have you been sleeping with him?"

"Daddy! What is wrong with you?"

"Couldn't you see it in his eyes? Maybe it's because I'm a man, but I could read his mind. He was thinking about fucking. That's why he was here. It's all part of the seduction. I'm telling you, sweet, stay away from him."

"And what, Daddy dearest, is on your mind when you run off to Hong Kong?"

Liam slapped her.

"Don't you ever talk to me that way again."

Rebecca ran to her room.

• • • • •

The next morning, Liam lingered at home. It was unusual for him, and he didn't explain himself to Aislinn, but as they sat on the terrace with their coffee, he often looked toward the hallway where his children lay sleeping.

"They might be waiting for you to leave, you know," Aislinn said.

"Then they won't hear my apology." He finished his coffee and went.

When Rebecca came out, she drank her orange juice in silence. Jason joined her.

"I think you put him up to being so rude," Rebecca said. "You don't like Martin, so you made Daddy do that."

"You know that's not true. There's no excuse for what your father did, but he was hoping to see you this morning to apologize."

"Whatever."

"Yes, whatever. Nonetheless, he wanted to say something to you. And we'll see him tonight at the staff Christmas party."

"What if we don't want to go?"

"Then you'll miss a chance to meet some new people."

• • • •

Aislinn led Rebecca and Jason into the restaurant where the party was being held. She waved to Liam, who hurried over, practically dragging a tall young man wearing a tan suit. Aislinn had to remind herself that although it was winter at home, they were still in the tropics.

"Rebecca Connolly," Liam said to his daughter, "meet Michael Oliver." He was slim, with close-cropped blond hair and impossibly broad shoulders. "Michael, this is my daughter, Rebecca." And then, as host, Liam slipped off to talk to newly arrived guests.

Aislinn leaned over to whisper to Rebecca, "A peace offering, I think."

"Hey, nobody told me the boss's daughter was a knockout," Michael said.

A corny line, but Rebecca blushed anyway.

"You really work for him?" she asked.

"Sort of. I'm getting my MBA at Columbia, and part of the deal is a rotating internship. Somehow I got lucky and they sent me here. It's pretty sweet."

"My father thinks I should go the MBA route, but I don't know."

Aislinn interjected, "You two get acquainted, and I'll see if I can find something to drink." Jason showed no sign of moving, however, so she took his arm to pull him away.

• • • • •

Aislinn found Liam talking to TJ Kwan.

"Michael seems like a nice young man. I think they hit it off."

"I thought she'd like him. I'd been meaning to introduce them all along, even before the shopkeeper showed up. I wish I'd done it sooner, but maybe she'll have some fun in the time they have left."

"Speaking of them, what about Jason? Have you got any more rabbits to pull out of the hat?"

"Well, I'm not going to fix him up with another intern, if that's what you mean. As for the swim team, I know I reacted badly. I just remember how important it was to me to swim competitively. I understand he doesn't feel the same way."

"For now, I would suggest that you say something to that effect to your son."

"You're right, love." He kissed her and went to find Jason.

• • • • •

Rebecca spent each evening the following week with Michael, coming in later and later each night. On Christmas day itself, Michael joined the family, since his own parents and siblings lived in Chicago. While dinner was in the oven—Aislinn wasn't capable of it herself, but Cecilia had prepared most of the meal the day before—they all went to the pool. Aislinn watched as Michael removed his T-shirt, revealing a supple, firm body. She saw the way Rebecca embraced him, and knew they'd been sleeping together. Liam might be able to read men's minds, but she could read their body language. And she knew that Liam had given her daughter to this man. To what end, she wondered. To ensure his loyalty? To buy hers? Was it worth the price?

• • • • •

That weekend, shortly before Rebecca and Jason were to leave for New York, Rebecca went out with Michael and didn't come home. At eleven, she called. Aislinn picked up the phone.

"I'm staying here tonight," Rebecca said.

Aislinn handed the phone to Liam.

She watched as Liam listened to Rebecca repeat what she'd just said.

"Use protection," Liam said, and handed the phone back to Aislinn.

"That's it? 'Use protection?'"

"Aislinn, you don't get it. Michael's from a good family. He's a thoroughbred. And I have no illusions that my daughter is a virgin. If she wants to have a little vacation fling with a quality racehorse, who am I to stand in her way? The shopkeeper was a different story."

* * * * *

The next day, Rebecca and Aislinn went shopping for the last time, visiting the luxury brand shops in one of the many high-rise malls on Orchard Road.

"You're dying to know, aren't you?" Rebecca asked.

"Know what?" Aislinn pulled a blouse off the rack and held it up. "This would look good on you, don't you think?"

"Too glitzy," Rebecca said and shook her head. "About me and Michael, of course."

"No, not really." Aislinn lowered her voice. "I assume you had sex, but it's none of my business, apparently. Your father gave you his advice on the phone. I hope you followed it."

"Please. I've been on the pill since I was 15."

"Protection isn't just about preventing pregnancy, you know."

"Duh. But Michael's clean. He told me so."

"Okay. He's clean. I'm happy for you."

"Isn't he beautiful, though? And you should see the rest of him."

"Becca! I don't want to know!"

"Don't lie to me. I saw you ogling him."

"I'll admit he's a very attractive young man."

"And he'll be back in New York in a few months. I'm thinking of looking at grad school. NYU, maybe. Let's go to Martin's shop. Shouldn't we apologize for Daddy's behavior?"

"Your father's the one who should apologize."

"Like that's going to happen. But I want to buy something for Mom. Wasn't that your suggestion?"

"I suppose it was." Aislinn didn't want to see Martin and hoped his sister was holding down the fort today, as she sometimes did when Martin took a break to go sailing. And yet she couldn't help but be pleased when it was Martin they saw as they entered.

Martin laughed when he saw them. While Rebecca was hunting through the maps for a gift for her mother, Aislinn looked again at the selection of old books, wondering once more if there was a connection there to Elizabeth Pennington. If not a diary, then her name written in one of the books? Martin stood nearby.

"I only went with her because I was desperate to see you," he whispered. "And I've been miserable since that night."

"Please. No. We can't."

"I have to see you."

"What are you two whispering about?" Rebecca called.

"I was asking the price on a couple of these books," Aislinn replied.

"When she's gone," he whispered again, "come to me."

Aislinn looked at him. She touched his arm. She wanted him so badly. She'd been miserable, too.

"Aislinn! What the hell?" And Rebecca ran out of the store. Aislinn ran after her.

"Rebecca, wait!" She caught up to her near the entrance to the mall.

"I can't believe you," Rebecca said. "No wonder you tried to stop me from seeing him—did stop me, thanks to Dad. You wanted him for yourself. Are you fucking him?"

"Don't be ridiculous."

"Why is that ridiculous? I know Daddy can be a jerk, and it wouldn't surprise me if he's screwing somebody else on his trips to Hong Kong. I don't blame you, frankly."

"Well…I'm not."

"Sure. Whatever. Like you said. None of my business."

15

25 January 1915

I feel so out of sorts this morning. I haven't any idea what might be the cause, but nothing tastes right. The girl brought me a lovely mango and at the first bite, I nearly retched. Even the tea tasted especially bitter. I asked for a bit of toasted bread, and that seems to have settled me, for now. When I bathed this morning, my skin was startlingly sensitive to the touch. It was a most peculiar sensation, nearly like the sting of a bee, though not unpleasant.

Perhaps I should stay in today, but Uncle Cyril has planned an outing, and I have been looking forward to it all week. We are to luncheon in the wild! He says there is a clearing in the jungle, newly made, where tables and chairs will be brought. I shall bring my pad and pencils—the paints and easel would be too much of a bother, I think—and will record the adventure. Of course, the entire island is a jungle, and Uncle's garden is little more than a clearing itself, but he says we will be out of sight and sound of the settlement, almost as if we were traveling back in time to when Sir Stamford Raffles first arrived.

Of course, it isn't safe, and we are to have an escort from the Regiment, Uncle assured me.

"Not safe?" I asked. "What dangers can there be just a few miles from our own home?"

"Besides the German spies, you mean? And the savage Malay tribes, some of whom are said to practice cannibalism? And the ravenous snakes, known to be as long as a church steeple's shadow at teatime and as round as a man's leg? And the tigers, of course. Mustn't forget the tigers!" Uncle laughed, and I joined in, although one or two of his fantastical demons do, I must confess, trouble me.

Snakes? Tigers?

26 January 1915
In the event, there were neither tigers nor snakes, although perhaps they were intimidated by the small army of escorts encumbering our party and found refuge deeper in the jungle. While duty kept Charles from joining us, even in the ranks of the guard, Lieutenant Raj was among those assigned to watch over us. When I saw him, I smiled and waved, trusting that Uncle would not notice. Raj nodded stoically, a gesture imperceptible to the others, ever the good soldier.

Our number included Mrs. Craddock and her children, a well-behaved pair of little devils who normally were not seen or heard when I visited the Craddock home. Mrs. Framingham, still a guest of the Craddocks, was there. Mrs. Burke and Daisy, although the girl seemed frightened of every shadow or bird call. One or two gentlemen of the legal profession also came along, as did a few government men I recognized.

The jungle itself was impressive, and it would be glorious to paint. My sketches will not do it justice. The clearing was small, not much larger than Uncle's garden, in fact, and was reached by a path that was almost invisible from the road, which at that point, far from the settlement and running through a Malay *kampong*, was barely deserving of the name. We attracted stares as we passed the houses, some of them built on bamboo stilts, and then, leaving the carriage, we disappeared into the undergrowth as if we ourselves were wild animals.

Especially given Uncle's comments about the man-eating snakes, I was more than a little careful of where I stepped, seeing a serpent in every root and fallen branch. There were none that I encountered, however, although that may have been because I had the good fortune to be walking behind several others, giving the slitherers plenty of warning before I came along. I had expected, too, that the jungle would be even steamier than Uncle's garden, but beneath the canopy, where the sun reaches only in narrow ribbons, it felt almost cool. Until, that is, we entered the full sun of the clearing, a bowl that captured not only the full force of the midday sun but also every insect and jungle sound you could imagine. The ladies each held a fan and we put them to good use. Hot, steamy, and cacophonous, with the smell of fruit that is overripe and beyond putrescent.

• • • • •

Luncheon comprised finger sandwiches, biscuits, a cake, and various peculiar fruits, some of which I gather we could have picked ourselves if we had gone searching in the jungle around us. I could barely eat, as I was not feeling at all well, and had no appetite. I did sip some tea, which had grown tepid in the transport, and Uncle produced a bottle of spirits, which I tasted. None of it pleased me, and I thought I might be ill.

When the party elected to "explore," to use Mrs. Craddock's word, by following a cleared path beyond the picnic area in search of a rumored pond and waterfall, I begged off. I would rather sit in the clearing and sketch, if they didn't mind. Mrs. Framingham offered to stay behind with me, as she said she was no longer of the age when traipsing through the jungle enticed her, but I knew she had made the offer solely for my benefit and was keen on finding that pond. Of course, they would not leave me entirely alone, despite my protestations that I would be perfectly all right, and that in fact I preferred the solitude for my sketching. Uncle decided that one of the Regiment would stay, and so it came to be that Lieutenant Raj remained with me.

Although I had wanted to be alone to sketch, I took the opportunity to pepper the poor man with questions.

"What do you hear from home, Lieutenant? Is there news?"

"No, Miss."

"No? There must be news. Does your wife not write to you?"

"She does not write, Miss. None of the women in my village read or write. It is not our way."

I'm sure I looked flabbergasted by this news. "I suppose it was not so very long ago that the same was true in England. And even now…. But then, the men?"

"Oh, yes, Miss. In Punjab we have good schools. For boys. My son will go to the village school."

"Your son, Raj? How old is he?"

"Only a babe, Miss. Not yet one."

"So, does someone write to you from home?"

"Yes, Miss. My brother."

"And what does your brother write?"

"I would rather not say, Miss."

"What could be so awful? That the work is hard? That the weather has been unpleasant? Or that something has happened in your village?"

"It is not the village, Miss. It is the stories. They say…."

"What do they say?"

"They say we will soon fight the Turks."

"The Turks have joined with the Germans, so, yes, they are now the enemy. We are already fighting them, I believe."

"I mean the Regiment, Miss. We are from the Punjab, and so we all hear from our families the same thing. They say we will be sent to Africa to fight the Turks."

"But are your orders not for Hong Kong? Preparations are underway. It's what everyone says. It's what Charles—Captain Bingham—says."

"It is what they say, yes."

"But it seems you do not believe what they say."

"It is not for me to say, Miss."

"And would that be so terrible, to be sent to fight the Turks? Fighting anyone must be terrible, of course, but you would be defending the empire, and your own homeland."

"Yes, Miss."

"Am I missing something, Lieutenant Raj?"

He hesitated, as if weighing what he might say to me, perhaps willing me to understand without his having to utter a word. I am afraid that I failed him in this, and he was forced to continue.

"The Turks, Miss. They are followers of Mohammed."

It took me a moment to understand what he meant. "Oh, I see." A monkey screeched in the trees above us, and another answered from across the clearing, but I dared not take my eyes from him. "Lieutenant Raj," I began, "are there not wars between Mohammedans, just as there are wars between Christians?"

"Yes, Miss. Sometimes. But the Turks are not our enemy."

I wanted to pursue the matter further, to understand why it was sometimes all right to fight other Mohammedans, but in this instance, when the Turks had joined forces with the Germans, who certainly *were* our mutual enemy, why it was *not* all right to fight them. But the others just then emerged from the path, having failed in their mission to find either falls or pond. Their arrival incited more shrieks and howls from the monkeys above us, and Uncle announced it was time to go home.

27 January 1915

The sketches I made yesterday—between waves of nausea and my enlightening conversation with Lieutenant Raj—delight me. No tiger appeared, despite my secret wish. But there is the monkey that descended the tree to investigate us, the flame bush that stood at one side of the clearing (making me wish I had brought my paints, after all, because I doubt that I will be able to recreate faithfully such a remarkable shade of red, which is not the red of a flame but more that of a most vibrant sunset), and of course our Lieutenant Raj, who allowed me to draw him while we talked about his village, his infant son, about the Regiment's reluctance to fight the Turks, and about living apart from his family.

He asked again if I had plans to go to Penang for the Chinese New Year holiday, but I explained that it was impossible. I had looked into it, but neither boat nor train were deemed safe for such a journey, thanks to the Germans. He looked as though he wanted to say more on the subject, but he restrained himself.

"What is so important about Penang?" I asked, but he did not answer. He gazed into the jungle, and it was then that I captured his likeness in a way that I had not been able to until that moment.

I had to close my pad when the others returned, but now, in the light of morning, I can see him again.

• • • • •

I am avoiding writing about my illness because I am afraid that I know its cause. Or at least, I suspect. There is no one I can discuss the matter with, of course. No one who could be counted upon for discretion. No one to offer wise counsel. And so I am left with a difficult decision to make. I do not feel desperate, in any sense. I am clear-eyed. I am not the first woman of this world to face this situation, nor will I be the last. I have recently concluded that our girl May, who disappeared and then returned and has disappeared again, may well have been in the selfsame condition.

By my reckoning, it is early days yet. What are my choices? Do I tell Charles? I suppose I must. Do I love him? I thought I did, and certainly, in a way, I do. I am not certain, though, that he is of a character that I would wish to marry. There is the matter of the demands he places on me, but also a question of certain rumors. They may be only that, but if they have come to my ears, then they no doubt are in wider circulation as well. However, for the sake of appearances, if I am to remain in the settlement, I believe marriage with Charles is the only course to be taken.

We have said to each other, excusing our behavior, that we consider ourselves already married, whether or not we truly meant it, and so it is not such a large step. He is leaving for Hong Kong momentarily, and what then? Not to mention that the war continues to rage in Europe and now Africa, and even on the high seas. Who is to say that hostilities will not find their way to our own front door? Perhaps it is time that I leave. I cannot return to England, of course, even if I had the means and somewhere there to go, which I do not. Aunt Margaret and Richard Bromley have seen to that. So then, where?

I have considered America as an option. I would not be greatly troubled there, I think. Whatever story I choose to adopt about the absence of a husband no doubt would be believed in these trying times. I imagine it would be possible to find passage on a ship to San Francisco, and then by train to New York. I know no one in America, of course. There is Australia, much nearer to us in Singapore. You see, I have many options.

28 January 1915

Charles has summoned me to the joss house, but I cannot go. I am not yet prepared to tell him of my condition, or to ask for his help. I do not know the degree of confidence that I must have that he will go along with my decision.

29 January 1915

Uncle has invited Charles to the house. I did not need to feign illness, but I could not bring myself to look at Charles, much less converse with him in Uncle's presence.

Another option has presented itself to me, one that appeals greatly. And that is to do nothing at all. Charles will be gone in little more than a fortnight. I do not wish to marry him. I wish to remain an independent woman, my own person. I believe Uncle has been right all along. Charles will go with the Regiment off to Hong Kong, to make further conquests of impressionable young women, and I will continue to flower here in Singapore, inevitably. I will bring shame to Uncle and myself, at least initially, but I will be forgiven. If Uncle allows it, I will remain in this house, which will take on new vitality and purpose, and I will take joy in our changed circumstances. If Uncle will not have me, I shall embark on the course I envisioned in Cape Town, to work as governess or tutor, and I will continue to pursue my art. I will not flee. I will stay.

But first, I must tell Uncle.

29 January 1915, evening
Uncle tells me that Charles was most frustrated that I did not appear for tea. Indeed, I could hear his loud voice asking Uncle why I would not come down, and what was the matter, and could a servant not be sent to assist me? It sounded as though Charles threatened to come up the stairs to my room, but Uncle stood in his way. In fact, though, I was tempted once or twice to emerge, to take this opportunity to unburden myself to both Uncle Cyril and to Charles. In the end, I stayed strong.

Eventually, Charles left, and, through the shutters of my bedroom, I watched him go. He looked back toward the house and gazed at my window. I stepped away, even though I doubted he could see me. Perhaps I did not wish to see him. I do not know if I shall ever see him again.

Is it not for the best? He will soon be gone, and the pain of separation is lessened if executed swiftly.

30 January 1915
I have considered calling off the exhibition. There are enough paintings and sketches now, but I am not feeling up to it. It is not just my physical condition that has laid me low, but the weight of my predicament. I prefer to remain in my room and allow the girl to come to me with my meals. I have my sketch pad here, but there is nothing more that I wish to draw.

Except....

The girl is back. She had returned once and disappeared a second time, but now she is here again. She came to me this morning with a tray as if she had never left. I am feeling better and could have taken more sustenance, but she, more than the rest, is sensitive to my special tastes and needs. Fruit would not do, she knew, for it is too acidic. Tea and toast are nearly all I could stomach before, but now there are preserves and a bit of cake. When she set the tray down on the table in my room, I asked her to stay, which she did reluctantly. I sipped the tea and took a bite of toast, but in that very moment, I was inspired to draw her. I picked up my pad and pencils, moved her into the light by the window and asked her to gaze out at the garden. She was quite beautiful that way, and I could see all of her, in her housedress and long braided hair. Her countenance was so melancholy that I could barely stand to look at her, and I wondered if she sensed what we shared. I longed to tell her, but because I had not yet told anyone, I did not. In the end, perhaps she guessed, because as I worked, she turned her gaze from the window and looked at me, more like a lover than a servant gazing at her mistress. A smile crossed her face, the light in her eyes turning bright with recognition.

It is now even more urgent that I share the news with the men in my life.

16

Aislinn spent more time in the office now, even when there was little work for her to do. There was nothing for her to do at home, either, and even the routine tasks at Bradford & Co. took her mind off her troubles. She couldn't bill clients for her hours spent researching issues of Singapore law about which she was merely curious, questions that had nothing to do with the projects she'd been assigned, but she enjoyed the distraction from the tension at home and Liam's odd behavior, not to mention her guilt for what she'd done with Martin.

• • • •

She reread the story in the Edmund Preston collection that included the character Molly, whom she was sure must be based on Elizabeth Pennington, and studied the portraits on her dining room wall. The two men had military bearing and uniforms, but one was light, the British officer, and one was dark, crowned with a turban. Indian, she supposed. Were these two men Pennington's lovers, as Preston had implied in the story? Is that why she painted them? The story was fiction, but it sounded so authentic, as if he had been writing only what he observed. In Pennington's portrait of the British officer, he gazes fondly back at her, imploring. He bears a secret, in which the artist is complicit. The artist loves him, but does he return her love? He doesn't seem to. He sees her as a possession, an object, a conquest. The expression on the Indian soldier's face is entirely different. In his eyes there is compassion.

She'd seen that expression in Martin's eyes, and the more she looked at the portrait, the more it seemed obvious. Molly—in Preston's story—had borne the Indian soldier's child, a mixed-race boy. Could that be Martin? But, no, Martin was born much later. His father? No, Martin had said his father had come here as a young man from India, so not him either. Just fiction, then, a reader's fantasy. Her fantasy.

• • • • •

Shan Lee called to propose an outing on a Saturday, which Aislinn was more than happy to join. They rode in Lee's MGB and parked near Chinatown on a side street in a spot that Aislinn was sure was illegal, but Lee didn't seem to notice or care. Was that another privilege of being the second wife of one of the most powerful men in Singapore? Park wherever you want, and the police won't bother you because they recognize your car?

"This festival is almost unbelievable," Lee said as they walked toward New Bridge Road. "Thaipusam is celebrated by Tamil Hindus, and the whole thing, as near as I can figure, is about proving your devotion to the deity, in this case a character named Lord Murga, who is supposed to be the embodiment of valor and intelligence. A man, of course." She rolled her eyes.

"And they prove their devotion how?"

"Ah, now *that* has to be seen. I could paint it, but words won't do it justice."

Normally a busy thoroughfare, New Bridge Road was devoid of traffic as they took their place among a growing throng that spilled into the street. A crowd, but not nearly as overwhelming as the Deepavali celebration had been.

"It shouldn't be long now," Lee said, and as she spoke, the first devotees appeared, accompanied by drummers, dancers, and teams of men chanting what sounded like cheers at a football game or a pep rally. Aislinn wondered if she'd stumbled into another anti-government demonstration, until she looked more closely at the approaching marchers.

"What's that he's wearing?"

"It's called a *kevadi*, an elaborate sort of shrine that he carries on his shoulders for the whole length of the march, something like four kilometers. But that's just decoration. Check out his body."

Aislinn studied the first pilgrim, not quite believing what she saw.

"Oh my God," she said, and could say no more. The man had a skewer piercing his mouth through both cheeks. Other men had hooks stuck in their chest and back, some weighted with metal balls, and others looked like porcupines with quills bobbing in their flesh as they trudged toward the finish line, a temple just another hundred meters away.

"How do they do that? Aren't they in terrible pain? It looks like torture."

"The pain is the point," Lee said, "although they claim they're in some kind of trance state and feel nothing."

There were dozens of pilgrims passing now, each more burdened than the last—larger *kevadis*, more hooks and skewers—most with an entourage cheering him on.

"I think I'm going to be ill," Aislinn said. "Can we go?"

The heat felt even more intense now, but it was a relief to be away from the crowd, away from the shocking sight of the Hindu devotees. She couldn't imagine being so committed to a religion or a cause to subject oneself to such disfigurement. As they drove back to Lee's house, she let the breeze wash over her through the tiny car's open windows.

When they had settled on the verandah with glasses of white wine, Aislinn felt better.

"So, what did you think?" Lee asked.

"I'm not sure what to think, honestly. I get that it's all part of their faith, but I can't imagine how anyone can do that to themselves."

"It's not unique to the Hindus, though. Even Christians have a history of mortification of the flesh. Why do any of us do what we do?"

Aislinn thought of the Muslim suicide bombers and the 9/11 hijackers who believed in the righteousness of their actions, although to her and people like her, it made no sense. It was beyond her comprehension.

"Oh, I know. We all have our reasons. We do crazy things for love. Or money, I guess."

Lee put down her wineglass and Aislinn realized she'd struck a nerve. She was about to apologize when Lee said, "And sometimes both." She stood up. "Be right back." She ran up the stairs and returned with a painting that she propped on a chair on the veranda. It was an abstract portrait, somewhat in the style of the Pennington portraits in Aislinn's dining room, but it was unmistakably a picture of TJ Kwan.

"He's going to hate it, I know, but he wanted me to paint him. I told him I didn't do portraits, but it wasn't really a request. So, this is what I did, and I don't think I can show it to him."

Aislinn grinned, imagining TJ's reaction, and looked closely at the painting. As she did, the mouth opened in a snarl and blood dripped from his teeth. The wineglass fell from her hand and shattered on the dark wood of the verandah.

"My God, Shan, I'm so sorry." Lee hurried to the kitchen and returned with a towel to clean up the mess while Aislinn knelt and picked up the pieces of broken glass, cutting a finger in the process. She barely felt it, but blood dripped toward her nail, and she stuck her finger in her mouth, something she'd done with cuts since she was a girl. The taste was metallic and salty.

"You've cut yourself," Lee said. "Let me get you a plaster."

While she was gone, Aislinn turned the portrait around. She couldn't bear to look at it.

"What was that about?" Lee asked when she came back with the bandage, helping Aislinn to wrap the wound. She glanced at the chair that held TJ's portrait. "You turned the painting?"

"I don't know how to explain."

"Try me."

"When I looked at it, looked into TJ's eyes, he spoke to me, and his face moved. It was a threat, I think."

"What are you talking about? It's just a painting."

She told her about TJ's visit to the office with the jacket she'd lost at the demonstration, how he had plotted with Liam to depose Liam's boss. "Maybe I was hallucinating, but I don't trust him, Shan."

Lee looked at the painting, the rear of the canvas visible, and began to cry. In a whisper she said, "Neither do I."

Aislinn got up and sat next to her, putting an arm around her shoulder. "I know it won't be easy, but maybe you should leave. I think he's dangerous."

"How? He would never let me. And where would I go?"

. . . . .

What had she been thinking? Martin was handsome, and his exotic blend of races was intoxicating. What woman wouldn't find him attractive? Surely, she wasn't alone. But it's not as if she slept with every attractive man she met. Was it that he reminded her of Clark in so many ways? Or just that Liam had been pushing her away ever since they'd arrived here. He'd changed so much, and he was probably having an affair. Letting Martin kiss her had been a mistake. Sleeping with him had been a worse mistake. And now she had to stay away from him, from the shop. This wasn't New York. Even if she wanted to carry on an affair with him, they wouldn't be able to hide it the way she and Liam had escaped detection for months.

And yet, she had to face the possibility that Liam already knew. Somehow TJ knew she'd been sailing with Martin, and maybe he knew more than that. Liam had met Martin and insulted him when Rebecca brought him to dinner, but surely there was something more behind those insults. Had TJ told him about Martin? And if he knew, why hadn't he confronted her? Possibly for the same reason she hadn't confronted him. They were both guilty.

Liam had been especially quiet since the kids left after Christmas. He said he had a lot on his mind, busy at work, despite the traditionally quiet period around the holidays. And Aislinn couldn't stand it. She was lonely, and found herself gravitating toward Martin's shop, despite her resolve to stay away. She wanted someone to talk to. Nothing more than that.

She entered the mall and then changed her mind. It was dangerous to go to him, so instead, she went in the opposite direction. She stopped in the antique store, unable to focus on the furniture or knick-knacks, then the rug shop, then the florist. She worked her way around the floor, until she came to Orientalia. The shop was dark. Brown paper covered all the shop windows, so she couldn't see in. Taped to the door was a "For Let" sign.

• • • • •

At dinner, she and Liam barely spoke. Her thoughts were with Martin, wondering what had happened and why the shop had closed so suddenly. Did it have something to do with her? Had he decided there was no future for them, and so he was free to go back to Australia? But he would have let her know, wouldn't he? Liam seemed lost in his own thoughts, and she wished he would talk to her. Something was troubling him, and she wanted to help, but lately, whenever she'd asked, he'd only bottled himself up tighter.

The next day, she set off for a walk in the Botanic Gardens. She told herself she wasn't going to Martin's house, but instead of entering the park, she found herself standing at his door.

She knocked, and Martin pulled her inside.

"What happened at the shop?" she asked.

He took her into his arms and kissed her, but she pushed him away.

"No, Martin, we can't. I only came because I saw the For Let sign and I wanted to make sure you were all right. What happened?"

"What didn't happen? First, I got a notice from the Registrar of Businesses that there was a problem with our license. Of course, my father had been renewing the same license for years, decades probably, but now suddenly there's a problem. They found a flaw. I don't even know what, except it was in his name, not mine. I said, 'Fine, I'll fix it, what do I have to do?' and they said, 'not so fast, it's not as simple as that.' And while I was trying to find out what they wanted me to do, the landlord told me I was in violation of the lease and that I had to close the shop and move. It's the same damn lease we've always had, and we haven't done anything different. The store is the same store, we sell the same stock. Nothing has changed except my father is gone and I'm the one running it. But now we're in violation of the lease? It makes no sense. And then, since I'd have to move the shop—if I could find a place to move to—I'm told the old license, which is flawed anyway, isn't sufficient. I have to apply for a new license. And so, effectively, I'm out of business."

"Have you checked with a lawyer?"

"Honestly, Aislinn, I can't afford a lawyer. We barely make enough in the shop to cover the rent as it is. What they're asking us to do will mean thousands more a month, and we just don't have it. And we don't have the fees to pay a lawyer."

"What will you do?"

"If it weren't for you, I'd seriously consider going back to Oz. Chucking it all and leaving. But I can't." He reached for her again.

"Don't do that to me. You know it's impossible. I've told you that."

"Yes, you've told me. And yet, here you are."

He put his arms around her and kissed her again, and this time she didn't push him away.

• • • • •

At home, she stepped out of the lift, still thinking about Martin—how comfortable she felt with him, how her own troubles fell away when she was with him, how much like Clark he was. She opened the apartment door and her breath caught at the sight of Liam sitting in their living room, gazing at the Shan Lee painting of the jungle's threatening tendrils, a glass of Scotch in his hand. His jacket was off, his tie loosened and shirt open at the neck. He didn't turn to look at her when she entered.

"It's early, Liam. What are you doing home? Is something wrong?" She remembered how he had behaved when he got the call about the Bali bombing, and she wondered if there had been another attack.

"Where have you been?"

"Shopping." She realized she had no shopping bags with her, nothing to back up her story, and she felt her face flush. "I couldn't find what I was looking for."

"What were you looking for, Aislinn? What do you need?"

"What happened? What's wrong?"

He took a long pull of Scotch. "We have a little problem at work," he said. "Not so little, actually."

She sat on the sofa. "Tell me."

He finished his Scotch, got up and went to his liquor cabinet, and poured a splash, then poured more. He came back and resumed his seat.

"You remember the deal TJ was so keen on? The Thailand loan secured by motorbikes and cars?"

"I remember. The leases were to be held by an agent."

He nodded. "It seemed like a great idea. Fool proof. Easy money."

"But?"

"But there was another bank that thought the same thing."

"Oh, no. The same borrower?"

He nodded again.

"How long have you known?"

"Since Christmas. A little before. It's the reason I was in a foul mood when the kids were here. One of the reasons."

It turned out that TJ's acquaintance, Khun Anuwat, had disappeared, leaving low-level managers to deal with the fallout of the fraud. Somehow, the title documents and leases had been duplicated and used as collateral for two different syndicates of lenders. And they were both looking at a total loss, unless the company could somehow continue to collect on the leases and service both loans. But that still wouldn't be enough, and they would book losses totaling at least fifty million dollars.

She remembered questioning Liam about this deal when she'd heard him discuss it with TJ. Thailand was a civil law jurisdiction, with a secured lending system that was completely different from what she was familiar with, so there was no way to be certain that assets were lien-free. And now it turns out they weren't. The deal seemed too good to be true, and so it was.

"What are you going to do now? What does TJ say?"

"I think," Liam said slowly, as if choosing his words carefully, not sure what he would say out loud, "that TJ is involved in the fraud."

"What makes you think that?" From what she was beginning to understand about TJ, Liam's suspicion didn't surprise her.

"It was all his idea, Aislinn. Khun Anuwat is his friend. It's not TJ's money at risk, it's ours. He gets paid for his connections, not to supply the capital. And he waited until Bruce was out of the way, pitching the deal to me, the eager new guy trying to prove himself."

Some of that made sense. Kwan thought he could manipulate Liam and helped maneuver Bruce out of the way. But it didn't entirely add up. The loss wouldn't look good for the bank, but it wasn't the end of the world, either. And how did TJ benefit from it?

"So you'll have to write off a bad loan. We saw that in New York often enough. It's not good, but it's not the end of the world."

"That's not all. There's something else."

"What is it?"

He started to say something, stopped, then began again as if something else had occurred to him.

"I didn't tell you before, but that artist, Shan Lee? TJ is seeing her. She's his mistress, I guess, and that's why he wanted me to buy one of her paintings."

"She told me."

He nodded. Nothing was going to surprise him, although Aislinn hadn't told him she and Shan had become friends because she thought it was best if TJ didn't know.

"I'm not sure she's safe."

"Liam, what are you saying?"

"She's been making noises he didn't like. About leaving him. About talking to the authorities about his shady deals if he didn't let her go."

"Do you think he might hurt her?"

He drained the Scotch. "Maybe not physically, but he could make her life hell."

"What can we do? How can we help her?"

"Stay out of it, love. It's none of our business and it would only make matters worse."

"I can't, Liam. She's my friend."

"I think maybe you should go away for a while. Visit your mother? Just until this gets sorted out."

"You think TJ is dangerous to me? Then what about you, Liam? We should tell someone. Tell your bosses you think he's a problem. We should both go." Could she tell him about the dossier Martin's father had built about TJ years ago? She couldn't, though, not without revealing too much, and she hadn't yet seen it, and didn't know its contents.

"I can't leave. Not with this mess hanging over us."

"Why not? Let's get the hell out of here. Quit the bank. We can go back to New York and get new jobs and rebuild our lives there."

"It's not that simple. I can't go. Not yet."

"Tell me what's going on. I don't understand." What had he gotten himself into that was so terrible?

"I don't know for sure."

Cecilia had emerged from the kitchen and was setting the dining table. Liam nodded toward the balcony and when they were both outside, he closed the door.

"TJ has apparently told Stephens that I got a kickback from Anuwat for doing the motorbike deal, but he's lying. My guess is that it's TJ who got the kickback, and I'm reasonably sure he knows where Anuwat disappeared to."

"Where were your lawyers? I thought you had a Thai law firm looking the structure over."

"I imagine they were in on it. Seems like the whole country was in on it. They all used me."

"What happens now?"

"To me? I'll be fired. At a minimum."

"Minimum? What else can they do?"

"Remember I told you about a trader here ten years back who nearly brought down the entire banking system with his phony trades?"

"Surely that's different."

"He's still in jail, love."

"Jail? You could go to jail?"

He nodded.

"But that makes no sense. It was a bad loan, not a crime. Why on earth would you be at risk of going to jail?"

Gazing out into the gathering dusk, he didn't answer, and she understood that he wasn't telling her all of it. It wasn't just the motorbike deal, and it wasn't just about TJ.

"Before it happens, Aislinn, you should leave."

"Liam, if you can't go, then I won't either."

• • • • •

Liam's revelation—his partial revelation, because Aislinn knew he hadn't told her everything about his predicament—put her on edge. He wanted her to leave, to get out of harm's way, but how could she do that? She couldn't leave without knowing what sort of trouble he was in. No matter how she felt about Martin, she hadn't stopped loving Liam, not really, despite the changes that had come over him.

He was going to need a lawyer, and Aislinn wondered if there might be a way for her to enlist the aid of Selvadurai or one of the other Bradford & Co. partners. Liam had hinted that beyond the loss for the bank, he might be facing criminal charges, like the rogue trader who had nearly caused a financial panic some years before. There was a lawyer at the firm, a Mr. Wong, who specialized in white-collar criminal defense. Maybe he could help.

And, besides, Liam wasn't her only concern. Martin's compounded problems with the authorities and his landlord were puzzling. She didn't know Singapore law, of course, and landlord and tenant disputes were out of her expertise. Plus, she suspected, in a commercial city like Singapore, leases would be skewed in favor of the landlord. There might be some recourse available, some tenant protections she didn't know about, but it seemed unlikely. As for the problem with the business license, that was even more bizarre, especially coming at the same time as the problem with the lease. Martin wasn't the type to give up easily, but the two blows at once were even more than he could cope with. He said he couldn't afford a lawyer, but maybe there was a way for Bradford & Co. to help him, too? If he were to surrender now and return to Australia, what would she do? Was a future with Martin even possible? Was that what she wanted?

Her life with Liam in New York had been nearly idyllic—maybe because it was so hectic, she hadn't had time to take a hard look at her marriage—but here in Singapore, she was miserable. What Liam had revealed only made it worse. Why couldn't he just leave? Was it really because of his legal troubles, or was it because of a woman? If they were going to save their marriage, if that was what she wanted at this point, they both had to go home.

Until they'd come here, she hadn't seen the side of Liam that drove him to destroy people like Bruce and Jenny Morelock. Or maybe she'd been too much like that herself in New York, competing with her fellow associates at the firm for a coveted partnership, and had been blind to it. Maybe it was because the situation was new and that allowed her to see clearly what he'd kept hidden from her. Maybe it was just that Liam was still insecure in his position, and once he'd solidified it and grown confident the job was his, he would become himself again. Or was the problem that he was under TJ's influence now? Had greed, the desire to accumulate more and more, to extract as much wealth from Asia as he could, overcome him?

Her only other choice, she supposed, was going back to New York, leaving Liam *and* Martin behind, and rebuilding the life she'd abandoned to come here. She might even be able to go back to her law firm. She hadn't been gone that long, but if Morrow, Dunn wouldn't have her, surely another firm would.

And what was she supposed to do about Shan Lee? Was she really in danger? What might TJ do to her?

How did she get herself into this mess? It was like some hellish maze. She'd taken one step and another step, and each one made sense at the time, or at least there had seemed to be no other choice, but now she found herself lost, with no way out.

• • • • •

Eager to get to Bradford & Co. and approach Selvadurai about Liam's difficulties, she went directly to his office. "If you've got a minute," she said when he looked up from his desk, "I wonder if I could talk to you about advising my husband on a legal matter."

He gestured to a chair and pushed aside the document he'd been reading. "What seems to be the problem?"

She filled him in as best she could—how TJ had brought a deal to Liam's banking joint venture that had now gone bad as a result of the borrower's fraud, how Liam suspected TJ had been in on the fraud to begin with but now blamed Liam, how Liam worried that he faced criminal liability in addition to the financial loss the bank would have to swallow. She suspected the problem was even bigger than that, but she didn't know how to explain it or even how to start.

When she had finished, they sat in silence. Selvadurai folded his hands in front of him. It occurred to her—why hadn't she thought of it before?—that Selvadurai and TJ might be friends. It was TJ, after all, who had talked to him about hiring her in the first place. This might have been a colossal blunder.

"Aislinn, I'm not sure we can be of direct help to your husband under the circumstances, but let me see what I can do." With that, he returned his attention to the document on his desk.

· · · · ·

Later in the morning, Selvadurai appeared and dropped a file on her desk.

"It's nothing urgent," he said, "but I wonder if you could review this file for me."

"Sure," she said, eager to start a new project, if only for the distraction it would provide. "What's the issue here?"

Selvadurai hesitated. "You tell me. Just don't discuss it with anyone else."

"Have you given any more thought to how we might help my husband?"

"Let's talk after you've reviewed the file," he said, closing the door behind him as he left.

She pulled the first of several manila folders from the accordion file and opened it, following the story like a detective novel. The next folder was just as riveting. The last was thinner, a criminal indictment for the firm's client, but the final document in the file gave away the ending of the story. The client was deceased from an overdose, an apparent suicide.

It appeared that the client was the principal owner of a Singapore importer of industrial supplies. At some point the company entered into a contract with another entity—one that looked from its incorporation papers to be a shell company incorporated in Hong Kong—and before long the two companies were in litigation over the Hong Kong company's multiple contract breaches, primarily a failure to pay sums owed. Very large sums. The paperwork in the file didn't indicate what industrial supplies were involved, but whatever they were, the letter of credit on which the client relied turned out to be fraudulent, leaving the client holding the bag. And instead of the Hong

Kong company paying the price, the Singapore authorities were hounding Selvadurai's client. Or, they were, until his death.

This wasn't a project for her. It was a warning.

There was one more folder, with background information on the Hong Kong company. The papers, many times photocopied and barely legible, traced the ownership of the company to a Cayman Islands entity and another intermediary back to a Singapore citizen, TJ Kwan.

She was now certain that TJ was the source of Liam's problems and probably Martin's, too. She understood there might be nothing they could do to protect themselves. TJ was too rich and too powerful, and would get what he wanted, no matter what. She returned the files to Selvadurai, who only shook his head.

She understood what he was telling her. Despite being well connected, a prominent lawyer and former Law Minister, he wouldn't be able to help Liam. TJ was too powerful.

• • • • •

At dinner that night, she opened a bottle of the Australian chardonnay she'd come to like, and Cecilia served a poached fish Aislinn had requested. Liam spoke about his day, in particular about a young secretary who had made some mistake for which he'd had to discipline her, causing much tears. He didn't seem in the least remorseful, and he showed none of the anxiety and dread from the previous night. She said nothing about her day of work or the information she'd discovered about TJ, still not sure exactly what it meant or why Selvadurai had put it into her hands, commenting only that the weather hadn't seemed as hot, as if the fact that it was January had any significance at the equator.

They dined in silence. As Aislinn gazed at the Pennington paintings, she realized that Martin's problems were probably not coincidental. Martin was an affront to Liam, his little joke about dating Rebecca having backfired. Liam was somehow punishing Martin, the shopkeeper. Was that it? Or was there more?

How could he have arranged Martin's difficulties? Did he visit TJ's office, TJ who knew everyone in town and had all the connections? Did they plot Martin's downfall just as they'd destroyed Bruce Morelock? No doubt TJ knew the landlord in the shopping center and was able to persuade him it would be good for business to do this favor for the bank. And TJ knew the government, even had a son who worked in some Ministry who had perhaps pulled strings with the Registrar of Businesses to make Martin's life miserable. To what end, though? What did Liam hope to accomplish by destroying him?

"How much do you really know about TJ?" she asked.

"Rich. Powerful. Connected."

"Right. So you've said." Liam didn't respond. "I came across some information at work today, some deals he's been involved with that look shady. I wonder if it wouldn't be a good idea to put some distance between TJ and yourself."

"TJ." Liam didn't look particularly surprised by what she'd told him. "I spent today convincing myself that we were OK, that TJ was going to find us a way out of the mess we made. He made. But I'm afraid he's only going to make it worse. For me."

· · · · ·

It was Sunday, and Liam was playing golf. He didn't particularly like golf, although he was good at it, as he was with all sports. But this was business, maybe a way to work himself out of his difficulties, and so, despite the intense heat, he was out on the course with a client. Aislinn was at the American Club, lying by the pool, reading a book and occasionally letting her mind wander to her problem. What she'd discovered in the files Selvadurai let her see had raised serious concerns about Liam's relationship with TJ, especially given the thin ice Liam seemed to be on at work. There was no solution other than breaking free from TJ.

She looked up from her book and saw a couple walking around the edge of the pool. She was sure she was unrecognizable behind her sunglasses and sunhat, but she was surprised to see Michael, Rebecca's Michael, walking hand in hand with a stunning Malay girl in a skimpy bikini. Aislinn had received a few emails from Rebecca since she went home, and although she hadn't gone into detail, she'd said that she and Michael had been carrying on a torrid online romance. Apparently, though, from Michael's viewpoint, their relationship wasn't exclusive. It occurred to Aislinn that Liam had used Michael to manipulate Rebecca. And now she wondered if Liam was really playing golf. He was experienced at deception, she knew. Would he come home with stories of birdies and pars, pythons on the fairway and rough greens? At this point, why should she believe him?

Was she any better? She hadn't seen Martin in days, but she thought about him constantly. And the more she thought about him, the more she needed to see him. She packed up at the club, changed at home, and walked.

· · · · ·

The sky clouded over, and the heat seemed to dissipate. By the time she reached Martin's house, a light rain was falling. She knocked on the door and there was Martin. She stepped inside and put her arms around him, made no effort to resist when he kissed her, or when he led her to the stairs.

Later, as they lay in bed, Martin said, "I'm glad you're here."

"Me, too," she said.

"And don't get me wrong, because I couldn't be happier, but why did you come?"

"I needed to be with you."

"Yes. But just for today? Will you go home now and climb into bed with your husband?"

"He's cheating on me."

"And you're cheating on him. Am I some kind of revenge for what he's done to you? Or maybe this is just a white woman's fling with one of the natives?"

"No, of course not."

"Then what are we doing? Because I can't do it this way, Aislinn. And I probably can't stay in Singapore. Things have gotten worse. Now the tax authorities have notified us of an audit at the shop. I've got a meeting with Inland Revenue on Monday. And a friend has been arrested in connection with some anti-government protest, a friend who had no more to do with it than I did, so when you knocked on the door, I expected to be hauled in."

"Liam."

"What?"

"I wonder if Liam's behind that. Not specifically the tax people, but I think he might have told his friend TJ to cause trouble. He was mad about Rebecca."

"That was nothing, Aislinn. Why would he try to destroy me just because I took his daughter to dinner? Or almost took her. It doesn't make sense."

"No, it doesn't, but you don't know my husband."

"You must be mistaken. And I told you, Kwan has had it in for my family for years. I wouldn't be surprised if he's behind it all."

"You're probably right, unless…. What if it's not because of Rebecca? What if he knows about us?"

"How could he know?"

"I don't know. I tried to avoid looking at you when you came over with Rebecca. I thought you were doing the same."

"I couldn't. A fool could have seen."

"Liam's no fool. And when I brought Rebecca to the shop before she went home, she suspected something. We were careless. What if she mentioned it to her father?" She remembered that TJ had warned her about friends with sailboats. He'd known all along, somehow. Had he told Liam?

"It might be your husband. Or it might be Kwan."

17

15 February 1915
The Chinese New Year celebration began last evening, accompanied by much chattering among the servants and the preparation of their traditional foods—steamed dumplings, balls of sweet rice, and delicious tiny oranges—all meant to bring good fortune. We are welcoming the year of the rabbit, apparently, according to their zodiacal system, which promises love and tenderness. Let us hope the prophecy is fulfilled.

This morning, then, Uncle and I were on our own, the servants having been given the day off to spend time with family, as befits the most important holiday of their calendar. While I do appreciate their daily labors on our behalf, I relished the peace and quiet in their absence and did not mind slicing the fruit and preparing the tea myself for our breakfast, although I could stomach only a bit of toast. We ate on the veranda, watched the breeze stir the palm trees in the garden, and thoroughly enjoyed the tranquility.

Soon, though, the time came to travel to Government House for the opening of the exhibition of my paintings. I was nervous, of course, not having any idea how my paintings would be received, and also increasingly uncomfortable, although my condition is still hidden, for the moment.

I tried to mingle with the guests who, when they saw me, expressed their admiration for the pictures, whether sincerely or not I could not tell. Even Governor Young put in an appearance and praised my work as being the equal of any modern drawings he had seen in London or on the Continent. There were those who expressed puzzlement, unaware that I could hear them, complaining that the portraits were not lifelike, or that the scenes depicted were not realistic. These reactions did not trouble me in the least, as I had learned long ago from Richard that such criticism was a signal that the work was not intended for that viewer and was not a judgment of its worth. All in all, though, the long-awaited occasion was a success far beyond my expectations. Nothing less than glorious, in truth.

As I moved from painting to painting, making contact with each cluster that had formed to study the art, feeling a bit like a bee that lands briefly on a flower before buzzing off to the next, I kept an eye on the entrance to the hall in the hope of spying the arrival of Captain Bingham, for it was his approval and recognition I craved above all others.

While there was no sign of Charles, I was amused to see Mr. Preston, who is still among us after all this time. There are rumors that he intends to return to England soon, and indeed he has made a number of visits to neighboring territories during his sojourn, despite the inherent risks from savages, not to mention the Germans. All fodder for his novels, I suppose. He also heaped praise on the exhibition, although I detected a note of derision for such a provincial effort. Perhaps I am imagining it, and he was in any case as unctuous as ever. At one point, I overheard him explain to Governor Young, "She studied with Richard Bromley, you know." So, he had not forgotten.

Eventually, the strain was more than I could bear, and I hurried to find a place where I could sit, alone or not. I did not mind. Soon Mrs. Craddock came to join me, however, so I was not looking quite so pitiful. She reported that she had heard nothing but praise for the pictures, and for that I was most grateful. There was champagne, to my surprise, and I found that the bubbles did help to settle my stomach. A servant, a Malay girl, wearing a colorful long-sleeved dress I learned was called a *kebaya*, brought slices of a mango cake, as well, and that was delightful. I suppose she was not released to partake of the holiday, as were the Chinese servants.

In planning the exhibition, we did not expect to become merchants. That was far from the point of the event, as I understood it. And while I had, when the subject first arose, no intention of selling the paintings, I do not know what I thought I would do with them once the show was over. I had learned from Richard Bromley that the making of art is its own reward, but that paintings are ultimately meant to be sold and displayed so that the artist might eat and prosper, however modestly.

Except for the one monkey portrait I'd given him, Uncle Cyril had shown no inclination to hang my pictures in his home, his taste tending more toward the peculiar artifacts that he has collected in his travels than to still lives and portraiture. He has a particularly gruesome collection from some primitive tribe in New Guinea that includes what he indelicately described as "penis sheaths" made of some knitted material or dried and elongated gourds. They are hideous things, but some of his other pieces—bronze statuary, wood carvings, intricate woven fabrics—are lovely, and I have urged him to display more of the latter.

Now, in my condition, and uncertain what the future holds, it occurs to me that I might soon be in need of funds and that perhaps I should have considered putting a price on the paintings after all. But who in the settlement would buy? And would I be all the more humiliated if it turned out that no one was willing to put forth even one pound for work that I had poured my heart into? So, ultimately, I am glad the paintings are not for sale. But, yet, what shall I do with them? Store them in a cupboard in Uncle's house where they will gather dust, never again to be looked upon?

And then it was all over, the guests dispersed, and Captain Bingham had not come. In fact, no one from the barracks was in attendance, which Uncle remarked was most peculiar. The war seemed so far away, but at the same time the absence of the Regiment made it feel so real, and I confess that I sank into a deep melancholy when Uncle brought me home before returning to his chambers in town to conduct some business or other that would not wait. I did not take tea and retired to my room to rest.

15 February 1915, evening
I do not know what to do. The servants have not yet returned, although they were due back before now, and Uncle is not here either. Where can he be? I sit in the dark with a single lamp so that I may write in these pages, but I am sorely afraid and wonder if I should not douse the lamp as well. I hear gunshots now and then, close by, then far away, and I do not know what it means. At least I believe they are gunshots, although they sound nothing like the hunters' shotguns I remember hearing in the English countryside. Have the Germans invaded Singapore? How is it possible we did not have warning of their approach? Would the watch not have spied them from the observation tower at Fort Canning? It was only this morning that we roamed the halls of Government House, and yet no one told us of any danger.

It began midafternoon. After the ordeal of the morning and the strain of exhibiting my paintings, I retreated to my room to lie down. I did not sleep. I can only think of the future and what will become of me and…the baby. The baby, whom I have not yet acknowledged. As I lay on the bed, I heard what I thought was a firecracker, of the kind that the Chinese seem to love. At first, I found it out of the ordinary, but then I remembered that, in fact, today is their holiday and so the lighting of their crackers is not terribly surprising. It was their way of celebrating.

Upon reflection, however, I thought it was odd after all. Because the Chinese were unlikely to light their fireworks in our district, as all the servants had gone. Rather, they would be down at the padang, or along the quay, or anywhere in the Chinese district of the settlement, gathering with their kind. Near the joss house, for example. If I were there, lying in the arms of my Captain Bingham, I would not be at all surprised to hear firecrackers erupting all around us. Or, perhaps I would be surprised, but I would recognize the custom and would be comforted by Charles, his closeness and soothing whispers, the moist touch of his warm body.

Then I heard more such crackers, and I realized the explosions were certainly the report of gunfire, not the tiny poppers that are familiar here. Unless the celebration had taken on a more rambunctious tone than I'd been led to expect, this was not mere fireworks. And, indeed, the sound came from much closer than the Chinese district. They seemed to be coming from very nearby, and then they were coming from everywhere at once, and I was sure the road in front of the bungalow was filled with them.

I was terrified.

When I heard more explosions that sounded as if they were just beyond my window, I squeezed inside the wardrobe. It seemed the only place that wasn't exposed to whatever was happening outside. I heard voices, shouting, but no words I could distinguish. I smelled smoke, and at first I thought Uncle's house must be on fire, but the smell diminished. It returned and left again, and I concluded that the flames were at some distance, the smell arriving and departing on the currents. I don't know how long I remained in the wardrobe.

All was quiet. I pushed the door open just a crack. I heard what I thought was another gunshot, but it sounded far away. At last, it seemed safe to emerge.

15 February 1915, night
Still no one had come. The servants, Uncle Cyril. The sky was nearly dark. I shook with fear and returned to the wardrobe to listen and wait.

I heard a voice. It called my name. I did not recognize the voice at first. "Miss," it called. "Miss Elizabeth!"

Raj. It was the voice of Lieutenant Raj, and I knew instantly that he had a message from Charles, or perhaps he had come to take me to Charles. I was safe. I threw open the door of the wardrobe and ran to the stairs, although I could barely see for the dark.

"Miss Elizabeth," he called again.

"Yes, Raj, I'm here," I said into the stairwell.

"Stay where you are," he said. "I will come to you."

I heard his steps treading the stairs and then he stood before me. In the dim light I saw that his uniform was smeared with black and that his face was also streaked with black. When I lit the lamp, I saw it was blood that had soaked his jacket and soiled his face.

"You're hurt," I said. "What is going on?" I sought out linens for bandages and a cloth to wash his wounds.

"There is no time," he said. "I only came to see if you were all right. And to tell you not to leave this house. You will be safe here. I have made certain."

"What do you mean, Raj? Safe from what? Is it the Germans? Have we been attacked?"

Now there was renewed gunfire, and it was not distant.

"I must go. You will be safe here. Do not leave."

"Where is Captain Bingham?" I asked.

"I must go," he said again.

He ran down the stairs. I think I shall never see him again.

17 February 1915

Uncle Cyril is dead. It seems impossible, but the clerk from his office, Mr. Avery Bradford, saw it happen. He came to tell me, and I cannot think just now of the scene he described. It is too horrible.

· · · · ·

The servants returned yesterday, after the holiday, full of their own trepidation and uncertainty, curious about the absence of Uncle Cyril. I had cowered all night in my bedroom, not knowing what to do, even turning the lamp off so as not to attract attention. I could not sleep, though, as I was alert to any sound. The shrieking of a night bird, the howling of a monkey, the croaking of a toad in the garden—every slight noise convinced me that an intruder was on the grounds and that I would soon be murdered.

But—Raj had said I would be safe in the house. Safe from what? I did not know until the servants came and found me in my room, where I had, at last, fallen asleep.

Poor, poor Uncle Cyril!

And this is what I understand now has happened.

There was a mutiny in the Regiment. No one knows exactly, but it seems that the sepoys, the Indian soldiers of which Lieutenant Raj is one, turned against the British officers. When I heard this, I of course thought of Charles, but did not interrupt the messenger. They captured weapons and rushed to the Tanglin Prison—not far at all from our house, so perhaps the source of the shooting I heard—to free the German prisoners who were interned there. I cannot imagine what they were thinking! The Germans are the enemy of India as well as England. But I remember that Raj once told me the men from Punjab did not want to fight the Turks, and they believed they were going to be sent to Africa for that very purpose, although Charles and his superiors had told them they were bound for Hong Kong to defend the colony there.

The sepoys—hundreds of them I now understand—simply ran wild. Bands of them went marauding, pillaging as they went, burning houses and shops. I am told by Mr. Bradford, the poor man who saw it all, that it was at a shop where Uncle was killed. They emerged from the establishment together to see what the commotion was in the street. A dozen or so sepoys opened fire—simply because they were Englishmen, it appears, and therefore the oppressors—and then moved on down the road toward the harbor. Bradford expressed shame that it was Uncle who was killed, and not him, but who can explain the workings of fate? One man takes a step and dies. Another man stands still and lives.

I am in a state of shock. What purpose did the killing serve? How did it aid their cause, which, it seems, was misguided from the beginning? Poor, poor Uncle Cyril! This tragedy recalls too clearly my own dear father's death, and now I am to be faced with the burial of yet another loved one.

17 February 1915, evening
There is still no news of Charles, and I am beside myself with worry. What has happened to him? There is word that some officers of the Regiment were killed during the mutiny. Surely I cannot have lost Uncle Cyril and Charles, too. Fate is not so cruel as that, I am certain. And yet, he would send a message if he could. He would know that I am worried, and he would also be worried for my own safety. I fear that he is hurt, or worse. I tried to approach the barracks to find him, but I was turned back. They would not let me near. Too dangerous, they said. And where, I wonder, is Raj?

The true danger, it seems, has passed. The Russians and the Japanese helped round up the mutineers, although not all, apparently. There are reports that some are still on the loose, as are many of the German prisoners whom the sepoys freed. Mrs. Craddock has insisted that I come to stay at her home until things have returned to normal, but of course they will never return to normal. I had thought to stay with Uncle Cyril when the baby came, if by then Charles and the Regiment had decamped to Hong Kong, if he would have me, but now what shall I do? In the meantime, I am with the Craddocks, but I have no comfort here. Poor, poor Uncle. And where is Charles?

18

By mid-January, the Christmas decorations on Orchard Road and inside the ubiquitous shopping malls had been replaced by harbingers of the Chinese New Year that this year would occur on the first weekend in February: faux cherry tree branches with pink silk blossoms, red paper lanterns, and wide banners that shouted slogans in Chinese and English—Happy New Year and Wishing You Prosperity and Wealth. In China, the holiday was known as the Spring Festival, but it was hardly spring-like in Singapore, with temperatures still over ninety during the day. At home in New York, according to CNN, temperatures hovered around freezing.

Aislinn realized too late that many expats would be leaving town for the holiday, and now she wished she and Liam had made plans to do the same. They desperately needed a break. Even though she still wasn't keen to get on an airplane, she could have summoned her courage, and perhaps a button, to make it to one of the relatively nearby beach resorts, Phuket in Thailand or Langkawi in Malaysia. With the recent bombing in Bali, she had no desire to go there, but there were other, equally exotic, destinations within a couple of hours. When she looked into the possibilities, however, it was too late. Resorts were full, flights unavailable, tour packages fully booked. Maybe next year she'd make the reservations in time. If there was a next year.

And next year, if she was right about what was happening to her body, there would be a baby to think about. She hadn't been ill yet, but there were other changes she'd noticed. Her breasts felt especially tender and there had been unusual cramping. It was possible she was imagining the source of these changes, but it had been more than a month since she'd stopped taking the pill, having come to the conclusion that a baby was what she and Liam needed if there was any hope of salvaging their marriage. She and Martin had been careful, so there was no doubt that, if she was pregnant, Liam was the father. Now that Liam had revealed to her some of his problems at work, she regretted letting it happen and looked into her options, discovering that Singapore was surprisingly progressive where abortions were concerned. She'd made this decision once before, with Clark. Could she do it again?

The arrival of the holiday on a Saturday, ushering in the Year of the Sheep, promising a docile period, was anti-climactic. Liam, still struggling to salvage his deal and his career, spent the day in his office. Aislinn gave Cecilia the day off and then went to the gym at the American Club, which was nearly empty, but that was fine. She wasn't in the mood to see Jenny Morelock's friends, anyway, certain they held her responsible for the Morelocks' abrupt departure.

In the evening, Liam still had not come home from the office and she began to worry. In the last few weeks, he'd been withdrawn and morose, and only shook his head when she asked whether she could help. She assumed he was distracted by the bad deals TJ had suckered him into, but he wouldn't tell her. Was there more to it than that? She thought he might be cheered if she told him she was pregnant, but under the circumstances, that might make things worse. She'd tell him when she knew for sure what she was going to do.

While she waited for him, she sat in the alcove where they'd hung Shan Lee's painting. She admired it again, the single glass office tower, threatened by black clouds above and the jungle below. As she watched, a tendril grew upward from the jungle and snaked around the building, its grip on the structure tightening as it rose. At the same time, the clouds rumbled, and bright ropes of lightning leaped toward the tower. She gasped when the top of the building burst into flames and the vines choked the burning building, bringing it crashing to the ground.

The phone rang, and the painting returned to its original, static form. The scene had been horrible, but what did it mean? Was it just a reflection of her own state of mind, her world falling apart, threatened from above and below? She picked up the phone.

When a man asked for Lizzie, Aislinn was at first confused, but then remembered what the name signified and coughed, the agreed response to confirm that the message had been received. She hung up. It was the call she'd been waiting for, that she'd hoped would never come, and she began to shake. It meant that preparations were complete. The cloak and dagger maneuver seemed absurd, but they didn't know what they were dealing with.

The plan was not without risks. She'd met Shan Lee one afternoon in the Botanic Gardens and sketched out the details as they strolled through the park. On a bench overlooking the small lake, as they watched the swans glide across the water, Aislinn explained to Lee what she thought might work. Lee had run out of options and nodded her agreement. That afternoon, in Martin's arms after they made love, she'd outlined the same plan to him. He was reluctant, because it meant leaving her, but he, too, had no choice, and agreed. She had done some checking at work and discovered that TJ had bought the building where Orientalia had been located, confirming that he had been behind Martin's troubles. TJ had set out to ruin them both, and they had both concluded they didn't have the strength to fight back. And he'd tried to buy Aislinn's silence by threatening her over the jacket she'd lost at the demonstration.

Now, she checked the slip of paper she'd tucked into her wallet and, still trembling, dialed the number Shan had given her for a new prepaid cell phone. The call went through, but there was no voice on the other end. Although that was as planned, too, now she hesitated. Should she speak? What if it was someone else on the line?

"I'm sorry," she said. "I think I have the wrong number."

There was a muffled cough on the other end. Message received. "I should go now," she said, and ended the call.

* * * * *

The next day, Sunday, Liam was at his office. Before he left that morning, he again urged her to make plans to leave the country, insisting that he had to stay to put things right at the bank and salvage what he could of his reputation. Was now the right time to tell him she was pregnant? She'd see a doctor after the holiday, and she'd know for sure. Either way, maybe she should make plans to leave.

First, though, she needed to check on Shan Lee. She considered calling a taxi, or walking down to Scott's Road to the taxi stand there, but who knew how closely TJ was tracking her movements, or who else might be watching? Would someone know she'd left her building and where she'd gone? It was no longer a question of her affair with Martin being discovered by Liam, but TJ might know her every move. Lee's house—TJ's house, she reminded herself—was nearly two miles from the apartment, a long, hot, two miles, and she'd be a sopping wreck by the time she got there, but it would give her a chance to think about what was happening to her and to plan her next steps.

She approached the house, then stopped in the shade on the opposite side of the road, watching. Nothing moved, except the palm fronds in the garden that rustled in the breeze and a pair of mynahs squabbling noisily in the grass. The gate was closed but unlocked, so she pushed it open, wincing at the croak of metal against metal. Next to the house was Lee's MG, and now she wondered if she shouldn't have called first. What had she expected to find?

On the veranda, standing before the front door, she hesitated again. "Shan?" she called. No reply. "Shan, are you here?"

She rapped on the door but didn't wait for an answer. She tried the latch and the unlocked door swung open.

"Shan?" she called again. The parlor was just as she remembered it, with the eclectic furnishings, the interior walls crowded with artwork, including the Pennington she'd seen on her first visit. She had never been to the upper level of the house, but now she found the stairs and made her way up. A guest room that looked unused. Another room, Lee's from the looks of it, a shambles. The bed clothes rumpled, more artwork on the walls, an open armoire, clothes still hung, but empty hangers, too.

The last room, her studio. On the easel, a self-portrait. As Aislinn studied it, she thought she heard it speak. She turned from the picture when she heard a car on the gravel drive and moved away from the window. In shadow, she watched as TJ emerged from the rear of his Mercedes.

His footsteps thudded up the veranda stairs and the door banged open.

"Shan!" he shouted. "Where the fuck are you?"

Aislinn retreated to the guest room to hide, because surely TJ would come up looking for Lee. She eased the armoire open, sat on the low shelf and lifted her legs inside, pulling the door shut.

"Shan!" TJ's voice was at the top of the stairs now and she imagined him racing into Shan's bedroom. When he saw she wasn't there, and not in her studio either, he would leave. Wouldn't he?

"I know you're here somewhere, you fucking bitch. You know you can't hide from me forever."

Now she heard his voice clearly. His heavy breathing. And then another voice, from further away, by the front door. "Mr. Kwan," the other voice called. "Phone for you in the car."

TJ said something then, in Chinese, and the sound of him faded. His footsteps rang on the stairs, and Aislinn knew she was safe. She only had to wait for the sound of the Mercedes pulling away on the gravel, and she could leave.

But nothing happened. Maybe she wasn't able to hear it inside the armoire. Curled up like that, she'd grown stiff and needed to move, to stretch. She willed herself to accept the discomfort, remain still. Time passed, but she couldn't say how much. Then she thought she heard the car leaving. No, she was sure of it. They were gone.

She pushed open the door of the armoire, squinting as her eyes adjusted to the light, and swung her legs free.

"Hello, Aislinn." TJ sat on the edge of the bed, watching her. "Have you taken up residence in the whore's closet?" He waited, but when Aislinn didn't reply, he continued. "Well, yes, I don't suppose there's a good answer to that question, but I do have some other questions I believe you can answer." He stood and extended a hand to help her out of the armoire, which she took. "Let's go downstairs, shall we?"

They moved to the parlor and TJ opened Shan's liquor cabinet, pouring them both glasses of Scotch. He directed her to the sofa and then sat across from her.

"Now then, Aislinn, I want you to tell me what the fuck you're doing here."

She sipped the Scotch, stalling, but she could tell him this much. It was true. "Looking for Shan. I'm worried about her."

"As well you should be. That little bitch is in way over her head. But I think you know where she is, and I want you to tell me."

"If I knew, TJ, I wouldn't have come here looking for her, would I?"

"Maybe you were looking for something else."

"And what would that be?"

"Not a 'what', my dear. A who perhaps. I also want to know where your charming husband is."

"Why would Liam be here?"

"No, he wouldn't be here, would he? Too close to home, too public. He finds his pleasures elsewhere. What was I thinking? So where is he?"

"He's in his office."

"No, he's not. I've just come from there. But I think you know where he is, too."

"Really, TJ, if he's not in his office, I don't know where he is. Honestly."

"I hope for your sake you're telling the truth, Aislinn, but if you're not, things could go very badly for you." The car's tires sounded in the drive again. Kwan finished his drink and stood, looking at his watch. "My driver is ever punctual. May I give you a lift home?"

She shook her head.

"Suit yourself, then. But if you hear from your husband, tell him I'd like to see him."

When he was gone, she went to the window to watch him get into the car. Even after it had pulled out of the drive, she waited. A quiet settled over the house and TJ didn't return.

She found the car keys where Shan had said they'd be, in the Chinese medicine chest, just inside the front door. She waited a long while, hoping that Kwan had truly left, and then climbed into the MG. It had been ages since she'd driven a stick shift, but it came back to her soon enough. When she pulled the car onto the road, there was no sign of Kwan's Mercedes, but now she wasn't sure what he might do, and hoped she wouldn't be followed.

She knew, even before she'd parked the car at the Changi Sailing Club and made it out to the jetty. She peered at the moorings, counting from the dock, as Martin had explained. Virtually every buoy was occupied, except the one she was looking for. Blue-hulled Lizzie was gone.

They had decided that any move by Lee to sell her car would be traceable by TJ, so Aislinn drove the MG from the sailing club to the Salvation Army Headquarters in the Bishan district and left it there in the open carpark with its keys and title certificate in the glove box. She would phone them later to let them know about the donation and hang up before they started asking questions. TJ would probably hear about it at some point, but by then, Shan would be long gone.

• • • • •

From Bishan, she took the subway back to the apartment complex and went up to their flat, expecting to be greeted by Liam. Instead, there was only Mack. "Apron," he squawked. "Bub!"

She called Liam's cell phone, which went straight to voicemail. When she tried his office number, there was no answer at all. Golf? She checked the closet where he kept his clubs, but they were right where they were supposed to be. Swimming? She ran over to the American Club and checked the pool, the library, the gym, the bar. No Liam. There was no sign of his car in the apartment's carpark. Where was he?

After dark, she was nearly frantic and didn't know who to call. Reaching out to Liam's New York office could cause trouble for him with the bank, and besides, it was still Sunday morning there. Hong Kong, like Singapore, was shut down for the holiday. She might have sought help from Shan or Martin, but now that wasn't possible either. Hospitals? There were so many, she didn't know where to start. If something had happened to Liam, someone would call. The police or…someone. So, nothing had happened. He was all right. He was with someone, or had gone to a bar, or…. Why hadn't he called?

Monday, also a public holiday, passed slowly. Cecilia returned to work and cleaned, as usual. Aislinn worked with Mack, who seemed to enjoy the extra attention, and wished again that she had her piano as a diversion. There was still no word from Liam. For the first time, she wondered if he might hurt himself. The stress had been building at work, more than he'd admitted to her. He was under pressure from TJ, too, and if he had learned about her relationship with Martin, it might all have been too much. It wasn't possible, though. Liam wasn't like her father.

· · · · ·

On Tuesday, not knowing what else to do, she went into work. Her fellow subway passengers seemed cheerful and energized after the long weekend. When she got to her office, she called Liam's bank. His secretary hadn't heard from him, and there were several urgent messages. Did Aislinn know when he might be coming in? She hung up. She thought of enlisting Selvadurai's help in finding Liam. He'd have a better idea of whom she might reach out to. But Selvadurai was with a client, and she'd have to wait. Why hadn't Liam called her to let her know where he was?

On her desk was a file Selvadurai had asked her to review and, briefly, she wondered if this was another warning about TJ. The task provided a distraction, at least, and she made an effort to push her worry aside. This time, the client was a Singapore corporation that was considering an investment in the US fast food industry. As it happened, one of the management buyouts she'd worked on before she left New York was a similar transaction, although from the lender's point of view. She felt like a spy conveying sensitive information to the enemy but made notes for the client on a yellow legal pad and was transported to her days as an associate at Morrow, Dunn & O'Brien.

She was thinking about how to tighten a particular clause in the client's investment proposal, took a sip of coffee, and was nearly thrown from her chair by a crack of thunder. But no, this wasn't thunder. She heard screams, and in what seemed like only seconds, the air filled with the wail of sirens.

"Oh, God, no, not again," she said, barely above a whisper, and then joined the staff gathering in the hallway to find out what had happened.

Safety procedures and common sense both dictated that they should stay away from the windows, but everyone piled into a corner conference room to watch the chaos unfold on the street below. If there was a second explosion, and if the window shattered, there would be casualties. But to hell with the risk, Aislinn needed to know what was going on, and she pushed through the secretaries, tiny young women all of them, to the window. As she peered out at the scene, her thoughts turned to Liam. He'd been near the World Trade Center when the planes attacked. Where was he now?

Directly across Raffles Place from their office building, a fire raged on the ground floor of the South Seas Hotel, which Aislinn remembered was a luxury hotel catering to Japanese travelers. She'd thought it odd that it was located in the heart of the business district, but it attracted primarily a business clientele and was highly successful, with a steady stream of limousines and taxis parked at its entrance. Through a scrim of smoke, Aislinn saw that windows had been blown out in the hotel and neighboring shops and offices, and already the surrounding streets and sidewalks and the small park in front of the hotel were crawling with first responders.

Surely, Aislinn thought, this was the result of a gas leak, or maybe a kitchen fire gone wild. A simple explanation. Her mind had jumped to terrorism—like New York and DC last year, like Bali in October—but it didn't have to be that. In Singapore? Singapore was wrapped up as tight as a drum, and there was no way something like the Bali attack could happen here. Other than the occasional spat with neighboring Malaysia, and the near-trivial complaints of the political opposition, Singapore didn't even have enemies. It was a multicultural society that welcomed everyone, with a thriving Muslim population alongside all the other religions. Why would anyone attack here? And why a hotel instead of a government building?

Might Liam have been there? His office was some distance from the hotel, but he wasn't at his office. She texted him again and didn't get an immediate response, which brought back the memories of 9/11 and the agonizing hours when she didn't know where he was or whether he was even alive. Where was he?

Selvadurai entered the conference room and herded his staff away from the windows and into the reception area, where he asked for quiet so he could address them.

"Nothing to be concerned about," he said, and there was a relieved murmur from the staff. "Nevertheless, the surrounding area will be the center of rescue operations for the rest of the afternoon and evening, so the firm will close for the day." Another murmur, this time of approval.

"The authorities tell me that the MRT is closed for now. Just a precaution. Buses are running, however, so that is probably your best choice for transportation. I'm sure business will be back to normal tomorrow, but call in the morning to make sure we'll be open."

Aislinn detected concern in Selvadurai's voice, so she lingered as the others filed out toward the elevators. She admired his calm reassurance to his staff, but having lived through this once before, she was certain he knew more than he was saying.

"What really happened?" she asked, her voice barely above a whisper.

Selvadurai turned to be sure that no one was nearby. He eyed her, assessing how much he could tell her.

"You know I was in New York on 9/11," she said, and he nodded.

"It was a car bomb just at the entrance, apparently," he said. "We've been instructed to evacuate, just in case, but not to cause a panic. No word on who did it, or why." And then he was called to the telephone, leaving her to gather her things and flee the office.

But she couldn't. As she lifted her briefcase, the tremors struck. At first, she was sure it was another bomb, rattling the building, or an earthquake. But it was her hands, her arms, her entire body convulsing uncontrollably. They had left New York to get away from this. They had come to the opposite side of the planet where they wouldn't have to deal with it, wouldn't be faced with the daily reminders of the horror. But here it was again, like a virus they couldn't shake, first in Bali and now right in front of her. The explosion, the sirens, the dust and debris, the wounded and the dead. Right here. Tears streamed down her face, and she made no effort to brush them away.

She wrapped her arms around herself, trying to stop the tremors. She closed her eyes, breathed deeply. The quaking wouldn't stop.

"Aislinn?"

She spun around to see Selvadurai.

"I'm sorry to startle you, but we need to go."

• • • • •

At home, she saw the television in the living room and remembered the endless replays of the Towers falling, and she couldn't bear the thought of seeing the aftermath of this attack, flames bursting from the hotel in a conflagration that seemed as if it would never be quenched. She didn't want to know what happened. She only knew that the world they'd tried to flee had followed them, and now there was no escaping it. This was the world they had created, America and the other world powers, with the help of people like her, like Liam, where resentment caused the powerless—people with justifiable grievances, their homelands occupied, their wealth exploited—to lash out at their tormentors. Where would it end? How many more people would die from this endless struggle? The thought of it brought back the tremors that had begun at the office, and she went to the bedroom to retrieve her buttons from their hiding place. She hesitated, thinking of the baby, if there was a baby, but she took one in the bathroom and then moved to the dining room to wait for the shaking to stop.

At the table, she gazed at the painting of the temple. Smoke rose behind the woman in the painting's foreground, not just from the urn where she had burned her incense, but from flames that had engulfed the building and perhaps the whole city. Now the woman rushed toward her. Aislinn couldn't hear her, but the woman was screaming at her, telling her to stop killing her people, to stop raping the land and enslaving her sons, her daughters. Aislinn backed away, nearly toppling the chair, the shaking now worse than it had ever been. Pain stabbed into her knee, burning upward into her thigh, and she doubled over when her stomach convulsed in agony. She had never taken two buttons before, but she reached for the silver box and took a second pill. Now she looked at the portraits. The two men, the British soldier and the Indian, looked at her imploringly, blood streaming from both their faces. The artist loved both men and wanted to be with both. But she distrusted them both, too, hated them for what they'd done to her. Aislinn could see that in the men's eyes, reflecting the painter's agony.

Where were Liam and Martin to comfort her? She was drifting now, falling, the room getting darker, and now it was completely black.

· · · · ·

She awoke, in bed, and light was streaming into the room. Liam was in a chair next to her, his eyes closed. Dark stubble peppered his jaw.

"Liam," she said, hearing the rasp of her voice. "Where were you?"

He opened his eyes and sat up, leaning toward her. "You had me so worried, love."

"What happened?"

"When I came home, I found you in the dining room on the floor. And I found this on the table." He held out the silver box with her buttons. "What are these, Aislinn?"

"Yesterday," she said, "it was too much."

"What are they?"

She turned toward the window, the light outside suggesting it was late morning. Now she looked at the beautiful box in his hands, the etched silver with the jade medallion, her lifeline for all these years.

"Percocet. Or something very like it. When the pain in my knee gets too bad, or the stress, they help me."

"You're addicted to painkillers?"

"No, of course not, Liam."

"What would you call it then?"

"Where were you? I couldn't find you."

"I needed time to think. But I'm here now."

• • • • •

She didn't know the details of what had happened at the South Seas Hotel until she read the newspaper. Liam had concluded he could leave her alone, but he took the silver box with him when he returned to his office. *The Straits Times* reported that the explosion had killed fourteen people, as yet unidentified. It was the work of terrorists, clearly, and an organization known as Jemaah Islamiyah, the same group that carried out the attacks in Bali, had claimed responsibility, although their involvement had not been independently confirmed. The goal of Jemaah Islamiyah, the article said, was to create a region-wide Daulah Islamiyah or Islamic State made up of Malaysia, Indonesia, the Philippines, Brunei, and Singapore. At press time, no arrests had been made.

She'd had no idea that such a group was present in Singapore. Their goals went far beyond those of the tepid opposition both Martin and Shan Lee had described to her, although she wondered if the dissidents would share in the blame for what had happened, just as politicians in the US often accused the other side or their allies for every tragedy that occurred, from hurricanes to train derailments. She knew, of course, that Indonesia and Malaysia were both close by and predominantly Muslim. She knew, too, that there had been demonstrations in Jakarta and elsewhere against the US because of the anticipated war in the Middle East. But she hadn't considered for a minute that Singapore was involved, or that it might be the target of terrorists.

• • • • •

After the attack, the police presence was increasingly evident. Now, every day was like the day of the demonstration Aislinn had witnessed—armed guards on subway platforms and street corners. There was even a police officer stationed at the entrance to their apartment complex, which Aislinn discovered had been arranged because one of her neighbors was an executive from an American company that had been threatened by Jemaah Islamiyah in the past. None of which eased her jitters and only reminded her of the tension everyone in New York had felt after the attacks there.

The newspaper reported new arrests of members of the organization, not only in Singapore but also in Kuala Lumpur and Jakarta. At first, the arrests were comforting, as if the authorities had eliminated the danger, but as they mounted, it seemed likely that the group had been buried like a rabbit warren, and it would be impossible to discover all the tunnels and cells. Surely, they'd strike again. And next time, it could be worse.

On the third day after the bombing, the paper published the names and nationalities of the victims. The list included two Japanese citizens and a German, as well as several Singaporeans. The paper also identified two Singaporean confederates of the bombers, individuals known to be tied to local dissident groups, as well as to Jemaah Islamiyah: Martin Roy and Shan Lee. The police had obtained warrants of arrest for both, but they had not yet been located. It wasn't possible, of course, and she knew immediately that TJ must have found a way to implicate them.

Although Liam had returned to work, Aislinn had stayed home, partly because she was afraid to be downtown in the event of another attack, and partly because she was afraid that stress would cause her to find a substitute for the pills Liam had taken from her. There was a third reason, too. She needed time to think about what she was going to do about her pregnancy.

Liam came home from work early, to check on her, she thought, and joined her in the living room. He poured a drink for himself and offered to get her a glass of wine, but she declined. He looked at her questioningly, but said nothing, and she wasn't ready to tell him the reason she wasn't drinking. Dinner passed in near silence. She didn't want to talk about the bombing. He didn't want to talk about work or the pressure he was under from TJ.

"Will you be all right if I go to Hong Kong for a few days?" he asked. "I need to talk to Richardson about what's been going on. I've tried to straighten it out on my own, but I just can't. It may be the only way out."

"Is there—," she said, but stopped herself. Is there a woman in Hong Kong, is what she wanted to ask. She wanted to confront him with what Jenny had told her, and what TJ had hinted at, but how could she?

Before she could say more, Liam spoke. "I've said this before. I want you to leave. It's going to get ugly, and I don't want you here. I mean it, love. Please go back to New York as soon as you can. When things get fixed here, I'll join you."

• • • • •

On Sunday, she lounged by the apartment complex pool. The water made her think of Martin and Shan Lee and the plan she had concocted to get them both out of TJ's clutches, and she wondered if it had worked. She hadn't heard from them, but they had agreed there could be no contact. Eventually, they'd find a way to let her know they'd made it, but for now, she was left to imagine it. Martin had sold his car and had been, basically, living on his boat. When he'd finalized the arrangements and put in the supplies they needed, he called her with the agreed signal. It was his sister, Isabel, who picked Shan Lee up and drove her out to the sailing club after Aislinn alerted her that the time had come. When Aislinn saw that the boat was no longer moored there, she knew the first part of the plan was underway.

· · · · ·

In the apartment, she looked at Lee's painting, the one that had foretold catastrophe. What was the right thing to do? She didn't want Liam to have to deal with his problems alone, but she'd already given up on the marriage. That's what her affair—was it an affair?—with Martin had been about. That was over now, too. She needed to look out for herself, she'd come to realize, and possibly a baby, and that meant going home.

A knock on the door startled her. Mack squawked. She opened the door and saw Shirley Lim.

"May I speak with you for a moment, Aislinn?" Shirley wore an elegant high-collared cheongsam, black with subtle red piping.

"Yes, of course, Shirley."

Shirley came in and waved off Aislinn's offer of tea, but sat, stiffly, on the edge of the chair opposite Shan Lee's painting. She gazed up at it, then turned away quickly, as if she recognized whose work it was and didn't want to see it.

"My husband and I bear you no ill will. I hope you know that."

Aislinn believed quite the opposite, and was in no mood for polite denials, but she was curious what had prompted such an assertion.

Shirley looked again at the painting. "I believe you are acquainted with the artist who made this picture, and I also believe you understand what she is to my husband."

"Yes."

"I want to know where she is."

"I don't know."

"Don't lie to me, Aislinn. It doesn't become you. My husband saw you at her house, and I'm quite certain you know where she's hiding."

"I'm telling you, Shirley, I don't know. As I told your husband, if I knew where she was, I wouldn't have gone to her house to look for her."

"Mr. Kwan didn't want to use threats, Aislinn, but here's the thing. We know you were at the Hong Lim demonstration, which could cause you grave difficulties with the authorities. We also know you have ties to Martin Roy, to put it delicately. Very close ties, which I think your husband will find most interesting. You must know that Roy is Muslim. It will soon be revealed that he is a member of the terrorist organization that attacked the South Seas Hotel, a property in which my husband happens to own a majority stake. If you don't tell me where my husband's whore is, I can make your life very difficult."

What did she mean about Martin? He was no terrorist, and she was certain he had no ties to them. And why was she so keen to find Shan Lee? Her disappearance should make her happy if it meant she'd have TJ all to herself.

"Shirley, I swear to you, I don't know where she is."

"We've given you a chance. I hope you don't regret your decision."

19

17 February 1915, night

Mrs. Craddock knocked on my door as I was writing the above lament. She said that her husband would like to have a word with me downstairs. And so I went to him in his study. He had a terribly somber expression, and I suppose I knew what he was going to say before he had uttered a word.

"Please sit down, Elizabeth," he said.

I complied. I saw he had poured a brandy for himself.

"It seems," he said, "that Captain Bingham is dead."

I nodded, because I knew.

"The wretched mutineers seized the armory and began shooting in the barracks. At least twenty of our men were killed, including two of the Double Company Commanders, Bingham and Elliott. Your Uncle Cyril was not the only civilian killed, either. More than twenty others perished. We have rounded up nearly 700 mutineers and before long will have the rest. A court of inquiry has been established. Justice will be served."

Charles Bingham, dead. "Charles," I said, touching my belly.

"Oh, my word," said Mrs. Craddock, catching my meaning, for I had until now told her nothing of my condition, although I thought she might have guessed. The expression on Mr. Craddock's face told me he did not understand the reason for his wife's exclamation.

"Mr. Craddock," I said, "might I bother you for a spot of brandy?"

19 February 1915
It has been decided. I will leave for Australia as soon as possible. Although there is the ever-present risk from German ships, we are led to believe that I will be safe on a Dutch vessel to Batavia in the Dutch East Indies, from whence passage to Australia can be arranged. I long to be away from here. I will take the name Bingham, which I will pass on to my child, and the name of Pennington will forever vanish.

Mr. Craddock has informed me of developments since the day of the mutiny. The court of inquiry will begin its work, but the case is already clear. Some 800 sepoys and Indian officers took part in the affair. They are being held and their fates will be determined by the court. Craddock says that many, the ringleaders certainly, will be executed, and that the public will be invited to watch. The practice of public execution has been banned here for some time, but owing to the crime against the empire that has been committed, Governor Young has determined it appropriate. I can't say that I disagree.

I have spoken Raj's name to no one. I do not think I can explain to Craddock my interest. I suspect, of course, that he is among the 800, and while I long to learn his fate, I can do nothing to affect it.

He knew in advance of the mutiny, of that I'm sure. Why else would he repeatedly urge that I remove myself to Penang? He knew perhaps that there would be civilian casualties and he knew—this in my mind is most certain—that British officers would be killed. Perhaps he himself participated in the killing. It is a most vile image, but I picture in my mind the gang of Indians breaking into the barracks and taking aim at the white men who ruled them, or who enforced the white man's rule, and firing their weapons. Did Raj take pleasure in killing Charles? Did he take satisfaction in this revenge on his oppressor? Did he think of me? Did Charles deserve to die like that? What purpose did his killing serve? What had Charles done to Raj other than command him?

I ask these questions, knowing full well the answers, and, despite my own unfathomable loss, I find myself sympathizing with the sepoys. Is my situation so very different from theirs? And did I not long to rebel against the course others plotted for me? Few will admit it, but the history of the empire's expansion, so often justified as the manifest spread of modern civilization, is one not of lifting up the masses but exploiting and subjugating people who did not ask for our help. Is it not understandable that they would revolt against the restraints under which we have forced them to live?

21 February 1915
The settlement is still much consumed with the catastrophe that has befallen us. It is known that I am with the Craddocks, and so there have been many visitors wishing to pay their condolences to me, but I have asked that they be sent away with thanks. I am not in need of the sort of comfort they can provide.

I have made two exceptions to this intention, however. When Mrs. Craddock informed me that Mr. Preston had come, I asked her to bid him wait in the parlor and I made preparations to see him. My tears had long since run dry, but my face was as red and splotched as a bruised apple, so I did what I could to make myself presentable.

When I entered the room, he stood, hat in hand, looking only slightly deflated by the recent events. He would move on, of course, unscathed if not untouched, and would perhaps write a novel about the mutiny. He would need to make it somewhat more salacious than it was, though, and so perhaps the affair between a captain of the Regiment and an Englishwoman would have to figure prominently in the tale.

"Miss Pennington," Preston said as we sat, "I hope you know I am most aggrieved by the incident, and I am terribly sorry for your loss."

It was highly inappropriate of me, but at the word "terribly," which Preston spat out with deep, guttural emphasis, I very nearly laughed. No, I did laugh. And my laughter brought a look of puzzlement to the man's face that only elicited more laughter.

When I regained my composure, I was able to speak. "Thank you, Mr. Preston. I appreciate your sentiments."

"If I may, Miss Pennington—Lizzie—I would offer words of advice. This from someone who has seen the world, loved and lost on more than one occasion, and sits before you now entirely alone in the world. Put the calamitous days behind you. I understand you are bound for Australia, and I endorse the plan, for it will allow you to fashion a new life. It is as if you have completed your painting of Singapore, and now it is time to start with a fresh canvas."

I was struck by the tone of Preston's words. Instead of making a pronouncement, as he was wont to do, he uttered his advice from the heart, as if to one's child, a loved one whom he truly wished well. I shall always remember Mr. Preston for this.

Later, Mrs. Craddock announced another visitor, Mr. Avery Bradford, Uncle Cyril's law clerk. Since the day of the mutiny, Mr. Bradford had been most attentive to the administrative details of Uncle's death and, apparently, the winding up of his law practice, or so the Craddocks had reported to me. It would take some time for Uncle's estate to be settled, his house sold, and so on, and Mr. Bradford would handle it all. Because I wanted to thank him for this work, I agreed to see him.

The poor fellow seemed genuinely distraught. As soon as I sat, he folded in upon himself in a chair opposite to me, his brown suit wrinkled and stained, showing signs that he had not been looking after himself. I remembered that not long after I arrived in Singapore, Uncle had suggested, in a tentative way that made me think he wasn't so terribly keen on the idea, that Mr. Bradford might make a suitable husband for me. While he was disheveled now, I had seen him in much better form on other occasions, and I knew him to be a handsome, if somewhat reserved, gentleman. In some ways, in appearance only and not demeanor, he reminded me of Richard, so chiseled were his features.

"Miss Pennington," he began now. "I do not wish to trouble you with business matters under the circumstances, but I understand you will be leaving us soon and there are a few things of which you should be aware."

"Thank you, Mr. Bradford. I do appreciate your attention to my uncle's affairs."

"Yes, well, the first thing you should know is that I have spoken to a few of your uncle's clients, and while they are of course devastated by the tragedy, they have agreed that it would be best if I continue to represent them. To that end, I am in the process of organizing a new law firm, to be known as Bradford & Company, and will assume the tenancy of your uncle's chambers. I hope that does not trouble you overly much?"

I had given no thought to Uncle's clients or his business affairs, but of course he had grown deep roots in this community and was highly regarded, so the need for those relationships to continue in some form should not have surprised me. "No, Mr. Bradford. Not troubled at all. I commend you for your attention to such matters, which are far beyond my understanding."

"Good. Thank you. The second thing I wished to discuss with you is of a somewhat more delicate nature."

"Delicate, Mr. Bradford?"

"Quite. I believe your uncle's household includes a number of servants, one of whom is a young Chinese woman by the name of May."

"Yes. I would hardly call her a woman, but, yes, May worked for Uncle. For us."

"Before his death, your uncle became aware that the woman, the girl, was with child."

"Yes, that came to my attention, as well."

"Your uncle, it seems, although I'm not sure how best to put this, felt some…responsibility."

"Responsibility? You're not suggesting…. Oh, my, that's exactly what you're suggesting."

"I'm afraid so. But your uncle had planned to bestow upon the girl's family a sum of money to ensure the proper care of the child, and that has been arranged. The payment will appear in the estate's accounts, and I wanted to apprise you of the matter before you saw it there."

Poor May. I do not condone what Uncle had done, nor do I understand what passed between them, although I doubt that their relations could possibly have been consensual on her part, but I was in a way proud of Uncle for attempting to do right by the girl. If all men, if the empire builders, made an effort to make amends to the people they have caused to suffer, perhaps we would not be in the midst of a great war.

"Thank you, Mr. Bradford. It's very kind of you to let me know." A thought occurred to me just then, and I asked Bradford to wait a moment while I fetched something from the room I occupied at the Craddocks'. I returned with one of the paintings from the exhibition, which seemed such a long time ago, so much had passed, and held it out to him. "Please accept this gift as a token of my appreciation, sir. It is a painting I did of the bird of paradise flower in Uncle's garden. Perhaps it will help you remember him, and me."

Bradford seemed pleased with the gift, admiring it as a student of art might, studying its brush strokes, the way the light caught on the whorls of paint, the way the flower seemed to glow and open as you looked at it.

"Thank you, Miss Pennington. I shall treasure it."

23 February 1915
Poor Charles. I was not permitted to see him, but I am told that he was given honors and buried in a grave on the Tanglin Barracks grounds. Uncle and the other civilians have also been buried, after a solemn affair that I could not bring myself to attend. Mrs. Craddock reported that much of the settlement was present, and kind words were spoken by Governor Young.

In the days after the mutiny, rumors spread that the killing had been indiscriminate, and that many white women and children were targeted. In the end, though, it appears that only one woman, Mrs. Woolcombe, whom I met briefly in the company of Mrs. Burke, died, and her killing may have been entirely accidental. I am glad of it. I do believe that Raj and his fellows would not have been so callous.

In any event, the inquiry is concluded. The executions have begun. So far, thirty men have been shot at Tanglin. Were I still in Uncle Cyril's home, I would surely have been able to hear the gunfire as these mutineers received justice for their crimes.

While I agreed the executions were necessary, I decided I must see for myself. And so, over the objections of Mr. and Mrs. Craddock, I made my way to Tanglin.

The message of the public executions is not meant for me, of course. It is aimed at the natives who might sympathize with the rebellious Indians who caused such suffering. It is the local people of Singapore—not just the Mohammedans, of whom there are many here, Indians and Malays both, and Arabs, but the Chinese as well—who need to be taught this lesson. Or so that is what Mr. Craddock explained to me. They are to learn that there is no escape, apparently. No way out from under the rule of the British except for the ultimate liberation we all will face. However enlightened the white men are, however beneficent they believe themselves to be, they must still deal harshly with those who break the law. So says Mr. Craddock.

There was a crowd assembled, and I joined. When the brown faces saw that I, a white woman, was among them, here also to see what they had come to see, they parted, as if by some pre-agreed signal, and let me approach the viewing area behind a fence. Six tall stakes had been erected, half-buried in the dirt, but still extending some eight feet in the sky, looking like trees stripped naked. I did not have to wait long before six men, each accompanied by two guards, were marched onto the grounds. Blindfolded, they stumbled among the rocks and debris as the guards pushed them forward. Then the guards tied the men to the stakes, none too gently, inflicting every indignity they deemed was due.

Other guards—all British men of the Regiment, perhaps men who had been under Captain Bingham's command—assembled between the prisoners and the crowd, although our view was not obstructed. I scanned the faces of the men tied to their stakes. Among them, as I had somehow known, was Raj. His uniform was still streaked with blood, as I had last seen him in my room. He did not look at the crowd, did not see me, but gazed skyward, as if tracing the path his soul might soon take. I was tempted to call out his name, but I would have interrupted what surely was his final prayer. I held my tongue.

Upon a command I did not see or hear, the guards fired into the bodies of the six prisoners, and they slumped at the stakes.

20

Aislinn had encouraged both Martin and Shan to leave, and now it was time to figure out her own move. It felt cruel to abandon Liam now, while he was facing the loss of his job and, he seemed to think, criminal charges. But he had long ago lost her trust, and she didn't know if he deserved her loyalty.

If she left, where would she go? To her mother's, at least at first. Then back to New York. She could probably stay with Jessica for a while, check in with Frank at Morrow, Dunn and, if that didn't work out, look for another job. She found the number for the United Airlines office and was reaching for the phone to book her flight when Selvadurai came into her office.

He closed the door and sat across from her. From his expression, somber and pitying, Aislinn knew that he had brought news.

"There is no easy way to tell you this, Aislinn. I've just had a call from the police." Her mind raced. Had something happened to Martin and Shan? A shipwreck, or had they been arrested in connection with the South Seas Hotel bombing? Or was she herself now in jeopardy because of her relationship with Martin? Or her attendance at the Hong Lim demonstration?

"The Singapore police have been contacted by their counterparts in Hong Kong. There has been an accident."

"Liam?" He'd gone there yet again, either in a desperate attempt to keep his job or to find comfort in the woman he'd been seeing there, or both. "Is he all right?"

Selvadurai only looked at her, and she knew.

"Is he all right?" she asked again.

"Aislinn, I'm sorry. He's dead."

She felt the trembling begin in her arms this time, swallowing her shoulders, and she wrapped her arms around herself to stop them. "No. It can't be."

Selvadurai related what he'd heard. The police had been closely following Liam's whereabouts because of a criminal investigation of a money-laundering scheme in which he was potentially implicated, and when they learned from the Immigration Authority that he had flown to Hong Kong, they alerted the Criminal Investigations Bureau there to keep an eye out for him.

"It seems that early this morning Liam fell from the balcony of his hotel room in the Admiralty district and died on impact."

Like the falling man, she thought, the horror he'd seen in New York on 9/11. A man jumping to escape the horror of the building collapsing under him.

"An accident, you said. No one falls from a hotel balcony by accident unless they're being foolish. Liam isn't foolish."

"You're quite right, and my thoughts, also. Probably not an accident."

Aislinn didn't know what to feel. She thought she might cry, but the tears didn't come. She had understood why her father had killed himself, a weak man suffering a blow to his ego, but Liam wasn't like that. The quagmire he'd found himself in, which was largely TJ's doing, was causing him unimaginable stress that he had refused to talk about, but she was certain he wouldn't commit suicide. He wasn't entirely innocent, she suspected, greed and a hunger for status having overcome him, but he wouldn't. He'd gone to Hong Kong to clear himself with his boss, to find a way out of the mess. And if he couldn't do that, he'd have faced up to it. He would have endured whatever consequences arose. That's how he was raised. That's who he was.

She looked at the bird of paradise painting. It looked different to her now, not vibrant and striving, but lifeless. Dead.

"Are you all right, Aislinn?" Selvadurai asked.

She shook her head. "I mean, yes, I'm OK. I...." How was she supposed to feel, exactly? A normal woman would be devastated by news that her husband had just died, but what did she feel? She was angry at Liam for getting himself into the mess, and she was angry at him for bringing her to Singapore, for treating her at times like a servant, still angry that she'd given up her career in New York. Why wasn't she crying?

So, it was no accident, but surely not suicide either.

The trembling began in her shoulders this time. She was cold and shaking, her jaw locked as the tremor engulfed her body. She'd kept buttons in the office, but when Liam flushed her supply at home, she'd done the same with those. She was on her own now.

"Aislinn, what's happening? Are you all right? Can I get you something?" Selvadurai was standing next to her now, a look of terror on his face.

She shook her head again. "Please," she said, barely able to get the word out, "go."

He backed out of her office and pulled her door shut. When he was gone, she slumped onto her desk and waited for the trembling to pass.

· · · · ·

At home the next day, she disconnected the apartment phone after it rang incessantly all morning and ignored her cell phone. She feared that someone—well-wishers, reporters, the police, maybe even TJ—would knock on her door, and she was relieved that no one came. Cecilia went about her work as usual. Aislinn fed Mack but mostly wandered from room to room in the apartment as if she didn't know where she was or what she was doing there. She made coffee and sat at the dining table, gazing at the Pennington painting of the temple. The woman in the foreground glared back at her. You see, she was saying, I told you. You shouldn't be here.

What should she be doing? She should tell Liam's children. His family. She should be making plans to leave. Should she talk to Liam's boss in Hong Kong? Or Stephens in New York? Or who?

At noon, the building's security guard delivered a message from Selvadurai, who hadn't been able to reach her by phone. Investigators wanted to speak with her that afternoon at the office. He would send a car for her.

At Bradford & Co., she joined Selvadurai in a conference room with a Chinese man. They both rose when she entered.

"Aislinn, this is Robert Ong of the Monetary Authority of Singapore. He has been investigating certain irregularities that have been reported at SJ Freeman's branch here, and he has some questions for you."

She nodded, although Liam had told her so little about his work, which at the time annoyed her because it seemed he didn't trust her or respect her expertise. Now, though, she wondered if he wasn't shielding her from possible culpability for his actions. In any event, she doubted she had any helpful information. Ong was taller than Selvadurai by nearly a head and had thinning black hair. He was jacketless, but he wore an elegant crimson tie that reminded her of one Liam had often worn, one he thought exuded power and authority.

"Mrs. Givens, I am sorry to bother you at this difficult time, but under the circumstances, we believe it is urgent to get to the bottom of these irregularities, as Mr. Selvadurai calls them."

"Mr. Ong, I don't think I can help, as I know very little about SJ Freeman's business. And, just to be clear, the office here is a joint venture between SJ Freeman and a syndicate controlled by TJ Kwan."

"Yes, of course. And we'll have questions for Mr. Kwan. But right now, I'm asking about your husband, Mrs. Givens. A great deal of money has vanished, and we think your husband knew where it went."

"My husband is dead, Mr. Ong."

"Yes, I'm sorry, my condolences. Mrs. Givens, do you know why your husband was in Hong Kong?"

"He was planning to meet with the head of SJ Freeman's regional offices."

"We've spoken to a Mr. Richardson there. He confirms your husband had an appointment to meet with him but failed to arrive for the meeting. Do you know anything about your husband's recent visits to Thailand?"

"Only that he had been working with TJ Kwan on financial transactions there."

"Did he mention that these transactions involved shipments of opium smuggled out of Myanmar?"

"God, no! They were financing a motorbike dealer, not drugs."

Ong continued his questioning, asking what sounded to Aislinn like the same thing over and over, until she stood up and left the conference room.

· · · · ·

She let Cecilia go. She apologized profusely, but the maid showed no emotion, no interest in Aislinn's explanation that she was going back to the US, stoic to the last. Aislinn didn't tell her about Liam, although, probably, she already knew. How could she not? With the arrival of flowers, the phone calls and visits, and surely the other amahs talked of what they heard from their employers. It had been in the papers, too, several stories about the prominent US banker who had committed suicide before the Monetary Authority could arrest him for a fraud scheme that netted a hundred million dollars or more. Cecilia was there with her one day and the next she was gone. She had thought, after overcoming the initial discomfort of having Cecilia live with them, that they might be friends of sorts, or at least develop an attachment, but that was fantasy. The maid would find a place immediately, Aislinn was sure, another low-paying menial job, and whatever it was, it was the least of Aislinn's worries just now.

* * * * *

She uncovered Mack's cage and, while he stumbled into wakefulness, continued packing. Had he noticed the changes in the apartment these last few days, the packing, the grief? He squawked "Bub" a few times, until Aislinn retrieved a bowl of grapes, the food he associated with Liam. She opened his cage, brought him out as he eyed the grapes, and fed him. "Bub," he said, but it seemed more of a question than a statement. Where is Bub, Mack wanted to know.

With Mack now perched on her shoulder, Aislinn opened the door to the balcony. Her fear of heights had dissipated in the months they'd lived in Singapore, but after Liam's death it had returned with a vengeance. She remained near the door so she would not see the ground, would not be forced to imagine Liam's plunge. She'd given it a great deal of thought and didn't believe for a minute he had jumped. He may have been despondent over his likely arrest and the challenges it would bring, but suicide? No, he didn't jump. And it wasn't likely an accident either. Given what Selvadurai had told her about TJ, or what he had allowed her to discover for herself in the files, Kwan must have been involved.

She moved Mack from her shoulder to a perch on one of the patio chairs. He was confused. He'd never been on the balcony before. His wings were not clipped, and he was capable of flight but, other than quick jaunts in the living room, he hadn't been given the opportunity in a long time. There above him was the wide-open sky, a path away from his captivity.

"It's up to you now, Mack. Make your own life. You're free." And she slipped back into the apartment.

* * * * *

When she returned to the Bradford & Co. offices to say her farewells and pack up her things, there was a DHL package waiting for her.

The cover note, written by hand in a script Aislinn didn't recognize but thought was feminine, said only: "Liam left this to deliver to you in the event something happened to him." Inside, in Liam's handwriting, was a timeline of his dealings with TJ Kwan, along with a dozen or more documents that implicated Kwan in various schemes to defraud the bank and other organizations with which he was involved. The fraud went far beyond the motorbike fiasco in Thailand. One of the documents alluded to a scheme to channel funds, the proceeds of a drug-smuggling operation, to a Saudi entity, but for what purpose wasn't clear. Liam suspected TJ's associates, including Khun Anuwat, were supplying arms to terrorists, and he was preparing to report his suspicion to the authorities.

She took the package to Selvadurai's office.

She was sure of it now. Kwan had Liam killed to silence him, and even if these documents wouldn't prove that, they should be enough to bring down his empire.

21

Christmas Day, 1915

I have little appetite for revisiting these pages, given the horror that the year has been. I shall bring it to a close from my new refuge. The war rages on, but far, far away. I am settled here in Melbourne, where Europe seems so distant, and yet it is not possible to forget. Even if I wanted to put the past behind me, the shame of England, the horrors of the last weeks in Singapore, I cannot, because there is little Charlie to remind me.

I suppose I could have stayed, although Mr. Craddock and Mr. Bradford, advising me on such matters, made it clear that Uncle's bungalow must needs be sold, as it would be too costly to maintain on the meager income Uncle's estate had provided me.

"I could teach," I insisted, or rather thought out loud, remembering my resolve at Cape Town to support myself as a governess or tutor to the children of British civil servants. "I can paint," I argued. But I believe my voice faded away to nothing as I recognized the futility of attempting to support myself and a baby in those circumstances. But did I not have friends? Would not the community come to my aid?

Craddock did not laugh, but gently shook his head at my folly. Mrs. Craddock, for her part, offered suggestions in private for how I might keep myself and the baby and have a reasonable life. I was not the first, after all, to survive in such conditions, nor was I the worst off. In the end, though, the notion of staying was too painful to bear. I believe Mr.

Bradford himself acquired Heatherleigh along with many of Uncle's furnishings.

It was concluded, then, more by Craddock than myself, although I must have acceded to the plan, because here I am, that once Uncle's estate was settled, I would sail to Batavia. From there, I found my way to Perth and then on to Melbourne.

The Craddocks provided me with an introduction to relations of theirs who quickly found a position for me with an elderly couple from Newcastle, Mildred and Walter Wrenn, childless, who have welcomed me into their home. It is not a job, exactly, as I receive no pay, but their home is comfortable, and I earn my keep with household chores and watching after them. The old gentleman is frail, and needs care, but the two of them seemed most pleased to have me around.

Charlie's arrival altered the dynamics in the household, but the Wrenns are unflappable. In fact, for a time after the birth, and even still, our situations were reversed, as Mildred looks after Charlie if I must be away, which happens each week when I am off giving piano instruction or drawing lessons, both of which I dearly love.

Mr. Bradford has written that May's child, Uncle Cyril's child, has also been delivered safely and is cared for by May and her family. The baby, he reports, is thoroughly Chinese in appearance except for a startling green shade to his eyes.

Between the Wrenns' generosity and the income I have from Uncle Cyril, along with the pittance I am able to earn, I believe we will be fine. Whether we will remain in Australia when the war is over, I cannot tell, as the future is not ours to know.

For now, though, I am at peace.

22

Aislinn settled into the chair behind her desk, taking in her new office. There were law books on the twin shelves behind her—primarily for show, as research these days was done online, although she still loved to browse through old cases—and both her Harvard Law School diploma and New York law license hung above the credenza directly behind her. The Miro lithograph Liam had given her gazed at her from the opposite wall. Now she saw the figures as sailing ships returned to port. The furniture in the office was solid, polished mahogany. One of the Persian rugs she'd bought in Singapore added warmth to the room. She felt at home.

A knock on the open door was followed by Hannah Boseman's cheerful voice and grinning face. She looked the same as always in an elegant suit and trademark brooch, a fuchsia scarf at her neck.

"Like the new digs?"

"They're spectacular, Hannah. I can't thank you enough."

"No, thank *you*, Aislinn. The chance to bring you on board gave me the courage to do what I should have done a long time ago. We're Boseman & Associates now, but maybe one day soon we'll be Boseman & Givens. Like the sound of that?"

"You bet I do," said Aislinn.

· · · · ·

Leaving Singapore wasn't as easy as she'd thought it would be. Mr. Ong at the Monetary Authority interviewed her a second time, repeating many of the same questions as before, although he found the documents Liam's friend had sent her most helpful, and requested that she stay in the country until his investigation was complete. Selvadurai confirmed her suspicion that this was not, in fact, a request, and that she would likely be stopped at the airport if she attempted to leave. There was enough to occupy her time while she waited for clearance from Mr. Ong, however, packing up the apartment and disposing of houseplants and appliances she wouldn't be able to take with her. To her surprise, when she took down the Pennington paintings to crate them for shipping, she discovered they had ceased to speak to her. The woman in the temple courtyard seemed benign, unconcerned by her presence, now that she was leaving. The two men in the portraits had blank, uninterested gazes, the longing gone from their faces. It seemed so long ago now, but Liam's colleague Stephens was right. Outside of Singapore, these paintings were unlikely to be of value to anyone. Even Shan Lee's painting had ceased to be menacing.

When Ong eventually concluded that Aislinn had no more information he could use, she left Singapore. She stopped first at her mother's condo in the Virginia suburbs of Washington, DC, only because she had nowhere else to go. She had dreaded spending time with her mother, especially given all that had happened, but it was surprisingly helpful and healing. Her brother visited while she was there, expecting momentarily to be deployed to Iraq now that the war had begun. The stay in Virginia gave her time to think and make plans.

She decided to keep the baby. She knew there were other options available, having been in this position once before, but this time it was the right choice for her. She'd stopped using birth control, thinking a baby might be the best way to bring Liam back to her, to heal whatever rift was threatening their marriage, as pathetic and misguided as that sounded to her now. Her situation had changed, obviously, but maybe a child was a way for her to contribute to a better future for everyone. She'd teach him a different way of interacting with the rest of the world, especially those less fortunate.

In any event, she planned to continue working. She needed to support herself and a child, and her only training was as a lawyer, so she would return to the practice, doing the work she loved. She'd been gone less than a year. Would Morrow, Dunn & O'Brien take her back? She called Frank and was forthright with him. Although initial reports had said Liam had committed suicide to avoid prosecution for fraud, the documents she'd given Selvadurai and that he'd put into the hands of the Singapore Police Force's Commercial Affairs Department had cast suspicion on TJ Kwan, and Liam's death was now officially listed as a homicide by the Hong Kong authorities, pending further investigation. Still, Liam wasn't exactly innocent, although if it was true he took some kind of kickback, she didn't know what had become of the money, as she'd managed to convince Mr. Ong of the Monetary Authority. Aislinn assumed she might be tainted by the hint of scandal. She hoped that wouldn't matter to the people who knew her.

"I'm not sure what you've heard, Frank, but I've come home. I'll be planning a memorial service for Liam, and then I'd like to come back to the firm."

When Frank didn't respond, she knew there was a problem. Might as well get it all out there.

"And the thing is, I'm pregnant. I realize that might make it awkward."

"I appreciate your candor on that score, Aislinn, but that's not the obstacle. You're a fine lawyer. However, a lot has happened in the last year. Our business hasn't rebounded the way we hoped it would after the attacks. We've had to let lawyers go, including a few partners. And we're considering a merger with another firm, one with a global presence, so there's a lot of uncertainty. It's a damn shame, but that's the reality of it. There's barely enough work to go around as it is. I'm sorry."

So, it wasn't going to be easy to get back on track. She was on the job market and so were a lot of other lawyers. America was at war, punishing a small country far away for failing to fall in line, and so much was uncertain.

She called her old friend and mentor at the firm, Hannah Boseman, to seek her advice. She told Hannah what had happened and asked if she had any suggestions for how she might find a job in New York. Hannah listened to Aislinn's story and paused for a moment before responding.

"It's horrible, dear. Truly horrible and I'm so sorry. But I'll be blunt. Your timing is perfect. I'll spare you the details, but I'm leaving Morrow, Dunn myself soon, and wasn't sure exactly what I was going to do with myself. But the picture is clear to me now. I've been wanting to run my own show for some time, and that's what I'm going to do. You need a job and I'll need help. I know you're a spectacular lawyer, and I know a young single mother needs flexibility, which I happen to have in abundance. This is going to be fabulous. We'll make a great team."

After a brief stay with Jessica, she found an apartment on the Upper West Side and started her new job. Working with Hannah was nothing like working for Frank or Selvadurai had been. They were friends. They lunched together. Aislinn told her about her marriage, how it had been falling apart even before Liam's legal troubles, largely because of her resentment over being dragged to the other side of the planet but also because of the change that came over Liam under TJ Kwan's influence, or maybe it was the manic environment in Singapore. She left Martin out of the story, but eventually that would come, too. She talked about her pregnancy. Hannah had never had children, but she still understood what Aislinn was going through and made sure she had lined up the medical help she was going to need.

Hannah was preeminent in the field of intellectual property and had secured commitments from several major clients to come with her when she left Morrow, Dunn. Now, Aislinn was learning the IP issues as well, and she found them just as intriguing as the banking work she'd done with Frank. She had also convinced two of Frank's clients, smaller lenders for whom she'd worked for years, to jump ship and retain Boseman & Associates to do all their legal work. It was the sort of validation she desperately needed.

• • • • •

Rebecca called and suggested they meet for lunch. They hadn't spoken since the day Aislinn called her to tell her about her father's death, one of the most difficult calls Aislinn had ever made. She still hadn't told her the entire story and wasn't sure she ever would. They agreed to meet at the same restaurant where they'd had lunch the year before, when Rebecca had let slip that Liam was planning their move to Singapore.

"How've you been?" she asked as they settled into a booth.

"Good. I'm taking a year off before I start grad school and found an au pair job, so I'm off to London soon."

"Oh, you'll love it there. I did when I was your age." Aislinn remembered that Rebecca had considered getting an MBA, in part because of her fling with Michael over the holidays. She hadn't told her she'd seen Michael with another girl, and it sounded like it no longer mattered.

"And Jason?"

"He just got his acceptance to study theater at Northwestern, but he's not sure he's going. He's been in a funk ever since…."

"I understand. I tried to call him, but he won't talk to me."

"I don't blame you, you know," Rebecca said. "For what my father did."

Aislinn didn't know how to respond. She had told her none of the details, only that Liam was trying to dig himself out of a mess at his bank and had gone to Hong Kong to meet with his boss, to see what they could work out. It had nothing to do with Aislinn, but Rebecca didn't know any of that. Would it be better for her to know he was murdered? That would come out in time.

"Also, for the record, I don't think he was cheating on you."

Aislinn wasn't so sure. What Jenny Morelock had reported was purely an act of revenge, true or not, but there was still some doubt in her mind, and TJ had hinted the same. Who was the friend who had sent the DHL package to her after Liam's death? Wasn't that the woman he'd been seeing there? She didn't think she'd ever know.

"Although with his track record, it was only a matter of time." Rebecca laughed, and Aislinn smiled along with her, but it was too painful.

"Even before your father died, I was planning to come back. In fact, we had talked about it, and he urged me to leave. I wasn't happy there, and, obviously, neither was he."

"What do you mean, 'he wasn't happy?'"

"It's hard to explain, but he had become a different person. He seemed to think he was owed something by…someone, I don't know who. The universe, maybe. His position was no longer just a job to him, it was an entitlement. He seemed to think he was part of this grand colonial history, that as an American he knew better than everyone else what was best for them."

"Can I ask you something?"

"Sure, of course."

"Is the baby his? Or did you really have an affair with that Martin guy?"

Rebecca had seen through her in Singapore. She'd been careless that day in Orientalia. "The baby is your father's, Becca. He'll be your half-brother. Liam wanted us to start a family. I didn't, at first, but eventually I came to think having a baby would solve the problems we were having. I don't think I was right about that, but here we are."

"And Martin? Where is he?"

"I don't know. He closed the shop and left Singapore. Honestly, I don't know where he is."

• • • • •

Aislinn was working on a loan agreement for one of her new clients, a project similar to the one she did shortly before she moved to Singapore, when Tawnisha delivered two packages to her office.

Tawnisha was still in law school at Cardozo, now taking night classes, but was grateful to be working with Aislinn again. One package was about the size of a book and the other was a long tube.

"Where's it from?" Aislinn asked.

"Australia, I think," Tawnisha said and pointed to markings that said NSW. "Isn't that New South Wales?"

Aislinn tore off the brown paper wrapping and then pried the end of the tube free. Inside was a tightly rolled canvas that she carefully removed and unfurled to reveal a painting of the bird of paradise flower. Unmistakably, it was another Pennington, signed and dated 1915 by the artist. It was every bit as vibrant as the one that had been hanging in her office in Singapore, a delicate flame that was also the head of a bird that seemed poised to lift off in flight. As she spread the painting on her desk and looked at it closely, the flower changed color, sprouting feathery green wings and a red-capped head. It had become an actual bird, flapping its wings and squawking.

"It's beautiful," Tawnisha said. "Who sent it?"

Aislinn was near tears, thinking of Mack and wondering what had become of him. She could only shake her head.

"Open the other one, girl!"

Inside the second package was a leather-bound journal and attached to the cover was a hand-written note that said: "Dearest, our friend says the enclosed will explain much that you have been anxious to learn. He suggests you turn to the last entry first, added much later than the others and in handwriting he recognizes as his mother's. He found the book and the painting among her belongings when he retrieved her stored possessions after our arrival. He also learned that his father's name underwent a change when he emigrated, and he believes you will understand when you have read the journal. Lovingly, Niao Hua."

Aislinn recognized the name Shan Lee had said she would use—Bird Flower. So she and Martin had made it to Australia. The plan had been for them to sail up the west coast of Malaysia, abandon the boat in Malacca, and then fly to Perth or Sydney from Kuala Lumpur. If TJ had been watching for Shan, he likely had Changi Airport covered, but they had gambled that he wasn't monitoring Martin's movements and that a boat from Changi Sailing Club would not be noticed. Was the code name still necessary? Selvadurai thought both Martin and Shan would be cleared of involvement in the South Seas Hotel bombing, which now appeared to have been a scheme by TJ that was meant to cover up one of his shady deals with the Saudis and Khun Anuwat, blaming Jemaah Islamiyah in the process. Selvadurai was making sure the authorities had access to all the information they had accumulated, but TJ was still a powerful man with connections everywhere. None of them were safe yet.

She opened the journal now and realized it was the diary of Elizabeth Pennington, the very book she had longed to find when she acquired the paintings. She turned to the last entry, as Shan advised.

April 1972

I am in tears as I write in these yellowed pages, so many years after my grandmother's final entry. Although I am named for her and am called Lizzie, as she apparently was known as a girl, I knew nothing about her past until I came across this diary while packing up her household belongings. What an amazing life she led, and what tragedies she suffered!

And now she is gone, and my father, Charlie, dead, too, when I was an infant, lost at Tobruk in the last war just as his father died at the hands of the mutineers in Singapore in the first war. Why did no one ever speak of it? My own grandfather murdered, and my grandmother's uncle as well.

There is nothing left for me here, but now I know what I must do. I have learned of a need for trained nurses in Singapore, a destination I would not have thought of until I read this diary, and I shall build a new life for myself there, where my grandmother's art blossomed.

GUIDE FOR DISCUSSION

1. As with many people, Aislinn's career is deeply tied to her identity and sense of self-worth. When forced to choose between her career and her marriage, she agonizes over her decision. What are the most important factors influencing her decision?

2. Liam's move to Asia to work for his bank's Singapore office seems to bring about a change in his personality. While Aislinn is disturbed by the change, she also makes excuses for him. How realistic is it for her to defend her husband, even to her own detriment?

3. Elizabeth Pennington's move to Singapore bears some similarity to Aislinn's. What are some of the reasons for her move? Given that she has a strong independent streak, might she have resisted the move?

4. What is the immediate cause of the 1915 Mutiny in Singapore? In what way is it similar to or different from modern acts of terrorism like 9/11 or the Bali Bombing?

5. Aislinn, a student of art history, sees movement in the paintings of Shan Lee and Elizabeth Pennington that others do not. What is she seeing? How and why?

6. Although Liam says that his marriage to Aislinn is a partnership, Aislinn feels they are unequal partners. What other examples of unequal power dynamics does the book explore? How are they similar or different and what are the consequences of disequilibrium?

7. Aislinn is resistant to Liam's desire to start a family. What are some of the factors that contribute to her resistance? Also, her relationship with Liam's children from his first marriage is fraught. Is this a common problem? How does she attempt to overcome it?

8. Singapore has a relatively short history, but by the early twenty-first century had grown into a modern metropolis and important financial center. What aspects of the city-state's history and political environment does the book reveal?

9. Both Elizabeth and Aislinn marvel at the diversity of cultures that make up Singapore but notice the disparities in their respective power and influence. Singapore isn't unique in this regard, but what might be some of the consequences of such disparities?

10. Elizabeth and Aislinn experience tragic losses but seem to have no choice other than carrying on with their lives. What do you think motivates them?

AUTHOR'S NOTE

This novel was a long time in the making. I first visited Singapore in 1978 as a young backpacker, touring Asia after spending two years as a Peace Corps Volunteer in South Korea. The history of the island nation fascinated me even then, though already some of its gritty charm was being erased by modernization. I returned six years later as an associate of a US law firm, helping to build an international legal practice, and watched the country's rapid development as a resident outsider.

In 1990, after a short assignment in one of our US offices, I again found myself living in Singapore, this time as a partner of the firm, and would stay there for another three years. In the process of decorating my new apartment that year, I bought a trio of paintings at Antiques of the Orient, a shop that became the inspiration for Orientalia in the novel. (Returning to Singapore in 2017 for research, I again visited Antiques of the Orient and acquired a facsimile print of a 1913 map of the city, showing the settlement much as Elizabeth Pennington's diary describes it.) The paintings I bought, all depicting the Thian Hock Keng Temple on Telok Ayer Street, a landmark I had enjoyed visiting over the years, are dated 1917 and signed by I. Codrington. As Aislinn Givens does in the novel, I displayed those paintings in my dining room, illuminated by the apartment's track lighting. They have followed me on every move since then.

Over the years, I've wondered about the paintings and I. Codrington. Who was she and what was she doing in Singapore? She was not Isabel Codrington, a British painter of modest renown who worked at about the same period in England. Most likely she was Mrs. Stewart Codrington, the wife of a British official in the colonial administration. News reports of the time list Mrs. Codrington as being active in the Singapore Art Club, an organization that annually displayed works by its members. In the novel, Elizabeth Pennington, the fictional painter of the pictures Aislinn Givens acquires at Orientalia, refers to one such exhibition. I should also note that the paintings by I. Codrington that hang in my home are not the same as

Elizabeth Pennington's paintings. Although Aislinn Givens does have one painting of the Thian Hock Keng temple, and it resembles one of my Codrington paintings, the portraits of Pennington's British and Indian army officers do not exist.

In wondering how I might employ the paintings or the painter in a work of fiction, I investigated what was happening in Singapore at around the time Mrs. Codrington was working and learned of the Singapore Mutiny of 1915. Because that event has modern echoes, I began to construct the fiction that became the novel. Some of the people mentioned in Elizabeth Pennington's diary are real people—Governor Arthur Young, for example—but most are entirely creatures of my imagination. Still, the basic outline of the tragic events of the Mutiny is accurate.

While the parallels drawn between the Mutiny and twenty-first century terrorism are my own, I was not surprised to find them confirmed in academic writing, particularly a working paper by Prof. Farish A. Noor ("From Empire to the War on Terror: the 1915 Indian Sepoy Mutiny in Singapore as a Case Study of the Impact of Profiling of Religious and Ethnic Minorities," published by the S. Rajaratnam School of International Studies in 2010.) This is one of the many sources I consulted during research conducted at the National Library of Singapore. Another resource that I found helpful is *The Mutiny in Singapore: War, Anti-War and the War for India's Independence* by Sho Kuwajima (Rainbow Publishers 2006). I am grateful to the staff of the National Library for their assistance.

It should be noted, also, that while the October 2002 bombing in Kuta Beach Bali *did* occur as Aislinn describes it, there was no hotel bombing in Singapore in February 2003.

A note of thanks: I am deeply grateful to the Virginia Center for the Creative Arts for providing the time and space (in both Virginia and France) to write in such an inspiring and supportive environment. Thanks also to the Ragdale Foundation in Lake Forest, Illinois, where I worked on this book during a Polar Vortex (a stark contrast to Singapore's tropical climate), which turns out to be great motivation to stay at one's desk to write. Sincere thanks also to my writing buddy Mary Akers who provided feedback on a near-final version of the novel after listening to me talk about the concept for years.

And, especially, thank you, readers. Thank you, independent publishers and booksellers. Thank you, book clubs.

ABOUT THE AUTHOR

Clifford Garstang, a former international lawyer, is the author of two previous novels, *The Shaman of Turtle Valley* and *Oliver's Travels*, and three short story collections, *House of the Ancients and Other Stories, In an Uncharted Country*, and *What the Zhang Boys Know*, winner of the Library of Virginia Literary Award for Fiction. He is the editor of the anthology series *Everywhere Stories: Short Fiction from a Small Planet*, and the co-founder and former editor of Prime Number Magazine. He is the recipient of a Walter E. Dakin Fellowship to the Sewanee Writers' Conference and an Indiana Emerging Author Award from the Indianapolis Public Library Foundation. His work has appeared in numerous literary magazines and has received distinguish mention in the Best American series.

NOTE FROM CLIFFORD GARSTANG

Word-of-mouth is crucial for any author to succeed. If you enjoyed *The Last Bird of Paradise*, please leave a review online—anywhere you are able. Even if it's just a sentence or two. It would make all the difference and would be very much appreciated.

Thanks!
Clifford Garstang

We hope you enjoyed reading this title from:

BLACK ROSE writing™

www.blackrosewriting.com

Subscribe to our mailing list – *The Rosevine* – and receive **FREE** books, daily deals, and stay current with news about upcoming releases and our hottest authors.
Scan the QR code below to sign up.

Already a subscriber? Please accept a sincere thank you for being a fan of Black Rose Writing authors.

View other Black Rose Writing titles at
www.blackrosewriting.com/books and use promo code
PRINT to receive a **20% discount** when purchasing.

Printed in the USA
CPSIA information can be obtained
at www.ICGtesting.com
CBHW020559260124
3765CB00004B/15

9 781685 133764